The Majorcan Affair

Keith Giles

Prologue

The twelve year old BMW three series motored along the Ma-11 towards Port de Soller, a small town on the north west coast of Majorca, the largest of the Balearic Islands. It was the twenty seventh of April.

After leaving the Ma-11 the driver, a dark haired Spanish woman of about thirty, slowed as she approached the narrow winding roads that led the motorist down into the picturesque little seaside town.

The woman, who had shoulder length black hair which ringed her rather attractive features, appeared on edge, continually shifting her small but well-proportioned body in her seat so as to allow her to see, through the interior mirror of the car, both the road behind the BMW and the child who was sleeping in the rear of the two door silver car.

She had been checking the road behind her ever since she steered the BMW off the main road, almost as if she were looking out for any other vehicles using the same stretch of road. Even though it was a warm and sunny April day, the road was quiet, no other vehicle was in sight, either in front of or behind the BMW.

As the car rounded one of the numerous sharp bends the road had to offer, it fell away to the right, to a drop of about a hundred and fifty metres.

Without warning, the driver lost control of the car despite the fact that she was not travelling quickly. The BMW slid, almost in slow motion, towards the edge. At the very last moment, the driver's door flew open and, literally as the front wheel on the passenger side found thin air, the driver threw herself from the car. As she hit the ground, the BMW went over the edge.

By the time the driver had got to her feet and gone the look over the edge, the car had bounced down almost to the bottom of the ravine. When it hit the rocks at the bottom, the car burst into flames. The driver appeared almost stunned as the car began to burn. When the flames reached its fuel tank, the BMW exploded.

As the Spanish woman stood and looked at the burning wreckage below, she became aware that a car had stopped on the road behind her. She heard doors open and people rush to her. The people from the car, a young couple, were able to tell the police when interviewed later that as they got to the driver, they both clearly heard the distraught woman call out the name 'Anna'. The couple, fearing that the driver could either collapse or try to reach the burning car, took hold of her and moved her away from the edge. As they moved her back to their car, the driver, whilst crying hysterically, called the name 'Anna' over and over. As his wife tried to comfort the distressed driver, the young man called the emergency services on his mobile telephone.

Whilst the call to the emergency services was being made, the driver of the BMW was able to tell the young woman who was trying to comfort her that her fiancé's daughter, Anna, was in the back of the car. When he discovered that there was a child in the car, the young man immediately looked for a way down to the inferno, feeling he had to try to save the child. He was unable to see a safe way down to the burning wreckage and reasoned that there was no point in trying to scramble down and risk falling into the flames, so wisely he decided to wait for the trained professionals, after all, no one could have survived what had quickly become an inferno.

The police were the first to arrive on the scene, some twelve minutes after the emergency call, they were followed moments later by the fire service. The BMW, which was by now, totally unrecognisable as one, was burning ferociously, out of control. The young man had notified the police, on their arrival, of the child trapped in the rear of the car and added that he had tried to find a way down but had not been able to identify a safe route. The senior of the police officers was able, to the relief of the young man, to state that it was his opinion borne out by long experience that it would have been impossible for anyone to survive the fire and that he need not chastise himself because he had not been able to get to the car.

By this time, the young man's wife had brought the woman over to where the police stood with her husband, she kept a tight grip on the hysterical woman as the driver managed to tell the police about the child in the car. She was also able to say that she had filled up the car at the last service station that she had passed on the main road. The two policemen exchanged a glance; that would explain why the car was burning so fiercely.

Whilst the police, driver and young couple were talking, the firemen had gone about their job quickly and efficiently and soon had their hoses trained on the fire. As they did so, one of their number was being rigged up in a safety harness and when the chief gave the go ahead, was lowered, along with a foam hose, down to the floor of the ravine. At the bottom, the fireman trained his foam on the still smouldering car until he was sure it would not flare up again, by the time he had finished, the water and foam ran away like washing up water.

Then, and only then, did he permit himself a look in the wreckage, what he saw caused him to turn away, murmuring a prayer before he fell to his knees and was violently sick. Once he had composed himself, he used his radio to contact his chief to confirm that the passenger in the rear of the car was most certainly dead. He also said that he was unable to give any clue as to the age or sex of the deceased person.

When he was told that the body was that of an eight year old girl. The fireman, a fifteen year veteran of the island's service was unable to stop the flow of tears from his eyes.

In due course, cutting equipment was lowered and the body removed from the wreckage. Once clear, the child's remains were strapped on to a stretcher and hauled up the cliff. As the stretcher came over the top, the cover that the firemen had used to hide the body slipped off leaving the charred remains in full view of everybody. The BMW's driver along with the young wife who had stopped with her husband to try to help, fainted at the sight. Her husband and one or two of the policemen present turned away to be sick.

When the BMW's driver had recovered sufficiently, the police, while feeling sorry, had their duty to do and breathalysed her. The test was negative to the relief of the policeman conducting the test.

The woman was then taken to hospital in the town of Inca, and told by the police that they would be along to see her later to obtain her statement. Once the ambulance had pulled away, the police obtained statements from the young couple who had stopped to help before sending them on their way. Then they looked closely at the surface of the road. No skid marks were visible leading the police to believe that the car had not been travelling too fast thereby causing the driver to lose control. A crime scene investigator had arrived to photograph and measure the scene of the accident. It was the opinion of the first policemen at the scene that this had been a tragic accident made worse by the recent filling of the BMW's fuel tank.

Later that evening, the police attended the hospital in Inca to speak to the woman they now knew to be one Inez Castillar of Santa Ponsa from the south coast of the island. When they arrived, Senorita Castillar was not alone, the man with her introduced himself as Raul Martinez, fiancé of Inez Castillar and the father of Anna Martinez, the little girl who had died in the crash. The policemen offered their condolences for their loss though both of them recognised the name of Raul Martinez, a man well known to the police in Mallorca.

Martinez then explained to the police that Inez was not in fact the child's mother, her mother was actually his former wife Patience, an Englishwoman from whom he was now divorced and had been for some five or six years. Anna was staying with him as she was on holiday, it had been the first time that her mother had allowed her to come. It was clear that Martinez and Castillar had been crying, both had red ringed eyes and looked distraught but the police had a job to do and took a detailed statement from Inez, within which she confirmed that the passenger who was in the rear of the car had been Anna Martinez.

Making use of the fact that Martinez was present, the police obtained a statement from him confirming that his daughter, Anna Martinez, had set off earlier that day to go for a drive with Inez Castillar. He gave the child's address in England and told of his wish to have his daughter visit him in his home, which had been his daughter's home until she was about two years old when his wife had left and taken the child home to England. He explained that the English Court had given custody to his former wife and he had, for the past few years, gone to England regularly to see his daughter. He had asked Patience, his former wife, if Anna could visit him and, after a great deal of thought, she had somewhat reluctantly agreed. He finished by saying that he wished he had never asked.

When they had their statements, the police told Inez that she would face no charges over the accident, she had had no trace of alcohol in her system and the road showed no evidence that she had been speeding, it had been a tragic accident, nothing more. The senior of the two officers asked if Raul would like them to inform the child's mother, he declined. However unpleasant a task it was, it was one that he had to do.

On the way out the senior office remarked to his colleague that though he had no time for Martinez, he was glad it was not he who had to break the news to the child's mother.

Chapter 1

Raul Martinez was waiting in the arrivals lounge at Palma airport, he was waiting for the flight from Manchester to arrive which was bringing his former wife Patience and her parents, Henry and Suzanne Jameson to his home island of Mallorca. They were coming for the cremation of Anna his eight year old daughter who had died in a car crash a couple of days earlier. Raul had arranged the cremation as quickly as he could knowing that his ex-wife would obviously come for the service, he did not want her hanging around his villa longer than was absolutely necessary.

Martinez was a good looking man of thirty seven standing six feet two inches tall. He had a well built, muscular body. To meet his former wife and her parents, he had chosen to wear a black polo shirt and black trousers. This dress, along with his jet black hair made him extremely noticeable. As he waited, he began to pace up and down, clearly agitated. Many women, both young and not so young, cast admiring glances in his direction. Today, they all wasted their time – he was oblivious to all, and everyone around him. The fact that he did not notice any of the women who looked at him, never mind respond to their looks, gave clear indication to his state of mind. He was not looking forward to meeting Patience again.

He remembered clearly what had happened when he had telephoned England two nights earlier. Patience had answered the call herself and had become hysterical when he broke the news, rather brutally he had to admit, about Anna's death. There is no easy way to give that sort of news. She must have dropped the phone as the next voice he had heard had been that of her father, Henry Jameson who had listened in silence as Raul had told him about the drive to Port de Soller and the accident on the winding roads as the car in which Anna had been travelling had gone off the road and plunged into a ravine. The silence at the other end of the phone unnerved Raul but he had no option other than to continue and told Jameson that the car had caught fire and that Anna had died. Finally Jameson spoke, he asked if anyone else had been injured or killed and made no comment when he had been told that Inez, the driver, had just managed to scramble clear. Naturally he had wanted to know what arrangements if any had been made and had questioned the setting for the cremation and said that Anna should have been laid to rest in

England but Raul had been able to convince him that getting the unpleasant deed done was more important than the location, Jameson had found himself agreeing. Then, Jameson had finished their conversation by saying he would make arrangements to fly to the island and would let Raul have the details, Raul had said he would meet them at the airport, now he was there, waiting.

The flight had landed some ten minutes ago and very soon the passengers would be coming through from baggage control and he would have to face Patience who, he thought, was a complete bitch.

His former wife was the fifth passenger through, supported by her mother, her father pushed the trolley with their luggage on. Patience was dressed in a black shirt and blue jeans. Despite the fact that she had obviously been crying, and probably had been since his phone call, Martinez could not help but notice that she was still an attractive woman. His view that she was a bitch was re-affirmed within seconds for the first thing she did when she saw him was to shrug off the supporting arm of her mother, hurry across to him and slap him hard across his face before calling him a bastard and demanding to know how he could let her daughter loose with some Spanish tart? Henry Jameson, wishing to avoid a public scene, took hold of his daughter, gently pulled her away, and passed her back to his wife.

'I'm sorry about that Raul,' he said, 'But as you must understand, since she received the news, she has been rather overwrought and has not slept for more than a few minutes at a time, I think it is catching up with her.'

'Please do not apologise for her Henry,' Martinez replied, holding out his hand which Jameson took after a momentary hesitation. 'I understand how she feels. I myself felt rage and anger when I found out about the crash. It was, still is and always will be a terrible thing, one that will take an awful long time to get used to. But please, come this way, I have my car waiting. Naturally you will stay at the Villa Borgosa while you are in Mallorca.'

Martinez then turned to Suzanne Jameson and kissed her on both cheeks and told her that he was sorry that they were meeting again in such circumstances. He then took both Suzanne and Patience's luggage and led them outside to his car, a black BMW 7 series. He settled them into the car making sure that Henry sat alongside him in the front before loading the luggage in the boot.

Once they had set off, Patience announced that she would like to see her daughter one last time. Raul was against the idea saying that she would not be able to recognise Anna and that it would be better to remember her as she had been rather than see her poor little body burned as it had been. Suzanne gripped her daughter's hand before saying that Raul was right, it was no use putting herself through such an ordeal and making herself ill.

They had cleared the airport and on the road to Santa Ponsa before Raul spoke again. He did not speak to any of them directly but addressed his words to them as a whole. 'Please do not blame Inez for the accident. She is my fiancé and she adored Anna. As a matter of fact, it was at the request of Anna that the two of went out for the day together. Anna wanted to spend time with Inez in order to get to know her.

The roads leading to Port de Soller are winding and Inez lost control of the car as she rounded one of the bends and the car in which they were travelling slid off the road and over the edge. Inez managed to get out by the skin of her teeth otherwise two people that I love would now be dead.

The police attended the scene of course. They gave Inez a breath test, it was negative. After examining the road, they found no skid marks or any other evidence that Inez had been either driving too fast or doing anything wrong behind the wheel. It was their opinion, and mine, having obtained all the evidence that this was a tragic accident made worse by the fact that the car had been filled with petrol minutes before the accident.'

No-one spoke for a few minutes, taking time to digest what they had just been told. Patience and her mother began to cry in the rear of the car and held each other's hands for comfort. Fortunately for Martinez, the information he had given them put an end to any further conversation and they soon reached the Villa Borgosa.

After their luggage had been unloaded and the guests shown to their rooms, they all met in the villa's spacious lounge where Raul told them of the arrangements he had made for the cremation. It was to take place the following day, Thursday morning at eleven. Cars had been arranged and afterwards they would return to the Villa Borgosa for lunch. Only family had been invited to the service. There was however two notable exceptions, Inez Castillar and Salma Guttierez. Inez was soon to be family and Salma had been nanny to Raul and his sisters Maria and Esther. Salma had also looked after Anna when Patience and Raul had been married and had been devoted to Anna. It would have been unthinkable for Salma not to attend the service.

That night, Martinez had arranged a simple dinner. In addition to the three from England and Inez, Maria and Esther along with their respective husbands and children were also staying at the villa and of course joined the others for dinner. Only the children were not present, having been fed earlier.

Before dinner, Martinez had spoken with Henry Jameson and had pleaded with him to ensure that Patience did not cause a scene either over dinner or at the following morning's service. Jameson actually thought this a good idea; he knew his daughter well. After his conversation with Raul, Jameson sought out his wife and daughter and spoke to them at length, stressing the need for the evening and the events of the next day to pass off without any problems. Both Patience and her mother agreed and promised not to cause a fuss.

Dinner passed off without a hitch. After they had eaten, Patience found herself alone with Maria and Esther. The three of them had always got along well and the two Spanish ladies had been supportive of Patience throughout the evening.

They took Patience out into the large garden for a walk. Maria and Esther walked either side of Patience and each took one of her hands in theirs trying to offer what comfort they could. They were clearly distraught themselves but tried for Patience. They told her that Anna could not possibly have suffered and that when the car went over the edge of the ravine, Anna had been asleep and that according to the emergency services, death would have been pretty much instantaneous. Whilst this did not help Patience feel any better, she did appreciate what she was being told and thanked Maria and Esther for their kindness.

Patience then asked about Inez. Maria, the eldest, answered, telling Patience that they had known Inez for some six months, since she had become engaged to their brother. She had presented herself as a charming girl, easy to get along with. Esther pointed out that clearly she adored Anna and was trying to spend time with her in order to get to know her better. Inez apparently had been devastated by the accident, continually apologising for what had happened. Patience listened politely to what Maria and Esther had to say about Inez but made no comment.

After half an hour or so, the three ladies went back indoors as the evening was growing chilly. Patience noticed that her father was in conversation with Raul and another man. She went over and joined her mother who was seated alone on a large sofa.

A few moments later, Henry Jameson beckoned over his wife and daughter. When they came across, Jameson introduced them to the other man, Capitan Caldano, the chief of the Santa Ponsa Police. Capitan Caldano bowed and shook hands with Patience and Suzanne and apologised for his English which he said was not very good. Patience did not bother to tell him that she was fluent in Spanish, nor did Raul.

Caldano's English was however more than adequate to tell them that he was deeply sorry for their loss and that he would be happy to assist them in any way while they were in Santa Ponsa. Suzanne Jameson answered for the family and thanked the Senor for his kindness which made him glow with pleasure. He was holding in his hand some documents which turned out to be copies of the report into the accident. He handed a copy to Raul and one to Henry Jameson.

'Please read this at your leisure gentlemen,' he said. 'If you will permit me, I shall give you the, how you say? bones of the report.' Without waiting for an answer he carried on. 'The police from Inca have compiled this report, my good friend Capitan Gento has looked into the accident, it was his men that arrived on the scene after the emergency call. The driver of the car, Senorita Castillar was given the mandatory breath test at the scene. This was negative. The officers inspected the surface of the road, they were looking for skid marks which would have shown that the Senorita was driving too fast. There were none. Several photographs were taken at the scene by our specially trained crime scene investigators and they are in the report, this will show you that the road was clear of any marks.

As for identification of the body,' at this point he looked at Patience and apologised for what he was going to say. 'The body received 100% burns making a physical identification impossible. Normally, we would request dental records, in this case from England however this case differs somewhat from the normal. In this case, we are in possession of statements from Senorita Castillar who states quite categorically that Anna Martinez was the passenger in the car at the time of the accident. The statement of Senor Martinez confirms that his daughter set off for a drive with Senorita Castillar from this very villa that morning. In the circumstances, we the police are satisfied with the identification of the body. As there has been no foul play, we are certain that this was nothing more than a tragic accident.'

On behalf of himself, his wife and daughter, Henry Jameson thanked Capitan Caldano for his courtesy. After a little small talk, Caldano excused himself and left. Raul showed him out. At this point, Inez came over to join them. Suzanne thought she looked shifty but said nothing.

After a moment or two of awkward silence, Inez turned to Patience and looked directly at her.

'Please do not hate me Patience, I adored your Anna and would not have hurt her for the world. I would do anything to undo the hurt this accident has caused, not only to you but to Raul as well.' Patience gave her what could only be described as a venomous look before turning her back and walking away, closely followed by her mother. This left Henry Jameson with Inez. Being the gentleman he was, he felt the need to say something. He apologised for his daughter's behaviour and went on to explain how Patience was unsurprisingly distraught at losing her only child.

'I thank you Senor Jameson for you kind words. Raul was quite right when he said you were a true English gentleman. I only wish that we could have met in happier circumstances.' At that point, Raul returned saving Jameson the need to respond to what Inez had said. Instead, he excused himself and returned to his wife and daughter.

Raul came across to go over the finer details of the following day's events, Patience had no desire to hear what he had to say and went to bed leaving her parents to listen to her former husband. Cars would collect them in good time to arrive at the crematorium in time for the scheduled start of the service at eleven. After, they would return to the Villa Borgosa for lunch. At three, a car would take Jameson and his family back to Palma airport for their flight back to England. Jameson thought Raul relieved that they were leaving right after lunch but reasoned that the circumstances would be as trying for him as for everyone else, after all, Anna was his daughter too. Once in possession of the details, Henry and Suzanne retired for the night.

Chapter 2

The morning of the cremation dawned bright and sunny, a beautiful spring Majorcan day. For Patience however it could have been pouring with rain. It was certainly raining in her heart. She could not come to terms with what had happened no matter how hard she tried. She kept expecting Anna to come running over to her with her ready smile lighting up not just her own face but also the face of the person she was smiling at. No parent should have to bury or cremate their child.

A knock at the door brought Maria and Esther into her room. They were subdued but had come to see if they could help. Their simple kindness reduced Patience to tears. Fortunately, Suzanne arrived and Maria and Esther were able to leave Patience in the competent hands of her mother.

How Patience got ready for the service she would never know. In fact it was her mother who got her ready. First, she sent Patience for a shower and then dried her daughter's hair. This made Suzanne cry as she recalled how she had dried her hair when Patience had been a little girl. Then she recalled how she had on occasions dried Anna's hair. Then she helped her daughter dress for the service before going and getting ready herself.

Once downstairs, Patience refused to eat anything but her father made her drink a cup of sweetened tea.

The cars arrived at ten thirty. A shining black hearse was at the front of the procession with its heart-breaking load. It was followed by three cars for the mourners. Patience, her parents and Raul got into the first of them, the others using the remaining two cars for the relatively short journey to the crematorium.

Patience was supported by her parents as they made their way to the pew at the front of the small chapel, taking their seats on the right. Raul and Inez sat in the front pew on the other side of the aisle with the other mourners filling the rows of seats behind Raul.

The priest arrived and the service began. Mercifully, it did not last too long and the curtains soon closed in front of the pathetically small coffin.

Then it was over. Patience found herself being ushered to her feet by her parents and helped out of the chapel into the bright sunlight. Patience caught a glimpse of Salma the nanny and after excusing and untangling herself from her parents, made her way over to the nanny. She was surprised that instead of coming to her, the nanny turned on her heels and walked away. Patience did not have a chance to consider this strange behaviour as she was then helped to one of the cars for the journey back to the villa.

Back at the villa, Patience had the idea that Salma was deliberately avoiding her. She had not seen the old nanny since they had arrived at the villa yesterday apart from the fleeting glimpse at the chapel. Once she had registered this, Patience was rather shocked as she and Salma had got along quite famously during her time in Santa Ponsa as Senora Martinez. During her pregnancy, Salma had been a huge help and the two women had become firm friends. Following the birth of Anna, Salma had always been there to help. She had been devoted to Anna and this was why Patience could not understand why Salma seemed to be avoiding her. It could not be that after the break-up of the marriage Salma had taken Raul's side, when she and Anna had left, Salma had promised to write and telephone and she had done so. It could not be that.

Once again, when Patience saw Salma, she approached her and was shocked to see that Salma was not crying, the only woman at the villa who was not. Looking at her, Patience thought that she had not shed any tears at all, her eyes were not red or bloodshot in any way. As before, when Salma spotted Patience coming towards her, she turned on her heels and hurried away. Patience was dumbfounded and did not know what to do. She was rooted to the spot, should she go after her or what? The decision was taken out of her hands by her father who came and led her to the table insisting that she ate something.

Patience sat beside her mother and did eat a small amount, the first solid food she had managed since she had heard the awful news. She told her mother about the strange behaviour of the nanny. Suzanne however was not concerned in any way, shape or form and told Patience that people grieved in many different ways. Patience accepted this as a fact but was not convinced. She was certain something was wrong but what could it be? It was a mystery to Patience but maybe mother was right.

Soon Raul came over to tell them that the car would be there for them in ten minutes to take them to the airport. He informed Jameson that their bags had been packed and would be at the door for them. Jameson thanked Raul for his hospitality which Raul shrugged away then went to round up his wife and daughter.

They said their goodbyes to Raul, Maria and Esther along with their husbands and children. It was rather awkward when Inez came to say goodbye, Henry and Suzanne did in fact say goodbye, Patience on the other hand gave Inez another withering look before walking past her to the waiting car.

The journey to the airport was made in silence, each of them lost in their own thoughts. Patience's thoughts were focused on the strange behaviour of the nanny. Despite what mother had had to say, as far as Patience was concerned, it was quite out of character for Salma to act in this way. It was not correct to say that Patience had been looking forward to seeing Salma again due to the circumstance but she had wanted to speak to the nanny and reminisce with her about the happy days they had spent together when Anna was a baby. Also, Patience had expected Salma to be at her side throughout the service and was at a loss to understand why this had not happened.

Thankfully, they suffered no delays in checking in. Patience was understandably very upset and her mother hung onto her as they waited in line at the check in desk. Her condition was noticed by the check in girl who alerted one of her colleagues who came over to see what the matter was. No doubt they suspected that Patience had been drinking.

Once they had been made aware of the circumstances, Patience and her parents were whisked through check in and taken to a private room to await boarding. They were also given priority at boarding and shown to their seats by a sombre member of the cabin crew.

The flight left on time though Patience was not aware of it. Sitting by the window with her mother next to her and her father on the outside, Patience spent the entire flight silently staring out of the window. Her mother had to both fasten and unfasten her seat belt.

Though silent, Patience was sobbing and did not notice when her mother took her hand, nor was she aware that her mother held her hand all the way back to Manchester.

Henry and Suzanne steered their daughter through passport control as Patience was unable to do anything for herself. In fact, Henry had to explain the circumstances to the man checking passports as Patience was unable to go to the counter alone with her passport. Luckily, the officer on duty was sensible and they went through without any problems.

In the car on the way home to Little Thornley, Patience sat in the back of her father's Mercedes S500 crying. In the front, Henry and Suzanne listened to their heartbroken daughter wracked by her grief. Either one of them would have willingly given up their own life to bring Anna back but that of course was impossible. For once, they were unable to say anything to make Patience feel better.

Chapter 3

For the first couple of days following their return from Majorca, Patience did not leave her bed. She did not eat but her mother was able to keep her hydrated by giving her water regularly.

With no sign of Patience coming round, Suzanne, on the third day, telephoned their GP, Dr Greene and told him what had happened.

Dr Greene had been their family doctor for many, many years and had been looking after Patience since she was eight years old, coincidently the same age that Anna had been. He came to the house after lunch and examined Patience. Over a pot of tea in the kitchen after he had completed his examination, Dr Greene explained to Henry and Suzanne that there was nothing physically wrong with Patience, just the heartbreak of losing Anna and the feeling of utter helplessness. He was certain that she would get back to a semblance of normality in due course. His main concern was that Patience should eat.

'Just give her time,' he advised. 'Obviously you will keep an eye on her and try to get her to eat something, in the meantime, you could get her a food supplement from the chemist which will help her to keep her strength up until she feels like eating again.

And she will. I cannot say when but mark my words, she will be back to normal and I would say it will be sooner rather than later.'

Once Dr Greene had left, Henry went out himself to purchase the food supplement that the good doctor had recommended. Suzanne went up to take a look at Patience and was pleased to see that she had fallen asleep. She had not slept properly since they had returned home. This time she managed a good hour before waking, calling out her daughter's name. By the time Suzanne reached her, Patience was crying hysterically. Suzanne, herself crying, hugged her daughter and tried to comfort her. Like any normal parent, Suzanne was in pieces seeing her daughter so distraught.

The following day, Patience got out of bed and went downstairs to join her parents in the kitchen. Suzanne made her a drink of the supplement recommended by the doctor. Patience managed to drink it all before going back upstairs. An hour later, Suzanne looked in on her and found her room empty. A quick look in Anna's room revealed Patience lying on her daughter's bed clutching Anna's favourite teddy bear. After hugging her, Suzanne gently took the teddy from her before leading her back to her own room. Then, by being rather firm with her, something she hated doing, Suzanne insisted that Patience took a shower. The main bedrooms of the house were all equipped with en-suite bathrooms.

When she came out of the shower, Suzanne dried her long blonde hair for her then made her dress which Patience did, if rather mechanically. The two of them then went downstairs where Suzanne made them both a hot drink.

'Mother, do you remember what I said about Salma?' Patience asked after a while.

'Yes of course I do darling,' her mother replied. 'I also remember saying that people showed their grief in many different ways.'

'I know that mother, but…,'

'But nothing darling,' her mother interrupted. 'Salma was too upset to come and speak to us. What other reason could there be? As I said, everyone is different.'

'Yes, but…,'

'Patience,' Suzanne spoke sharply to her daughter who stopped speaking immediately, 'Please do not torture yourself. Anna has gone. We are all devastated and would do anything to turn the clock back but we cannot. It is impossible as you know. You must not keep hurting yourself by this thought about Salma.

Your father and I do not want you to harbour any false hopes as it will only make things worse in the long run. Please darling, do not do this.' By now Suzanne was crying. Patience hugged her mother before going back to her room where she lay down and tried to rest. Finding herself too restless to settle, Patience went back over recent events. Something was troubling her but due to her lack of sleep and deep upset, she was unable to bring the thought to the forefront of her mind.

Despite her grief, Patience was a sensible woman and told herself not to try to force the thought out as it would come to her in due course. The rest of that first week passed for Patience in a tear stained daze. At night, when she managed to fall asleep, a recurring nightmare woke her repeatedly.

She imagined herself sat by a road in Majorca watching as a BMW came round a bend right in front of her. The car was travelling in slow motion, the driver was Inez. Then Raul would appear. He was dressed as the devil complete with the regulation pair of horns, forked tail, goatee beard and trident.

As the car rounded the bend where she was sitting, Raul would open the driver's door and give his hand to Inez as she stepped out. The car continued in slow motion to the edge. Raul and Inez stood and waved to Anna who was screaming and trying desperately to unfasten her seat belt and get out of the car.

Then, the car went over the edge and plunged down the ravine bursting into flames at the bottom. Patience, now standing, watched in horror. She was then joined by Raul and Inez. Raul told her that if he could not have Anna then neither could she have her in this world. Anna would join him in hell.

Anna then stepped out of the car, flames completely covering her small body. Raul and Inez disappeared from her side only to reappear at the bottom of the ravine with Anna. Each of them took one of Anna's hands, turned and walked away. They only ever took two steps before vanishing completely.

At that point Patience would wake up, covered in sweat, calling Anna's name aloud, over and over. Her parents would rush in to her bedside and comfort their distraught daughter.

After a few nights of this, Dr Greene was again called in and he prescribed a sleeping draught which managed to get Patience through the night.

With the sleeping draught at least giving her some rest, Patience finally remembered what had been troubling her. Her parents were in the kitchen eating breakfast when Patience burst in.

'Mother, daddy, I must talk to you urgently,' Patience cried, joining her parents at the kitchen's centre island.

'What is it darling?' her father asked, kindly.

'It is about Salma. No please mother, just listen, I beg you,' Patience pleaded. Exchanging a look with his wife, Henry smiled at his daughter.

'Of course we will listen darling. What is it you want to say to us?'

'As I said, it is about Salma. When we were in Majorca, Salma didn't once either speak to me or even look at me. Don't you find that at all strange?' Patience demanded of her parents.

'No Patience. As I said at the time, and have said since, people show their grief in different ways. You accepted this then, why not now? You keep torturing yourself with this, going on about Salma and I cannot see why.

I do not wish to seem harsh darling but continually going on about Salma will not bring Anna back.'

'I'm afraid that I agree with your mother darling,' added Henry. 'Neither of us want you to keep this up. We both love you and like you, we will never get over this but time does help one come to terms with grief.

If however you keep worrying about why Salma did not speak to you, you will never be able to come to terms with the situation and move on. We do not want you to forget Anna, on the contrary, you must always remember her but do please darling let this unhealthy obsession with Salma go.'

For several seconds, Patience faced her parents, the tears streaming down her lovely face. Then she spoke, her voice so quiet, her parents had to strain to catch her words. 'I'm sorry, I just can't.' Then Patience turned and left the kitchen. Suzanne made as if to follow but Henry put his hand on her arm and shook his head.

Back in her room Patience sat down, her mind suddenly clear. 'I know Anna is alive,' she said aloud to herself. 'What I don't know is how I know this.'

Patience there and then vowed to write down everything that she could remember from the cremation and then go over it again and again until the answers came to her.

Taking pen and paper, Patience began to assemble her thoughts on paper under the heading 'Salma'.

It was perhaps a couple of weeks later, about the twentieth of May, Suzanne asked her daughter what was on her mind. The past two weeks had seen Patience's health improve, she was now eating, not as much as in the past but a definite improvement which had come as a relief to her beleaguered parents. The two women were alone, apart from Aggi the maid, in the house, and were sitting in the TV lounge. Henry Jameson was out at a golf dinner.

Suzanne had killed the sound on the TV as she asked her question. She had waited for this moment to ask though she had wanted to bring this up for a few days now. Having asked the question, Suzanne was well aware of what the answer would be.

Patience looked at her mother, the two of them were sitting side by side on the sofa. 'Mother, it's Anna of course. Please bear with me and hear me out.' Suzanne nodded for Patience to continue. 'I simply cannot get over how Salma acted at the cremation and after at the villa. I know you said that people grieve in different ways and I agree with that. Also, everything that you and daddy said is right and I agree, or in other circumstances I would. You won't be surprised to know that I don't agree in these circumstances. It was just so out of character for her. In fact, I was expecting Salma to be at the door of the villa waiting when we arrived.

You know as well as I do that she was devoted to Anna, I will not accept that she was so grief stricken that she would not at least speak to me.' Suzanne sat in silence for a few moments digesting what Patience had said, before telling her daughter that she would speak to her husband once again about the matter. She would however wait until she thought the time was right to broach the subject. Patience smiled gratefully at her mother before hugging and kissing her and saying how pleased she was that they had had this conversation. Patience added that she had wanted to speak to her father but that she had been afraid to do so because he was so upset at losing Anna.

Now that she had spoken to her mother about her thoughts, Patience began to feel better and regained some of her appetite, something that was not missed by her parents.

Suzanne did not mention the subject again until the Thursday of that week, the twenty fifth. They had all sat down to dinner that night when Suzanne said that Henry wanted to speak to them. He asked Patience to go over her thoughts and feelings about Salma and her strange behaviour for his benefit. Patience was happy to do so.

'It all started when we arrived at the Villa Borgosa. During the flight out to Majorca and the ride from the airport, I had been expecting Salma to be at the door waiting to greet us. I thought that she would be in as much distress as we were over the accident and would want to see us as soon as we arrived, I was quite surprised to say the least when she was not there. I thought perhaps she was doing something and did not worry at the time.

When, after we had eaten, I went for a walk in the garden with Maria and Esther, I looked for her, expecting her to appear at any moment. Even when I came back indoors and found you in conversation with the police Chief, I expected Salma to come and find me. She had to have been as upset as I was but she never appeared. I remember lying in bed that night thinking how strange it was.

The following morning I confess that Salma went completely out of my mind, that was no doubt due to the cremation. I am sure I saw her outside the church after the service and, I am sure, I started towards her and she turned her back on me and walked away.

I saw her again later at the villa and again made to go to her. Once again, she turned on her heels and walked away. I noticed on both occasions that she was not crying, nor did it appear that she had been. My initial reaction when she turned her back on me was one of shock. I told mother about it but she told me not to worry as people show their grief in different ways.

At the time I accepted that because, to be honest, I was too upset to really think too closely about things but the more I thought about it, the more strange it became and the more out of character her behaviour at that time was. Something was nagging at the back of my mind but I could not think of what it was. I didn't worry because I knew it would come eventually and it has. It is the fact that Salma was not crying then, nor had she been crying at all.

Salma was devoted to Anna, I remember once when Anna was a year old, she fell and cut her knee. Salma could not stop crying, in fact, she cried about it far more than Anna did. I cannot believe that she would cry over a cut knee yet not cry because the child had died. It does not make any sense nor does it ring true.

The only reason that I can come up with to explain Salma's behaviour is this. Anna is not dead. I know that this sounds really silly in view of the cremation we attended but I have been thinking of nothing but this almost ever since we returned home.

It is inconceivable to me that Salma would not cry over Anna or come to me to comfort and be comforted.

I am aware of how controversial my thoughts are but please believe me, I have not come to this conclusion lightly or for that matter, quickly. It is how I feel and I am sure that I am right.'

Patience could not have caused more of a stir even if she had danced naked on the table while the vicar was dining with them. Before either of her parents could say anything, she continued.

'Salma would have been devastated by Anna's death, as we are, and no way would she have not been there to comfort me and have me comfort her. Remember how close we became during my pregnancy, when Raul was away on business or whatever it was he was doing, Salma was more often than not my only companion. Oh, Maria and Esther came round from time to time but in the main, it was Salma and I. We spent hours sitting and chatting, Salma knitting little bootees for the baby, going for walks and so on, anything and everything, we did it together. If I had been here, then I would have had you mother for this but stuck in a foreign country I needed someone and Salma was there for me.

Then, when Anna was born, there were times when I could literally not get near her for Salma. She was absolutely brilliant with Anna and I have no idea what I would have done without her. I know that if she and I had become close, then she and Anna became inseparable. As Anna grew, Salma was always there for her. After I left Raul and came home, not a week went by without either a letter or phone call from Salma, as you both well know. I always replied to her letters and sent her countless pictures of Anna as she grew. No, I cannot accept that Salma would not come to me and, if not console, hug and kiss me, then at the very least, speak to me.'

Jameson did not reply and carried on with his dinner. Patience knew her father well enough to realise that he was thinking over what she had said so she did not interrupt, but carried on with her own dinner. Suzanne had sat silently throughout.

Eventually, Jameson looked across at his daughter. 'Before we or I do anything about this, I want to spend a day or two going over what has been said, to get things clear in my own mind. Then I want to speak to Martin

Keogh about this. Is this all right with you two?' Martin Keogh was the family solicitor and a close friend. Patience and Suzanne both voiced their agreement to Jameson's terms before he continued. 'If you are correct, and at this moment in time I am not saying you are either right or wrong, unless the whole crash was a sham and included in the deception was a false police report, which I cannot accept, then someone perished in that car. If it was not Anna, then who was it?'

Patience looked at both her parents in turn before saying that she had not considered that point. She just knew it was not her daughter who had died in that crash. She then wanted to know when her father would see Martin Keogh.

'Monday next over a round of golf,' was his answer.

Patience was hardly the embodiment of her name over the next few days. She had begun to sleep better, the nightmare had been replaced by dreams but all her dreams centred on Anna and she awoke every morning with her daughter's name on her lips. It was not until after dinner on the Monday that Jameson sat down with his wife and daughter and told them of his discussion during his round of golf. He had told Martin everything he knew about the situation, the details they had of the accident, the thoughts of Patience about the nanny's actions, everything he knew the solicitor now knew.

'We are meeting Martin for lunch Wednesday at the Lansdowne to discuss matters further.' Again Patience could hardly contain herself as she waited for the meeting with Keogh.

Finally, Wednesday arrived and they met the solicitor for lunch as arranged. Apart from being the family solicitor, Martin was a valued friend of the Jameson family. He greeted Suzanne and Patience with a kiss to their respective cheeks and Henry with a handshake. Once they had settled down with a drink and their lunch order taken, Martin told them that he had considered very carefully what Henry had told him over golf. He went on to say that at the moment they had no evidence to support the theory. As Patience made to protest, he smiled and held up his hand, asking her to bear with him. She smiled in return and kept quiet.

'Please don't get me wrong,' he said to Patience. 'I appreciate your feelings and accept that you know Salma better than any of us. The simple fact is that we are unable to do anything about this without hard evidence to back up the claim.

We cannot go to the police as it seems that the Chief, Senor Caldano is a friend of Raul and if we do approach him, he will likely as not go straight to Raul and tell him of our suspicions. Just as we cannot speak to Caldano, neither can we go to any other Spanish authority without evidence. Without using any names, I have spoken to a contact in London who has extensive European contacts. He is going to find the name of someone in authority for us to talk to once we have the necessary evidence to back up our theory that Anna is alive and well.

Incidentally, I want you to know that I believe you without question that Anna is alive.'

'Thank you for that Martin,' Patience replied. 'How are we going to get the evidence that we need?' she then asked, the anguish in her voice there for all to hear. Martin was able to reassure her by saying that he had ways and means at his disposal to gather the evidence they needed. Patience was reassured, she had known Martin for several years and in fact he acted for her when she had divorced Raul. She trusted him totally.

Their lunch continued with the conversation touching on Anna, as well as on other topics. At one point, Martin waved to a man on the other side of the room. As Patience looked, he waved back. Patience saw a good looking man of about her own age, she recognised him from having seen him in the gym and pool area of the hotel but did not know who he was. He was about six feet tall with a medium build. His brown hair was worn rather long but suited him, she thought. He was tanned and walked with an easy, graceful step. He looked quite athletic and exuded strength in an understated way. Dressed in a blue polo shirt and black trousers, he had a nice, kind face. He looked to be the type of man she wished she had met at some point in her life.

'A friend of yours Martin?' she asked, trying not to sound too interested.

'Yes, a good friend actually. His name is Matthew Bentley. He used to work with me at Claytons before he jumped ship and started his own business,' Martin replied, thoughtfully. 'He is a private investigator and he does a lot of work for me.'

After lunch they went their separate ways, Martin returned to his office, the others back to Little Thornley. They did not hear from Martin until the thirtieth of May when he telephoned Jameson to say that he had spoken with a Senor Almunia, the Majorcan Minister of Justice who had told him that if or when they had the evidence needed to support their claim that a crime had been committed on the island, then he should contact him and he would look into it on their behalf. This is what Martin had been waiting for.

'We now have a place to go with our evidence,' Jameson said to his wife and daughter after his call with his solicitor. 'All we need now is just that. Martin is coming here Monday evening, the third of next month and is bringing with him the private investigator he pointed out the other day when we were having lunch. Martin speaks very highly of this chap and cannot recommend him enough however, Martin will not say anything to him about the case, we will tell him all about it when he is sitting down here with us.' The two ladies were delighted with the news and at last that something was going to happen.

Chapter 4

It might have been the beginning of June, Monday the third to be exact, but at five am it was a bit chilly, especially if one was lying in the back of an old van, waiting to see if a crooked baker was at work.

This was the first morning watching the back of Linley's bakery. Mr Linley, the owner, was convinced that the two bakers who came in early to do the actual baking, were on the fiddle. Why did he think this? Well, in my office, the Friday before, he said this.

'Mr Bentley, we are producing the same amount of goods that we have produced for at least twelve months but in the last few weeks, the amount of ingredients I have had to purchase has increased by a third, so, the only reason can be that they are making extra goods which are not for sale in the shop. I am sure that they are selling the extra loaves and the other items elsewhere, and that's why I need a private investigator, you Mr Bentley, to get me the evidence I need to prove this theft.'

So here I was, silly o'clock in the morning, uncomfortable in the back of my van with my trusty Nikon at the ready.

It was at times like this that I questioned my decision to leave the relative warmth and comfort of a solicitors office to become a private investigator, had I not left the firm where I had worked for a few years and gone to be self-employed, I would not be crouched in the back of my van waiting to see what happened next to Mr Linley's stock.

I had been a clerk with a firm called Claytons who practised in Greenfield. When I started, another lad of around my age, Martin Keogh, was working there, but while Martin wanted to go on and qualify as a solicitor, I had no such ambitions, content to work as a clerk, doing mainly divorce and matrimonial work. This type of work was all right but could be a bit depressing at times. Still, Martin and I had become good friends and I had a great secretary called Daisy who also became a good friend.

Over a period of a couple of years though, I became disillusioned with the job. During my time with Claytons, I had become friendly with a retired police officer called Paul Hilton who, after his retirement from the force, set up a small business as a private investigator and process server, he called it

Hilton Investigations. Over the few years he worked it, he had built up a decent client base, I used him for all my serving and out of office work.

During one of our conversations, Paul told me that he wanted to retire properly and indulge his passions for fishing and golf and to spend more time with his wife, presumably as long as that didn't interfere with his hobbies.

Knowing as he did that I was fed up with the law, Paul offered me the business of Hilton Investigations. We discussed this at length, Paul was sure that I had what it takes to make the business a strong one, he himself played at it, and pointed out that if anyone knew what solicitors needed then it was me. It made sense and it could be a good move for me.

I discussed the idea with both Martin and Daisy, both of whom I trusted implicitly and whose opinions I respected. Both were adamant that I should go for it. I wanted to and as the two people closest to me both thought so too, then go for it I would.

Paul and I met and I asked him to name his price, a statement that had him chuckling before he told me that he wanted nothing for the business, he was giving it to me. He told me that it had been his intention to simply retire and walk away but knowing of my disillusionment, he spoke to his wife and told her what he planned to do, she was in total agreement with his decision so here we were. I was speechless, it was a staggering thing for him to do but it turned out that he actually liked me and wanted to do this for me.

Naturally, I tried to get him to name a price but he steadfastly refused so I gratefully accepted his generous offer.

So I left Claytons and began to trade as Hilton Investigations. The fact that I knew, or was known to most of the solicitors in town was in my favour and most were happy to send me their work. Martin at Claytons was brilliant, he promised me Claytons work and kept his promise, he also paid promptly which really helped me out in the early days.

That it worked out was now history, otherwise I wouldn't be in the van at five am. I worked alone for the first year or just over before I decided that I needed some help. I was doing everything, serving all the papers, doing all the observations, tracing all the missing persons, in fact anything and everything. In addition, in the evening I was working late preparing all the reports, affidavits, statements and bills which was tiring to say the least. To put it bluntly, there was no way that I could carry on without cocking something up due to being shattered all the time so I went to see Daisy and asked her to come and join me. She jumped at the chance.

We had worked well together at Claytons and did so again. With Daisy's considerable help, the business went from strength to strength, a fact that I would never forget; without her, there would be no business. She did all the admin leaving me to do the other things; it was a good system and worked well for us.

We had always been good friends but the fact that now, it was only the two of us, and the close proximity in which we worked, meant that we became more than just friends, we became lovers though I don't think that either of us wanted to settle down.

Greenfield is a northern town with around three hundred thousand residents, plenty of commercial business and some industry round the place. It boasted between thirty and thirty five firms of solicitors so there was plenty of work for us. The town also had a busy County Court as well as a Magistrates and Crown Court which provided us with plenty of work.

Quite a lot of people came to the area to settle as jobs were available, the town had good rail links, was easy to get to the motorway system and, we had an airport though for some reason, it never seemed to really take off. No pun intended. From time to time, international flights were available but the airlines seemed to come and go.

Towards the end of last year, it had been Daisy who had pointed out that we really needed more help, we had become really busy with a lot of out of town work coming in so we took on two retired police officers, Karen Adams and Tony Burton, the four of us got on and worked well together, things were good and the future looked bright.

In time, I was able to persuade Paul Hilton to accept a cruise for him and his wife with my grateful thanks.

My reminiscing passed on some time and while it made me feel good, it didn't do much to keep me warm. I was shaken out of my reverie when a Transit van drove past and reversed up to the back door of the bakery. This was promising. The driver got out and took a long look round which was nice of him as it allowed me to take his photograph, by now it was light enough. Satisfied that no-one was about, he rapped on the door of the bakery which opened seconds later. As the driver opened the van, the two bakery workers brought out several trays of goods, bread, barm cakes and so on. I was able to photograph them as they loaded up the van. Mr Linley was right then. I kept snapping away as the thieves loaded up, unaware that they were being captured on disc which doesn't sound right, not like in the old days when we captured stuff on film. Oh well, progress.

Pretty soon they were finished, the van drove off and the guys locked up. I gave it ten minutes before clambering into the driving seat of the van and going home for a hot shower and breakfast.

In the office later, Daisy took the disc from the Nikon and downloaded the pictures, all were pretty good, and clearly, the people could be identified from them, Mr Linley anyway would know his staff, maybe he would know the other one as well but we would see. As Daisy prepared our report, I rang Linley and told him the news.

As for us, another job successfully completed, which was good. Now for the next one. It wasn't long in coming.

Chapter 5

Later that morning, the telephone rang, Daisy answered it and smiled before passing me the phone, it was Martin Keogh at Claytons.

I was pleased that Martin had telephoned as I wanted to ask him who the attractive blonde I had seen him with at the Lansdowne Hotel last week was. Now was my chance, I had been meaning to call. Since I had left Claytons, Martin had done very well. He had qualified as a solicitor with honours and a year later had been offered a partnership which he had gladly accepted. Now, thanks to some retirements and a little bit of falling out, he was senior partner in the firm.

'How are you Matt?' he greeted me. Before I had a chance to respond, he continued, 'Are you by any chance free this evening?' he enquired, 'And if not, can you get out of whatever you are doing as I need you to come with me to meet some rather important clients of mine.'

'I am free actually Martin, who are we going to see?' I asked.

'Later please Matt. For the moment, they are not only clients but close friends too, and they have a serious problem. I have recommended you. Can you be ready for seven and I will pick you up at home?'

'Seven is fine Martin. Who are your clients?' I asked. Surprisingly, he would not say anything else, either about the job or his clients. Very mysterious, I did however press for at least a name and in the end, he relented.

'My clients are Henry Jameson and his family. You saw me having lunch with him, his wife Suzanne and their daughter Patience at the Lansdowne last Thursday.' I had recognised Suzanne Jameson as someone I saw at the hotel's leisure club though I did not know who she was and we had not spoken.

'So the blonde was Patience Jameson eh,' I said, 'Very nice too.'

'You don't change Bentley,' he retorted. 'See you at seven.' Then he was gone.

Naturally, Daisy wanted to know what was going on so I told her what Martin had had to say and how I had seen him at the Lansdowne last week. Daisy wanted to know what I knew about Henry Jameson. I thought for a moment or two before answering her.

'Well, he is a multi-millionaire, I believe he made his money in property in Manchester before moving over here. He inherited several buildings from his father but as far as I know, he has trebled the amount that he now owns.

He also has bought out several businesses that were on the verge of liquidation and turned them round before moving them on at a profit. One thing he has got Daisy is a good reputation, not easy for a man in his position.'

'What about Patience?' Daisy asked. 'An odd sort of name don't you think?'

'What's in a name,' I said. 'Patience is a very beautiful woman, something of a businesswoman in her own right as far as I know,' I mused. 'She too has a good reputation or at least I don't know of anything bad about her.' In my business, you got to hear a lot about all sorts of people but the Jameson's were well regarded. 'I know Suzanne Jameson by sight,' I said to Daisy. 'She uses the leisure club at the Lansdowne and I have seen her there several times but I don't know her. I think that I have seen Patience there too but without knowing who she was.' Suzanne was actually a very good looking woman who had kept herself in good shape, it was easy to see where Patience had got her looks from, though I didn't say this to Daisy.

Daisy was pleased though, any work for a multi-millionaire was good news in her book. Anyway, that was for tonight, we still had the day's work to do. While Daisy went through the post and allocated the work for Karen and Tony, I brought our work book up to date. The work book was the book in which we entered all the work that came into the office and gave it a reference number. When the job was completed, the date was entered along with who had actually done the job, the date of the bill and the date of payment. A simple system but it worked for us.

During the morning, Karen and Tony popped into the office with their weekly work records for Daisy. The two of them were self-employed and each week they gave me, via Daisy, a work sheet totalling all that they had done. It served as their invoice to me and satisfied my accountant in the bargain. I then paid them a week behind, a system which suited everyone. Daisy then gave them their new jobs and they drifted off to make a start. Karen and Tony did almost all the serving of papers on people between them and also did some missing person work though in the main, I did most of that. I also did most of the accident reports too. There was enough work for all of us. Both Daisy and I thought that they had something going but as they never mentioned anything, then neither did we. It was their business.

For lunch, we usually had a sandwich in the office so that the phone was covered all the time. I did not like to miss anything though the phone could be switched to either mine or Daisy's mobiles if need be. Today, Daisy wanted to go out so I would stay in and answer any calls that came in. I popped out to get myself a sandwich from the nearby sandwich shop and by coincidence, Martin was in there doing the same thing. He was rather reluctant to say anything about the evening meeting but did say that it was a serious matter and concerned Patience and her daughter, Anna. He refused to say any more and went back to his office. What he had not said intrigued me rather more than if he had said a lot however, it could wait.

After lunch, I took a walk to the bank to pay in the cheques that we had received that morning, quite a few which pleased me. As it was a lovely June day, I took a walk round and bought a CD before heading back to the office around three thirty. Martin had phoned while I had been out and left a message that I was to dress in a businesslike manner that evening. Daisy suggested a nice suit without a tie. That would do.

At four thirty, I left for the day as I had had enough, Daisy would leave at five. At home I put a Santana CD on having left my new one in the office, Caravanseri actually. The music of the Santana band always helped me to relax. I went and prepared myself something to eat while I listened to the music then sat down with a drink and watched a little sport on TV. At six, I went for a shower and shave and got ready for my meeting with Henry Jameson and his family.

I dressed in a lightweight navy suit with a pale blue shirt and black shoes and thought I looked fine; professional enough to meet Jameson at any rate. At six thirty, Daisy rang to ask what I was wearing, after I told her she considered for a moment before announcing her approval. Her parting remark was that she did not want me turning up at the home of a multi-millionaire looking like the village idiot. Charming but that was the nature of our relationship, she could say what she wanted to me and I would never be offended.

Chapter 6

Martin arrived promptly at seven in his new car, an Audi Q7. It was the first time I had seen the Audi though I had heard plenty about it from him. It was really nice, black with a black leather interior with all the latest refinements, I was extremely impressed with it and said so which pleased him.

Martin was thirty four years old, some four years older than me. He was married to Carole and had been for eight years now. They had two children, John, six and Chloe who is just four. I am actually godfather to Chloe who is a gorgeous little thing.

On the way, Martin told me that the Jameson's lived in a village called Little Thornley which was about fifteen miles from Greenfield, and went on to say that the job they wished to speak to me about was very delicate and a lot would depend on them taking to me. I did not mind that, they needed to have confidence in me if they were to employ me.

As he would not say anything else about his clients, we chatted generally in the half hour it took us to get to Little Thornley. I had been to the village before, many times in fact for one reason or another. It was a charming little place with a good pub, selling good beer and good food. The village boasted a bakery and a general shop with a post office as well as the pub, the Saracens Head. The large residential properties in the village cost from about a million and I was interested to see Jameson's place.

Martin drove through the village taking a right turn part way through continuing out into the country. 'This land on our left,' he offered, his voice matter of fact, 'all belongs to Henry, around twelve acres in all.' Then he pointed out a wall, just visible between some trees.

'Around the house is a ten foot wall with two or three gates which let you into the grounds.' Then we turned left. On our left was a two storey building though the only windows I could see were in the upper storey.

Martin pulled off the road to the left and we came face to face with a huge pair of iron gates which filled an enormous archway. The gates were closed. A well maintained grass area with a few young trees separated the building from the road. To the right of the gates sat another two storey building again with the windows in the upper storey only. While I sat in the car,

Martin nipped out and rang a bell in the wall. Almost before he was back in the Q7, the gates had started to swing open.

We drove through into a large, paved courtyard and I was able to take a look at the Jameson residence. A long, two storey building, it looked to have three sides. Facing the gates was a large double door. I counted four windows to the right of it and three to the left.

The house continued round to my left as I looked with more windows and a door. Next was two garage doors. The wing, I could not think how else to describe it, was also two storey. I got out of the Audi and looked behind me. That must be the two storey building I saw from the road. Two more garage doors then the gates, at the other side of the gates, two more garages. Six garages in all, but, I reasoned, with three adults in the family, they would have more than one car.

To the right of the house, was what looked to be an extension, then a high wall with a gate set into it.

'That leads in to the grounds,' Martin advised, having followed my gaze.

As we approached the doors, the one on the right opened and a rather attractive oriental girl admitted us. She obviously knew Martin who introduced me. Her name was Aggi and she was the maid. She smiled and bowed slightly as we entered.

Inside, a long corridor ran the length of the house, all the windows letting the evening sunlight in. Along the corridor to the right was a pair of double doors which no doubt led into the extension on the end. It turned out to be a guest suite as I later discovered.

To my left, an imposing archway led off somewhere, in front of me a large staircase. The floor was covered in a burgundy carpet, the walls plain white. Paintings adorned the walls at intervals lending a splash of colour to the white walls. Two or three narrow tables were placed up against the wall in the hallway, each contained a vase with flowers adding yet more colour, it looked like a typical English country home and looked as if it could feature in one or other of the glossy magazines.

The two of us followed Aggi who led us to a doorway on the right. After knocking and opening the door, the maid stood aside to let us enter. I went in after Martin. The room he led me into must have been thirty feet square, it seemed huge to me, being used to my little lounge. The same carpet had been laid in here too with the same white walled colour scheme. More paintings hung on the walls to provide the colour to break up the white.

The room contained only four items of furniture, three rather large white leather sofas were arranged round a huge coffee table which looked to be made of solid oak. I would not have wanted to try to move it. The fourth side faced the fireplace. As I looked round, I noticed double doors out into the garden, all I could see of this was a well-manicured lawn and some flower beds which were ablaze with colour.

Now though, it was time to meet my prospective clients.

In the room, three people awaited us and rose as we entered, a man, Henry Jameson no doubt, his wife and daughter. Jameson stepped forward to greet us. He stood about six feet tall and was of medium build. His hair, of which he had a full head, was grey and well cut. I guessed him to be in his sixties. He was wearing a grey suit and looked as if he had been dashingly handsome in his younger days, he had a sort of Stewart Grainger look about him. After shaking hands with Martin, Martin introduced me. His handshake was firm, this was something I liked in a person.

'I am very pleased to meet you Mr Bentley,' he said. 'Martin has told me a great deal about you. I smiled and said hello as we shook hands. Then Suzanne Jameson stepped forward as Jameson introduced her. We shook hands, her grip was firm too.

'I know Mr Bentley at least by sight darling,' she said. 'You use the leisure facilities at the Lansdowne Mr Bentley, I have seen you there.' Suzanne Jameson was very attractive as I had said to Daisy, about mid-fifties, five four or so, blue eyes, fair hair. She wore a dark blue silk dress which fitted her curvy body very well.

'Hello Mrs Jameson, I'm delighted to meet you,' I responded. 'I have seen you at the Lansdowne many times though we have not spoken before so it's nice to meet you at last.' It was too, she was quite a good looking woman. As he shook hands with her father, Patience was at last able to take a close look at the man she knew to be Matthew Bentley. Last week, when she had first seen him from across the bar of the Lansdowne, she had had a feeling that his eyes would be blue, how she did not know. And now that he was here being introduced, she could see that she had been right.

He was just a little shorter than father and looked to be fit and healthy. His brown hair was just a little too long to be fashionable but it did suit him. Not movie star handsome, he was nonetheless a good looking man. When he smiled, which he seemed to do regularly, it always reached his eyes which twinkled in the evening sunlight.

To Patience, Matthew exuded a quiet confidence and she guessed that he had hidden strength, not a man to indulge in idle boasting or one to make rash promises.

With a sigh, Patience thought that this was a man she should have met earlier in her life and instinctively felt that she could trust him with anything.

Now it was time to for me to meet Patience. From across the Lansdowne she had looked great. Now, close to, great did not do her justice. She was simply stunningly beautiful. About thirty or so, about five feet six or seven, a blue eyed blonde with a body to die for. Firm looking breasts, I just happened to notice, a slim waist and long legs which she had dressed in a pair of tight jeans. A grey tee shirt completed her outfit. As she turned to sit, I could not help notice that the jeans fitted in all the right places.

It was evident where she got her good looks from and I said so. Both mother and daughter smiled at the compliment though I suspect that it was not the first time they had heard it. When she shook my hand, Patience said that it was nice to meet me. Like her parents, she too had a firm grip. She was smiling as she spoke. Somehow, I felt like I had passed the first test.

One thing that I noticed about my prospective clients, though they all smiled, none of them looked really happy. I did sense that when Patience smiled properly, and it reached her eyes, it would transform her entire face.

When we had all sat and received a drink from the maid, Martin opened the proceedings. He told me that he had met Henry Jameson some twelve years ago, Jameson had been a client of Claytons when he had joined the firm. After he had qualified, he had taken over looking after Henry's business following the death of old Mr Clayton. They became good friends as well as solicitor and client. He concluded by saying that the Jameson's needed some very discreet enquiries carrying out in Majorca and that these enquiries could possibly take several weeks to complete.

'Could you be available to go to Majorca for a few weeks work any time soon?' he asked me.

After a moment or two thinking, I looked at him. 'Yes I could. Daisy is more than able to run the office, Karen and Tony can do the work that comes in, it will not be a problem for me to be away.' I thought I noticed a look of relief on the faces of the other four people in the room.

Now it was time for Jameson to take over. He stood and began to pace as he spoke. He said that he had asked Martin for the name of an investigator whom he trusted completely, one who would do a thoroughly professional job at all times and who could keep things to himself. Martin had had no hesitation in recommending me. I looked at Martin and nodded my thanks before saying to Jameson that I appreciated what Martin had said about me and that it was my aim to do as good a job as was possible for all my clients.

'May I call you Matthew?' he asked, and when I said of course, he continued, 'I am Henry. What I am about to tell you happened on the twenty seventh of April this year in Majorca and concerns my granddaughter Anna. To give you the complete picture, I must ask you to bear with me, I will try not to bore you but I do feel that it is important for you to be aware of everything including the background.

Our daughter Patience is our only child and we love her enormously, the only other person we love in the same way is her daughter, our grand-daughter, Anna.

When Patience was young, we always went to Majorca for two weeks holiday each year. We stayed in Santa Ponsa. In time, we became friendly with some local people, the Martinez family. They had three children, Raul, Maria and Esther. The children got on well together as did my wife and I with their parents. Senor Martinez and I did some business together and we all became firm friends, so much so that we began to spend our fortnight at their villa, the Villa Borgosa. The villa backs on to one of the golf courses which is near the seaside in Santa Ponsa.

Anyway, I digress. It was, with an almost certain inevitability that Patience and Raul would fall in love and so it happened. As far as we were concerned, the man was all right and they married, sadly by this time Senor and Senora Martinez had passed away and the daughters had left home, married themselves. Patience and Raul lived in Santa Ponsa in the family villa which passed to Raul as the eldest.

A couple of years after the wedding, they had a child, Anna who is now eight, our only grandchild and the apple of our eyes.' By now, I was certain that the problem was with the kid.

Jameson continued with his story. 'Sadly, the marriage did not last very long, Patience and Raul separated when Anna was two, the two of them returned here to live. On behalf of Patience, Martin obtained a divorce in the Greenfield County Court where Patience was granted sole parental responsibility. Raul accepted this without ever being too happy about it. The ancillary matters were concluded without any problems and Raul naturally wanted contact with his daughter and we as a family never had a problem with that.

He would come to England every two or three months for a few days and spend time with Anna. The child seemed to enjoy the experience and her behaviour was never an issue after one of his visits.

When he last came in February of this year, he asked if perhaps Anna could go to stay with him for a week in Santa Ponsa in April during her school holidays. Patience did not answer straight away saying, quite rightly, that she needed time to consider the request. Raul accepted this without fuss. Patience came home and discussed it with her mother and I, Martin was consulted over the legal implications. In the time that Raul had been coming to visit, there had never been a problem so we, that is to say Patience, decided to let her go. Anna herself wanted to go, she is a well-adjusted child and we all felt that she should know of the request and give her opinion.

Looking after the young child would not be a problem. Raul and his sisters had a nanny, Salma, when they were small. Salma still lived at the villa and while Patience was there, and pregnant, Salma looked after her as she did with the baby following the birth. She had been devoted to Anna so the decision was taken to let her go.

Martin made the necessary application to the court for permission to take the child out of the jurisdiction, which was granted. Raul was to fly to

Manchester to collect her, then the two of them would fly back, this was on the twenty fourth of April, he would bring her back on the fourth of May. Patience took her to the airport to meet her father and off she went without any problem whatsoever.

On the evening of the twenty seventh, as we sat watching the television, the telephone rang, Patience went to answer it. Suzanne and I heard her cry out and as we turned to look at her, we saw her drop the telephone and slump to the floor. My wife ran to her and I picked up the telephone. It was Raul, he told me that there had been a terrible accident that afternoon. The car in which Anna had been a passenger had run off the road on the way to Port de Soller which is on the west side of the island. The car had gone off the road, gone down some sort of cliff and had burst into flames and Anna had died in the inferno. The car had been driven by Inez Castillar who is the new girlfriend of Raul, she by the way managed to get out safely.'

I was stunned. All along I had expected the problem to be that Raul would not send the kid back to her mother and that my job would be to travel to Majorca to serve some sort of court order on him requiring him to hand the kid over, presumably to Patience, it would have been nice to go to Majorca with her but that was a none starter. I wondered what they wanted me to do, if the kid was dead I could not imagine what I could do for them. I looked across at both the women, the two of them had tears in their eyes but a look of steely determination was on their faces.

Jameson continued, 'We took the first available flight to the island and Raul met us at the airport. He took us back to the villa where we stayed overnight. He had arranged the cremation for the twenty ninth of April. Patience did want to see the body but Raul persuaded her not to as the poor child had suffered 100% burns and was totally unrecognisable.

The evening before the cremation, the twenty eighth, the Chief of the Santa Ponsa Police, Capitan Caldano came to the villa with the police report into the accident. As far as the police were concerned, it was a tragic accident. The driver, Inez, had been breathalysed at the scene, the test proved to be negative. There were no skid marks on the road to indicate that she had been driving too fast. Raul and Inez certified that Anna had been in the back of the car, Raul when they had left the villa and Inez when the car had gone over the edge. There was no indication anywhere of foul play therefore there was no need for any further investigations, the autopsy said that Anna had died from the burns she had received when the car had blown up at the bottom of the cliff.

On the day of the cremation, Patience had got her way and had viewed the body. No doubt she regretted doing so as she promptly passed out.' I looked across at Patience and caught her eye, giving her a little sympathetic smile which she returned. The others were looking at me too.

I said the usual things whilst wondering what I could do for them. As I spoke however, Patience interrupted me and dropped something of a bombshell.

'Anna is not dead,' she said. 'It was not Anna who had been in the car at the time of the accident therefore she is alive.' Needless to say, that perked up my interest but before I could speak, Jameson spoke again.

'Someone certainly died in that car, we do not know who. We are however almost certain that it was not Anna.' I could feel all the eyes on me, no doubt waiting for me to ask the obvious question. I did not disappoint them.

'How do you know that it was not Anna who was in the car?' The answer came from Patience.

'We have no hard evidence yet to support our theory however, something happened at the villa the night before the cremation and again at the service, or rather, just after, then once again at the villa which, over the last few weeks, has made me sure that I am right and that Anna is alive.

What happened was this, the Martinez family has employed a nanny, Salma Guttierez, for many years. You remember earlier daddy mentioning Salma? Salma looked after Raul and his sisters when they were little. When I was pregnant and living in Majorca, Raul quite often went away on what he said was business. Salma and I became very close. After the baby was born, Salma helped me an awful lot with her and became devoted to Anna. As she grew, Salma seemed to spend more time with Anna than I did, that's not actually true of course but you know what I mean. When we arrived at the villa for the cremation, I had expected Salma to be at the door waiting for me. That first day, I did not see her at all which was somewhat unexpected.

I did see her after the service outside the church, as I started to go to her, she turned her back on me and walked away. The same thing happened back at the villa. I was, to say the least, surprised by her actions and mentioned it to mother who told me that people showed their grief in many different ways. This I accepted but over the past few weeks, I have thought of little else and am certain that Salma would not have ignored me knowing how she had been with both me and the baby. It simply is inconceivable.

Anna is alive and Salma is aware of it. That is the only reason why she did not come to me.' Having said her piece, Patience sat back on the sofa, looking at me, having edged forward as she became more animated

This was their theory, nanny didn't talk to me. It seemed a load of rubbish to me but when I looked at Martin, he certainly believed it. The Jameson's were sure the child was alive so I bit back the remark that had been on my lips and asked my next fairly obvious question.

'If it was not Anna in the car, then who was it? Raul and Inez have made statements to the police and both say that it was Anna who had been in the car at the time of the accident. Certainly someone had been in the car and had died.' I looked round the room before continuing 'Are we suggesting that Raul a), rigged the police report or b), deliberately crashed a car with someone in it then lied to the police by saying it was Anna, if so, what has he got to gain?'

'It really is very simple,' Patience replied quietly, looking me directly in the eye. 'He wants Anna and I, for one, feel he is capable of anything to get what he wants.'

Jameson said that they had considered going to the police with their theory but had decided against it. Without any evidence it was a little far-fetched. I had to agree. Raul would deny it and anyway, this Captain Caldano was a friend of Raul and as such, unlikely to take it seriously.

What they needed was hard evidence that Anna was alive and to get it, they needed someone out in Majorca for as long as it took, carrying out observations. This could take several weeks. Whoever went, and it looked like being me, would look for any sign of Anna. It would be boring. Jameson was well aware of this but conceded that it was the only way. He said that he

Keith Giles   The Majorcan Affair   44

would pay very well for the service even if the results were not what he was hoping for. Then he asked the question.

'Would you undertake these observations for us Matthew? According to Martin, you are the best man for the job and since he recommended you and we have met you, I agree with him entirely. I think I can safely speak for my wife and daughter when I say you are the man for us.' I was quite flattered and looked at first Suzanne then Patience. The beseeching look on both their faces ensured that the only answer that I could give was to accept.

The two women were openly crying by now. Suzanne stood up and came across to me, I stood up wondering what was going to happen. Nothing alarming as it turned out. She hugged me, thanking me through her tears. Jameson had a tear in his eye as he shook my hand then Patience came over and hugged me. All this and all I had agreed to do was go look for the kid. What would they do if I actually found her? Martin too shook my hand and smiled.

The conversation then turned to when I could go. I felt that I needed a week to prepare and suggested next Monday, the tenth of June. That was not a problem for them. From my point, Daisy could run the office, she did now anyway. Karen and Tony would do the work and Daisy could share out the stuff I did. The only possible problem would be paying them. I usually did this myself on a Friday but surely we could work something out between us, or at least, Daisy and I could.

More to the point, I would need to plan the equipment that I would need to take with me to Majorca, also I would need some sort of a base on the island, a hotel or something. I mentioned this.

Martin answered. 'I had been sure that you would accept the job Matt, and also sure that Henry and family would be happy with you once you had all met. Henry has a good friend on the island, Diego Calva and he has obtained an apartment which overlooks the Martinez villa. It's a couple of hundred metres away but there is nothing nearer. It's on the top floor of a five floor block and our apartment actually overlooks the rear of Raul's villa.

If there is anything else that you need when you are over there, Diego will get it for you. He will meet you at the airport in Palma and leave you the car that he picks you up in. Do you have any preference by the way?' I said that I did not, just as long as it was inconspicuous. Finally Martin confirmed that he had been put in funds by Jameson. This was good news and meant that I would get paid.

We agreed to meet again this coming Friday for an update. Martin again offered to collect me from home and run me back after our meeting.

Then Patience said 'I will get some photographs ready for you to take with you Matthew, when you go.' She had pictures of Anna of course, Raul, Salma and even one of Inez which was taken, she assured me, by her mother.

I thought that it would be very helpful to have pictures of the main players, if I got them Friday I would scan them on to my laptop over the weekend. 'Thanks Patience,' I responded, 'A good idea. I will scan them on to my computer then I can identify all the players easily.' She looked pleased that I had accepted her idea.

Martin and I left the Jameson residence at about half past ten with Henry showing us to the door.

'Matthew,' he began when the three of us were out of earshot of the ladies, 'I must warn you about Raul. My friend Diego has told me that Raul is in fact a criminal and a thoroughly dangerous man. I did not want to say anything to you in front of Suzanne and Patience as I don't want them worrying about Anna, not that I think there is any cause for concern there, the man, whatever he may be, loves his daughter and I am certain that he would not harm her.

That said, I think there is a real possibility that he might harm anyone trying to take her away from him. I just wanted you to be aware of this Matthew, from the outset and to be sure that you take care of yourself.'

'Thank you Henry, it is as well to know these things. I will make sure that I am careful at all times. The thing is, Raul is not expecting me so I should be able to do my work without him knowing.'

On the way back to Greenfield, Martin asked me what I thought. I told him.

'To be honest mate, I'm not too sure about this. Nanny didn't speak to me, it's a bit thin but saying that, they all clearly believe that the kid is alive so who am I to say that they are wrong. In any event, the worst case scenario is that I get a few weeks in the sun and well paid for it.'

'I don't know Bentley, you are a cynical sod. I have to say that at first I thought like you that it was a bit thin but over the past few days, they have convinced me that it is all kosher after all, Patience does knows the nanny and if the two of them got on only half as well as Patience says, then it really is odd that Salma didn't speak to her at the service or at the villa before they came back to England.'

Well fair enough, she could be right, and as Martin said, she did know this Salma better than any one of us. Whatever, I would go and do my best for them.

Chapter 7

I arrived in the office just before nine the following day. As I expected, Daisy was already there and dying to hear about my meeting with the Jameson family. First things first, we needed tea. I made a pot for the two of us and sat down with my cup before I would say anything. Daisy was burning with curiosity but managed, just, to keep her impatience in check.

Eventually I was ready to start. I ran through the details of what I had been told by Henry Jameson and his daughter, missing nothing out. As I spoke, Daisy made no comment nor asked any questions, she was however absorbing all the details and I knew that the questions would come. Once I had finished the story, she was silent for a few moments before she spoke.

'That poor woman, in fact those poor people,' she said. 'I am inclined to agree with Patience and her parents. Without knowing any of them, including the nanny, it does seem that Salma was passing on a sort of message. As she works for Raul she could hardly go up to Patience and say 'Hey Patience, Anna is alive. Your ex has staged a crash and killed a kid so he can take Anna away from you.' Maybe she was under duress from this Raul character who certainly sounds like a piece of work. When we are in possession of all the facts and details at the end of the case, I will bet you, dear boss, that this is what has happened. Wanna take me up on it?' To be honest, I didn't. Daisy was usually right about things like this.

'Also Matt, Mr Jameson is quite right, it will be boring stuck over there on your own just watching and hoping for a glimpse of Anna; what it won't be is anything new to you, after all, you have been doing the job long enough. When are you either intending or hoping to go to Majorca?'

'I told them I would need a week to get everything here sorted out which they accepted as both reasonable and sensible. I hope to go next Monday, the tenth.'

We continued to go over various aspects of the job. Daisy was particularly concerned about Raul and what Henry had said.

'If he is capable of kidnapping his own daughter, possibly kill or arrange to have killed another child, then he will need to be watched very carefully and you will have to watch your back.' I agreed.

The discussion then moved on to the equipment that I would need over there. Daisy, as usual, was way ahead of me.

'Does this apartment have broadband or whatever the Spanish equivalent is, already installed? If not, can it be installed asap, you will need to be able to email me your reports. Also, if you do see Anna and get some pictures, you can send them back too. I can then print them for Martin. Broadband is a must.' She then began to compile a list of questions for Martin with broadband at the top.

Then came the question of photographic equipment. I had, and used a Nikon D80 digital SLR. I had bought the body only and had purchased lenses specifically for my needs. I had a 55-200 mm zoom, an 80-400 mm zoom and a 600 mm telephoto lens. I would take them all, which would be probably one too many but it was sod's law that the one I left at home would be the one I needed.

'What about binoculars Matt?' Daisy posed the question. It was a good one. They would be useful for looking in to the garden of the villa, the trouble was, I just did not fancy carrying them with me because of the extra weight.

'Put a pair of binoculars on the list for Martin please Daisy. I'm sure that Mr Jameson's friend Diego will be able to get his hands on a good pair. Oh, I might as well ask for two tripods as well. I can use one with the binoculars and one with the camera, that way I can have both set up and pointing at the villa just in case I see anything. If I have the 600 mm lens on, that will attach straight on to the tripod and can stay there all the time. If I need to go anywhere with the camera, I can just take the camera off the lens. Easy.'

'You had better not forget to take the laptop with you Matt, be mighty hard to send reports back without it don't you think?' This she said with heavy sarcasm. Once, I had gone to London on a job and forgot to take the laptop along. I had never been allowed to live it down. 'While I get on with opening the post, why don't you phone Martin and get him look in to the broadband situation and the other things on your list?'

A good idea. I rang Claytons and fortunately, Martin was in his office.

'Morning Martin, how are you?' I asked after I had been put through. 'Listen, Daisy and I have been planning, and we have a couple of things for you to do if you will. First, has this apartment got broadband or whatever they call it over there installed? If not, can it be done before I get there? I will need it to email reports and pictures back to Daisy. The second thing is this, can Diego get hold of a good pair of binoculars and two tripods for me to use? I can take them with me but it's just extra things to carry on the plane.'

'Okay Matt, I don't know the answer to the broadband query but I will phone Henry now and get him to call Diego and ask the question. At the same time, he can ask about the tripods and binoculars. When I get an answer, I will call you straight back.

Have you had any further thoughts since we spoke last night?'

'Yeah, I keep thinking about Patience and her obvious belief that her daughter is still alive. It's kind of infectious, isn't it. Also, Daisy is convinced that the nanny, Salma, was, in a roundabout way, sending a message to Patience that only she would understand. I sincerely hope that Anna is alive and well and I can get the evidence needed to get her back. I've never met this Raul but I think he is a complete tosser and I would love to help have him sent to prison for what we think he has done.'

'Are you sure or do you just fancy Patience and want to succeed so you will be in her good books?'

'How can you say such things, I'm shocked and hurt.'

Martin cut the connection, laughing. Did he have a point? Certainly Patience Jameson or Martinez or whatever she called herself now was a beautiful woman. Nah, it was just business but that said, I did want to be the person who got the evidence for her.

While I was on the phone talking to Martin, Karen and Tony had come in to the office. Daisy made us all tea then I sat down with them and told them of my forthcoming trip.

'Next Monday, I am going to Majorca on an observations job. I have no idea at all how long it's going to take but from what I have been told by the client, I expect it will be a few weeks.' Naturally, both Karen and Tony offered to take my place.

'Who is our client Matt?' asked Karen. 'It's going to cost rather a lot to send you out there indefinitely.'

'Our client is Henry Jameson.' I saw no point in being evasive. In any event, no-one had said it was a secret and Daisy, Karen and Tony were very discreet, I trusted the three of them implicitly.

'The multi-millionaire,' Tony mused. 'While I have never been properly introduced to him, I did meet him once when I was on the force. Seems like a nice man.'

I then got down to business.

'While I am away, Daisy will run the office and allocate the work, just as she does now. As far as I can see, things will be pretty much the same as always except that I won't be here. This will mean more work for the two of you but by the same token, this will mean more money. You will need to do between you the stuff I do but I have every confidence that the three of you will manage just fine.'

It was Karen who replied on behalf of the three of them.

'Don't worry Matt. With Daisy in the office and Tony and I out and about, we will make sure that things run smoothly in your absence. One thing though, what about wages?'

This was the area that was giving me something to think about. At the moment, the way we worked was that Karen and Tony were self-employed. They received their work from either Daisy or me, then they went and did it, whatever type of work it was. Once they had completed the job they would give Daisy a report. This report would have their personal reference number on it and would show where, when and at what time the job was done. It would also show all work, times and mileage they had done in order to get the particular job done. These reports were also their invoice to me for payment though they did supply a schedule each Monday. I paid them the Friday of the week following. Karen and Tony received cash, Daisy had hers paid into her bank. Daisy received the same every week and was not self-employed, the others differed each week according to how much work they had done..

I thought that I could do one of a couple of things, I could sign a load of cheques and let Daisy have them, she could then pay Karen and Tony with a cheque or I could ask the bank what they thought about Daisy actually signing company cheques while I was away. As I did not fancy leaving signed cheques, I would ask the bank about the second option.

'I will speak to David at the bank and see about Daisy being allowed to sign cheques then you two can continue to be paid in cash. Is that all right for everyone?'

Tony answered first, 'That's fine with me Matt, the weekly cash saves me a lot of messing about.'

Karen simply nodded her agreement to the proposal. Now it was up to Daisy.

'I don't mind getting cash for Karen and Tony,' she said. 'As my wages are paid into the bank it will be no different for me. Do it this way Matt, providing the bank will agree to it.'

As Karen and Tony both had work to do, they left soon after. As it was almost lunch, Daisy popped out to get sandwiches for us. I took the opportunity to phone David Williams my business manager at the bank. He was not in but I was able to make an appointment to see him Wednesday morning at eleven thirty.

Over lunch, Daisy and I chatted about the Jameson job as we tended to call it. Strictly, it should have been the Martinez job but never mind. We talked over other on-going matters too. As she was going to be on her own Sunday, her husband John was going to be doing some overtime, Daisy offered to come to my home in the afternoon and help me to pack for the trip. That was good, I hated to pack. Martin phoned me back around two thirty.

'Hi there Matt. Henry has spoken to Diego in Santa Ponsa. Wireless broadband is installed at the apartment. He also has a good pair of Zeiss binoculars that he is happy to loan you for the duration of your stay. Also, he will get the two tripods that you need and put everything in to the apartment before Monday. Why do you want two tripods by the way?'

'One for the binoculars, the other one for my camera.'

'Oh, I see. Have you sorted out the office yet?' I told him what I had agreed with the staff and that I had an appointment to see David in the morning. David and Martin were old friends, in fact when I went on my own, Martin introduced me to David who was Claytons banker, and we had become friends over the years. David had set up a business account for me which I had used ever since I had had Hilton Investigations. Martin, David and I played golf together regularly.

I think Martin was pleased to know that everything was under control, he wanted me over in Majorca as soon as possible, I thought that he must be under pressure from his clients all time but the circumstances must be awful for them.

For the rest of the afternoon, I busied myself with the work of the office. That night I sat at home and gave a great deal of thought to the Jameson job. The more I thought about it, the more I began to feel that Patience had a very valuable point. Yes, at first I was sceptical, the nanny didn't speak to me. I mean, it sounds totally daft but the actions of the nanny could be described as strange. Yes Salma could have been too upset to talk to Patience but I thought not. Not in the case of a child's death. Patience knew this woman well and if Salma had only been half as close to Patience and Anna as she had said then it would have been inconceivable for her not to grieve, as in fact Patience had said. It had to be worth the effort of me going to Majorca, if only to put Patience and her parents minds at rest.

I attended the bank the next morning for my meeting with David and we spent the first few minutes chatting generally before he steered the conversation round to business and asked how he could help.

'Next Monday,' I began. 'I am going to Majorca on a job. It's quite likely that I will be away for a few weeks but at this moment in time I just don't know.

Daisy and I have been discussing how I can pay her and the others while I am away. One possible solution would be to make Daisy a signatory to the account until further notice. Is that something that the bank would condone? If so, what do you think David?'

'That would work Matt. I know you pay Karen and Tony in cash and Daisy has hers by transfer. You want that to continue as so far, it has worked well, therefore we can make Daisy a signatory to the account so she can draw cash for the others.

For the safety of both you and the bank, we would want a limit on the amount of cash she can withdraw. I would suggest a maximum of £1500. How does that sound to you?'

It sounded fine to me. Karen and Tony usually earned around £350 to £400 per week but with me being away, that figure could well rise. Personally,

I would be happy if they both earned £1000 per week. That way, I would be earning good money too. I paid them £20 per hour and charged £35, in addition, I paid them 25p per mile and charged 35p. The more work they did, the more I charged. I could make a living without doing any work, point was though, I enjoyed what I did.

David wanted a letter from the firm authorising Daisy to become a signatory, he also needed the two of us to sign a new mandate. Finally, he wanted to introduce her to the senior counter clerk. They would not hand over cash without these things being done which was fair enough. We made another appointment for Thursday afternoon for Daisy and I, I would ask Karen to man the office while we were out.

David and I then went for lunch. He was curious about the Majorcan job. I did not go into details, just told him I was looking for a missing person and that it was very delicate. He knew enough about my work not to press for any more.

Back in the office I asked Daisy to do the letter the bank required then I left. I had a job to do out of town, some enquiries about a missing husband which I wanted out of the way before I went to Majorca. My trip was a success but I was late home, around nine thirty.

Daisy and I attended the bank Thursday afternoon. David accepted the letter we had done and we signed the new mandate before going down to meet the senior counter clerk. We were back in the office by four twenty five, Tony arrived at the same time having been to the County Court to collect some work. He and Karen shared them out then left to get on with them.

At five John, Daisy's husband came to collect her. As he and I got on well, we talked for half an hour before they left. I stayed behind in the office as I wanted to clear some paperwork and as I was in the mood, decided to get it done.

At around six fifteen, the door buzzer sounded. I was surprised to discover that it was Patience at the door, I buzzed her in and met her at the top of the stairs. Our offices were the top floor of a two story building. Patience looked really nice, wearing a blue tee shirt and a black pencil skirt to her knees, at least that's what I thought they were called. Her hair was tied back in a ponytail which I thought suited her, with bare legs and black shoes she looked wonderful but I said nothing.

'Hello Matthew, I hope that you do not mind me calling, I got your office address from Martin the other day. As I was passing I thought I would see if you were still here, as you are, would you like to come for a drink and a chat with me?' She sounded quite shy, maybe she did not usually ask men out, I would think that it would be the other way round. As it was not every day that I was asked out by a millionaire's daughter I gladly accepted. Patience suggested the Hare and Hounds, a pub just out of town. As it was a glorious sunny evening, I could think of nothing I would rather do than sit and have a cold drink with Ms Jameson.

We left the office together after I had shown her round. Her car was parked at the front by mine. I was pleased that I had not used my van, I would not have wanted to accompany Patience in my old van. I drove an Audi A4 Estate, Patience a Mercedes CLK AMG. She led the way to the pub, as I followed her, I noticed that she handled the powerful car well; she seemed to have no need to either speed or show off in any way. My estimation of her rose because of this. It would be too easy for her to flaunt her wealth, she did not. I parked at the side of the Mercedes and went to open her door. In the bar, Patience asked for a small glass of Chardonnay, I had a bottle of Coors Fine Light Beer, she tried to pay but I was having none of that. As it was such a nice evening, we decided to sit outside in the beer garden. As we walked out, quite a few people stared, quite openly, at us. This was no doubt because she was both beautiful and rich, the guys who stared were obviously jealous which gave me a good feeling, they would be thinking that she would be better off with them, I didn't care as my ego was taking quite a boost. We found a secluded table and sat down.

'I'm sorry for coming to your office without phoning first.' I waved her apology away.

'No need to apologise Patience, I'm always ready to go for a beer and a chat on a nice evening like this, especially with such lovely company.' She smiled at the compliment.

'Have you had any thoughts about Majorca?' she asked. Actually, I had had plenty.

'The more I think about it, the more convinced I am that your reasoning is sound. I don't know Salma, you do and you strike me as being a sensible woman, I don't think that you would delude yourself no matter how much you want a result to go your way.

As you feel that Anna is alive and in Santa Ponsa, then I am more than happy to go over there on your behalf and look for her. I am sure that you would not ask me to undertake something that you thought was a wild goose chase.

You have my assurance that I will do everything possible to both find her and obtain sufficient evidence to satisfy any court that Anna is alive and well, or devise a plan to get her back home to you.'

I seemed to have developed the knack of saying the right thing around the Jameson family. Having said that, I noticed tears forming at the corner of her eyes making her rummage in her bag for a tissue. It was my turn to apologise.

'I'm not upset, yes I am sad but these tears are, oh I don't know, maybe I'm just pleased that you believe me and are prepared to go to a strange place by yourself for goodness knows how long, to help me and find Anna for me.'

As she wiped her eyes a couple of guys came over. One of them I knew. Jason Topping was a complete arsehole. We, Hilton Investigations that is, had served papers on him several times because he regularly used to hit his girlfriends, big tough guy.

'Is this fellow bothering you Patience? Just say the word and we will get rid of him for you.' I burst out laughing and was just about to tell him where to go when Patience beat me to it.

'Clear off you boring little jerk,' she said sharply. 'I am having a drink with a good friend and neither need or want you poking your nose in. In any event, the only person I can see you removing would be a girl and only then if she was small and vulnerable. With a man, especially Matthew here, you would have no chance. Now, just go away.' His friend began to laugh as well which only made his temper worse, going bright red Topping flounced away, his friend muttered an apology before following him.

'You know, I thought he was going to stamp his foot,' I laughed. Patience laughed too, something I don't think she had done for quite some time.

'Oh Matthew,' she said, 'I have not laughed in weeks. Thank you so much for cheering me up. If anyone can find Anna for me, it will be you.'

We stayed talking for another hour, Patience was great company. Also, she was a good listener, interested in what I had to say. Her questions were about my work and me as a person. She had no airs or graces and the time unfortunately passed far too quickly. Neither of us had another alcoholic drink as we were both driving but we both had a soft drink to help the evening along. As we left and walked back to where we had parked our cars, I found myself wanting to do this again, especially as she slipped her arm through mine as we walked along.

'Thanks for stopping by,' I said when we reached the cars. 'I have really enjoyed this,' I chanced my arm, 'Perhaps we could do this again one day?'

Smiling, she replied 'Yes. It has been lovely to have a drink and a talk. I have not felt like doing anything for ages now, since, well you know. Meeting you the other night has made me feel human again and it has also filled me with confidence that there will be a successful outcome.

In this last hour, I have laughed and smiled, at one point I thought I would never do so again so it's me who should be thanking you Matthew. And, yes, I would like to do this again, soon.'

Wow, that was a great response. In truth, I had not expected her to agree but I was delighted she had. When she unlocked the Merc, I opened the door for her. Before she got in, she kissed me, just a quick kiss but on the lips, not my cheek. Then she got in her car.

'I will see you tomorrow,' I said as I prepared to shut her door.

'I am looking forward to it already,' she replied, smiling. I closed her door, then she was gone. I drove home thinking about the evening. Patience was certainly a very interesting woman, I wondered if I would get to know her better but immediately discounted it. What could the beautiful daughter of a multi-millionaire possibly see in me?

Chapter 8

Friday was usually a really busy day, today was different, it was just busy. By two thirty, I had had enough and decided to go to the Lansdowne for a sauna. If any more work came in, I was confident that Karen and Tony could handle it. I had prepared their wages so I left the money with Daisy who reminded me that she would be coming round to my place Sunday afternoon to help me to pack, as if I would forget someone doing my packing for me.

I left the office and drove to the Lansdowne. The hotel had a leisure club which included a well-equipped gym, several studios for yoga and so on together with a pool area. In this area, as well as the pool, us members had a sauna, steam room, Jacuzzi and sanarium which was like the sauna but not as hot, to play in. Normally, I would spend at least an hour in the gym before going through to the pool but today, I just did not feel like the gym, I just wanted to loaf around for an hour or two. After all, I was working that night, at least, that was what I told myself. It was of course to be the second meeting with the Jameson family, the last before I went to Mallorca as the Spanish called it.

Fifteen minutes after leaving the office, I was rinsing off under the pool side showers before making my way over to the Jacuzzi where I intended to start my loafing. It had room for about eight or nine people but when I got there, only two people, a couple I did not know, were using it which was good, plenty of room to relax in. I climbed down the stairs and sat down in the hot, bubbly water. Closing my eyes, I relaxed allowing the hot water to surge around me.

'Hello Matthew.' The sound of my name caused me to open my eyes and I saw Suzanne Jameson smiling at me from the top of the steps leading in to the Jacuzzi.

'Hello, how are you?' As I spoke, I stood up and offered her my hand as she came down the steps. Taking it, she came down in to the water. She was wearing a dark blue, one piece swimming costume, the costume looked good on her and she looked extremely attractive though I did not tell her. We sat, side by side, chatting.

'Patience tells me that you had a drink with her last night. You know, it has done her the world of good. She actually came in with a smile on her face, you will believe me when I tell you that I have not seen her smile since this awful affair began.

I was hoping to run in to you before tonight's meeting to thank you, not just for taking the case on, but for believing in us. It means a lot to us that someone who does not know us believes what we say, and I accept that it does sound rather far-fetched when you look at it, and is prepared to go overseas alone for an indefinite period and look for Anna for us. I know that you will be paid and rightly so however both Patience and I know very well that you are not doing this for the money, you are doing it for us and I will always be grateful to you for this, whatever the outcome.' As she spoke, Suzanne had taken my right hand in both of hers and was squeezing it, hard.

'As I said to Patience last night, I am honoured that you have asked me to go and look for Anna for you. It means a lot to me that you, as a family who had not met me before Monday, trust me enough to go and do this vital job for you.

As I said to Patience, you have my assurance that I will do everything I possibly can to bring this horrible situation to a successful and speedy conclusion.' Suzanne had started to cry, a condition that both she and Patience must have experienced too many times over the past few weeks. Not wishing anyone to see her crying, we left the Jacuzzi and went through to the sanarium which was fortunately, empty. It turned out to be a good job too because she was crying openly now. Without thinking, I took her in my arms to console her, holding her close as she sobbed. She fitted into me easily.

'I am sorry Matthew, what must you think of me?' she said eventually. Despite saying this, she made no attempt to move away from me, she simply stood there, her head against my chest, her arms round my waist, mine were round her shoulders.

'Think nothing of it,' I responded. To be honest, I was quite enjoying the feeling. 'I am just glad that I was here and able to help. There is no shame in crying and don't forget, one of my strong points is that I know how to keep quiet so unless you say something, no-one will ever know.' She looked up at me and smiled gratefully.

We climbed up to the top tier of seats and sat facing each other, backs to the wall with our legs on the bench, feet almost touching. Suzanne began to talk, she told me about Patience when she had been little and how she had not wanted her to marry Raul, not having any trust in the man, of her love for her granddaughter and how she and Henry were struggling to cope without her. Finally, she told me how their hopes had been transformed by what Patience had noticed in the behaviour of the nanny though she did confess that at first, neither she nor Henry had taken Patience seriously.

'We all have faith in you.' Then came a rather tricky question. 'What do you think our chances are, truthfully?'

I looked her in the eye. 'I will not lie to you Suzanne. It will be really difficult. If Anna is alive, then Raul is hardly likely to parade her through the streets of Santa Ponsa. That said, he cannot keep her hidden away forever. I do not know Raul but the impression of him that I get from Patience and you, though neither of you have said so in so many words, is that he feels he is superior to everyone else. If that is the case, and I am hoping that it is, then it's my betting that it will not be long before he thinks that he is in the clear and Anna is out and about, not on her own but certainly visible.

This is only part of the problem though. When and if I see her is only one part of the job, The other and more difficult part of the case is to get her away from her father.

Yes, Martin can get a court order and we can serve it on Raul. Bear in mind though, this man has probably killed someone to make this deception work. How much notice will he take of a piece of paper, an English piece of paper at that? Not too much I suspect. No, when I find Anna, the hard work will only just begin.

But that is for the future, for now, I think you owe it to yourselves and Anna to fully investigate the one chance the nanny has given you. If you don't take the chance, then you will forever ask yourselves why you didn't. For my part, you all know that I will do everything that I can to bring this to a satisfactory end.'

She was crying again now and came over to me. 'Hold me again Matthew, I felt so much better when you did earlier.' She then sat on my lap, Christ, it was a good job the place was quiet. But what could I do other than comply with her wishes? She was my client after all. After a few minutes sitting clinging to me, she sat up and looked up at me.

'I can see why Patience thinks so much of you. If I were twenty years younger, she would have a rival.' She glanced at her watch. 'Anyway, its four fifteen now and I have to go. We will see you later this evening Matthew. Thank you for your kindness, understanding and above all, honesty this afternoon. I do appreciate it.' With that, she kissed me lightly on the lips and was gone.

Well, that was a turn up for the book, Patience it seemed, did like me, mother too. I sat there grinning like the village idiot and received funny looks from a couple of women who came in to the sanarium, I left, quickly.

I was ready that evening when Martin came to pick me up. For this meeting with the Jameson's, I wore a grey Boss polo shirt with black trousers, Daisy and I had decided that a suit was not needed now but that I still needed to look smart and professional. On the way to Little Thornley I told Martin that I had gone for a drink with Patience the night before and of my chance meeting and conversation with Suzanne that afternoon. I mentioned that I thought that the two of them were maybe seeking reassurance from me. He considered before replying.

'It's possible of course, more than possible. I know that both of them have been devastated since they were told that Anna had died in that crash. Being reassured at any time is a great comfort, especially when the reassurance comes from the man who is going out to the island to look for Anna. But more than that, I think that finding a stranger who believes in them and what they have to say has given them a tremendous lift. It also helps that Patience quite fancies you.' He finished speaking with a broad grin on his face.

'In that case, I suppose it helps that mother fancies me too.' He looked across questioningly so I told him what she had said about being twenty years younger.

'I don't know how you do it,' was all he had to say, shaking his head as he spoke.

As before, the family were sat in the lounge waiting for us as we were shown in by Aggi, the maid. Jameson was wearing a white shirt with grey trousers and looked very distinguished. Suzanne looked good in a blue cashmere sweater with dark trousers. As we shook hands, she smiled an almost shy smile at me. I had been worried about seeing her after the afternoon at the Lansdowne but the smile told me that maybe Suzanne was feeling a little embarrassed about what had happened between us though in reality it was nothing. She had every right to be upset. She needn't have worried, no way would I say anything about it.

Patience wore a simple blue tee shirt with a short denim skirt and looked fantastic. When she smiled at me it made me feel, I don't know, kind of special somehow. Whatever, it was a smile that reached her eyes and brightened my evening at once.

She beckoned me over to sit beside her which I was happy to do. As I sat, she passed me an envelope which I opened to find several photographs.

'These are the pictures I mentioned Monday evening. In total, there's seven of Anna, all taken within the last six months. It is possible that he will have had her hair cut short by now. These two are of Raul, I have written his description on the back. This is Salma and is a very good likeness, she has not changed much over the past few years. Finally, this is Inez.'

I took the pictures from her. Inez looked rather pretty but of course I didn't say so. Salma looked to be a nice lady in possibly her sixties though her age made no real difference to me one way or another. Raul looked to be a bit of a hard case and had the type of face that suggested he didn't like to be messed with. I wasn't going to mess with him, a low profile at all times was the secret to successful observations. I turned the picture over to read the description, six feet two inches tall, large build, age thirty seven, longish black hair.

I then turned my attention to Anna. She looked adorable and I could easily see her mother and grandmother in her looks. I looked at Patience and smiled.

'Anna looks a lovely little girl, you must be very proud of her.' I held up the shot of Inez. 'She looks a bit shifty to me.'

'That's exactly what I said,' Suzanne responded triumphantly, 'I told you that she was shifty when we first met her.'

I returned the photographs to the envelope as Aggi came in with a tea tray. After she had poured and left the room, Jameson began to speak.

'Diego telephoned earlier Matthew. He confirmed that two tripods and a pair of binoculars, Zeiss apparently, have been placed in the apartment for you. We have booked you on the eleven thirty BA flight from Manchester to Palma on Monday morning, a one way ticket. We will sort out coming back in due course. Now, check in opens at nine thirty and Patience will drive you to the airport if that is okay with you.' I said it was. 'Diego will meet you at the airport, now if you don't mind Matthew.' He produced a digital camera and took a couple of shots of my face. 'I will send these too Diego in the morning so that he will be able to recognise you at the airport. This is at his request by the way.

He has a Renault Megane Scenic for you to use over there, it's anonymous as you specified. I think you already know the situation regarding the broadband and he tells me that there is even a safe in the apartment.

Diego is an old, dear and trusted friend who has no love whatsoever for Raul Martinez. He is from Santa Ponsa therefore he knows the lay of the land. If you have any questions or need anything, please do not hesitate to ask him. I am sure he will tell you the same thing when you meet Monday.

Finally, I have one question Matthew if you do not mind, why two tripods?' I smiled.

'The apartment is a couple of hundred metres from the villa, on one of the tripods, I will fix the binoculars, and train them on the villa. On the second, I intend to fix my 600 mm telephoto lens which I can attach my camera body to. If I need the camera and a different lens I just whip the body off.

Having the two tripods means I can watch through the binoculars and also be ready to take any pictures if the opportunity arises.'

'I see,' Henry said, 'You will be well prepared.' He looked pleased.

'Thanks for the ride to the airport,' I said. 'That's very welcome, and thanks for the heads up regarding Diego. I won't hesitate to contact him.

You will be pleased to note that my business here is sorted so I will be going to Majorca with nothing but Anna on my mind.'

Then the shit hit the fan so to speak. Things had been going so well that I should have expected something to go wrong. It did, in a big way. Patience announced that she was going to go to Santa Ponsa with me.

'I should be there daddy. When Matthew finds Anna then I will need to be there for her.'

Jameson was clearly rattled, he had not foreseen this, nor had Suzanne who began to cry. Now was not the time for me to comfort her. I looked over to Martin and shook my head, this was right out of the blue. I didn't want Patience there until I was good and ready and that would not be until I had found Anna and a way of getting her away safely. The Jameson's were all talking at once, Patience trying to justify her argument, her parents trying to talk her out of her course of action. Martin looked at me as if to say 'Do something.' I did.

'May I say something please.' They actually shut up and looked at me. 'In my opinion, it would be counter-productive for Patience to be in Santa Ponsa until I think it necessary.

You are paying me to do a job of work for you, paying in fact for my expertise in these matters as it is after all my job. At the risk of sounding big headed, which is not my intention, I am good at my job.

In an observations case of this type, I prefer to work alone because I am able to concentrate more this way. One thing that you must take into consideration is that nobody in Santa Ponsa knows me. There must be many people there who know Patience or at least who she is, people that she does not know.

If Raul gets wind of the fact that Patience is on the island, he could do anything, if he has done just a fraction of what we suspect then we are not in any way exaggerating. He is capable of whisking Anna away somewhere, anywhere, maybe even off the island altogether. Then where would we be? At the moment, we have a pretty good idea where Anna is and I would like to keep it that way. It really does make things easier for us.

And another thing, again based on what we suspect Raul of doing. If he does discover that Patience is in Santa Ponsa then she may well be in some considerable danger. I will then have to look after her.' I looked at her and smiled. 'Don't get me wrong, I would look after her and protect her from any danger and be pleased to do so, but that will take me away from my primary function which is first to find Anna, then get hard evidence and finally get her off the island. I will have enough to do without worrying about Patience.

Oh yes, I don't want Patience to see Anna and go rampaging over to the villa all gung ho and giving the game away. Then where would we be? Up the creek, that's where.'

By this time, Patience was crying hysterically. I felt really awful but it had to be said.

She jumped to her feet and cried 'Anna is my daughter, none of you understand that.' Then she ran from the room.

For a few stunned moments nobody moved, we were all frozen to our seats, then Suzanne rose as if to follow Patience.

'May I go and speak to Patience?' I asked Henry. 'After all, it was my words that upset her, I feel that I want and need to explain my position to her.' Jameson gave me his permission and Suzanne showed me up to her room. The house was huge, Patience's room seemed to be in a wing over the side of the house. Maybe she and Anna had this part of the house with Henry and Suzanne over the main part. Who knew. Suzanne knocked at a door and called out that I wanted to come in and talk.

After a moment, the door opened and Patience's tear stained face peered out. At that moment, my heart went out to her and I vowed there and then that I would bring Anna home to her. I also thought she looked lovely, vulnerable but lovely. She stood aside to let me in. It was a large room and I could see two other doors, no doubt an en-suite and a dressing room. A large double bed dominated the room with night tables at either side. She had a leather armchair in another corner and a large TV set. A dressing table sat alongside one wall with a small chair in front of it. Patience sat on the edge of her bed, I took the armchair.

'You are quite right, I do not understand how you, or any mother could possibly feel. What I do know is that you love your daughter more than you can possibly say. That I can understand. I also understand that you want to be in Majorca looking for Anna but what I said about observations is true. It is boring and you need infinite patience.' I stopped suddenly, realising what I had said. Before I could carry on, she began to chuckle. The mood was instantly lightened so I carried on.

'Please let me to do my job in my own way. It is for the best, I could not do it properly if I was worrying about you or if you were pacing about the apartment, bored. If you were to go out alone I would be too worried to concentrate on what I was doing. I would be concerned that Raul or someone would see you and it could well affect my work and I don't want to risk that.'

She was crying again now so I went over to her and knelt at her feet. As she looked at me I took both her hands in mine.

'Please trust me Patience. You know I will do all I can for you. I promise that when I have found Anna and have a plan to get her away, I will let you know and you can come over and join me. Deal?'

She smiled as I released her hands and stood up. She stood too.

'You are right Matthew, I would just be in the way. I'm so sorry, I just feel so useless.' She began to sob again. I held out my arms and she came to me. I held her close as she cried herself out, stroking her hair but saying nothing. What was it with the Jameson women, whenever I was around them they were always crying and I was comforting them. It was a tough job but hey, someone had to do it, might as well be me as, after all, I seemed to be rather good at it. When she finished, I let her go and looked at her.

'I must look a right mess,' she sighed.

'Actually I think you look absolutely gorgeous. Now, no more thoughts of Majorca for the present?'

'Deal.' She said, kissing me on the lips. I left her to clean up and found my way back to the lounge.

As I walked in both Henry and Martin stood up, Suzanne sat looking worried. I gave them a reassuring smile.

'Mutiny over,' I said. 'Patience understands my position and has agreed to wait for me to say when she should come over before she does anything.' I could almost feel the escape of the tension from the others as I explained what I had said to Patience and that she had accepted my reasons.

When she came back in to the lounge, Patience hugged her parents and apologised to everyone.

We then continued with our meeting though there was little else to say. I took all their mobile numbers and entered them into my phone and gave them mine, Martin of course already had it as I had his. Henry mentioned that he had forgotten to tell me that Diego would put some bottled water in the apartment's fridge for me then Martin handed me an envelope with a bundle of Euros inside, 10,000 he said, for expenses on the island. He then gave me a printout from BA, I would collect my ticket Monday at the airport. I decided then that working for millionaires was really rather nice.

It was then time to leave, they all wished me luck. On the way out I received another apology and kiss from Patience. I was getting to like this.

'I will pick you up at seven Monday morning Matthew. I know it's early but better early than late and you know what the traffic is like on the way to the airport. I already have your address and I will see you then.'

Chapter 9

Saturday morning, I thought I had better do some washing ready for Daisy to pack when she came round on Sunday. What a great way to spend a morning, it did have to be done though. Once washed and dried, I then had to iron which I really did not like. Still, I reasoned, once it was done, it was done. Great thinking on my part, deep and profound.

At five, the call I had been half expecting, came. It was Patience.

'Hello Matthew, it's me, Patience. I'm not interrupting anything am I? I just wondered if you were doing anything special and if not, would you like to meet and have a drink?'

'Hi Patience, good to hear from you. I'm not doing anything at all, I would like to meet you for a drink. Tell me when and where.'

'I was thinking about seven thirty at the Ship at Great Bidding. Do you know it? Maybe we could have a bite to eat as well?' The Ship was a nice country pub situated in a small village between Greenfield and Little Thornley. I had been there but not for a year or two.

'The Ship will be fine, I will see you there at seven thirty and I would enjoy having something to eat.'

Plenty of time for a shower and shave, I could not meet Patience Jameson looking scruffy. Then there was the question of what to wear. I was beginning to sound like a big girl but wanted to look nice for her. After a few minutes pondering my wardrobe or lack of one, I decided on a clean pair of jeans and a blue linen shirt. Thank goodness for my morning's work.

I left home just after seven, giving myself plenty of time and arrived in the Audi just before half past. No sign yet of her Mercedes but I had only been there a moment or two before it rumbled in to the car park. Today she had the top closed though it was a fine June evening. She pulled up next to me and when she turned the engine off, I opened her door. She had on a blue shirt, a similar colour to mine and a pair of jeans. Her hair hung loose around her face making her look angelic. I mentally slapped myself for becoming a soppy git. Patience was smiling as she got out of her car.

'Hello Matthew, it's good to see you again.' She kissed me on the cheek. 'I hope you don't mind me calling out of the blue like that, I just feel comfortable with you, and you know and understand what is going on. Also, if I do cry, you will not become annoyed with me and will help me through it.'

'To tell you the truth, I was delighted when you called. I had been looking forward to seeing you again after last night but I expected it to be Monday (little liar) so this is a nice bonus. Tell me, who becomes annoyed with you?'

'Some of my so called friends would you believe. One of them, Fiona Bartlett, actually said I should pull myself together and get a grip. Needless to say, I shan't call her again, the insensitive bitch. Now, shall we go in?'

We did. Since my last visit the place had been done up. New, ultramodern tables, in beech, dominated the room, large plants had been placed strategically around the place, the floor too was also new, no carpet, varnished wood and a new bar in the same beech. All in all, it was a tasteful renovation.

'No arguments from you today Mr Bentley, I am going to buy the drinks. I had a bottle of Coors and Patience had a glass of Chardonnay. When pressed by her, I chose a chicken sandwich on brown to eat. The menu said that it came with chips. Patience ordered the same then we took our drinks to a table in the corner where we could talk without being overheard.

'There is so much I want to say to you Matthew. The first thing is to apologise properly for my behaviour last night.' I tried to protest but she silenced me. 'Please let me finish then you can argue.' This was said with a twinkle in her eye, something I had not seen before; it actually pleased me. 'Yes I did behave badly last night, I cannot excuse my conduct but I want you to understand that I am not usually like that, it's the business with Anna that has affected me more than I care to admit or would admit to anyone other than you. I miss her terribly and am sure that she is alive and that Salma was trying to tell me in a roundabout sort of way.

Thank you for what you said to me when you came to my room. I know you are going to Majorca to do a job of work and the last thing I want to do is interfere in any way. I want you to know that I have complete faith in you and I will not say again that I want to come to the island until you are good and ready for me.'

Then our food came so we settled down to the serious business of eating and neither of us spoke until we had finished. Seemingly, it was still not my turn to speak.

'At first I was not sure that my father believed what I was saying to him about Anna and neither did mother but they have now both come round to my way of thinking, as you well know and now they agree with me. Mother said that she spoke to you yesterday at the Lansdowne.' I looked closely at her but her expression did not change so mother had not mentioned the fact that she had been sitting on my knee, a good job too. 'It is good to know that you believe in us as a family and me in particular as really, it's my theory. I will never be able to thank you enough for believing in me, whatever happens over there.

Most people think that I am a typical blonde, empty headed with nothing going for me except money. I know you are not like that. When we spoke the other night in the Hare and Hounds, I could tell that you enjoyed my company for who I am not what I am. That is so refreshing.' Now it was my turn.

'Well as for last night, there is no need whatsoever to apologise as there is nothing at all to apologise for. You are a mother who is worried for her child, it is only natural that you want to be where she is but I am glad that you have come round to my way of thinking. It isn't that I like the sound of my own voice, it's just that what I told you is fact, plain and simple.

You know I believe in you and what you say, it actually makes perfect sense. Daisy, who works with me, wants to have a bet that when we bring Anna home, it will turn out that Salma was sending you a message. Daisy has the nasty habit of being right more or less all the time so no way will I bet with her any more. Anyway, I am sure she is right. I did speak with your mother yesterday at the Lansdowne and believe in you totally. As for our having a drink the other night, I enjoyed myself more than I have for a long time, just as I am enjoying myself now.

I also think that It is a load of old rubbish for anyone to say that you of all people are empty headed, you are anything but. Patience, you are a very intelligent woman and the people who say otherwise can't know you. I am more than happy spending time with you and the more it happens, then the better I will like it.'

At least she looked pleased by what I had said. More than that, she looked, what was it? At peace, that was it. For the first time since I had met her, and it was not quite a week yet, she looked at peace and if I had had something to do with that, then good.

Our conversation turned to things in general, it transpired that we both liked to read and shared a passion for adventure thrillers and had actually read the some of the same books though Patience had read Dickens and some of the classics which I had not.

We had another drink, this time I insisted on buying and we talked for ages. The pub had filled up whilst we talked and I noticed several people looking at us and nudging their companions. Stuff em was what I thought.

'Tell me about Anna, I have her picture but know nothing about her?'

'Anna, what can I say about her, she is my whole world. When I heard that she was dead, I wanted to die too. I could not see a way to carry on living, nor did I want to. Simply put, I had no reason to carry on. Now I do, more than one.' She reached out and took my hand, which was nice, I could feel the eyes focused on us.

'I have not told you my natal history, actually, I have not told anyone this, even my parents. When I was married to Raul, I had two miscarriages and was told by the gynaecologist that I would not be able to conceive, something was wrong with my womb. Don't worry, I won't go in to details.' She had seen the look on my face.

'Then somehow, I became pregnant again. For the whole nine months I had to take it easy. Salma was indispensable to me at that time. Throughout the pregnancy I was scared, scared for two reasons, obviously another miscarriage but much more scary was the thought that I could not help thinking, that my child would be born with abnormalities caused by my condition. I could not talk to Raul about my worries, he was only ever interested in himself and he made no secret of the fact that in his opinion, I had let him down by miscarrying. In the end, I carried for the full period and gave birth to Anna but now I am unable to have any more children, that is why

I am so upset, She looked upset now, I took her hand and squeezed it but said nothing. Then she smiled, a little sad smile.

'I am sorry, you asked about Anna. What can I say about her? She is a polite well-mannered little girl. I think these things are important. Too many children are not taught how to behave these days. She is doing well at school and enjoys going.

When she finished Rainbows she moved up to Brownies and loves to go with her friends. I think she is a well-adjusted child, she certainly had no problems as a result of the divorce, she loves her father, I have never tried to stop that or said things about him. When he came to this country for his visits, she looked forward to spending time with him. When she told me what the two of them had done, I was sure that she had really enjoyed the time spent with him.'

'Thank you for sharing these things with me. I'm pleased that you trust me enough to tell me these things, things that you have not told anyone else. I am looking forward to meeting Anna, she sounds quite a girl.'

'I told you these things Matthew because I wanted you to know, it is important to me that you do know them.'

It had gone dark outside, we had been in the Ship for quite a while now and it was time to leave. As we made our way to the cars, Patience again slipped her arm through mine, she had done this last time too. At the cars she unlocked her Merc but made no move to open the door. Did she expect me to kiss her? I had no idea but the way she looked at me encouraged me to go for it. I held out my arms to her and she came to me quickly. Our kiss was passionate and seemed to last for ever. When our lips parted, she stayed where she was, resting her head on my shoulder. It was nice standing there, holding each other. Then it was time to go. I waited until she was sat in her car with her seat belt on before leaning in and kissing her again. She seemed to enjoy it; I certainly did. I drove home happy with the way things had gone between us. The only down side was that apart from the trip to the airport, I would not see her for a while.

As arranged, Daisy came round Sunday afternoon to help me pack. Actually, she did not help, I let her do it all. She was most impressed that I had done the washing and ironing though, a brownie point to me. As she packed my stuff, I told her of the phone call from Patience and our evening out. I knew she was thinking about Patience as she packed so I kept quiet. She packed a couple of pairs of trousers, the same in jeans, several tee shirts and polo shirts, four pairs of shorts, socks and underwear, flip flops, shoes and trainers and my leather jacket, just in case. No doubt if I was there a long time, I could wash things. Finally she threw in three baseball caps. These she said could be a disguise. Sunglasses I would have on. Eventually she mentioned Patience.

'She certainly seems interested in you Matt. I just hope that she does not see you as her knight in shining armour and when you bring Anna back safe and sound she has no further use for you. I am sorry, I don't want to be negative but, well you know me.'

'I had already thought of that Daisy. Don't worry, you know full well that you can say anything to me and that I won't be offended. Truth is, I don't think she would do that, I have an inkling that her feelings are genuine but, as always, time will tell.

In any event, after she takes me to the airport tomorrow, it will possibly be quite a few weeks before we see each other again. If she is not interested it will surely be clear when I do see her again.'

'That's true Matt. I hope that it works out for you. It's about time you had a good woman in your life.'

Chapter 10

I was ready when Patience arrived for me Monday morning. She arrived on the dot, it was a miserable rainy morning but hopefully the last one I would see for a while. I had wondered how she would be after Saturday, I need not have worried, as I opened the door for her she was smiling and greeted me with a kiss and a hug.

'I have missed you since Saturday. God knows how I am going to go on while you are away.' She certainly knew how to cheer a guy up.

I had a suitcase and my Adidas holdall as luggage. In the holdall my laptop was in its own case, a Samsonite. Also in there was my camera gear. A few months ago I had bought a special backpack for the Nikon stuff. Both the laptop bag and the camera bag went in to the holdall which was quite heavy. In my case I had packed several books and my Ipod. I liked to read though not when working as if I did, I was sure to miss something, listening to music helped while away the hours when I was watching and nothing was happening.

A final check that I had my passport, travel printout and money then I was ready to go.

That morning Patience wore a simple pair of jeans and a white tee shirt and had her hair fastened in a ponytail. As always, she looked wonderful, at least, I thought so. The bags went in to the boot of her car, just and I settled down in the passenger seat thinking it was a nice change to have someone drive me around.

When I followed her to the Hare and Hounds I had thought that she handled the power of the Mercedes well. Now, in the car with her on the motorway, I was sure of it. She controlled the power with ease, driving fast but well within her own capabilities and those of the car. The CD she had on was U2, greatest hits, I actually had my own copy, something else we had in common.

As we got to Manchester, the traffic got heavy though we did keep going. As we drove we talked of many things, Anna of course, music, books, she asked about my family. She was great company, empty headed? Not a chance. I did wonder if anything would happen between us, her demeanour suggested that it might. As Daisy said, see what happens when Anna is home and she does not need me anymore.

All too soon we were there. Patience pulled up at the drop off area. Once my stuff was out of the boot we stood and looked at each other before we came in to each other's arms and kissed, quite tenderly as it happened considering we were in public.

'Good luck Matthew,' she said when we had finished. 'Please take good care of yourself and do keep in touch.' All her hopes for the safe return of her daughter were pinned on Matthew, she was literally in his hands.

'Thanks. I will. Don't worry I have a good feeling and I'm sure you will be joining me soon.'

'That good feeling you are having, it's me,' she said laughing. With that it was time to part. She climbed back in to the AMG and drove off. I waved until she was out of sight before sighing deeply, collecting my bags and going off the find my ticket.

The ticket was waiting for me, first class no less so I got priority check in which was very nice thank you. Once through, I went to find some breakfast, as a first class passenger, I was able to go to a nice part of the VIP lounge to eat and had a full English breakfast which was far nicer than I would otherwise have had. I had finished eating and was drinking my tea when my mobile bleeped, a text. Opening it, it was a good luck message from Patience.

I replied to the message then bought a magazine for the flight and soon it was time to board. The first class section was not full. I was pleased as it gave me the chance to have a think about things.

My thoughts turned to Raul, in effect, he had allegedly kidnapped his daughter. I was sure that the crash actually happened, I didn't think that he could have arranged a police report even though he was friendly with the local police chief. In any event, had not the report been prepared by the police in Inca rather than the Santa Ponsa boys?

The fire service had confirmed that there was a body in the car at the bottom of the cliff and of course, did Patience not say she had viewed a body which was unrecognisable because of the burns. This was a fact.

As it was fact then Raul and Inez must have staged the crash with a child in the car, on the face of it, they had sacrificed a child to create the illusion that it was Anna in the car, that was the only possible way to describe it. They had killed once, they could do it again but would they? To preserve their secret and liberty, of course they damn well would.

Now that these thoughts were out in the open, I would have to be extremely careful. I always took great care when doing observations as obviously I had no wish to be seen by whoever it was that I was watching but this was different. Thank goodness I had not let Patience come with me. She would have to come at some point, I would have to be certain that it was safe, something else for me to think about while I was working on everything else.

I was interrupted in my thinking a couple of times during the flight when a darling of a stewardess or cabin crew as they seem to be called now, brought me a drink. Her name was Cherry and she had a great personality. If I hadn't been working, still that was another story. My thoughts did have one good point though, the flight seemed to be over quite quickly, we had hardly seemed to get going before Cherry was round making sure all seat belts were fastened.

I went through passport control with no problems and was waiting at the carousel when the baggage started to come through. Once I had my case I wandered into the arrivals hall and stopped dead. I had no idea what Diego looked like. As ever, several people stood about holding up cards with people's names on them, not mine. Great. Suddenly, a guy appeared at my shoulder, he was about 60, tall with light brown hair, quite a patch of it actually. He was well built though not fat and had a rugged, good looking but pleasant face. I suspected he could handle himself in a rough house should the need arise.

'Matthew?' he enquired, tentatively. I smiled and held out my hand.

'Yes, I'm Matthew, you must be Diego.' His face broke into a huge grin as he shook my outstretched hand.

'I thought it must be you, I have the photo Henry took and sent me. Come this way Matthew, I have a car waiting.' He took my case from me and pulled it along leaving me struggling to keep up with him.

Diego led the way outside and to the car park. The heat hit me as soon as we stepped out of the air conditioned terminal. God, it was hot. This rate I would soon have a nice tan. We stopped beside a dark green Renault

Megane Scenic which Diego opened and put my bags in the boot. I joined him in the car and we set off to Santa Ponsa. On the way, he told me about the apartment, which was on the top floor of a five story block, in addition to the view of the Villa Borgosa, if I looked to my right from the balcony, I had a view of part of the golf course.

Majorca is a lovely island, I had been a couple of times in the past but not to Santa Ponsa so I enjoyed the ride. On the way, Diego acted as tour guide. He was very proud of his homeland and pointed out many items of interest. He then drifted back to the job in hand and confirmed that the villa was about two hundred metres from the apartment and that I could see one side and some of the back from the balcony but unfortunately, neither the front nor back doors. I would have a view down into the apartment's garden and the pool.

'I have put some bottled water in the fridge for you and the tripods and binoculars in the apartment. I do not mean to sound as if I am telling you your job but I think you could set up the tripods just inside the lounge, I am sure that they cannot be seen from the villa,' he informed me.

'Thanks Diego, for everything, the water, tripods and binoculars. I'm sure you are right about where to site them and now you have said that, it will save me a job looking for the best position.'

It did not take too long to get to Santa Ponsa and the Apartments Playa Rosa. The town seemed quite pleasant as we drove through to the sea front. We went round a roundabout and along the promenade with the sea on our left for a couple of hundred yards or so before Diego turned right along a one way, busy street. It housed gift shops, a hotel, some bars, a market, supermarket and the apartment block towards the top of the road. As he pulled into the car park, I took a look at what was to be my home for the next few weeks.

What I saw was a pleasing, substantial building which was finished in white with terracotta roof tiles. Flower beds were all over the car park with a dazzling array of multi coloured flowers blooming in the bright sunlight. It was certainly an impressive display. As we parked and I got out, I noticed Diego take a carrier bag from the glove box and wondered what could be in it, probably nothing to do with me.

Inside, the large reception area was cool with a couple of overhead fans turning. Plain tiles covered the floor and our footsteps sounded as we walked on them. At the desk, a beautiful dark haired girl was on duty, Michelle according to her name tag.

'Hola Michelle,' said Diego to this vision of Spanish womanhood. 'This is Senor Bentley, he is going to be in 5a for a few weeks, a private rental so you will see him going in and out.'

I held out my hand and she took it. 'Nice to meet you Michelle,' I said.

'Ah you are English Senor Bentley,' said Michelle in a husky, sexy voice. 'That is good, I will be able to practise my English with you, no.' That was all I needed, the lovely Michelle practising her English on me. Oh well, could be worse, she could be ugly.

Diego was grinning broadly as we got into the lift but said nothing. When the lift stopped on the top floor, I followed him out and to the left as he walked down the landing to the end, the apartments were to the left, the balcony to our right overlooked the car park. Handing me the keys to the apartment, I unlocked the door and went in.

The interior was pleasantly cool as I walked in to the tiled hallway. After a few paces, I came to a door on my left. Looking in, it was a bedroom, next door a bathroom. The hall led into the large open plan lounge which was tiled the same as the hallway but had a rug or two dotted about. The furnishings consisted of a three piece suite in a green colour, it was material and not leather. A TV set stood on its stand in one corner, a coffee table in front of the sofa was the only other thing in the room.

On the left between the lounge and the kitchen, again tiled, was another bedroom, like the first, a double. This one had an en-suite bathroom, I would use this one. A large bed with tables at either side dominated the room. For some reason, I thought of Michelle, the receptionist. The room had a walk in wardrobe and a couple of chests of drawers, plenty of room for the things I had brought with me.

In the kitchen, the units had been built in, in an 'L' shape and contained a hob and oven. On the worktops, I had a kettle, toaster and microwave, which was all I would need. The drawers held cutlery, crockery was in the wall cupboards, the fridge was built in under the worktop. The kitchen also had a table and four chairs.

A balcony ran outside the whole apartment with doors leading out from both the lounge and the kitchen. A sun lounger was on the balcony together with a plastic table and four chairs. I would be fine here. I went out and looked across at what I took to be Raul's villa, no sign of Anna in the garden; that would have been too easy. As I had been warned, I could not see either of the doors to the villa but a driveway went down towards what I assumed to be the front of the villa. I took a look over at the apartment's pool area too, very nice gardens with plenty of flowers adding colour to the scene, and a nice pool in which people splashed about.

Between the apartments and the villa there seemed to be some sort of rough track, the apartments had a wall round the garden, about seven feet or so I estimated, Raul had the same round his villa.

When I went back in, Diego asked me what I thought.

'It's a great apartment,' I said. 'I will be fine here for however long it takes.' He then offered me the carrier bag he had taken from the glove box of the Scenic.

'Here is something I hope you will never need Matthew but I know Raul Martinez of old and I want you to be prepared for anything and everything. Rest assured, it is legal in every way.'

I opened the bag, four boxes. The first contained a Glock 19, 9mm semi-automatic handgun, the second, three magazines and the third, a box of bullets, in the other was a Fobus holster, the GL-2 as I found out later when I looked properly. The gun did not have a magazine in the butt. I looked questioningly at Diego.

He handed me a piece of paper. 'Here is your permit to carry the weapon. It is in Spanish of course but you will recognise your own name.' I did. 'Do you know how to use it?'

As it happened, I did. I had a friend, Scott, who lived in Florida. When I had been over there, I had gone with him to the gun range he used regularly, he had had a Glock 19, amongst others, and I had used and become familiar with it. After checking that the safety was on, I quickly loaded a magazine and slipped it into the butt cocking the gun in the same movement.

'Yes, you do know how to use it,' Diego observed lightly.

'I certainly hope I don't need this Diego.' In truth, I was rather shocked.

'Martinez is a known drug dealer and has plenty of muscle at his disposal. He also has a string of girls working for him and a whole host of informers throughout the island. It is rumoured that he also plans and finances robberies throughout the length and breadth of Spain and finally, there are stories of gun running. On the whole, he is bad news. So far, he has never been caught, actually, that is not true, he was once but someone else took the prison sentence for him. In a phrase, he is bad news but I understand that Henry has already passed on this information to you.

I know that soon, Patience will be coming to the island, I hope you do not need the weapon but when Patience comes, you may be glad of it. Whatever, please be careful Matthew.'

We then exchanged mobile numbers. As he took his leave, he said 'Anything you need or any help no matter how small, please contact me right away.' Then he was gone.

I took my case and holdall through to the bedroom I was going to use, found the safe into which I put my passport, the money, keeping some out for immediate use and the gun and all its accessories. The gun, this was a turn up but if Martinez was half as bad as Diego had said, then it could come in handy though I really hoped not. Once I had put all my clothes away and changed into shorts and a tee shirt, I checked over the kitchen. Diego had put several bottles of water in the fridge but I was rather hungry, more than I was thirsty, time to go shopping. It was half past four, Spanish time.

I went down but Michelle was nowhere to be seen, I was going to ask about supermarkets. Going out, I wandered down towards the sea and found one not too far away. Getting a basket I got some tea bags but put them back as I didn't like the look of the milk and got some Redbush tea bags instead, I could drink it without milk. Two litres of mango juice then went in followed by some fresh bread, margarine, ham and tuna, I paid and went back to the apartment, again Michelle was nowhere to be seen.

While the kettle boiled, I made a ham sandwich and took my late lunch out on to the balcony.

As I ate, I took a good look at Raul's place, I rather hoped that Anna might come out to play in the sunshine but it was never going to be that easy.

After I had eaten, I set up the tripods, with the binoculars in place, I could look right into Raul's garden. From the position Diego had suggested, I had a good view, as the room I was in would be in darkness to anyone looking up, I was sure that no-one could see me.

Then the 600 mm lens went on to the other. With the Nikon body fixed I was sure I would be able to get shots of Anna when she eventually appeared. I was now ready for work so I went for a nap waking up at seven fifteen. After a shower and shave, I went out for a drink and a good dinner, but the drink first.

I walked down to the sea front and on the way, passed a nice looking Spanish restaurant, I would eat there later. On the sea front, several bars vied for the passing trade, I chose the one that had the good looking girl serving the outdoor tables. Sitting down outside, I waited for her to come over and when she did, I ordered a beer.

'Oh, you are English, I'm Sam from Lincoln,' she said.

'Hi Sam from Lincoln, my name is Matt.' She was attractive, maybe about 25, shoulder length auburn hair, a full figure but no visible fat and an infectious smile. When she brought the beer, she pulled up a chair and sat down for a chat.

'Don't tell me that a good looking guy like you is alone Matt, you must have a wife or girlfriend around somewhere.'

Daisy and I had discussed this at length, and we had a story ready for me. 'No Sam, I am on my own. I have just gone through a messy divorce and decided that I needed to get away from it all for a while, you know, a change of scenery and the scenery has improved 100% in the last few moments.' This made her smile, hopefully with pleasure. She then had to go and serve some customers. When she came back, I was ready to go.

'You are not leaving so soon are you?' My new friend sounded disappointed.

'I'm just going for something to eat then I was thinking I would come back and have another couple of beers and maybe a drink with you.'

'That's great, I will be finishing a bit earlier tonight as I started earlier. We can have that drink then if you like.' I liked.

The Spanish restaurant I had seen turned out to be very good. I had fish with another beer before heading back to Sam's bar. Thinking about her made me feel a bit of a git as I was lying, not that I could tell a stranger the truth. For some strange reason, I also felt that I was being unfaithful to Patience which was a right load of old rubbish, but the feeling was there nonetheless. Ridiculous really, yes I liked her and she seemed to like me, but at the moment, that was it. Maybe something would come of it but that was the future. Also, I reasoned, Sam could well be good cover for me. A couple does not stand out as much as a person on their own.

Back in the bar, once Sam had finished work, she brought drinks for us over to where I was sitting. During our conversation, she told me that she had all day Wednesday off. That would be a good opportunity to visit Port de Soller and take a look at the crash site. I asked her if she would like to go for a day out with me and she accepted gladly.

It was soon time for her to get the bus home, I walked with her to the bus stop and as it approached the stop, kissed her. Fortunately, she responded.

'Will I see you tomorrow?' she asked, expectantly.

'Of course you will,' I answered. 'We have to arrange our day out Wednesday. I will be in to see you.'

I waved as the bus pulled away and strolled back to the apartment feeling pleased with myself. For the first day I had done okay. I was going to see the crash site and wouldn't stand out. Not a bad night's work.

Chapter 11

I was awake by eight Tuesday morning, ready for my first proper day's work in Santa Ponsa. It was the eleventh of June. After showering and shaving I made breakfast which I had on the balcony. It was a glorious June morning in Majorca. Already it was hot and would get hotter as the day went on. It occurred to me that the one thing I had not brought with me was sun crème, I would need to get some before I burned. After breakfast, I went out and bought some. Then it was up to the room to start work.

The tripods were set up, it was now time to wait and watch. The Ipod came into its own at times like these. At eleven, a black BMW 7 series came round from the far side of the villa. Looking through the binoculars, I was able to identify Raul at the wheel. He appeared to be speaking to someone but I could not see anyone in the car with him, he could be on the phone of course. No doubt the car was equipped with Bluetooth, I would need to get the registration number in due course, it was no big deal.

At half twelve, I made a sandwich and cup of tea and ate on the balcony and spent a half hour or so reading. The sun was shining directly on to the balcony now and I was down to a pair of shorts, not a pretty sight but I didn't need to look. If the weather was going to be this good, I would end up with a fine tan by the time the job was finished.

The BMW returned to the villa at three thirty. As it came slowly up the drive, I took a couple of pictures of it, hoping that I could possibly blow it up a little on the laptop and get the registration. There was a woman in the passenger seat, Inez I presumed. The car went round the far side of the villa which no doubt was where the garages were. I wanted to take a look round there and wanted it to be sooner rather than later.

I watched for another half hour without seeing anyone or anything. By then, I had had enough, it had been a long, hot day and I was ready to relax. Taking the sun crème, book and a towel, I wandered down to the pool and found a sun bed free and lay down to read, staying there until five thirty.

I was ready to go out for food and beer by seven. Before closing the balcony door, I took a last look at the villa, through the binoculars, I was glad that I had done for walking down the drive was none other than Salma, the nanny. This was a good opportunity, having locked the door, I put some money into my pocket and went out. I was hoping that she might just be going to one of the shops on the street outside the apartments. Not being sure, I just hung around out front, hoping.

After ten minutes she still had not appeared and I was giving up hope of her coming this way but then I saw her, coming slowly down the road. I was not sure how far away from the apartments the entrance to the villa was, something else that I needed to check. It took Salma almost fifteen minutes but she was in no hurry.

I slipped out of the car park once she had passed and strolled slowly down the road. Salma went in to the supermarket that I had used yesterday, I followed. It was not too busy but never mind, it couldn't be helped. I found her on the aisle that sold biscuits, crisps and sweets. As I checked out the stock, I had an opportunity to have a good look at Salma. I had the impression, a gut feeling, that she was not a happy lady but of course, I did not know her, just my gut feeling. Maybe this was something we could use later, when Patience had arrived. We would see.

I decided to buy some biscuits and crisps myself and picked a packet of chocolate Hobnobs, but carried on looking. Salma had a basket and had put some chocolate biscuits and sweets in. Were they for Anna? As she made her way to the till, I picked some plain crisps and followed her, arriving just behind her. As she emptied her basket, a packet of sweets fell to the floor, I quickly bent down and picked them up.

With a smile I put them back. 'Those look good, does your little girl like them?' Salma returned my smile.

'I have no children Senor,' she said in slow, deliberate English. 'They are for a friend.' She paid and was gone. I paid for my things and decided against following her back to the villa. I was not in any way sorry that she had not blurted out Anna's name, I had not expected her too but it had been worth a try. I was under no illusions about this job, it was going to be a long, hard slog but I was confident about the outcome, more so now that Salma had been buying sweets, unless of course Raul and Inez liked them.

Back in the apartment, I put my purchases away then the tripods which I put in the other bedroom. I didn't want them on show, just in case.

Now for a beer. Naturally, I went to Sam's bar and was greeted warmly by her.

'Have you eaten yet?' she asked as she brought me a cold beer.

'Not yet Sam, why?' I took a sip of the cold beer which was actually lager, whatever, it was nice and cold.

'I just wondered, are you coming back here and are we still going for a drive tomorrow?'

'Yes and yes. I will be back when I have had something to eat and of course we are going out for the day tomorrow. I am looking forward to it.' She beamed with pleasure. I enjoyed the beer and told Sam I was going to eat when I had finished it. She was serving a group of lads who were a bit noisy.

'See you soon Matt,' she said as if to let these lads know that she was unavailable.

'Back in an hour or so,' I said, giving her a wink. I went back to the Spanish restaurant, why not, last night the food had been good, it was again. This time, I had paella, the Valencia one with chicken and chorizo rather than seafood. Then I went back to see Sam. The bar was busy but she spotted me right away and brought me a beer which she handed over with a big smile.

'Thanks for earlier, all those lads fancied me and were trying to decide who should have a try to get off with me. Idiots, still, they were harmless, just having fun.' She carried on serving the throng but came over to where I was standing whenever she could. At one point, I slipped my arm round her and gave her a cuddle which she seemed to enjoy, I know I did.

'What time do you finish tonight?' I whispered in her ear, my arm still round her.

'Midnight tonight Matt I'm sorry to say. Are you going to wait for me? It's just less than an hour but if it calms down, I will ask if I can go early.'

'That would be nice but I will wait.' I kissed her cheek and patted her bottom as she went to take an order. Each time she passed, she gave me a big smile. At eleven forty five she came across to me.

'I can go now as its gone quiet.' We left the bar and outside she took my arm and led me to a quiet part of the sea front. She then kissed me and me being me, happily let her. We carried on like this for a bit but things were becoming too heated for the great outdoors so I took her hand and led her up the road.

'Are we going to your place?' she asked shyly. I smiled and nodded.

'If that's all right with you.' It was. Sam left at two in the morning, I went down with her and waited for the taxi she had ordered to turn up. We had arranged to meet outside the bar at eleven the next day for our outing.

Back in the apartment, I went straight to bed, tired out.

I was up at nine though and showered and had breakfast before having a look over the balcony. Nothing to see. For the trip, I wore a tee shirt and shorts as the weather was hot again.

After getting some cash from the safe, I left in the Scenic to collect Sam. She was waiting for me and had on a short denim skirt and a tee shirt. She looked rather fetching and I told her so.

I wanted to look at the scene of the crash, if I stopped and looked alone, it could look suspicious, but not if there were two of us looking. At least, that's what I figured. Having studied the police report before I came, I was sure that I could find the place.

On the way Sam asked 'Why do you want to go to Port de Soller Matt?' I was ready for this one.

'Some friends have been and say it's a really nice place and that I should go if I got the chance. When you said that you were off it seemed like a good opportunity to do two things I want to do, see Port de Soller and spend time alone with you.'

'We spent some nice time alone last night,' she said, giggling.

'Play your cards right and we can do it again tonight,' I said, laughing. It was a lovely day, hot and sunny, the good weather seemed to have brought plenty of people out on to the roads but we were in no hurry.

Sam was good company, different time and place, who knows, still, work first.

We eventually came to a service station so I pulled in to fill up, wondering as I did whether or not, this was the same place that Inez filled up that fateful day. We soon left the main road behind and took the winding road to Port de Soller. As we rounded a bend, I became sure that this was the place, especially as Sam pointed to some flowers at the side of the road. I pulled the car off the road and got out and Sam followed me out of the Scenic.

'Why have we stopped here Matt?' she asked as I walked to the edge.

'Oh, just being nosy. When you pointed out the flowers, I wondered what had happened here.' I looked over the edge and down to the bottom of the ravine. 'Look down there Sam, it looks like a car has gone off the road, there seems to be an area at the bottom of the cliff that is burned. If a car did go over, maybe it caught fire.' Sam came to the edge and I held on to her as she looked over.

'You know, I seem to remember hearing something about a crash on this road, at the end of April or the beginning of May I think. A little girl on holiday from England died in the crash.

If I remember right, the driver was the kid's father's fiancé and she got out. How could she do that? Leave the kid in the car and save herself. I could not do that.'

I looked at the road, no skid marks, just confirming what the police report had said. I had not thought that the report would have been rigged and this seemed to confirm that it was authentic.

Then I looked back at the bend, to me, it was not a sharp one, the drop was almost on the bend itself. I could not see how Inez had possibly lost control of the car as it had rounded the bend. She must have been going slow to have given herself time to open the door and jump out. I thought that she and Raul might just have been up here before the crash, looking for a suitable place for it to happen.

As far as I was concerned, there was no way that the car could have gone over the edge by accident. It was murder, plain and simple. My opinion was not just that though. I had done an extensive accident investigation course before trying to obtain work from Insurance companies. I got plenty of work from them so I knew what I was talking about. I had brought the Nikon with the 80 – 200mm zoom lens and went to get it from the car. The photographs I took were quite comprehensive, from the bend to the drop and back, the road and the drop in to the ravine.

As I photographed the scene, I was as sure as I could be that Raul and Inez were the only people involved in this, I was convinced that Salma was not involved. But for her behaviour at the cremation, Raul and Inez may well have got away with their plan meaning that what Salma had done had been done intentionally. That made Patience right. It also made Daisy right and I would never hear the last of that.

If Raul ever found out what Salma had done, she could be in some danger, I would have to tread very carefully when it came to getting Anna back.

I turned round and saw Sam, Christ, I had forgotten all about her as I looked and photographed the scene. She was looking at me with a puzzled look on her face. Being nosy was one thing, doing what I had been doing, another thing altogether.

'Let's get back into the car Sam, and go down to Port de Soller for a drink and some lunch. How does that sound?'

'It sounds great Matt.' Her voice though did not sound like it was great. I was sure that she must have a multitude of questions.

'Bear with me please, Sam, I will explain everything over lunch.' I smiled at her, hopefully reassuringly. I had decided to be honest with her, up to a point anyway. To her credit, she asked no questions as we drove into the little town. Once there, we parked the car and found a nice looking little tapas bar with outside tables. Very chic. After ordering both food and drinks, I looked directly at Sam.

'Look Sam, I owe you an explanation, I am not here to get over a divorce. Before I say anything else, will you give me your word that what I tell you will go no further?' I thought myself a pretty good judge of character and felt that if Sam did give me her word, she would honour it.

'Yes of course I give you my word that I won't say anything to anyone Matt. Are you in some sort of trouble?' I smiled at that.

'No Sam, I'm not in any trouble, it's nothing like that.

The position is this. I am a private investigator from Greenfield in the north of England. I have been retained by the family of the little girl who allegedly died in that crash that you remembered hearing about earlier in the year. I am here in Majorca looking for the little girl as the family believe that she was not the passenger who died in the crash. That's why I took all those photographs at the scene.' She looked upset

'You just wanted to use me to find an excuse to come here. So last night you were just using me too.'

'That's not true Sam. Last night I was with you because I wanted to be. I want to be with you today too.

If I am honest, then yes, I did want to look at the scene of the crash but I could have done that at any time on my own, couldn't I?

My thinking was that I could do a little bit of work then have a brilliant day out with you. I still hope we can, I can't see any reason why we can't.

I am really sorry if I have upset you, no way did I want to do that or would have done intentionally. You will appreciate that I can't go round telling people why I am really here. I have told you because I like you and trust you. Would I tell you this if I were just using you?'

She thought about that. 'I guess not Matt. You could have come on your own. I'm sorry, I am being silly.' Just then, our lunch arrived and we ate before I spoke again.

'The thing is Sam, the family of the little English girl do not believe that she is dead. They think another child was put in the car and the crash staged. The reason behind it is that the parents of the little girl, Anna, are divorced. The mother is English, the father, who lives in Santa Ponsa, Spanish.

I am here to look for the child, to gather evidence that she is still alive and find a way to get her back to her mother.

This is why I have to be very discreet, I am truly sorry that I deceived you but I hope that you now understand why I had to.'

'Yes I do now Matt. Thank you for explaining the situation, I will not breathe a word of what you have told me. Those poor people, they must be going through hell.' Her eyes widened. 'If it was not your client's daughter in the car, then who was it? Who was the child who died?'

'The million dollar question Sam. That's not one for me to answer I'm pleased to say though when I get my evidence it will be passed on to the authorities here and then, up to them.' I changed the subject. 'You are not working tonight, are you Sam?'

'No. it's a full day off.'

'Good, then why don't we take a drive out of Santa Ponsa and find a nice restaurant to eat in. You must know a place. What do you say?' She smiled, the first natural smile since we stopped on the road, a good sign.

'That will be nice. I do know of a place that is supposed to be very good though I am told it's a bit expensive. Is that all right?'

'That's no problem Sam, as long as it's good, that's all that matters.

After lunch we had a walk round Port de Soller, it was every bit as nice as I had been told, then we headed back to Santa Ponsa. I took her straight to the apartment and made love to her. She seemed to enjoy it, I know I did. Sam did seem to have forgiven my little deception.

After she had left, I took a look at the villa, nothing was going on, outside at any rate, inside, that was another matter.

I picked Sam up at eight as we had arranged. She looked sexy in a little black dress and black stockings. When I complimented her on how nice she looked, she kissed me, I guess I was forgiven. She directed me out of Santa Ponsa towards Andratx. On the way, she told me of her family in Lincoln. Her gran had been poorly but she was hoping that she was on the mend. She suffered from angina which was not good. I made the usual noises.

As we pulled up into the car park of the restaurant, Sam apologised for earlier, which I waved away.

'No Sam, I should be the one to apologise for misleading you. When I came here, I had no idea that I would meet you. The story I told was the one we had got ready as a cover because of the nature of my work.

Now that I know you, I am happy for you to know what I am doing here. I also enjoy being with you, especially when you look like that.'

Things were fine after that and we had a really good evening. The food was excellent, Sam had been right though, it was expensive, still Henry could afford it though I would have to find some way of accounting for this meal in due course.

Back in Santa Ponsa, I took the car back to the apartment. Once parked, Sam led me up to my flat, one thing led to another and she ended up staying the night. I drove her home first thing in the morning.

As I drove back to the Playa Rosa, I passed Raul going in the opposite direction. I was sure Inez was with him in the front. I had the impression that someone else was in the back of the car but of course I could not be certain. Once I had parked, I went for some fresh bread and back in the apartment I made some breakfast. I was tired and hungry, I needed an energy fix after the night with Sam.

While the kettle boiled, I set up the tripods for the day's work. The BMW returned around eleven thirty. About half an hour later, two more cars turned up, A BMW 5 series and a Mercedes, I think an E class. Like Raul's BMW, these cars went round to the far side of the property.

About ten minutes later, three kids came into view in the garden, they were all boys, then a little girl joined them. She had on a sun hat which covered most of her head. It did not stop me getting pictures of all four kids. I was not able to get a clear head shot of the little girl, which was a downer, I thought it was Anna but I could not be sure. Patience would know her daughter though, that was for sure. Having said that, I had not got a photo that clearly identified one of these kids as Anna Martinez. It was one thing a mother saying 'Yes, that is my daughter.' It was quite another proving it to a court of law. After being out for half an hour or so, during which time I still had not been able to get a clear face shot of the little girl, they went in, no doubt for lunch. That seemed to be a good idea so I ate too.

The other two cars left at three thirty. Nobody had been outside since the kids went in for lunch, a siesta no doubt. I decided to upload the pictures on to the laptop, which I did. I then did an interim report to Daisy and sent it off with the pictures. The report included my thoughts on the crash site and the pictures I had taken there.

No sooner had I sent them than my phone rang, it was Martin.

'Hi Matt, only me, this is just a quick call to see how things are going out there and to see if you need anything?'

'Hello Martin, you must be able to read my mind. I have just sent an interim report to Daisy with some photographs. Some of the pictures are of the scene of the accident. I have had a good look and in my considered opinion, it had to be a staged crash. No way should Inez have gone off the road there unless she was either pissed or driving like a mad woman. As they breathalysed her and it was negative and there were no marks on the road to suggest fast driving, it had to have been staged. Also, at the bottom of the ravine, there is an area where there has been a fire quite recently. This proves that the car did catch fire, and there was a dead kid but who that kid was, God knows.

On Tuesday, I followed Salma in to the supermarket where she bought sweets, I guess they could have been for Anna. I spoke to her but surprisingly, she didn't tell me who was getting the sweets. Can you believe that?

Earlier today, three young boys came to play in the garden of the Villa Borgosa, they were joined by a young girl.' I heard his sharp intake of breath. 'Sadly, the girl had a sun hat on which concealed quite a lot of her face. I have sent the pictures to Daisy with the report. I am sure it's Anna and I am convinced that Patience will be able to identify her but the problem is that we do not have a clear picture of the girl's face. It's all very well Patience saying its Anna but a clever lawyer would be able to argue that it could be anyone.

You will be getting them any time from Daisy, see what you think.'

'Hang on a sec Matt, something is coming through now.' Daisy had been quick in getting the pictures out to Martin. I hung on while he took a look. 'I agree with you Matt, there is no way that these enable us to go before a court and say 100% that this child is Anna. A clever lawyer will make us look stupid.'

'There is another point too Martin. If we go with these, then friend Raul will know we are sniffing around and he could well move Anna away somewhere.

As I said to Patience before I came, at the moment, we are in the driving seat, more so now because if this is Anna, then we know definitely that she is at the villa.'

'True enough. I will print these off and take a drive out there now and show Patience and ring you later to let you know what she says.'

'Did you know that Diego left me with a, er em...' I tried to think how to phrase this over an open line. 'With what all cowboys had, Mr Colt's product.'

'Jesus Matt, a gun. For Christ's sake, be careful. I'm beginning to regret getting you involved in all this now you have told me that.' So much for my attempt at being discreet.

'Don't worry mate, you know me, Mr Careful. I will not take any chances.' We talked for a few minutes more before he hung up. A few minutes later the phone rang again, it was Daisy.

'Hi Matt, everything has come through okay and I have sent the pictures on to Martin. How are you and how is the weather?'

'Hi Daisy love, I'm okay. As for the pictures, Martin rang out of the blue and was on to me when he received the pictures from you. He is going to print and go and see the Jameson's his afternoon.

As for me, I am fine ta love, it's going the way we expected. I think one of those kids is Anna but I said to Martin, the pictures are not good enough for a positive identification.'

'I thought that but I didn't say anything. Just keep trying. Everything is fine in the office so don't worry, just do the job,'

A few minutes later, yet another call. This time it was Patience. As soon as she spoke, I knew she had spoken with Martin.

'Matthew, it's me. Are you all right? Martin says you have a gun, what are you doing with that?' So much for discretion, it seemed that the world now knew about the gun. 'Please, please be careful, I don't want anything to happen to you.' The words tumbled from her mouth.

'Patience don't worry, everything is fine, honestly. Nothing is going to happen.' I was pleased that she was concerned though. 'I have sent some pictures over, three boys and a girl. The girl could be Anna but unfortunately, I can't get a clear shot of her face, she had a sun hat on. You may well recognise her, but as Martin will tell you, it isn't enough to take to a court. By the way, what type of cars do Raul's sisters drive?'

'I know about the pictures, he told me and also mentioned about the identification, if it is Anna then we will know. As for Maria and Esther, they both have four wheel drives, one has a Range Rover, the other a Mercedes ML, I don't know which is which though. Why?'

'Two cars came to the villa earlier, one was a BMW 5 series, the other a Mercedes E class. I wondered if it might be the sisters but apparently not.' I paused, 'Would you do something for me please?'

'Anything Matthew, is there something you need?'

'No, it's nothing like that. I want you to promise me that you won't worry. Everything is good. I feel it's just a matter of time before we get what we need. I just don't want you to worry any more than you will do anyway, if that makes any sense.' She laughed at that before giving me her promise. Before hanging up, she made me promise to be careful, it felt nice that she cared

Later on, I went for a beer before eating. For some reason, Sam was not in the bar. The other girl I had seen working there, Gail, brought me a beer and an envelope.

'Hello Matt,' she said. 'Sam asked me to give you this when you came in.' I thanked her and opened the envelope which contained a short handwritten note.

'Dear Matt, I am sorry that I am not here to say this in person but I have had to go back to Lincoln. You remember I said that my gran was not well, she is much worse. Mum rang me and asked me to come home. Don't know if you will be there when I get back, if not, good luck. I enjoyed meeting you. Love Sam.'

That was a shame, I hoped her gran was all right. Next time Gail came past, I called her over.

'Thanks for this Gail. If Sam rings give her my love and tell her that I hope her gran is fine.' She promised to pass the message on. While I was enjoying me beer, the phone rang, it was Patience.

'Hello Matthew,' she sounded down. 'The girl in the picture is not Anna, I have no idea who it is.' Shit, that did not help.

'Never mind,' I said brightly, 'We never get a result in the first couple of days. We all knew I was here for a while. Next time it will be her, I am sure of it.' I don't know why I added the last bit but I would have to deliver now.

'Thank you for that Matthew, whenever I talk to you I always feel better, you are good for me.'

'I am very positive about this, I am having one of my good feelings, even though you are not here. It won't be long before you come to join me.' She laughed, remembering what she had said at the airport.

After eating, I was back in the apartment and in bed by ten thirty.

Friday dawned bright and sunny, another glorious Majorcan day. From around nine, people were down splashing about in the pool. I decided that I would take an early morning walk around the villa and would go early Saturday morning. I really wanted to see the far side.

Raul left in his BMW at eleven, a few minutes later, Inez came out into the garden to lie in the sun. I watched her through the binoculars, as far as I could see, she was alone. As I watched, she stripped off to bikini pants, I felt like a voyeur but this was work after all, I would just have to grin and bear it. At times, this was a tough job. Not a bad body on her mind, small boobs but nice anyway. She stayed out till just after one: at one point, Inez raised her head and had a conversation with someone who maddeningly stayed out of my vision. That was annoying, it could well have been Anna but just as easily, it could have been Salma.

At two fifteen, a Seat Leon left the villa, Inez was driving, I could not tell if anyone else was in the car with her from my vantage point. As both Raul and Inez had gone out, maybe with Anna, I decided to take a walk and get some sun.

I was out for over an hour having donned sunglasses and a baseball cap before I left. The day was so hot that when I found myself down at the sea front, I ended up taking a paddle, carrying my trainers in my hand. It was really nice, something I had not done for years, the sea was cool and it felt good on my hot legs and feet.

As I strolled back to the Playa Rosa, the Seat passed me. Up ahead about a hundred yards, a bus was holding up all the traffic on the road, the Seat stopped about fifty yards from where I was. This was too good an opportunity to miss so I set off running and got to the Seat just as it pulled away. In the back was a young girl but was it Anna? I thought so but could not be 100% sure so I decided to say nothing about this. By the time I was back on my balcony, the Seat was nowhere to be seen, no doubt in a garage on the far side of the villa.

That night I had a couple of beers and a nice but solitary dinner and was in bed for just after ten, I wanted an early night in preparation for the mornings walk around the perimeter of the villa.

Saturday morning and I was up just after five for my look round the far side of the villa. It was almost light when I set off, straight across the Playa Rosa's grounds to the wall which was about eight feet high. Despite that, I was able to get over without too much difficulty. On the other side, I waited for a few moments in case of a shout but none came.

Last night, whilst eating, I had thought about what to take with me, binoculars or camera. Finally, I had decided to take the camera, I would be able to get some pictures and that would be more use in the long run than looking at the place close up.

Turning to the right, I set off towards the golf course, Raul's grounds backed onto one of the fairways. I came, after a short walk to a wall and fence, the wall to Raul's garden, the fence to the course. I went over the fence on to the golf course and followed the wall round.

Up ahead stood a large tree with plenty of branches; if I climbed up, I would have good vision in to the villa's garden. Hurrying over to it, I began to climb and went up about fifteen feet to where I had an uninterrupted view of the back of the villa. It was a large home on two stories, which I knew already. It was obviously an expensive villa, a luxury home. If Diego was right, the upkeep was from the proceeds of crime. It had a single door to the right, probably the kitchen door, and double doors to the left as I looked. A plastic water butt stood to the side of what I thought was the kitchen door.

They had a pool which I could not see from my balcony, it looked inviting and had a few sun beds scattered around it. To the far right I could see another building, possibly the garages. As I had expected, nobody was around.

I took several pictures with the 80 – 400 zoom, this was the one I had thought of leaving at home. Now I was glad that I had carried it with me. On its 400mm setting, the lens gave me a good close up of the back of the villa.

I didn't feel it a waste of time, I wanted to see the back of the property, no way could I do it later when the golfers were about, it would have been nice for Anna to come out but what the hell.

Over to my right, along my way round the perimeter, I could see another tree, it would give me a view of the other side of the villa. I climbed down from mine and set off again. I would have to be quick, in the distance I could see the first pair of golfers on the fairway.

Getting up the second tree was more difficult than the first but I managed. From my perch I saw Salma outside the kitchen door taking the early morning air. I took a few shots and hoped that Anna would appear but she didn't. I could not hang around on the off chance that she was up and came out, a golf ball had landed about fifty yards away so I would have to go, and quickly.

Once down from the tree, I rushed round and nipped over another fence, it was all climbing, and found my way to the front of the villa from where I took some more shots. From there, an easy ten minute stroll back to the apartments.

I went back to bed for a couple of hours before getting up again and making some breakfast. I watched the villa all day, after lunch the BMW left and did not return until late. No other movements at the villa so in the middle of the afternoon I went out and had another paddle in the sea, which was nice.

That night I went out and ate another good meal and had a few beers. I seemed to be drinking rather a lot but never mind. There was not much else for me to do in the evening.

Sunday was another long, slow day. The BMW left at ten thirty and returned at six thirty. An hour after the BMW left, Salma left, alone. I did not follow her deciding instead to have the afternoon in the sun. Armed with book, sun crème and towel, I spent the afternoon down by the pool, topping up my already good tan.

For my evening's entertainment, I had another good dinner and a few more beers and got chatting to some people from London which helped to pass the time. It was a hard life.

Chapter 12

Monday morning dawned bright and sunny. The seventeenth of June which meant that I had been in Santa Ponsa for a week now. Sitting on the apartment's balcony with a cup of Redbush tea, I reflected on my first week.

What had I discovered? Well, it did seem that a child was living at the villa but was it Anna? If she had come out to play with those other kids, then great. That she had not did not really mean much. Truthfully, I was in no different a position than I had been when I arrived. Just keep watching and waiting, it was all I could do and all I had been expecting to do.

I thought about the two cars that had come with those children, why would people bring children to Raul's villa if there was not already a child there? Of course, the cars drivers may well have had business with Raul but why bring your kids? That did not make any sense to me. What did make sense was this, whoever had come to see Raul had brought with them their kids to play with Raul's kid whilst the adults discussed business. That was the only logical reason for any of this as far as I could see. As far as Patience was aware, Inez had no kids so my reasoning had to be right. All I needed was proof.

Not much happened during the early part of the morning but at twenty past eleven, Salma walked down the drive towards the road, she was carrying a shopping bag. After about fifteen or twenty yards, she stopped and looked back, as if waiting for someone. Could it be? I was ready with the binoculars to my eyes and into the frame came a little girl, running to join Salma. Could this be Anna? The hair was shorter than in the pictures Patience had given me but there was a definite resemblance. I almost whooped with joy. She was wearing a white tee shirt and blue shorts and looked well from my distance. I watched them walk down the drive, if only they were going to the supermarket. This could be my chance to get some good full face shots.

I had about ten minutes before they would be outside the apartments, time to make my move. After grabbing the camera, I got some cash and a baseball cap and the apartment keys, then ran down to the car park.

It was about seven or eight minutes later that I saw the two of them walking down the road. I was now certain that this was Anna. I took a couple of quick shots before legging it out of the car park and rushing down the road on the opposite side to get ahead of them. A few more shots followed, of the two of them but in particular of Anna. I was able to get some good, full face shots of the child, Patience would be over the moon to have it confirmed that Anna was alive and well, we now had the proof that would stand up, if we chose to use it.

Looking at Anna, I thought that she looked a little sad but then, the poor kid would be missing her mother and she was only eight years old.

They went not into the supermarket but an ordinary market that I had not noticed before. I followed on behind them. Salma led the way to the fish counter and proceeded to have a conversation with the lady behind the counter. Anna just hovered about, slightly behind Salma, who spent about five minutes chatting and picking her fish. This gave me an idea. I left the market and was outside when they came out, as they did, I took several more full face shots of Anna. Magic, I could hardly wait to phone Patience to give her the news. On the way back to the apartment, I rang Daisy.

'I have found her,' I said when she answered. 'She went with Salma to the fish market, I have just left there and I'm on my way back to the apartment, as soon as I am in, I will upload the pictures and send them you. Get them to Martin as soon as you can please love.' Daisy was thrilled with the news and would copy the pictures to Martin as soon as she got them.

She must have phoned Martin, as I was uploading the pictures, he rang.

'Fantastic news Matt. Just brilliant. Now we know. When I get the pictures I am going straight round to see the Jameson's though I expect that you will ring Patience in the meantime.'

'Well I did think of giving her a ring, thought that I might be the one to break the news. Don't forget though, this is only the start. We still have to get Anna away from here. I will work on a plan over the next few days.

I am ready to send the pictures to Daisy now so you should have them in a few minutes.

Listen Martin, as you are going up to see the family, for God's sake, don't let Patience near a plane. I don't want her here yet. The good thing is that we know Anna is alive and well and, more importantly, we know where she is. If Patience comes here we just don't know how Raul will react. Diego has told me that he is a dangerous man and I see no reason not to believe him. If Patience comes before we are ready, she may well be in danger. It's up to you to make sure she stays at home until I am ready for her. If he gets wind of us then he could well move Anna away, maybe off the island altogether, then where would we be? At the moment, we are in a good position, let's not lose our advantage eh.'

'Fair point Matt, I will make sure that Henry lays down the law to her. I will ring him now to make sure that they will be there when I get there. I'll go so that you can ring Patience. See you soon.'

I rang Patience. 'Hi, it's me. How are you?' I said easily. After she had responded I gave her the news. 'This morning, I saw Salma going shopping, and guess who was with her.' Her shriek nearly deafened me.

'Are you sure? Is it really her? Is this the proof we need? How is she?' The questions came thick and fast.

'Patience, please calm down, just listen for a second. I am certain it's Anna, 100%. I have several pictures which are, as we speak, on their way to my office. Daisy will send them on to Martin and he is going to bring them out to you as soon as he gets them.

They went to the fish market actually and I took the shots on the way there and as they came out. Now, I am going to devise a plan to get her away from there but I need you to bear with me.'

'Matthew that's wonderful news, thank you so much. When can I come out there?' There it was, the question I had been dreading.

'Please listen to me Patience, I know you are desperate to get over here but I am not ready for you yet. Please leave me here alone until I am ready. That will be when I have a workable plan to separate Anna from her father. At the moment I have no idea when that will be so please, be patient. I will work on getting her away, don't you worry.

When I am sure that we have a foolproof plan to get her away and safely off the island then you can come, not before. I am sorry if I sound a little harsh, I don't mean to, I know what Anna means to you but consider this; we know Anna is alive. We also know where she is. This is in our favour and enables us to plan.

If you come over and go banging on Raul's door, he will not admit that she is there, he will call you a crazy woman and no doubt get his friend Capitan Galdano or whatever his name is, to remove you.

He will almost certainly move Anna, probably off the island, then where would we be. We may never find her again. At the moment, we know exactly where she is and this is to our advantage so she is really in the best place from our point of view.

Another thing, I feel that when you come, you may well be in some danger so when you do come, I want to have everything just so for you. Remember, Raul, or someone at his bidding, has already killed once. Would he kill again? To protect himself, I am certain he would, without hesitation. What has he to lose? I do not want you hurt or worse so please, just trust me, it's for the best though I know you will not agree with me. Please Patience, do as I ask.' It was quiet for a moment, I held my breath.

'Oh Matthew,' she sighed. 'I know you are right. Everything you say is right. I do want to come, desperately so but I will wait for you. I trust you totally and will do as you say.' Thank goodness for that. I slowly let my breath out.

'Thanks love. I have the beginnings of a plan but I need time to check things out and work it out properly. As soon as I am ready, I will send for you, I promise.'

'Here's dad, just hang on please Matthew. Its Matthew dad, he's found Anna, she is alive and well. I will put you on to dad Matthew.'

'Matthew,' Henry's voice came over the phone. 'I have just spoken with Martin. This is wonderful news, thank you so much. You have done a marvellous job so far but I suspect that this is only the beginning. You need to find a way to get Anna away from Raul so don't rush your plan. I suspect that we will only get one chance so take your time to ensure it works. I will hand you back to Patience. Again, well done.'

'I heard what dad said Matthew only don't take too long, please. I miss her so much. Do you know something, I miss you too.' Well, that was a surprise.

'I miss you to and want to see you, in fact, the sooner the better.' This would give me the incentive to plan both well and quickly. 'Let me think it through and I will speak to you soon.'

All things being equal, I thought that I deserved the afternoon off so I took myself out for a bite to eat and a couple of beers and ended up having another paddle in the sea. Whilst it was soothing, I didn't relax, I was thinking all the time.

At five, Martin rang, he had just left the Jameson's. The three of them had been overjoyed to see the pictures of Anna. Despite what she had said, Patience, understandably, wanted to get the first flight to the island, until she was reminded about what she had said by her father,

'By the way Matt, I took the opportunity to establish some ground rules for when she does come over. Patience has agreed that you are the boss and she will not do anything until she has obtained your approval. She will not go out of the apartment without you being with her. In a word, she will do as she is told.' I had to laugh at that.

'If she does as she says then we will have no problems when she arrives. I want at least another week to watch and see if any pattern emerges that we can use to our advantage. It's no use her coming until I have a way of getting Anna away from Raul and off the island.' After a few more words of thanks, Martin rang off.

Seconds later, the phone rang again. This time it was Patience.

'Hello Matthew, only me. Martin has just left. He brought up the pictures that you took. Poor Anna, she looks so unhappy, I just want to hold her and tell her everything is going to be all right. Before you say anything, I know I cannot, yet. I just want to, that's all.

I know we spoke earlier but I wanted to talk to you again. Thank you so much for finding her, I will never be able to thank you enough. Is there anything I can do for you? Anything you think we might need when I come over? No, don't worry, I will only come when you say it's all right for me, even though I can't wait to see Anna ….. and you too.'

'I want to see you as well but I want to be in a position to move when you get here. I am sure Martin said that there was no point in going to the authorities at this stage, we need to do this ourselves. I will have a plan for us, rest assured. There is one thing though, I am sure that Raul must have Anna's passport, can you get a new one or a duplicate or whatever. We will need it at some point.'

'Yes, he has it. I will phone the passport office right away and make an appointment. Please come up with a plan soon Matthew, I do miss her.' She began to cry. Before I could speak, Suzanne came on the line.

'Matthew, Suzanne. Patience is a little upset so I thought I would take my chance to thank you for what you have done. You have given us the best news that we could ever have. I will always be grateful to you.' Then Patience came back on the line.

'Sorry about that, I'm all right now. Is it okay for me to ring you later in the week? I don't want to pester you.'

'You can ring me at any time you want to, I am always pleased to hear your voice.' We spoke for a few minutes more then hung up. I was hungry and quite fancied a beer. I was ready to go out just before eight.

As I went through reception, Michelle, the stunning receptionist, was leaving. Naturally, I held the door for her and we began chatting. She told me that she had finished for the day. On impulse, I invited her for a drink which she readily accepted. I was feeling good after my discovery earlier. Michelle was good company and we chatted easily.

'Would you like to join me for something to eat?' I asked after a while.

'That would be nice, I am enjoying talking with you. I hope my English is all right.' It was. We went to a different restaurant in case I took Patience out to eat when she arrived, whenever that would be.

'Michelle, I don't know how to say this delicately so I will just say it. I am expecting a lady to join me in the apartment in maybe a week or so.'

'In a week you say, perhaps we could work on my English before she comes, eh.' She looked at me coyly.

'No strings?'

'No strings,' she confirmed. That was fine, it would help to pass the time, and pleasantly too.

We spent a satisfying time together before Michelle left for home around one.

As he had done last Tuesday, Raul left the villa around eleven and returned around half three. While he was out, I saw no other movement either to or from the villa but I was not disappointed. It gave me time to think. If Salma and Anna went to the fish market next Monday, which would be the twenty fourth, then I would assume that it was a regular thing for them on Mondays.

That being the case, I was sure that between the two of us, Patience and I could get Anna away from Salma whilst the two of them were in the market the following Monday. Yes, we could manage this but Patience had to be there with me, if I tried to get Anna, she would scream the place down. No, her mother had to be there. An opportunity would present itself at some point, most likely when Salma was buying her fish. That seemed to be one problem resolved, now, as far as I could see, only two more to solve.

The first of these was Patience herself, or more accurately, how to get her to the island. The obvious way was for her to do what I had done and fly direct to Palma. I didn't want her to do this though, if Raul was the type of man that Diego had alluded to, a criminal with plenty of people to do his dirty work, and a network of contacts or informers, then I figured that he would have eyes and ears all over the island reporting to him. No doubt he would have someone at the airport on his payroll, and no doubt that this person would be checking every flight in from the UK ever since Raul had kidnapped his daughter, I certainly would have done if I was in Raul's position, and they would be looking for the name Patience Jameson or Martinez, I didn't know what name appeared on her passport.

Anyway, if she appeared on any passenger manifest, I assumed that friend Raul would be notified at once and Anna would be whisked off somewhere and we would have lost her.

No, Patience had to appear on the island discreetly. She could fly into somewhere like Valencia and get a ferry to Palma. That would be a good idea, surely Raul would not expect her to do this. Daughters of millionaires don't put themselves out. I guessed that he would think that if she was to come to the island then it would be by direct flight. The more I thought about this, the more I liked it. If Patience came as a foot passenger, surely she would not be on any passenger list. I could then collect her from the port at Palma. I liked it.

Two down, one to go, and this was the big one. Getting off the island with Anna. Once he realised that she was gone, Raul would do everything in his power to find her. I was confident that he would not or could not contact the Police. How could he possibly say to them 'Excuse me, my daughter is missing. Yes I know I told you that she was killed in a car accident back in April but I was only joking. I think her mother has got her.' No, that was not going to happen. He no doubt had a team of his hatchet men that he could call on at a moment's notice so this would rule out flying from Palma, for the same reason that Patience could not fly in. How else could I get them off? I needed a guide book so I went out and got one. Back in the apartment I made a drink before going back out on to the balcony to look at the book.

Looking at the map of the island, an idea came to me. If Patience came by sea, we could all leave by sea. Not the ferry but by a private boat from somewhere which could take us to the mainland. Looking again at the map, I thought that if we could get someone to take us somewhere near Barcelona then we could get the train to Paris and either fly to England from there or even get the Eurostar.

I was sure that my ideas were as good as they were going to be, save for a little fine tuning. I would ring Patience in due course and have her travel via Valencia. I didn't expect that this would be a problem for her. Also, I would get her to change her appearance. A haircut and colour change ought do the trick, it should be enough to throw anyone who knew her when she lived here off the scent. As for Anna, I would discuss this with Patience when she arrived. The bit about getting off the island, I would discuss with Diego, he was a practical guy and in any case, he had said to call if I needed anything. I did, a boat, maybe he had one, he seemed to able to get his hands on most things. It was a comforting thought.

Nothing of interest happened at the villa for the rest of the day. That night, I went out and had a couple of beers in a different bar, and enjoyed people watching. After the beer, I went for some food before heading back to the apartment for a good night's sleep.

Martin rang me first thing Wednesday morning, the nineteenth.

'Just a brief update,' he began. 'Patience has an appointment at the Liverpool passport office at noon today. Unless something goes wrong, she should have Anna's duplicate passport when she leaves.'

I took the opportunity to run by Martin the thoughts I had had whilst sitting in the sun.

'I like the ideas,' he said. 'I cannot see Patience having any problem going via Valencia. You can tell her about her hair when you next speak to her, I happen to know she is very proud of her hair so I don't envy you. As for getting Anna away from Salma at the market, I agree with what you say, it should not be too difficult for you and Patience between you to get her away without a fuss. Speaking to Diego about boats is a good idea, he will know someone if half of what Henry says is true. Give him a call.' I did.

'Diego, it's me, Matthew.' I introduced myself when he answered.

'Hello Matthew, I understand from Henry that things are going well.'

'They are but I need some help and some advice if that's all right?'

'Of course my friend. Today I am busy but tomorrow I am not. Can you meet me for lunch in Inca? Yes, good. In Inca there is a bar, the Bar Aztec, meet me there at one pm.'

Diego then proceeded to give me the directions I needed to get to Inca and once there, to enable me to find this bar.

It sounded straightforward enough but I would give myself plenty of time, just in case I got lost.

Nothing was happening at the villa so I decided it was time to do some shopping. While I was out, I saw Raul and Inez in the BMW 7 series. Was anyone in the back? I thought so. As they were out there did not seem much point in my hanging around the apartment. I decided to send a text to Patience, just to wish her good luck with her attempt to get a duplicate passport for Anna.

Chapter 13

Since returning home to Little Thornley from Majorca following the cremation of Anna, Patience had, understandably, been depressed. Each morning getting out of bed to face the new day had become progressively more difficult, and more than once, she had contemplated suicide. However, once she had interpreted Salma's actions at the cremation, Patience faced each new day with growing optimism. Her dreams about Anna were now happy ones, the two of them together again. And, once or twice, Matthew had featured in the dreams as well.

Meeting Matthew Bentley had played a major part in Patience's new feel good factor. He had a quiet strength about him, was not prone to making excessive claims about what he could or would do. His confidence had rubbed off and Patience was sure that one day soon, Anna would be back home with her.

When she had first seen Bentley across the bar at the Lansdowne Hotel, the day she had lunched with her parents and Martin Keogh, their solicitor, she had thought that he looked to be a nice and considerate man, the type of man that she would have loved to have met a few years ago. Now that she had met him and had been for a drink with him on a couple of occasions, she had not been disappointed. What she now wanted was to get to know him properly. Patience felt sure that Matthew was also interested in her and sensed that his interest was in her as a person, unlike most of the men she met who saw her only as a sex object and meal ticket.

Their drinks together, first at the Hare and Hounds and then the Ship had gone a long way to her forming that opinion. He had been very good company, as keen to listen to what she had to say as to speak himself. When they had spoken of Anna, he had made no wild promises to her and had told her of the difficulty that they faced with this job. He had spoken sensibly of how he intended to carry out his observations of the villa and had given off an air of quiet confidence. He had also treated her as a woman, was interested in her opinion of the topics they discussed. Like her, he was an avid reader and they had both read and liked some of the same authors. Patience sensed that Matthew liked her and wanted to get to know her better, call it women's intuition but that was how she felt. She hoped that her intuition was correct.

Their second meeting at her home had reinforced her feelings. Patience recalled running, crying from the lounge where she, her parents, Martin and Matthew had been discussing the case. She reddened as she recalled her hysterical outburst as she ran from the room.

As expected, someone had come up to see she was all right and to speak to her. What had been a surprise was that it had been Matthew and not mother who had come though mother did show him up. She recalled inviting him into her room and he had spoken to her. He had asked her to be patient, she remembered them both laughing at that. Then, Matthew had told her what he would be doing over in Majorca, as he spoke, Patience began to understand just what would be needed to find Anna. It sounded impossible that she would ever be found and her insides were in turmoil.

When she had cried, he had come across the room and knelt down in front of her and held her hands as he had spoken. Patience tingled with pleasure as another memory from that night returned, how Matthew had held her in his arms, stroking her hair until she stopped crying and then telling her that she looked adorable. He was quite a man and she simply had to get to know him better.

Now, he was in Santa Ponsa looking for her Anna. She had driven him to the airport and they had kissed as they parted. He had looked both surprised and pleased at the kiss.

Patience had failed to notice her mother come into the room, so lost was she in her thoughts.

'Is everything all right darling? Suzanne posed the question. 'You have the most enormous smile on your face.'

'I'm fine mother, really thanks. Things are getting better and I feel quite certain that Anna will soon be home with us.' Patience saw the concern on her mother's face and continued, 'Please don't worry, I am not going to let my hopes and wishes get the better of me. Of course I am hopeful but I do know that there is a lot to do before she is back home.'

'I'm relieved to hear it darling but I do know how you feel. I have confidence in Matthew Bentley too.'

Did mother know how she was feeling about Matthew? It would not surprise her, over the years, mother had been able to read her like an open book.

She suddenly remembered the gun. Martin had spoken with her and her father and had let it slip that Diego, her father's friend in Majorca, had supplied Matthew with a gun. She had immediately phoned Matthew, worried about him. He had been pleased to hear from her and had assured her that he was fine.

The next few days had passed slowly. In finishing her last call to Matthew, she had told him she would call him Tuesday. What she actually wanted was to speak to him on a daily basis, she would not do so but it was hard for her to stop herself calling.

Since leaving Raul and returning to England, Patience had again been working with her father. She did not really need to work but rather enjoyed the world of business. Her father had a number of business interests and was on the boards of some high profile companies. Patience to, was retained as a non-executive director with three companies.

The family also had an extensive property portfolio, both commercial and domestic. Patience, on behalf of her mother and father, managed the portfolio and received an income from it. They also had interests in frozen foods, computers, clothing and operated an extremely lucrative escrow company and she and her father had contacts all over the world. These business interests kept her busy and she had her own income from her efforts. Since this business with Anna, her involvement with work had understandably declined and her father had drafted in one of their employees to take over from Patience until she was good and ready to return to work.

Now, she felt like working again. Like her father, she too had an office in the family home, hers was in the wing over the kitchen where she and Anna had their bedrooms. On the morning of Monday the seventeenth June, Patience had gone into her office for the first time in many weeks. She had gone in to clean. Aggi had wanted to do it but Patience would not let her, she felt that it was her responsibility. The hoovering had been done and she was dusting when her phone rang. It was Matthew.

'Hi, it's me. How are you?' had been his first words. Then he gave her the news. Patience had shrieked, alarming Aggi, who had been by the door, so much that she ran off to find somebody. A few moments later Jameson entered her office, he had been on the telephone to Martin and looked ten years younger. Henry then had a brief word with Matthew before handing her back her mobile. She spoke to Matthew for a while longer before hanging up.

The news was fantastic, Anna was alive and well and Matthew had the pictures to prove it. Damn that bastard Raul, how could he have done what he did.

Martin was coming over in the afternoon and bringing with him copies of the photographs Matthew had taken.

The wait for Martin was indeterminable. Even mother, who was blessed with more patience than most, was pacing up and down. Finally, Martin arrived. They could hardly contain their impatience as he opened his briefcase and took out several colour photographs which he quickly passed round. All the pictures showed Anna, some alone, some with Salma. Both Patience and her mother were crying, even Henry Jameson, normally the most undemonstrative of men had to wipe away a tear.

'I understand that you have spoken with Matt,' Martin said to Patience, 'And that you are happy to leave things to him for the moment.'

'That's right Martin. I will not do anything until Matthew says it is all right.'

Martin left after an hour or so, leaving behind him four very happy people. Suzanne had called Aggi down to share in their happiness too.

At last Patience could see the light at the end of what had been a very long tunnel. She decided on impulse to telephone Matthew again as she wanted to thank him all over again for finding Anna, but really, she just wanted to hear his voice.

During their conversation, Matthew asked if she could get a duplicate passport for Anna, Patience was delighted to be asked, at last she felt that she was contributing something useful to the business.

Once they had finished talking, Patience rang the passport office in Liverpool and was fortunate to find that they had just had a cancellation for Wednesday at noon. Patience was happy to take the appointment. Having just phoned Matthew, she decided instead to ring Martin and tell him, being wary of pestering Matthew while he was working. That done, she finished off her cleaning, as she did, she put on a CD and began to sing along. Outside the office door, Henry and Suzanne listened to their daughter sing, happy themselves with the news, they were delighted for Patience that Anna was alive.

After finishing her cleaning, Patience switched on her computer for the first time in weeks. Many, many emails awaited her attention. She made a start on them, anything with an advert was deleted without being opened. Once that was done, she began to read, Rodney, the man her father had brought in had dealt with quite a lot of the work but some things needed her personal attention. She began to answer some of the mail, by way of explanation for the delay, she told people that she had been ill which wasn't altogether untrue. She also said that she would be going away to convalesce for two or three weeks and Rodney would look after things for her until she was well enough to return.

When their evening meal was ready, Patience found that she had recovered her appetite. Aggi had excelled herself with dinner and Jameson opened a special bottle of wine to celebrate their news.

'When Anna is safely back in this house with us, we must have a celebratory dinner. We will invite Martin and Carol and, of course, Matthew,' Suzanne announced after they had eaten. Patience looked at her mother gratefully, now certain her mother was aware of her feelings for Matthew.

Wednesday morning, first thing, Patience took her Mercedes to the local garage where they filled it with petrol and checked the car over before her trip to Liverpool. She set off at ten thirty thinking she had plenty of time but due to the traffic, she did not get parked up until eleven forty five. As she walked to the office, she checked her phone, one unread text. It was from Matthew wishing her good luck. She was delighted, and would phone him when she came out of the passport office.

All went smoothly and she was outside with the duplicate by one fifteen. As it was such a nice day, Patience sat at one of the pavement cafés that had sprung up in Liverpool over the past couple of years. After ordering tea and a sandwich, she phoned Matthew.

'Hi, it's me,' she said when he answered, pleased to hear the happiness in his voice as he spoke to her. 'I have just left the passport office with the duplicate and I am having tea and a sandwich sat outside. What are you doing love?' she asked.

'Just sitting, watching the villa with nothing to report today, so far. I'm glad you rang, apart from wanting to know about the passport, I just wanted to talk to you.' Just by saying that, Matthew made her day.

'I assume Martin has spoken to you and told you that I have agreed to do as I am told. You must have something about you Matthew,' she mused, 'I cannot ever remember agreeing to do as I am told before, especially by a man.' She wondered if he could hear the happiness in her voice. They spoke for a few minutes longer before hanging up.

Patience drove back to Little Thornley happier than she had been in weeks. To her surprise, she found herself singing along with the CD player as she drove.

Chapter 14

Thursday the twentieth of June dawned bright and sunny as each previous day had. My tan was quite good now even though I had not been trying. Over breakfast, I considered my three plans; Patience to Majorca, Anna back with her mother and all three of us off the island. The only one of the three that I could not plan down to the last detail was the second, separating Anna from Salma. In truth, we would have to wing it but I was confident that an opportunity would present itself for us to do the deed quickly and quietly.

Mid-morning I took a shower and got ready for my trip to Inca to meet up with Diego. I was not due at the bar until one but having said that, it was my intention to leave about an hour and a half earlier and check for any tail. I was probably being paranoid but with Patience possibly coming in the next week, I was not about to take any chances.

When I went out to the Scenic, I dropped the keys and had a good look round as I bent to retrieve them. As far as I could tell, no-one was hanging around by the car park, nor did anyone jump into a car as I got into mine. Before starting the car, I lowered all the windows. When I started the engine, I counted to three then turned off. Silence. I was not able to hear any other cars start up. That was fine, another good look round, nothing seemed out of the ordinary so I put the windows up and started the car again: I pulled out of the car park into the road which was, at the moment, quiet, and accelerated away. After about fifty yards, I pulled up suddenly and checked my mirrors. No cars had pulled out into the road behind me so I continued on my way feeling quite happy.

I took the road for Palma keeping a careful eye on my rear view mirror, then the Ma-13 to Inca. I continually monitored the rear view mirror. As far as I could tell, nothing was following me though I did keep slowing down then speeding up. Nothing seemed to be taking any notice of me.

About half way to Inca, I spotted a little taverna sitting just off the road, without a signal, I pulled sharply off the road into the car park of the taverna. Apart from a couple of blasts on the horns of cars behind me, nothing happened, no cars slowed down or pulled over further up the road, though to be truthful, I would not have expected them too, but then, not everyone was perhaps as professional as I was. After ten minutes, I continued on my way.

Whilst parked, I had been keeping a close eye on the cars that went past, as I continued towards Inca, though obviously I could not be certain, I did not think that I saw any of those same cars.

I arrived in Inca at twelve thirty and found the leather goods store exactly where Diego said it was which pleased me. It was only a little thing but it reinforced my opinion that Diego was a man who could be counted on. Turning right, I found the car park and parked up, took a slow look round before strolling off to find the Bar Aztec.

It was ten to one when I went into the bar. Diego was already there and rose to shake hands as I crossed to his table.

'Beer?' he asked. I noticed that he already had one. As it was a hot day, I nodded and smiled my thanks. He merely looked at the girl at the bar who immediately poured a beer and brought it over.

'I have ordered a selection of tapas for lunch, I hope you like our traditional food.' He did not wait for an answer. 'It will be served now that you are here Matthew, after that, we will talk business. I have spoken with Henry and he tells me you have found Anna and that skunk of a father had her, as we thought. That does not surprise me, he is an evil bastard, that one. Nothing like his father, a fine man and a dear friend, God rest his soul. If I had my way I would break down the door of the Villa Borgosa and take Anna and give her to you to take home but the law says I cannot, bah, the law is stupid. Ah, here comes the tapas, let us eat my friend then tell me how I can help.'

The selection he had ordered was very good and included patatas bravas, albondigas which turned out to be meatballs, chicken and fish dishes, all of which were extremely tasty. Neither of us spoke until the little dishes were empty.

'Diego,' I said, 'That was excellent and I enjoyed every bite. Whoever the chef is, he has done a great job.'

'I am glad you enjoyed it Matthew, the chef is my brother Fernando, Angelica there is my niece, I own the bar,' He pointed to the pretty girl at the bar who smiled and waved. 'Now Matthew, what can I do to help?'

I took a breath and began to speak. 'As you know, Anna is living at the villa with her father and Inez. Also Salma the nanny is living there. On Monday, Anna accompanied Salma to the market on the street outside the apartment, they went to the fish counter where Salma seemed to be quite friendly with the woman working there, certainly they talked for a time and did seem to know each other. Anna just stood by, waiting patiently.

I intend to watch this coming Monday to see if they go again. One thing I have noticed is that the people in the villa do seem to do the same things each week so I am hopeful that the fish market will be a regular thing on Mondays. If they go next week then I think it safe to assume they will go the week after which will be the first of July. My intention is this, if they go next Monday then I will have Patience come over towards the end of next week.

Now, as I see the situation, there are three things that I have to do. The first of those things is getting Patience safely on to the island without Raul knowing she has arrived. The second is Patience and I have to separate Anna from Salma at the fish market and lastly, I have to get them safely off the island. Agreed?'

'Agreed. I presume that you have thought about this and have a plan or maybe three plans and you are going to tell me them.'

I smiled. 'You are quite right. I will start with Patience. When I arrived here and we first met, you told me a few things about Raul which I have taken on board. If Raul is the type of man you say, and I believe you, totally, then I would assume that he has many people on the island who work for him, either directly or indirectly, also that he has informers throughout the island supplying him with information for which he pays, depending on the value of the information to him. Would you say that is right?'

'Quite right Matthew, he has a network of contacts throughout the island.'

'Okay, then I would further assume that some of these people will know Patience by sight from when she lived here as his wife. From her point of view, she would be unlikely to know many of these people, why would she know the hired help? Oh, one thing, she never mentioned to me that Raul has a shady background.'

'I do not think that she would be aware of what he does Matthew, if she knew then she would have told you. Henry knows of course for I have told him about Senor Martinez and he of course warned you.'

'Fair enough, back to Patience, if one of these people saw her they would report the sighting to Raul and get a reward. All things being equal, an English expression, I expect Raul to have someone at Palma airport who is able to check passenger manifests of all flights coming to the island. Since he kidnapped his daughter, I expect that this person at the airport has orders to check every flight in for the name Patience Jameson or Martinez, I don't know which name is on her passport. Now as soon as the name is spotted, Raul will be told, then I expect that Anna would be moved to God alone knows where and we will be in a much worse position than we are at the moment.

To get round this, what I propose is that Patience flies to Valencia and from there, takes one of those ferries into Palma. I feel sure that Raul will not be checking passenger manifests at Valencia. If she boards the ferry as a foot passenger, I doubt very much that they would even take names. Also, I will ensure that she changes her appearance before she leaves England.' I took a welcome drink of my beer.

'I think that is a very good idea Matthew, I would be pleased to have thought of that myself. You are right about Raul, he does have a contact at Palma airport, Carlos Luis Sanchez. Now, this Carlos is in Raul's debt, I do not know how or why but it is safe to assume that Carlos will check every flight into Palma and warn him where necessary. We cannot take the risk of Raul discovering that Patience has come to Mallorca, so the ferry from Valencia is a good idea.' He looked at Angelica who brought two more beers.

'Secondly, getting Anna away from Salma. I don't have a hard and fast plan for this, I propose that Patience and I follow them to the market where an opportunity to act will present itself, of that I am sure. If Patience is right, and I am sure she is, then Salma indirectly passed her a message at the cremation.' I went on to tell Diego what had happened at the cremation and the villa. 'I think that if Anna sees her mother then she will want to be with her.'

'Yes, I am inclined to agree. I was aware of what Salma had done, Henry passed this information on to me, it does seem like she was sending a message. As you say, if the child sees her mother than she will go happily with her, and Salma shouldn't present a problem.'

'The last part is the tricky part, getting the three of us off the island after we have got Anna. I imagine that when Raul finds out that Anna is gone, his first thought will be that Patience is involved and that we are flying her off the island, and will get in touch with Carlos at the airport and take the necessary steps to prevent that happening.

My idea is that we go nowhere near the airport at all. We would leave Santa Ponsa by road and head for one of the ports on the west of the island, from there we go by boat to the mainland, somewhere near Barcelona, a place rather more quiet than Barcelona. From there, we make our way into Barcelona heading for the railway station where we can take the train to Paris. From Paris we can either fly home or take the Eurostar back to England.'

'I like this, it is devious, my sort of plan. Leave this to me. I have a friend who has a boat and I will talk to him about this.

Now one thing, what about the police? You have not mentioned them Matthew, why?'

'I have not mentioned them for a good reason, I do not think that the police will come into this in any way whatsoever. As far as I am concerned, Raul cannot involve them, despite his possible friendship with this Caldano fellow, without leaving himself open to an intensive investigation. How can he say 'My daughter is missing.' The police will surely say 'How can this be Senor Martinez. Your daughter was killed in a car crash in April, we have a statement from you and one from Senorita Castillar stating clearly that your daughter was a passenger in a car than went off the road and burst into flames. We recovered a body from the wreckage, if not your daughter then who was it?' Somehow, I cannot see Raul wanting to answer questions like those.'

'Good man, that's just how I see things. We are on the same wavelength you and I. Now Matthew, please leave this to me. Can you meet me here Sunday at the same time, we will talk again and I will have news about a boat.'

'Thanks Diego, Sunday at one is fine, I will look forward to it. Now, please let me pay for our excellent lunch.' He would not hear of it, we left the bar together, shook hands then he was gone, in the opposite direction to me.

I wandered slowly back to the Scenic keeping a close lookout, nothing caused me any alarm. As I drove back to the apartment, I kept my eyes open but saw nothing to concern me. I was back by half four, nothing seemed to be happening at the villa so I decided to go down and read by the pool in the sun. Michelle was in reception as I passed, she told me that she finished at nine that night and would appreciate another English lesson if I were free. That seemed like a good idea so I arranged to meet her at nine.

Outside, I found a sun bed and settled down where my thoughts turned to Patience. I was really looking forward to seeing her and hoped that she could come out next week.

I went out at seven thirty and had a beer and something to eat and was back at the apartments at nine to meet Michelle. We then went and had a drink before heading back to my apartment. At one point, she asked if I was still expecting someone, the fact that I was made no difference to her English lesson. Michelle left around two. No strings.

On Friday morning, things seemed quiet at the villa so I took the opportunity to send another interim report to Daisy. She rang me a little later to update me on things at the office.

'We have become rather busy over the past few days,' she told me happily. 'Both Karen and Tony have been doing plenty which is great. Do you know Matt, we have had some business from Carstairs & Co.' That was interesting, Carstairs & Co was a firm of solicitors in Greenfield who did not use our service, they used our main competitor.

'How come they have used us?' I asked, 'Has someone cocked up somewhere along the line?' Daisy was laughing now.

'You're spot on Matt. You know Mike Weir.' She named a guy who worked for our competitor, EB Investigation. I did not like Weir, had never liked him. I thought him a slimy little shit. 'Well, friend Weir served a Statuary Demand on someone, this person did not respond so a Bankruptcy Petition was issued.' A Statuary Demand was a demand for payment of a fixed sum. Failure to respond to the demand was to commit an act of Bankruptcy, and a petition could be issued against the debtor.

'Weir swore an Affidavit of Service of the demand but someone else from EB served the petition, I think it was EB himself. The debtor turned up at

Court for the hearing of the petition and proved to the District Judge that at the time Weir swears that he served the demand, he was in the United States. He brought with him his passport, stamped at entry, and papers from the airline he flew with.

The DJ was furious, it was Jenkins by the way.' The District Judge she named was a stickler for things to be just so. He would not be impressed by this. 'He threw out the petition, ranted and raved and ordered the costs of the day to be paid by Carstairs & Co.

That's not all. Weir has been sacked by EB, Carstairs have demanded that EB pay the costs ordered by the Court, they have also reported the matter to the police and have basically instructed EB to double check all their cases where Weir has served things for them.

The Judge has also instructed the court staff to look at every affidavit Weir had filed, not just for Carstairs but for all the other firms in the area.'

I had to laugh. Edward Burns, the owner of EB, was a pretentious prat, every bit the tosser, just like Weir. I had no sympathy for either of them. On the contrary, we could benefit by getting the work from Carstairs & Co, and with luck, plenty of the other firms that used EB. Shit, as they say, sticks.

'Daisy, make sure that Karen and Tony know all about this, find some way to make sure that neither of them take a short cut like Weir has obviously done.'

'Already done Matt, we all had a good laugh at their expense. No problem with our troops, they are good guys and know better. I thought of doing a mail drop to all the firms who don't use us. I will not make any mention of this incident but putting our name in front of them at this moment in time can only do us good. What do you think?'

'Go for it Daisy. It's a damn good idea.' We talked for a while about the Jameson job before she hung up. Well, that was great news, if we could pick up more business while I was away then I would be delighted.

I then went out on to the balcony and saw Anna in the garden, went back in to look through the binoculars. As far as I could tell, not knowing her, the poor kid looked really sad and lonely. She was no doubt missing her mother. So was I, I admitted to myself. As I continued to watch, I found myself thinking aloud. 'Don't worry kid, in little over a week, you could well be back with your mom.' Thinking of Patience, I would phone her later and mention that when she came to the island, I wanted it to be by way of Valencia.

It did seem that friend Raul was now getting confident, allowing Anna out in the garden and to the shops and certainly looked like he was not worried about anyone seeing her. I guess he thought Patience had accepted what she had been told, maybe he was too arrogant to think anyone could challenge him. He would get a shock soon enough.

Having checked my cupboards when I got up that morning, it was clear that I had to go and do some shopping, I went at lunch time and had some lunch in a sea front bar first. It was very nice here in Majorca even though I was working. I was able to enjoy the sun, the time that I had been here had given me a good tan though I needed to do more to my back. I also felt really well, much better than I had in a while, was it the sunshine or was it Patience?

After lunch I went to the supermarket and stocked up with the items I needed. Back at base, I checked out the villa which was all quiet, siesta time, so I had one too. There was not a lot I could really do now, it was a case of waiting for Monday to see if Anna and Salma went to the fish market. As long as they did, we were on.

Raul left in his BMW around ten or so on Saturday morning, someone was with him, I thought it was Inez. I watched for an hour and saw nothing so I decided to go down to the pool and get some sun on my back. It was quite busy but I managed to find an empty bed by a couple. She looked to be around fifty, he was a good bit older. I asked if the bed was free and received a nice smile, it was so I settled there. I got out my sun crème and tried to put some on my back, not the easiest thing to do. My new friend, who had introduced herself as Consuela took the bottle from me and playfully slapped my arm.

'Silly man, struggling like that. Lie down and let me do your back.' I did so and rather enjoyed her oiling me. She had a lovely, gentle touch, she did my back and my legs, starting at my feet and working her way up. It was heaven lying there while she did this. As she did the back of my thigh, I wondered how far she would go. I soon had my answer as she pushed the legs of my shorts up a bit. I was wondering what her husband was making of this but didn't like to ask. Then she was done.

'My turn now,' she said. I looked but hubby seemed to be asleep which I was pleased about. She handed me her bottle before removing her bikini top and showing me a rather nice pair of boobs. Then she lay down and I did to her what she had done to me. To be honest, I don't know who enjoyed it most, Consuela or me? Me I guess though she did squirm when I did the top of her legs. The two of us chatted for an hour or so before her husband woke up and wanted his lunch. She sat and faced me as she put her top back on. For her age, she was really rather good looking and had a good body on her. Lunch, that seemed like a good idea so after getting ready I wandered back down to the sea front and went to the same place I had been to yesterday,

The BMW returned around six and all at the villa remained quiet. Round about half past seven, I was ready for a drink and some dinner which I went for and enjoyed and was back in the apartment and in bed by eleven.

Chapter 15

I retraced my steps to Inca Sunday morning to meet up with Diego once again at the Bar Aztec. By taking the same precautions I had previously engaged, I was able to feel confident that nobody was taking an interest in me or my movements. Parking in the same spot, I was again ten minutes early arriving at the bar and, once again, Diego was there, waiting for me.

This time, he did not have to ask. As soon as I walked through the door, Angelica poured me a beer and brought it over. I had just shaken hands with Diego when she arrived with it. I thanked her for the beer, it was a hot day and I was ready for it. No sooner had we sat down when Angelica was back, laden with a tray of tapas. As before, we ate the delicious food before we got down to business.

'Matthew, I have arranged the boat for you to leave the island on. What I propose is this, and this is of course subject to your agreement, Oh, and of course, this is dependent on our going ahead on the first of Julio.

I will come to the apartment around ten that morning, I think you said that Anna went to the market after eleven. We will load your luggage into the Scenic, then we wait.

When you and Patience go for Anna, I will be behind the wheel of the car, when you return with her, I will drive us out of Santa Ponsa and we will go to Port de Soller where we will meet my good friend Sergio Bosko. Sergio has a Sunseeker Predator 75, a cabin cruiser. This boat will make short work of the Med though in reality, it will take about seven to eight hours. Sergio will take the three of you to Canyet de Mar which is a small fishing village to the north of Barcelona. There, the boat will be met by another friend of mine, Miguel Ramos who will drive you to Barcelona railway station. From there, you can take the train to almost any place you like. How is that?'

'Diego, that is great. Thank you very much indeed, I am very grateful to you for this.'

'Think nothing of it, I am happy to help. Henry and his family are dear to me, I also despise Raul Martinez.' He said this as if it explained everything, I suppose it did.

'Now Matthew, I have also looked into the ferries from Valencia. It takes just short of ten hours for the ferry to make the crossing, one leaves at eleven in the evening and arrives before ten the following morning. I will leave it to you and Patience as to when she comes to Spain.'

'I will phone her in the morning, as I see it, she needs to arrive in Valencia late in the afternoon and go straight to the ferry port.' He agreed. For the next hour, we pushed the ideas around, neither of us could really do any better. Again, he would not let me pay for lunch. I was back in the apartment by four, another siesta.

Monday the twenty fourth of June. D day, or to be more accurate, Anna day. It was a glorious sunny day, just the sort of day to go and buy fish. I sat on the balcony after breakfast just watching and hoping that Anna and Salma would appear. I knew that several other people were sat, biting their finger nails in England waiting for the same thing, I tried to read but couldn't concentrate. I put my Ipod on but heard none of the music. The waiting was hell, each minute seemed like an hour. It was bad enough sitting here looking over the balcony. I could not imagine how it was for those at home, waiting and praying.

'Yes,' I cheered when I saw them walking down the path. It was eleven fifteen. I was overjoyed as I went down to pick them up in the street. This time, I had no camera, I didn't want to draw any attention to myself. I also had on a baseball cap and sunglasses. It was an outside chance that Salma would recognise me from the supermarket which was now quite a few days ago, she may have also seen me last Monday so I was taking no chances.

As before, I saw them on the other side of the road and slipped out of the car park once they had passed, and followed from the other side of the road.

When they got near the market, I found that I was holding my breath, until they went in. What a relief. When I got in, they were at the fish counter and again Salma and the fish lady were deep in conversation. It really did look like a regular Monday event. While they were choosing their fish, I took a quick look round the market. I was looking for exits. Surprisingly, I found only two. The main one where we had come in, the other was a small one at the rear which led into an alley which was no use to me. We would leave by the main door, if the timing was right, we would be away before Salma had her fish. With luck, it might spoil Raul's dinner that night. Oh dear, how sad. Never mind.

By the time Salma realised something was wrong, we should be at the car. A quick jump in and we would be off to Port de Soller. As I left the market, I came face to face with the two of them. All I could do was smile, Salma wished me 'Buenos Dias.' She did not seem to recognise me which was a relief, I rushed back to the apartment and rang Patience who must have had the phone in her hand as she answered immediately.

'Matthew, what's the news?' she asked urgently.

'The news is good. I have just followed them to the market where the lady at the fish stall spoke to Salma as if they knew each other. I am sure that they will go again next Monday.' I could hear her sobbing.

'Matthew that's wonderful, when can I come? Please say I can come soon.'

'Yes you can come soon but listen, I don't want you to fly to Palma. I will explain why later, but for now, please do as I ask. Get a flight on Thursday to Valencia. From Valencia I want you to take the ferry to Palma which takes around ten hours, one apparently leaves at eleven pm so please try to get on that one but don't book or pay by card, use cash. What I suggest is that you try and get a flight that gets you to Valencia around tea time, no later than say seven. Then get a cab to the ferry port and pay cash for your passage to Palma. You could probably get a cabin so that you will be able to rest.

I will meet you at the ferry port in Palma on Friday morning. Can you do that?'

'Of course I can. I know you will have a reason for this and it will be a good one.'

'There is one more thing I need you to do for me before you come. Believe me, it is necessary or I wouldn't ask.'

'What is it Matthew? I will do anything you ask, you know that.' I was dreading this, I took a deep breath, here goes.

'Patience, I want you to change your appearance.' Something like a wail came down the phone.

'Do you mean cut my hair?' She sounded incredulous.

'Not only cut it my love but change the colour too. I want you to look as different as possible from the last time you were here. It is important otherwise I would not ask.'

'All right Matthew, I will do as you ask. I told you the other day that you must have something, I would not do this for anyone else.'

'In that case, I feel suitably honoured,' I joked. After she said she would book a flight then let me know, we hung up.

As I made some lunch and a drink, I realised, with a jolt that I had called her 'my love' and she had not complained. Wow.

She called back an hour later.

'I have booked my flight, it is due in Valencia at six pm Thursday evening. I think that will give me plenty of time to get a cab to the docks and get the ferry. Dad will drive me to the airport Thursday. Oh, I have booked an appointment for tomorrow with my stylist.'

'Don't go to mad or I might not recognise you Friday morning.'

'You had better recognise me Bentley otherwise you will be in serious trouble.' That told me. Patience went on to tell me what she was bringing with her, the way she told it, she made it sound like she was travelling light. I thought it sounded rather a lot but had the good sense to keep quiet. She was also bringing more cash, just in case we needed any. I did not think we would but you could never tell.

'Will you take me to the scene of the crash please Matthew? I know it was not Anna who died but I want to see it anyway.'

'Of course I will. We can go either Saturday or Sunday but let's decide when you are here.'

Next, I phoned Diego to tell him where I was up to. He suggested that I bring Patience to lunch at the Aztec on Sunday, that way we could finalise our plans for Monday. That was fine with me, we could look at the crash site on the way then continue on to Inca.

Well, only four more nights for me to eat my meals on my own. I was really looking forward to seeing Patience again. The memory of the kisses we had shared at the Ship and at the airport were fresh in my mind. Not for the first time, I wondered if we could possibly have any future together after this business was over. Time would tell, for sure.

After the highs of Monday, Tuesday was always going to be an anti-climax. As usual, Raul left around eleven and returned just after three. In a way, this was quite pleasing as he had done the same thing the last two Tuesdays. It was obvious to me that the inhabitants of the villa were creatures of habit and reinforced my view that Salma would take Anna to the fish stall next week.

I got a brief glimpse of Anna that evening, she appeared in the garden with Salma, the two of them picked some flowers.

Wednesday was not much better, now that we had settled on a plan and Patience was coming to the island, time, for the first time since I had been here, began to drag. The hard work was done so I decided to work on my tan. Outside, my new friend Consuela waved to me, there was a sun bed at the side of her and hubby. Why not. I went over smiling. She again wanted to rub the sun crème over my back and being a weak individual, I let her. Then I did her. Her husband was oblivious to all this which was probably just as well as we had both been squirming a bit while the other rubbed.

After an hour or so, he got up and left, he had gone to do some shopping. Consuela was now free for three hours and did I want to take her to lunch? That was a good idea so I agreed. At twelve thirty, we went in to get changed for our lunch. I walked her to her apartment intending to go to my own and shower, then come back down for her. She however had other ideas and almost dragged me into her apartment. I left just after two having missed lunch altogether. Back in my apartment I took what I thought was a well-deserved siesta.

Thursday I relieved what had now become a bit of a drag as the hard work had been done, by taking the car out for a drive and filling the tank ready for my trip to Palma to collect Patience.

I got a call from Daisy just after lunch. 'We have had calls from three more firms who used EB Matt. They all asked for you but when I told them you were away on business, they seemed happy to talk to me.

I hope you don't mind but I told them that as you were out of the country, I was in charge, it didn't seem to make any difference and they all sent work: Tony dealt with their jobs right away which must have done the trick as all three, Garraway & Jones, Randall, Randall & Simms and Hunt &

Co have all said that we will get all their work from now on. I did say that you would call them on your return. Have I done right?'

'Of course you have. I don't mind who you tell that you are in charge if it continues to bring in work. You can be in charge all the time Daisy my love. When I come back, remind me to give you a big bonus.'

She would as well but I did not mind as we were taking business of that shit Edward. At some point, I would sit down with Daisy, Karen and Tony and discuss business in general and ask them if they thought we needed anyone else. That could wait of course, until I was back home which the way things now seemed to be going, would not be too long off.

Chapter 16

Harvey, the stylist Patience had used ever since she returned to live in England, could not believe what she had just said to him. It was Wednesday, the day before she left for Spain.

'You want me to do what, darling,' he trilled, standing there, hands on hips and a disbelieving look on his face.

'You heard me well enough Harvey, I want you to cut my hair reasonably short and in any event turn it into a totally different style, and colour it. Auburn I think,' Patience replied, trying to act as her name suggested.

'But darling,' he gushed, 'Your hair is perfection itself. I should know as I created it. Why meddle with something so wonderful. If a thing isn't broke, why fix it.' He stood there, arms folded looking stern, or at least, trying too.

'It's a long story and concerns Anna. One day I will tell you but for now, please do as I ask.' Harvey huffed and puffed but had his assistant wash Patience's hair before going to work.

When he had finished, he stood back and surveyed his work.

'Mmmmmm, though I say so myself, it looks good and actually suits you. I would hardly recognise you if I saw you in the street.' Patience was pleased, she also thought the style and colour suited her. The important thing was that Harvey had said he would not recognise her and that was what she wanted to hear. Matthew would be pleased with her and pleasing Matthew was something she definitely wanted to do.

'Harvey, you have done a great job. Not being recognised is what I wanted to achieve.' Harvey clearly did not understand and was desperate to ask questions however Patience did not give him the opportunity, paying and leaving before he could ask her anything.

Donning a large pair of sunglasses, Patience strolled round the centre of Greenfield for half an hour. It was lunchtime and the town was busy. As she walked, Patience saw several people she knew, none of whom recognised her. That was great, just the result she had wanted to achieve.

When she arrived home, her parents too were amazed at the transformation of their daughter.

'You had better be careful darling,' her mother joked. 'Matthew may fail to recognise you when you leave the ferry.' The scowl that appeared on her face left Henry and Suzanne in fits of laughter.

That night, with her mother's help, Patience packed for her trip. The two of them had spoken at length on the subject of whether to take any clothes for Anna. In the end, they had decided not to because of the extra weight. Any items Anna needed could be purchased in Majorca. She had both passports and her travel documents, then her father handed her €5000.

'Just in case of emergency, my darling,' he said easily.

As her flight was due to depart from Manchester at two pm, they decided to leave for the airport at ten thirty. Henry and Suzanne would take Patience to the airport. After a late breakfast, they were ready to set off just before half past ten. Traffic was as usual rather heavy meaning they didn't arrive until just after twelve.

After checking her documents, Patience kissed her parents goodbye.

'Please take care of yourself darling,' her father said. 'Let us know that you have arrived safely. Listen to Matthew and follow his lead. He knows what he is doing and your mother and I think that he cares for you, he will look after you so please let him.'

Then they were gone. Patience felt momentary alarm as she realised that until Matthew met her in the morning, she was alone. Telling herself not to be stupid, she went in and found her gate which was number fourteen, when she arrived only two people were in front of her which was nice. Once checked in, like Matthew, she was travelling first class, she went through to the vip lounge and bought a couple of magazines for the flight. Then with about forty five minutes until boarding, she got a glass of wine and sat enjoying the taste. Her phone bleeped indicating a text message. It was from Matthew. 'Have a safe journey, see you soon love M xx.' His thoughtfulness pleased her so she rang him and enjoyed talking to him until they announced the flight.

Boarding went without a hitch, it was a scheduled flight rather than a package so she found herself alone on the row of seats, at least a peaceful flight.

When the trolley came round, she had another glass of wine and regarded the two very pretty girls who were serving from it. When she had been just eighteen, Patience had considered applying for a job as a stewardess as they had been called in the days before political correctness and women's lib and that was before her father had said that he wanted her to work in the family business with him with a view to eventually taking over. She joined him willingly, learning from him. In addition, she did a business studies course with the Open University, graduating at nineteen. She enjoyed working with her father and had learnt an awful lot from him.

Marrying Raul and moving to Santa Ponsa had, predictably, caused her to lose touch with the business however, since her divorce and return to Little Thornley, she had thrown herself wholeheartedly into her work and had no regrets about her career choice. Working from home in her own office within the large family home, Patience and her family had a portfolio of around a hundred and forty properties, both commercial and domestic. They had interests in several other businesses and between them, sat on the boards of nine companies. All in all, Patience was a busy woman, not rich but financially independent of her father.

Despite her busy schedule, Patience always had time for Anna. They spent their evenings together, after tea they would go over Anna's school work, play games or just read together. Weekends too, were spent together, swimming, walking or just doing nothing but doing it together.

What if Raul had turned Anna against her? No, whatever he might say, Anna would always know that her mother would never stop loving or looking for her. It was a worry though. What would Majorca bring?

Alone with her thoughts, the time passed and before she knew it, the Captain was calling the cabin crew to prepare for their decent in to Valencia. Patience had flown many times but it was always the landing she dreaded.

This one passed, as had all the others, without incident. Quickly off the plane and through passport control, Patience waited at the carousel for her case which soon appeared. It was seven, Spanish time.

Outside, a row of gleaming Mercedes taxis waited for fares. Joining the queue, Patience got the sixth in line. Fluent in Spanish from her time with Raul, Patience directed the driver to take her to the ferry terminal for boats to

Mallorca. He did and chatted pleasantly on the way, giving Patience the time
and opportunity to brush up on her Spanish which she had not used for a
while. They arrived at the ferry terminal at seven fifty. The first job was to book
a cabin on the eleven pm sailing which she did without any problems,
boarding was to take place from nine. Time to get a bite to eat. Patience
wanted somewhere nearby, the clerk in the ferries office was able to direct her
to a nearby restaurant which he claimed was excellent.

After ordering, Patience took out her phone and first called her parents
to confirm that she had arrived safely. They were pleased to have heard from
her. Then she called Matthew to advise him that she was now in Valencia. He
too was pleased to hear from her. They chatted until her dinner was served.
She took her time with the meal and joined the queue to board the ferry
shortly after nine thirty. She was on board and had been shown to her cabin
by ten.

The ferry sailed on time, Patience had been reading until the boat left,
once it had, she undressed and slipped into bed.

She woke up at seven, wondering at first where she was. Then it all
came back, she was on a ferry going to Majorca where she would team up
with Matthew to get Anna back from that bastard Raul. The thought of so
doing made her smile and she sang quietly to herself whilst under the shower.
After breakfast, she readied herself for disembarking which, according to the
tannoy message which had just been broadcast would take place at nine
thirty. At nine, she received a text from Matthew in which he said he had
located where the ferry docked and was waiting for her. She felt a tingle run
through her at the thought of seeing Matthew again and wondered if he would
kiss her as soon as they were together. She rather hoped he would.

Wanting to be off the ferry as quickly as possible, she got in the queue
that had formed by the gangplank, she was about twentieth in line. Looking on
the quayside for Matthew, she received a jolt to her system. With trembling
hands, she reached for her phone, found the number she wanted and pressed
the call button.

Chapter 17

I left for Palma to pick up Patience at eight, it was not a long run but I had no idea where these boats docked and would need to find out. Having checked carefully for any tail, I was in Palma for eight forty and had found where the ferry docked some fifteen minutes later. Strolling along the quay looking for anything untoward, I decided that everything was all right. At nine, I sent Patience a text to say that I was there waiting for her. That done, I settled down to wait for the boat to dock. I could see it coming into port. Quite a few people had begun to arrive at the dock, it was not just me that was meeting people from the ferry.

Then my phone rang, it was Patience and she didn't give me a chance to speak.

'Matthew it's me, I can see you.' She sounded in a bit of a state but before I could ask what was wrong, she continued. 'About twenty yards away from you to your left are two men, one has a black shirt on, the other, red. The one in the black is an associate of Raul. Oh God, you don't think he knows I am coming do you?' She sounded near to hysteria. I looked at the two men she was referring to. Shit, shite and bewilderment, that's all we needed, but hang on, it didn't look to me like they were doing anything other than meeting a friend.

'No love, they are not waiting for you, their body language is relaxed, not tense as I expect it would be if they were on the lookout for and going to grab you. In any event, how could Raul possibly know you are coming, as far he is concerned, he is in the clear, no I think it's just a coincidence that they are here.'

'What are we going to do?' She was clearly afraid.

'Patience, please just listen to me. Walk down the gangplank, look straight ahead and walk directly to me. Don't look at those guys, just look at me. Have a huge smile on your face like you are pleased to see me, the sort of look you would give your boyfriend if you have not seen him in a while. I will be watching them from here, if they make any sort of move, I will deal with it but I am sure they are simply meeting someone from the ferry. It will be all right, I promise you. Is that you waving, in the blue top?'

'Yes that's me. I will do as you say Matthew.' All I could do now was wait and hope that she did as I had said. I kept a surreptitious eye on the two guys, they didn't look like they were waiting to grab someone. I hoped I was right. We would soon know as the gangplank was down and people were coming off the ferry.

I had to admire Patience. Scared or not, she did as I asked, a huge smile all over her face as she made her way to me. Behind the two men she had pointed out, I watched them closely. Yes, they did look at her but only in the way any guy will look at an attractive woman.

As she got near to me, I went to meet her. Holding my arms out, she rushed the last couple of paces and threw herself into my arms. I held her close and found that she was trembling. I kissed her as passionately as I could under the circumstances then held her close. From over her shoulder, I watched the two guys, they were walking away from us, going to meet people off the boat.

When I was certain they were not interested in Patience, I cupped her chin in my hand and kissed her again, lightly this time. Then I told her that the men had gone. The relief in her face was obvious. Then, for no reason other than I wanted to, I kissed her again, properly. I was pleased that she responded.

'I've missed you Matthew.' That was all she said, all she needed to as far as I was concerned.

We set off to where I had parked the Scenic, I pulled her case along with my right hand and held her hand with my other. It seemed natural somehow.

Once in the car, I took a discreet look at her, her hair in particular, it was different, shorter and a different colour. She had on a blue tee shirt and a pair of jeans and looked lovely. I had not realised that I had been staring until she spoke.

'Do I meet with your approval,' she asked.

'Well, um, er yeah, you do actually. In fact, you look great.' I started the car and moved away.

'Harvey, my stylist, almost had a fit when I told him I wanted it cut short and the colour changed. I almost had to talk him into doing it for me.'

'Well, he has made a good job of it whether he wanted to do it or not. Apart from the last few minutes, how was your journey?'

'It was fine thank you Matthew. The flight to Valencia was uneventful, I had a cabin on the ferry and I had a good overnight sleep as the boat sailed. You know, I had such a shock when I saw that man, I was sure he had come for me but as usual, you were right. By the way, that first kiss was so realistic, anyone looking would have been fooled. I did not know you were such an accomplished actor,' she added mischievously. Luckily, the car was moving so I didn't have to look at her as I could feel myself going red.

'As a matter of fact, I can't act at all,' I managed to say then risked a quick look at her, she was smiling. Eager to get off the subject, I told her of the plans that I had made for Monday.

'I asked you to come via Valencia because Raul has a contact at the airport, this guy will be checking all passenger manifests, I think since Raul kidnapped Anna, he would have to be checking things. This way, no-one knows you have arrived which suits me.

On Monday when they go for the fish, Diego will wait in this car while you and I follow Salma and Anna to the market. At some point, and we will have to wing this bit, you and I will separate the two of them and leg it back to the car which Diego will then drive out of Santa Ponsa for us.

We are going to Port de Soller where a friend of Diego will take us to a little village on the mainland, just north of Barcelona, from there, another friend of Diego will take us to the train station in Barcelona, there we can get a train to almost anywhere but I thought Paris from where we can either fly back to England or take the Eurostar but we can decide that later.

If it's okay with you, we can go to see the crash site Sunday morning as we are meeting Diego for lunch in Inca at one. What do you think?'

'I think they are good plans Matthew. I did wonder why I was coming by way of Valencia.

As for Salma, I don't think we will have a problem with her, after all, it's because of her and what she did, that we are here now.

Your plan to get us off the island is just brilliant, he will never think of looking for us at Port de Soller. I knew you would have good plans Matthew.

Now that we have sorted that out, could we do some shopping sometime, maybe tomorrow as Anna will need some things, toiletries and the like, not to mention some clothes as she will only have what she is standing up in on Monday and will need a change.'

'Of course we can. Should we come into Palma, I would expect them to have a much better choice than Santa Ponsa?'

'Good idea, the more we are out of Santa Ponsa, the better I think.' Then silence, Patience was thinking about something, I kept quiet, she would tell me soon enough what was on her mind. I was right.

'Matthew, I have been thinking. I am sure that if Salma was aware that it was me taking Anna, she would make no fuss or try to prevent it.'

'You could well be right. I don't know Salma but you do and if that's what you think then I am more than happy to go along with it. If that is the case, it will make things so much easier for us on the day.'

By now, we had reached Santa Ponsa. Patience was quiet again, no doubt thinking about the last time she had been in this little town. She did not speak until I had parked up in the Playa Rosa's car park. Then she looked round.

'This looks nice, we will be fine here until Monday.' She looked and sounded quite positive which was a good sign. I collected her case from the boot and led her inside. Michelle was on the reception desk, she simply waved. Patience either did not notice the wave or simply chose not to comment.

Once inside the apartment, I put her case inside the first bedroom, she followed me in but said nothing. I then showed her the rest of the apartment before opening the doors to the balcony. I let her go first and followed her out. She looked across at her former home and tensed. I followed her look, in the garden stood Raul and Inez.

I moved in between her and the wall, leaned against it and drew her to me.

'Look over my shoulder,' I said to her. 'That way, should anyone look, all they will see is my back.' She didn't speak, just put her arms round my neck and looked. We stayed there, like that for a good few minutes, I could have stayed there for hours. Then she spoke.

'They have gone.' I let go of her but she made no attempt to move away, her arms were still round my neck so I wrapped my arms around her again and held her close. This time she rested her head on my shoulder. Moments later, she looked up and kissed me.

'I hope you don't mind Matthew, I enjoyed our kiss earlier but I enjoyed this one better and I will enjoy the next one even more.' That was too good an invitation to miss so I kissed her. When we had finished, Patience looked like I felt, very happy. She then went to unpack while I made us a nice, cold drink.

We sat on the balcony and chatted generally until it was time for some lunch, which I made for us. At three, Patience went into her room for a siesta which I thought was a very good idea and did likewise, my room that is.

Back in her room, Patience sat on the bed and thought of her daughter, only a couple of hundred metres away. It could have been the moon, Anna was still unreachable. The thought brought tears to her eyes as she sat there. The whole situation was so frustrating, she wanted to march round to the villa and demand Anna's return but she knew that was a none starter. For one thing, Matthew simply would not let her, for another, what he had said about having Anna in the villa was to their advantage especially as Raul did not know that she was across the way. No, hard as it was, she would try to live up to her name.

After her nap, Patience felt a little better, the frustration was still there but she felt better equipped to handle it.

I heard her moving around about seven. By then, I had had my nap, showered and shaved and was sitting on the balcony reading wearing only a pair of shorts when she came to find me. She wore only a short blue silk robe, it revealed a lot of very nice leg, I could not help looking. Up until then, I had only seen her legs from the knee down apart from one fleeting view when she had a denim skirt on.

'Are you looking at my legs Bentley?' she demanded. I assured her that I was. By way of punishment she came and sat on my knee and kissed me before running off to the shower.

Things were going rather better than I had dared hope for. We were totally at ease in each other's company. She was ready to go and eat by eight, the hour had been well spent, she wore a simple blue dress with a white belt and looked stunning, I told her so and noticed that she looked happy to receive the compliment.

When we went out, I had the Glock in its holster with me, you just never knew. The holster was covered by my shirt which I wore out of my trousers.

To start, we went to one of the sea front bars, not Samantha's for obvious reasons, and had a drink. Then we went to the Spanish restaurant where I had been eating. She surprised me by speaking to the people there in Spanish, I had not known she had the language though I suppose I should have thought of it as she had lived here for a time and had been married to a local. To eat, we shared a Valencian paella. Our conversation was far reaching, we spoke of Anna of course and her hopes for the future. She wanted to know more about me, my work, parents, whether there was anyone special in my life and when I told her that she was the only special person, she reached for my hand across the table. I guessed that I was getting soppy in my old age, still, it was rather nice.

We were back in the apartment by eleven fifteen. In the morning, we were going to Palma to buy things that Anna would need.

Back in the apartment, I think we were both a little unsure of what if anything to do so she gave me a quick kiss and disappeared into her room. Me, I got ready for bed, before I turned in, I went round and checked the doors and windows, all secure.

I was soon asleep but woke up with a start. What had I heard, a footstep, there was another. The Glock was under my pillow, I had carried it with me in its holster since the morning when I went to meet Patience at the ferry though I had been careful to ensure that she was not aware of it. I had it in my hand when the door opened.

'Matthew, are you awake?' I heard Patience whisper.

'Yes, what's the matter, are you all right?' By then, she was at the side of my bed.

'I heard something outside the front door, I'm scared.' She was shivering. All she seemed to have on was a tee shirt and pair of knickers. All I had on was shorts but I got straight out of bed, trying to hide the Glock behind my back.

'Don't worry, wait here,' I whispered in her ear. I slipped the safety off the Glock and went out. First I checked the balcony, which was clear. Then to the front door, I listened for a few seconds without hearing anything then quietly unlocked the door. Taking a deep breath, I wrenched open the door and quickly stepped out, the Glock held in front of me in the two handed grip with my knees bent as I had been taught in Florida. Nobody there thank goodness. Releasing my breath, I went back inside and re-locked the door. Then I put the safety back on the Glock and went back to my room.

Patience stood where I had left her, still shivering.

'It's all right, there is no-one about,' I told her. 'Are you okay?' As she was still shivering with fright, I reasoned that she wasn't okay and took her in my arms, well arm, I still had the Glock in my hand.

'I'm cold and scared Matthew, please can I stay with you tonight?' She looked at me, imploring me to say yes.

'Of course you can,' I told her. 'Get in to bed.' She climbed in and I got in beside her and slipped the Glock back under the pillow. She was still shivering.

'Hold me.' That was all she said. I reached for her and she came back into my arms, her head resting on my shoulder and chest. I had one arm under her and used this to pull her closer to me.

'I always feel safe when you hold me.' I did not reply but stroked her hair with my free hand until her breathing became even. I lay awake for a time, listening to both Patience breathe and for any sound that should not be there until I too, fell asleep.

I was alone when I woke up, slipping out of bed, I went into the kitchen and found Patience, still in her tee shirt, making breakfast. She looked fine.

'Morning Matthew,' she said brightly. 'I am sorry about last night, for disturbing you I mean and thanks for looking after me. I seem to spend a lot of time saying sorry and thank you to you, don't I.'

'No thanks necessary, I rather enjoyed looking after you.' She smiled shyly at that before placing a mug of Redbush tea and some toast in front of me.

We left for Palma around half past ten. I had the Glock in its Fobus holster which was hidden by the tee shirt I was wearing. There had been no sign of Anna in the garden before we left which on reflection was probably just as well as I didn't want Patience to become upset. I kept a discreet but careful watch on the mirrors as we drove to the Majorcan capital but saw nothing to alarm me. I made no mention of the precautions I had been taking as I didn't want to worry Patience. We were parked up in the capital within the hour.

Firstly, Patience decided we would shop for necessities and soon found the right shop where she bought a toothbrush and paste, a hairbrush, soap, shampoo, deodorant and some towels. Then she bought a nice toilet bag to put the things, towels apart, in. Then we looked for clothes, I say looked advisedly. We made no attempt to purchase anything. When I questioned this, she told me that one never bought the first thing one saw, but had a good look round. Not the way I shopped but hey, whatever. By one, I was hungry and ready for a beer, I had spotted a nice looking pavement café, so we stopped and had a drink and a snack.

Pretty soon we were back shopping, in the same shops that we had been in earlier. This time, she did buy some things for Anna. Underclothes and socks, a couple of pairs of shorts, three tee shirts and a cardigan and finally, a backpack to put them all in. Needless to say, I was given the lot to carry. Then it was time for another beer. Patience seemed to have something on her mind, I decided to sit quietly until she was ready to tell me. It didn't take too long. She was worrying about Anna of course.

'I want to buy something special for Anna, a teddy or something like that. The poor child will be in a state of shock when I turn up and take her away from what she must have become used to by now.

She must also think I have abandoned her, I am sure that he will have told her that I do not want her any more, I just think that a cuddly toy will help, that's all.' She looked close to tears so I reached out and took her hand, she gripped mine tightly. After a moment she smiled but before she could speak, I got in first,

'No thanks needed, I am happy to be here shopping with you.'

We had a good look round before she decided on a teddy bear, not a particularly big one but a cuddly one with floppy ears. Then I got a call from

Diego. He was checking that all was well for lunch on Sunday. The trip back to Santa Ponsa was uneventful, back in the apartment, she got out a book to read so I went for a lie down. When I woke up I was not alone, she was lying next to me, asleep with her left arm draped across me. It felt nice. I didn't move as I did not want or need to disturb her. I must have lain awake for half an hour before she stirred. After kissing me, she went through to her own room to start to get ready to go and eat. I went and got a drink and took it out on to the balcony. Anna was in the garden of the villa, I ran through to her room.

'Quick,' I said. 'Anna is in the garden.' As she turned to rush from the room, I noticed that all she had on was bra and knickers, the sight was heavenly but I kept quiet and followed her on to the balcony, Anna was still there. She stood, still, seeing her daughter for the first time in weeks, and after being told that the child was dead. What was going through her mind, I had not a hope in hell of knowing. Quickly, Patience grabbed me and stood me back to the wall before standing close and looking over my shoulder. Her arms round my neck gripped me tight as the tears rolled down her cheeks. As she cried, I put my arms round her and held her close which, considering her state of undress, was really rather nice.

'She looks so sad and alone,' she sobbed. We must have stood there for at least ten minutes before she moved back a pace, her arms still round my neck.

'That bitch took her inside.' She almost spat the words out.

'Don't worry love. Before you know it, we will have Anna back where she belongs then I will make it my business to ensure that Martin nails the bastard legally so that he cannot bother us anymore.'

'I know you will Matthew. Do you know, you said 'bother us' and not 'bother me' just then.'

'I know what I said, I meant it too.' She leaned into me and we stood there for a few minutes before she went in to get ready to go out.

Despite the excitement, we were out just after eight. Tonight, she wore a green silk blouse with black trousers and looked sensational. We went to the same bar and same restaurant as we had the night before; we enjoyed a good dinner before returning to the apartment.

As usual, before going to bed, I went round and checked the doors and windows. Patience was nowhere in sight, I imagined that she was using the bathroom. She was not. When I went into my room, there she was, in bed waiting for me.

'I don't want to be alone tonight Matthew having seen Anna. Please let me stay here with you.' She looked at me with those big blue eyes. How could I refuse her? It was simple, I couldn't. I merely nodded and turned off the light, got undressed, put on a pair of shorts and climbed in next to her. She came to me and kissed me.

'Not yet,' she whispered before turning her back to me and reaching round to pull my arm across her.

'In your own time darling,' I whispered back, knowing what she meant. She took my hand and squeezed it, tight. I lay awake listening for a while before drifting off to sleep.

This time when I woke up, she was still there, sleeping with her head on my chest and her arm draped round me. I didn't move, just lay there watching her sleep. I enjoyed watching her like this, in fact I just enjoyed looking at her full stop. I thought that I was definitely getting soppy.

'What are you thinking about?' I had not noticed that she had woken up.

'Well, you as it happens,' I replied. 'That's if you can believe that.'

'What about me?' she continued playfully.

'How nice you look when you are asleep and how peaceful you look now compared to when I first met you. Oh yeah, and how much I want to kiss you.' She looked at me expectantly so I didn't disappoint her. She responded quite enthusiastically as our lips met. Hers parted, allowing my tongue access, and one thing led to another. Our lovemaking was quite urgent and passionate. It seemed to me that we both desperately needed the love of the other. After, we lay, content, in each other's arms.

'Matthew, when this business is over, you will still want to know me, won't you?' The concern in her voice was clear.

'Of course I will Patience. There is absolutely no way that I ever want you anywhere other than with me.'

'I wish we had met years ago.' Looking me in the eye, she continued. 'You do realise that I have fallen head over heels in love with you.' If I hadn't before, I knew now. My feeling must have shown because she smiled happily.

'You know something, I think I fell in love with you that Friday evening at your parents' home, remember when I came up to your room to talk to you. I knew you were someone special before that but seeing you there, in your room, then I knew I loved you. I'm here for as long as you want me to be.' There was nothing left for me to say so I kept quiet and let Patience speak.

'That's all right then. There is only one thing that can make me any happier.'

We were due to meet with Diego at one. I did not think Patience would want to spend too long at the scene of the crash but with women you can never tell; we left at eleven. I took the same route that I had taken with Sam, which seemed a long time ago now. I filled the Scenic up at the same petrol station that I had used before. If Patience wondered if it was the same one Inez had used, she did not say so.

It was just after midday when I pulled off the road at the site of the crash. I got out, followed seconds later by Patience. I was not going to rush her. God only knew what she was feeling at this moment. As we moved to the edge, she took my hand. There, she stood in silence which I respected, I just stood at the side of her, holding her hand. After a minute or two, she spoke.

'I know it was not my child who perished here, it was someone else's child though. Unless the poor thing was an orphan, surely someone somewhere is missing her.' I gently turned her away from the edge and putting an arm round her, I led her back to the car.

'Matthew, will you please try to find out who that child was. If nothing else, I would like to at least let her parents know that she will not be coming home. Then, at least they can have some closure, and stop waiting for her.' I guess that it was the type of person she was, finding the time to worry about a total stranger when she herself was in bits over Anna.

'I expect that Martin and I will come here in the next few weeks to present our case to the authorities, Martin has already spoken to someone here as you know, I will try to make sure that they do everything possible to find the child's parents.' Her smile was all the thanks that I needed, not that I needed thanks to do something that she wanted.

Neither of us spoke as I drove into Inca, each of us was alone with our own thoughts. Coming into Inca from a different direction, I nonetheless found the car park without any problem.

As I expected, Diego was in the bar when we arrived.

'Patience,' he boomed, hugging her and kissing her on both cheeks. 'I have not seen you for oh I don't know, too many years. Let me look at you. You look well considering all you have been through. Come and sit here by me. Matthew can sit there.' I sat down where I was directed. Angelica brought me a beer, Patience asked for one too and was introduced to Angelica and her father.

'Diego it's wonderful to see you again after all these years. It has been too long. I know you speak regularly to dad but both he and mother send their love.'

Angelica arrived with the beer and a tray full of tapas. They talked, in Spanish mostly, I ate, not all of it, they ate too. I just listened, happy to take a back seat and observe Patience looking happy as they reminisced.

'That Raul,' Diego almost spat the word out, 'He was never good enough for you. You deserve someone much better, like Matthew here. He will be good for you.' I almost choked on my beer as Patience smiled sweetly at me. Was this guy psychic as well as everything else he was? Then, he got down to business, speaking in English for my benefit.

'The last two Monday's Salma has taken Anna to buy fish. Tomorrow, we expect them to do the same. I will be with you by ten in the morning. If you can have your things ready when I arrive, we will load the Scenic. The tripods and binoculars I will give to my wife to take away.

Then, when you have Anna, I will drive us to Port de Soller where my good friend Sergio will take you to a little place to the north of Barcelona. Sergio speaks a little English, not a lot. From there Miguel will take you to the train. He speaks no English, not that that matters, Patience can speak to him. I will not travel with you, I will return to Santa Ponsa to try to find out what if anything Raul is doing about all this.'

That was it for business. They continued to talk. He spoke fondly of Henry and Suzanne. It was clear that he had great affection for the Jameson family. Patience did not leave me out of the talk, filling me in on things that Diego had said. At one point, he looked at me sharply then smiled. That was something I wasn't filled in about. Oh well, never mind. The time passed very quickly, and at four, it was time to go. Diego kissed Patience on the cheeks again and shook my hand vigorously.

'Look after this woman Matthew. I know that she likes you very much. One day she will meet a proper man who will appreciate her and she will make him a wonderful wife. I think she might have already met him eh Matthew. Until the morning.' He winked at me then was gone.

Walking back to the car, she slipped her arm through mine.

'Nothing to say?' she asked, coyly.

'Plenty probably, possibly. That is, when my mind stops spinning.' She laughed and kissed me before we got into the car. Our trip back to the apartment was without incident. Back in the apartment we decided that it was time for a nap. Taking my hand, Patience led me through into my room.

'There seems to be no need for separate rooms now Matthew.' she said. I had to agree. We fell asleep in each other's arms, it felt right but I wondered what Jameson would have to say about it.

For the third night in a row, we ate in the same restaurant and finished off with a couple of beers at a bar on the front. We strolled back to the apartment hand in hand. The night was warm, the lights on the sea front were twinkling, the bars and eateries doing good business. All the people sitting there looked like they had not a care in the world. Soon, neither would Patience if I could do anything about it.

As usual, I made sure that everything was secure before joining Patience in bed.

This time, our lovemaking was slow and gentle, we took our time, kissing and exploring each other thoroughly. Both of us found the experience more than satisfactory and we fell asleep, happily in each other's arms.

Chapter 18

Monday dawned bright and sunny as usual in Majorca. Oh to live in the sun, what a dream. After breakfast, we packed our things, ready to load in the Scenic when Diego arrived. Patience was understandably nervous but to her credit, she did not complain or moan at any time, she just got on with what she had to do.

At one point, I took her in my arms. 'Don't worry about a thing darling, everything will run smoothly and before you know it, it will be Anna you are hugging. As the hour of ten approached, I received two calls in quick succession, the first was from Martin, to wish us luck. The second was from Daisy, for the same reason. Patience also had a call, from her father. From what I could gather, both he and Suzanne were as nervous as we were. Yes, I was nervous even though I was not family, I was involved and had been for a while now and wanted this to end well.

Diego arrived just after ten bringing with him his wife, Constantina, a handsome woman of about fifty. Of course she and Patience knew each other and hugged and kissed. This left Diego and I with the job of taking the bags down to the car. We loaded our stuff into the Scenic, the tripods and binoculars went into a Seat Leon, no doubt Mrs Diego's. I did not know what Patience had been saying to Constantina but when I got back in the apartment, I was the subject of a close scrutiny before she said something in Spanish that had the three of them laughing. I guessed from the laughter that it was not something bad. Constantina then left after hugs and kisses all round. Nothing for us to do now, but wait.

I still had the Glock and had mentioned this to Diego who told me to hang on to it for as long as I needed it. If I didn't need it, then I could give it to either Sergio or Miguel.

It was quite a tense wait. The clock hardly seemed to move. It was ten forty, then ten fifty, finally the hands dragged themselves round to eleven. Any time now. It was eleven twenty before I finally saw them on the drive.

'They are leaving the villa.' I announced quietly. Patience ran to look from the balcony.

'How are we going to do this?' asked Diego, suddenly sounding nervous. It was time for me to be decisive and put my professional expertise into practise.

'We will go down to the car park in a couple of minutes and wait in there. When they pass, Diego, you go to the car and get it ready for our leaving, by that, I mean at the exit.

Patience, you and I will follow them to the market and wait for our opportunity. Trust me, we will get one. Then we will come back to the car and you Diego will get us out of Santa Ponsa as quickly as you can. Okay?' I looked round. Diego nodded, Patience wore a look of steely determination on her face which broke up when she smiled at me.

As we waited in the car park, Diego announced that he would come back and clear out the fridge and cupboards later on. I had forgotten that and apologised which he waved away. He had the keys to the apartment now.

Anna and Salma passed us after about twelve minutes. Patience and I slipped out of the car park and trailed them from the other side of the street. When they entered the market, we crossed and followed them in. We had been, and still were, holding hands. I was unsure who had taken whose hand, not that it mattered. The market was not as busy as I had hoped it would be, it was certainly not as busy as it had been last Monday. I would have preferred a crowd but it was not to be. At the fish stall, Salma stood chatting to the lady on the counter, Anna stood just behind. This was our chance.

'Wait here.' I whispered to Patience and walked over to where Anna stood. I crouched down beside her and put a finger to my lips. As the child looked questioningly at me, I simply pointed behind her. She turned and saw her mother. Before either Patience or I could react, Anna cried out and ran to her mother. Salma of course heard and turned round. I had by now stood up. Patience was on her knees hugging Anna and I heard the child say that she thought her mother was dead. This was said through her tears, both mother and daughter were crying. That must have been what Raul told her, what a bastard.

This was not how I imagined things would go, I expected Anna to run to Patience and the three of us could slip away quietly. Not gonna happen now was it. Bugger. I could only hope that what Patience had said about Salma was right. We would find out any second now. I noticed Salma cross herself as she walked over.

'You came, I knew you would,' she said, as Patience stood up.

'At the villa, the way you ignored me, it was deliberate wasn't it. You knew that that would arouse my suspicions.'

'Yes I did. It was the hardest thing I have ever done in my life. I wanted to speak to you, to let you know it was all false but Raul frightened me. He threatened me and also made threats about you so I came up with my plan to warn you without speaking. I see that it worked well.' The two women hugged.

This was all very nice but I was impatient. All the time we stood here chatting meant that someone could ring Raul and he could come down here with some of his goons, I had the Glock but did not want to get into any fire fight, I would rather just leave.

'Come on Patience, we have to move, now.' As I spoke, I began to usher Patience and Anna towards the exit.

'I will return to the villa in an hour and tell Raul that I have lost Anna. An hour is reasonable for me to look for her, any longer and he would become suspicious.' That was fair enough. Patience hugged and kissed Salma, as did Anna who was looking rather bewildered by events, not really a surprise. Then, much to my surprise, Salma hugged me.

'Look after them both,' was all she said.

'I will.' Then on impulse, I gave her Diego's phone number, just in case.

'Go now; she urged. I did not need a second invitation and hurried the girls back to the car. I put the two of them into the back of the Scenic and jumped in the front. When he had seen us, Diego got the car running so we were quickly out of the car park and away before anyone spoke. It was eleven fifty.

'I assume everything went to plan?' Diego asked. I quickly took him through the events and told him that I had given Salma his number, he was fine about that.

'No problem Matthew, she may have useful information for us at some point.' I looked into the back, Patience and Anna were sat close, Patience had her arms round her daughter, both were crying. Patience saw me looking and smiled through her tears.

'Thanks love,' she mouthed to me. I smiled back at her but didn't speak. Then I noticed Anna's new bear on the floor. I picked it up and handed it to the child. She smiled when she saw it and took it from me.

'That's for you my darling, I thought you might like him.'

'He's lovely mummy, I will soon think of a name for him.' Then she started sobbing, really hard. Between her sobs and her gasping for breath, she managed to say that she thought her mother had died in a car crash in England. It struck me that as well as being something of a bastard, Raul was a bit simple. The only thing he could think of was a car crash. Prick. Then she looked at me.

'What's your name?' she asked. Patience answered for me.

'This is Matthew darling, he is a private detective and has been here looking for you. The man driving is Diego, a friend of granddad.

'Please call me Matt, Anna. I am pleased to meet you, I have heard a lot about you from your mother.' I reached behind and held out my hand which she took in her small hand and shook.

Our journey to Port de Soller was both quick and uneventful and it was getting on for one pm when we arrived. That meant that it would be around ten when we landed on the mainland, not much chance of a train at that time.

Diego pulled up alongside a sleek boat, the Sunseeker Predator 75 no doubt. He had been right, this thing would make short work of the Med. As we got out of the car, a guy jumped down from the boat and spoke to Diego, he introduced us, this was Sergio. There was bad news, Miguel in Barcelona had had an accident and could not meet us at Canyet de Mar. Diego looked at me and held his arms out apologetically, it was not his fault. There was another guy on the boat, a younger version of Sergio, who no doubt was his son.

'Could we get a bus to Barcelona?' I asked Diego. We could but possibly not until the morning. Did we want to go now or wait until morning, we could probably get a room for the night here. I thought about it, for all of a second.

'We will go now,' I stated. 'I want to get off the island as quickly as I can and will worry about getting to Barcelona when we arrive at the other end.' I looked at Patience, she nodded her agreement. That was that. Quickly I unloaded our stuff from the car and passed it down to Sergio.

Patience hugged Diego before being helped on to the boat by Sergio, then I passed Anna to her before turning to shake hands with Diego. I thanked him but he would have none of it.

'Matthew I have been pleased to have been able to help you. The child should be with her mother.'

'I will be back soon, Raul needs to be brought to justice. I will see you then.'

'Until then,' he said. 'Please take care of Patience my friend. She loves you and I think you feel the same about her.' Definitely psychic.

Sergio had untied the rope at the bow, I did the one at the stern and jumped on board as the younger version took us away from the quay. We stood and waved to Diego then Sergio began to tell us about the boat, it had twin MAN 1300 Diesel engines actually. His enthusiasm was infectious and I found myself telling him that it was a magnificent boat.

As junior made his way to the port exit, slowly, we could see a number of sailboats coming in. I noticed one guy on one of the boats taking a great deal of notice of us. I assumed that he was one of those purists who only liked boats with sails.

Once clear of the harbour, junior opened up, it was now one twenty five pm. Sergio went to join his son at the controls, I joined Patience and Anna who had gone to sit in the cabin or whatever the nautical term was for the seating area just behind the controls. The two of them were sitting very close, Patience had a protective arm around her daughter.

'We should be there around nine or maybe a little before or a little after,' I said as I sat down.

Sergio came down and showed me the galley. The fridge was full of food, he explained that it was for the three of us, he and his son had theirs up top. When I mentioned food, Anna's little face lit up, the poor kid was starving, though as I was to discover, she normally was. That said, she had no fat on her as far as I could see. Patience and I sorted out lunch for us. Sergio had done us proud, we had fresh bread, chicken, assorted meats and water. Enough to keep us going during the crossing. Once we had eaten, Anna told us her story.

'It was nice coming to Majorca with dad,' she began. 'When we arrived at the villa, Salma made me feel very welcome. There was another lady there, Inez, dad told me they were going to be married. Inez was nice to me and told me she wanted to be my friend.

On my first night, Salma showed me some photographs of you mum, you were with Salma. Some were of you when you were carrying me in your tummy. Salma told me that you and her had been great friends and that she knew me when I was a tiny baby.

When I had been there two days, a family came, they had two daughters and they took me away with them to their house. I did not want to go but dad said that I had to. I kept on crying and saying I didn't want to go. He made me, he said I had to go, I was frightened of him then.' Patience and I exchanged a look that said that was what he had done with her. The child saw the look. 'What?' she asked.

'Nothing darling, please carry on with your story.'

'I was away for ages. The people were nice and the children too, they were nice to me but I could not speak to the children as they only spoke Spanish, I could speak to their parents though and they told me what the children were saying. I was lonely and wanted to go back to my dad's but really, I wanted to come home to you mum.' Patience was about to speak but I caught her eye and shook my head, I wanted to hear the rest.

'When I went back to dad, he sat me down and said that you, grandma and granddad had been killed in a car crash. I cried and cried. Salma tried to comfort me but I could not believe it, that I would never see you again.' She was crying now, as was her mother.

'I cried myself to sleep every night, Salma was great, she kept saying that everything would be all right soon. I didn't know what she meant but I do now, oh mum, I don't ever want to be away from you again.' The two of them were crying now, to be honest, I was not far off myself, it was a heart wrenching story. Raul was a cruel, heartless bastard to do this to his own daughter. Anna had told her story in a level, even voice, she had not sought to sensationalise what she had said in any way, nor did she seem to be looking for pity. Then, she came to me and gave me a hug.

'Thank you Matthew for coming to find me and for helping mum to take me home.' What a kid, I felt a big lump in my throat.

'It was a pleasure Anna. It is also a pleasure to meet you. I have heard an awful lot about you.'

'Is Matthew your boyfriend mum? I hope so, he's very nice and you do need a boyfriend.' I almost choked, the kid was perceptive. I didn't know where to look and kept quiet. Patience though, had to reply.

'Yes he is darling, I am pleased that you approve.' I checked the time, we had been going for almost two and a half hours now, only five or so to go. There was a cabin nearby with a bed in, Patience took Anna in and suggested she have a lie down, it was a lot to take in and the poor kid looked shattered to me. She came out and told me Anna had gone to sleep.

The two of us retired to the stern and held hands as we talked. I had to tell her that I thought her daughter was adorable, she was pleased by my reaction and told me that Anna liked me very much. That was nice.

After about five hours at sea, Sergio took over the wheel and his son went somewhere for a nap. I went to speak to Sergio but his grasp of English wasn't enough for him to understand what I wanted so I had to get Patience to speak to him in his own language.

What I wanted to know was whether there was any hotel accommodation available at Canyet de Mar or could we get transport, a bus or a hire car when we got there.

Unfortunately, the answer to all my questions was a definite one. No. No hotel, no car hire but there should be a bus in the morning, as far as he knew. It sounded like we were going to the back of beyond. Sergio smiled apologetically but it was not his fault in any way. Patience and I retired to discuss our options, which in truth were rather limited. Sleeping on the beach seemed to me to be our only alternative. Not something I wanted to do with the two girls. Sadly though, it seemed that that was all that would be available to us. At Patience's suggestion, I went to have a sleep, if we had to sleep rough tonight, I would need to stay awake to look after the two girls so it made sense to sleep now, while I could

I must have been tired because when Patience woke me, it was seven thirty pm and we were not many miles away from our destination. The evening was chilly, due no doubt to our being at sea but someone, Patience I guessed, had covered me up.

'While you were asleep Matthew, a helicopter flew overhead, it hovered above us for a time, Sergio waved to it while Anna and I kept out of sight. I went below as soon as I heard its engine and stayed there until long after the noise had gone. Do you think it could be Raul?'

'It's possible I guess love but I don't see how it could be. How could he know we are on a boat? I cannot see how he could possibly know that.' She thought about what I had said before agreeing.

We landed at Canyet de Mar ten minutes before nine, on a deserted quayside. It was dark hereabouts, Sergio was most apologetic but in truth, it was not his fault. Patience convinced him that we would be all right though it was with a certain reluctance that he and his son steered the Sunseeker away from the dock. We stood and watched the boat disappear then turned and made our way off the quay.

What to do for the best. Canyet de Mar looked to be a quiet place, we could see no sign of a hotel, we did look even though we had been told that there wasn't one. Very little stirred in the village, one or two cars were parked and a few people wandered about. We had thought of paying someone to take us to either a hotel or Barcelona but I didn't really like the look of anyone that I could see.

Then we saw the woman, she was walking down the road, alone. Patience spoke to her in Spanish and she stopped to talk. The two women spoke for a few minutes, it seemed to be a pleasant conversation as they were both smiling. Finally, Patience turned to Anna and I.

'This is Paulina,' she told us, 'She is on her way home from work and lives nearby in this village. I have asked her about getting out of here to go to Barcelona, there will be a bus in the morning, not before.

It is possible that she may be able to arrange a ride for us, we need to go with her.' I was a little nervous putting ourselves in a stranger's hands but there seemed no alternative. Anyway, I still had the Glock and was confident that I could handle any problems especially as I would be on the lookout for them.

'Okay, let's go.' I made the decision and pulled mine and Patience's cases along with my holdall thrown over my shoulder. Patience had her shoulder bag and Anna's backpack, we must have looked a bit of a sight here in this little village. We followed Paulina for three or four minutes until she stopped at a small cottage and said something to Patience as she knocked on the door.

'This is her cousin's house,' Patience translated for Anna and I. The door opened and a guy who looked to be about forty stood in the doorway, a big guy running to fat, he must have been six feet tall, he was going thin on top but he seemed to have a kind face, I certainly hoped it was.

Paulina spoke to him and he nodded rapidly. Again, Patience translated.

'She has told him that we are in trouble and need to get to either Barcelona or a hotel for the night, he has agreed to take us, how much should I offer him, do you think?'

'Offer him €200, see how he reacts to that.' He reacted nicely thank you very much and went to get his shoes. Patience tried to pay Paulina for her help but she refused point blank and said, so Patience told me later that it was her pleasure to help such a nice family as us. That was nice of her. She left us when the cousin, Pablo came out, he led us to his car, a Seat Toledo, not a new one but it started right away. I sat upfront with Pablo with the girls in the back. I got out the €200 so he could see it. Patience asked how long it would take, about an hour to Barcelona. I looked at my watch, nine fifteen, we would be lucky to find a hotel on the way so I asked Patience to tell Pablo to get us to Barcelona as fast as possible and tell him that there would be another €50 for him if we got there before ten. He smiled at that and put his foot down, the Seat did not actually spring forward but it did begin to go faster.

Chapter 19

When Salma returned to the Villa Borgosa at around one thirty, Raul and Inez were sitting in the lounge, quietly.

'Raul, something terrible has happened,' she began as soon as she entered the villa, crying. 'Anna is missing, she has either run away or someone has taken her. It happened while I was in the market, I have been looking all over for her.'

'That is terrible news,' he replied calmly. 'I cannot believe this has happened, can you Inez?'

'No Raul, I am shocked.'

'So Salma,' Raul went on, 'My daughter is missing, what time did you last see her?'

'It was about eleven thirty, at the market,' Salma began to feel afraid, he was not reacting as she had expected, he was far too calm

'Let me see if I have this right, you last saw Anna at the market at around eleven thirty. It is now one thirty and you are only just bothering to tell me. This I cannot believe.

Shall I tell you what I believe has happened?' Salma could only nod her head, a feeling of trepidation growing inside her. 'I think that Patience has been here in Santa Ponsa and Anna has gone with her mother. She has not run off, she would never leave me. Yes, she has been taken but by that English bitch that I had the misfortune to marry. Do you want to know how I know this?' His voice was dangerously calm, Salma could only nod her head. 'Good, then I will tell you. My good friend Rodrigo de la Pena actually saw Anna and her mother a matter of minutes ago, you know where they were? No, then I shall tell you. They were on the deck of a sea going motor cruiser which was sailing out of Port de Soller as Rodrigo came into port on his yacht. He thought he recognised that cow even though she has had her hair cut but what convinced him was that he recognised Anna, he has been here a couple of times recently with his boys. What do you have to say to that, old woman?'

'Patience has not snatched Anna, Anna went gladly with her mother, she was delighted to see her and only too pleased to leave with her.'

'That is rubbish, you are lying. Anna hated her mother and loved being here with me and would never voluntarily leave. In any event, how did

Patience know that Anna was still alive and to come here looking eh? Can you answer that?'

'No I cannot, you forbade me to speak to Patience at the cremation, either at the villa or the church and you had this woman follow me around to make sure I obeyed your instructions, so you know that I did not tell her. You are deluding yourself boy if you think that the child does not love her mother, that child loved her mother with all her heart and never once believed that she was dead. I always told her to keep the faith, she did and she has been rewarded. Raul Martinez, you are a wicked man and I am just relieved that your dear parents are not here to see how you have turned out.'

'Inez,' Raul growled. Inez sprang up out of her chair and grabbed one of Salma's arms, which she proceeded to twist up the elderly nanny's back. The pain was excruciating but Salma kept quiet.

'Now my faithful old nanny, you are going to tell me where they have gone, are you not.'

'I do not know where they have gone, they never told me and I did not ask. All I know is that the child is away from you and good luck to her.' Raul's hand shot out so quickly that Salma did not see it coming, she felt it though, when it smacked her, hard, across her face. He looked at Inez who immediately forced Salma's arm further up her back. Salma thought it only seconds before it broke. Mercifully, Raul believed her.

'Let her go Inez, she does not know where they have gone, it must be either the mainland or possibly Menorca. I would think the mainland. Go and lock this old hag up in her room then come back down here and we will decide what to do.' Salma was dragged unceremoniously away, she thought about struggling but did not have the chance.

Inez was soon back in the lounge.

'Right, where would you go if you were fleeing Mallorca?' Raul asked as soon as she reappeared.

'The mainland, Barcelona. From there, I could go almost anywhere.'

'Yes, from there, they could go anywhere they chose, the airport will take them to any country in the world though I expect she will head straight to England. I will contact Carlos in Palma, he will be able to find out, before I do, let's look at the other alternatives, how else could they leave Barcelona, I

think we both agree that that is where Patience will have the boat take her.'
Inez nodded in agreement. 'They could go by road, from there it is an easy
drive into France, I think that the nearest airport to the border is at Perpignan.
Unfortunately, Carlos has no influence with the French authorities.

Now, where else could they go by road?'

'She could hire a car and drive across country to say Bilbao in the
north. From there, it would not be too hard for her to leave Spain with Anna.'

'That is true. I will phone Carlos now.' Raul reached for the phone and
placed the call to his contact at Palma airport. When Carlos came on the line,
Raul briefed him in a few minutes and he agreed to do as Raul required and
promised to call back.

Once that call had been made, Raul placed another call, this time to an
associate in Marseilles, Christian Faubert, the two had done many deals over
the past few years.

Raul explained his predicament to Faubert who immediately agreed to
send some of his men to the airport at Perpignan to watch out for Patience
and Anna.

'You know,' Raul mused when he had finished his call to Faubert, 'I
cannot believe that Patience has had either the wit or the courage to come
here and do what she has done.' Before Inez had a chance to respond, the
phone rang.

'Carlos, what news?'

'Raul, I can tell you that your ex-wife is not booked on any flight out of
Barcelona in the next forty eight hours. I have persuaded a friend of mine to
ensure that should she try to get a flight, he will alert me. My friend will pass
the word throughout the airport, I took the liberty of promising a reward for the
right information, I hope that is all right? Anyway, if she tries to buy tickets,
she will be told that that no seats are available until at least Thursday, that
should give you time to get there and take back your daughter. I will also now,
check with all the other airports that she could use, Girona, Valencia and so
on, I will let you know in due course.'

'Gracias Carlos, possibly you could check the northern airports as well,
in case she chooses to drive across county.'

'I will my friend.' After hanging up, Raul relayed the details of his conversation to Inez who studied him thoughtfully for a few moments.

'Raul. Consider this, they could take a train from Barcelona, from there they could get to Madrid or even Paris.'

'My God, you are right, I think we need to get to Barcelona this afternoon. If they are on a fast boat, they could be on the mainland by what, eight thirty tonight or thereabouts, I need to organise a helicopter.'

While Raul was on the phone, Inez quickly went and packed a bag each for them. When she came down, Raul was taking cash from his safe.

'The chopper will not be ready to leave until four, even so, we will still be on the mainland well before Anna and her mother. We will leave the car at the airport. Are you ready, good, let's go. It's now two fifteen, we can have a drink before the chopper leaves.' The two of them left, completely forgetting that Salma was locked in her room.

Salma heard them leave. As soon as the car pulled away, she reached for her phone intending to ring Diego Calva and have him warn Patience. Where was her phone? Then she remembered, it was in her bag, her bag that she dropped in the lounge when Inez twisted her arm.

'I must get out of this room,' she said to herself. 'Should I break the window and try to get down? She looked out of the window, her room was on the first floor but quite a way up. There was no way that she could jump down without breaking her leg or ankle, in any event, the villa's doors would be locked and the windows were toughened glass. It had to be this door.

She looked round for something to use to break down the door. Checking her watch she saw that it was now two twenty, Patience and the others should be well under way by now. Eventually she settled on a chair and began to batter at the door, it was not as easy as it appeared on the movies, for one thing, the doors at the villa were all solid wood original doors, none of that flimsy rubbish they made these days. That thought did not help, she shook herself and carried on.

Predictably, the chair gave way long before the door but the old nanny kept on battering away with each of the chair legs in turn until they too, broke. Another check of the watch, 'My goodness,' she thought, it was now four thirty, she had been trying to break down the door for over two hours and she was still nowhere near through. She simply had to rest, it was exhausting work and she accepted the fact that she was not as young as she used to be. Feeling faint, she sat down on her bed. All of a sudden, rather overcome, she fainted, waking later feeling unsure about what had happened. Slowly, she managed to piece her last memories together before realising that she had actually fainted, how long had she been out. With a shock, a check of her watch revealed that it was now seven thirty, she had been unconscious for some three hours. She renewed her attack on the door, finally breaking through at a few minutes to nine.

She rushed down stairs for her phone and dialled the number Patience's young man had given her. Busy. She swore then quickly crossed herself before getting through to Diego to give him the news. Diego told her to pack her things and that he would have someone collect her from the villa in half an hour, in the meantime, he would get the message to Patience.

Raul and Inez had their drink while waiting for their helicopter to be readied for the trip across to the mainland. Over their drink, Raul phoned a friend in Barcelona, Juan, with whom he had done several criminal deals. Juan agreed to pick Raul and Inez up from the airport and mobilise his team ready to track down Anna and her mother. Raul told him they ought to land around four thirty five which would give them plenty of time to be at the waterfront, to spread out and watch for the boat Rodrigo de la Pena had seen.

The chopper took off on time, Raul knew the pilot, he had smuggled drugs on Raul's behalf in the past. As they crossed the coast of Mallorca, Raul told the pilot, also called Juan, why they were going to the mainland. Juan agreed to fly up the coast to Port de Soller before heading across the Mediterranean towards Barcelona.

They had been in the air for just over an hour when Juan spotted a boat ahead, they flew over before circling round a couple of times. The guy driving the boat waved up happily at the chopper, they could not see anyone else on board.

'That does not mean that there is nobody else on the boat,' said Juan. 'All it means is that we can't see them.' Raul wanted to keep circling but Juan was unable to do this, he only had sufficient fuel to get to Barcelona and back when he started, the detour to Port de Soller meant that he would need more fuel to get back to base.

'Never mind,' Raul said. 'We know where they are going, it is not a problem Juan, just get us to Barcelona.'

Chapter 20

Cousin Pablo earned his bonus, getting us to Barcelona just before ten. He dropped us off somewhere, I hadn't a clue where but I didn't care, at least now we were in a large city, we could find rooms for the night.

My phone had rung at round about nine fifteen, it was Diego, what he had to tell me was not good news. I thanked him for the call and promised to keep him updated, then I remembered the Glock.

'I'm sorry Diego, I still have the Glock, I completely forgot to pass it to Sergio.'

'Never mind Matthew, perhaps in the circumstances, it is maybe for the best. Take care of the girls and yourself.' I could see the concern clearly on the face of Patience but I didn't want to alarm Anna so I said nothing about the call; that would keep for later.

After Pablo had dropped us and gratefully received his tip, I flagged down a passing taxi and Patience asked him to take us to a hotel near the train station which he did, dropping us across the road from there. The hotel had a family room available, a double and a single bed, so we took it and paid in cash.

The room was pleasant and clean, Patience sent Anna to use the bathroom, while she was in there, I brought Patience up to date on Diego's phone call. She was horrified.

'What are we going to do Matt?'

'The first thing we are going to do is to stop worrying,' I told her. 'While I am with you, nothing is going to happen, I give you my word on that. Now, it seems that Raul does not know of my existence, Salma said that all he spoke of was you and Anna, the guy on the boat must have taken me for part of the boat crew so I am an unknown quantity, which gives us the edge.' Just then, Anna came out of the bathroom, so I shut up while Patience got her into the double bed. Patience and her daughter would share the large bed while I took the single. The child dropped off to sleep almost straight away, it had been a hell of a day for her. Once she was asleep, I continued.

'As I say, he does not know about me so we have an edge. If I walk behind you two, as if I am not with you, I can intervene if he appears, take him by surprise and you know, get you away.' She looked doubtful.

'I know what you mean Matthew but I will feel much better if you are at my side.' The look on her face said it all. I smiled.

'No problem love, I will be with you all the way, wherever I stand or walk.' That seemed to do the trick as she came to me for a hug and kiss, before going to the bathroom to get ready for bed.

Over breakfast in the morning, we decided to take the train to Paris, Patience discovered from the receptionist that the next one left at eleven thirty. We left the hotel to walk across the road at ten forty five.

Patience held on tight to Anna as we entered the station which was rather busy. I certainly felt anxious and I was sure that Patience did too. She was continually looking over her shoulder. I was pulling my case with my holdall and Anna's backpack over my shoulder, Patience had her own case and bag. I spotted a couple of benches at the top of some steps which led to an emergency exit, I sat the two girls down there and went to the ticket office where there was a large queue. It took twenty minutes for me to get our tickets. As I was coming out of the ticket office, I saw two men grab Patience and Anna and begin to pull them away. Shit, shite and bewilderment! They had to be Raul's men. No time to pussyfoot around, I needed to get the two girls away from these guys and us away from the station as quickly as I could. Drawing the Glock, but not arming it, I rushed up behind them and smacked the one holding Patience across the back of his head, hard. As he dropped, I put the gun under the nose of the other, and gestured for him to put his hands up which he did. Patience rushed to Anna.

'Get our bags,' I instructed her, she did without question. 'Pick him up,' I ordered the thug. He did not understand English but when I pointed to his mate, he got the picture. As he picked the other one up, I took a look round. No-one was taking any notice of us. At the top of the steps leading down to the emergency exit, I made him stop. Then I hit the conscious one on the side of his head with the Glock, he went straight down the steps, as he did. I pushed the other one down on top of him. Then I went for Patience and Anna, tucking the gun away into its holster which was down the back of my jeans.

'Did they say anything?' I asked Patience as soon as I re-joined them.

She nodded. 'The one holding me said 'Raul wants you, bitch' then they started to drag us away. Then you came and saved us.' At that point she threw her arms round me and hugged me. We didn't have time for that. Quickly, I untangled myself from her arms.

'We have to go, now.' The urgency in my voice got through to Patience immediately. She took her case and Anna's hand, I got the rest of the stuff and led the way to the exit. 'He is not getting them now, as long as I can do something about it,' I said to myself as we made our way out of the station. I could see a road called the Av De Josep Tarradellas across the road from the station. That would do for starters. I led the girls down it. We were heading away from the station which was what I wanted to do, fast. After a few minutes fast walk, we arrived somewhere called the Placa De Francesco Macia.

'Matthew, can we rest for a few moments please,' Patience said, sounding out of breath.

'Okay, just for a minute or two. By now I would imagine that Raul has met up with his two goons and will know that we are aware of his activities in the area.

Also, he will now know about me and be wondering who the hell I am. He will also know that I am armed so it may make him keep his distance. We need to get away from here though and fast.' I looked around, plenty of taxis cruised up and down, I was reluctant to take a cab, Raul had guys out and cabbies liked to talk. Just then, a bus trundled past. I looked at Patience and we both smiled. Of course, take the bus. Who would expect people to do a runner on the bus? No-one, or so I hoped.

We spotted a bus stop and went to wait. One came along within five minutes, Patience spoke to the driver and beckoned Anna and I on. We sat down as Patience paid. When she joined us, Anna sat on my knee to make room for her mum.

'This takes us to the main bus station, we should be there in ten minutes, from there, we can get a bus anywhere. I hope he won't be there.' So did I.

We arrived at the bus station without any more excitement, thank goodness. Before we got off the bus, we took a good look round, neither of us saw any threats so we were happy to leave the relative security of the bus.

Now, where to go from here. Patience spotted a map so we went over to look. We decided to head for Tarragona, a town to the south of Barcelona.

First though, food. We bought some things to eat on the bus and some water to drink then went to find the bus, which was not too difficult. Sticking together, we bought tickets then went to the stop, the bus was in with three or four people waiting for the driver who arrived moments later and began checking tickets as the people got on. Noticing our cases, he said something which had Patience nodding and answering. He opened the luggage area and helped me load our stuff on. We kept the bag with the food in with us of course. Anna led the way to the back of the bus, more of what us English would call a coach really, so that we could all sit together. Then we were off, neither of us had bothered to ask how long the journey took, I for one did not care, we were getting out of Barcelona and that was all I was bothered about. Patience, sitting between me and her daughter, took hold of my hand, I found that she was trembling so I squeezed her hand and smiled, hopefully, reassuringly at her.

'Do you think he will find us?' Her voice betrayed her feelings, she was scared. It was up to me to keep both hers and Anna's spirits up.

'Of course he won't find us now love. How could he, who runs away on the bus.' She laughed at that. 'He will find his pals, the ones with the sore heads but they will not be able to tell him much about which way we went. Yes, he will know we have left the station but how could he know which way we went. No chance. I am hoping that he thinks that we will still look to take the train and that he searches the station thoroughly, by the time he realises that we are not taking the train, we will be long gone.' I was pleased to see that Patience was reassured by my words. It was now noon.

'What shall we do when we reach Tarragona?' Patience asked after we had been travelling for an hour. I had been thinking that same thing myself.

'I think we should hire a car and head down to Faro airport in Portugal,' I answered. 'At the moment, I would expect Raul to still be looking for us in Barcelona. If we go that way, I am hoping that it will be the last place he thinks to look for us. Don't forget, he has his mate at the airport at Palma. No doubt this guy will be checking all flights out of this part of Spain, if not all Spanish airports looking for us, I am betting he has no contacts in Portugal. What do you think?'

'I like it. Knowing Raul, he will expect me to do the easiest thing possible, he always maintained that I was a lazy so and so who would not do anything for myself, that's not true by the way, it was just the vision of me that he grew to have. Anyway, the thought of me driving all the way to Portugal would not enter his head. Let's do it.' That was that.

We arrived in Tarragona around two fifteen, while the two girls went to use the bathroom, I rang Martin and brought him up to date.

He was horrified when I told him of our adventures, though I glossed over the incident at the train station.

'What is your plan now?' he asked.

'I thought that we might hire a car and head down to Faro in Portugal and get a flight home from there.'

'That's a good idea, I may be able to help from this end, let me make some calls and get back to you.'

I told Patience what was going on when she and Anna came back. Then we looked for a car hire office, after asking a policeman, we found a Europcar, I walked past the office, much to the confusion of Patience.

'I don't want anyone in the office to see you love,' I told her. 'As far as these people are concerned, I am travelling alone. That way, if by some strange stroke of luck, he comes to this place, none of the staff will have seen either you or Anna, therefore they will not be able to tell him anything.' She liked that. Then I spotted what I was looking for, a café, I sat the two girls down inside then went back to the car hire office where a very attractive Penelope Cruz lookalike saw to my needs, well, she rented me a car. She also spoke English, which was a bonus.

Having told this vision that I was holidaying alone and wanted to do some touring up to the French border then towards the Basque country, I asked what they had in large, comfortable cars and chose an Audi A6 2.0 Diesel. The girl confirmed that I could drop the car off anywhere that suited me, which was handy to know. Once the formalities were completed, she took me outside to the car, a silver one, one of thousands of that colour on the roads, which was good for anonymity. After a brief run through of the controls, I was on my way. My first stop was into an underground car park, I wanted to get Patience and Anna into the car without anyone seeing us. Then I went back to the café for them. As I did so, Martin rang back.

'Hi mate, it's me. Listen, I have spoken with Henry, he has a friend who has his own plane, he will fly over to Faro and meet you and fly you back to Greenfield, how does that sound?'

'Great Martin, if we push, we can be there in the morning, with luck.'

'There is just one thing though Matt, he can't be there until Thursday morning so in reality, you have just under two days in which to get there.'

'Oh,' I said, the disappointment in my voice evident.

'Not to worry mate, I am sure that the bad guys will never expect this, and anyway, look on it as a bonus, you get to spend more time with Patience.'

'That is true,' I conceded. 'Shame about all the thugs chasing us though.'

He was immediately contrite. 'I'm sorry Matt, this is serious, I shouldn't joke.'

'It's all right mate, don't worry, I will look after us and get them back safe. Me and Mr Glock anyway.' That sobered him up instantly. 'Don't worry, I will get rid of it over the channel.' He was relieved to hear that.

I sat with Patience and Anna and explained what we were going to do, drive to Faro and there we would be met by a friend of Henry's who would fly us back to England.

'Just one thing though,' I finished. 'This friend cannot be there until Thursday morning so in effect, we have about two days in which to get there, not that that is in any way a problem.' I smiled and I was glad to see that both of them smiled back at me.

Chapter 21

The helicopter carrying Raul and Inez landed in Barcelona just before five. Once clear of the authorities, Raul phoned Juan and arranged a place to meet up.

The two men shook hands when they met up, then Raul introduced Inez as Juan led them to his car, a Mercedes, behind the wheel sat another man who Juan introduced as Gonzalo.

'Raul,' Juan began as the car set off. 'I have my men ready and waiting for your orders, we are yours to command.'

'Thank you Juan my old friend. I knew I could rely on you. Now, as I see it, my ex-wife and my beloved daughter are, even as we speak, crossing the sea towards Barcelona on a power boat. Even a fast boat will not get them here much before eight so we have time in which to take a look at the likely places that they could dock, then we can get them all covered. How does that sound?'

'That sounds fine to me my friend, Gonzalo, the marina.' Gonzalo drove away from the airport and headed for the marina, not a long journey but due to the time of day, it took them well over an hour to get there. Once they did, they split up and wandered about asking questions of the locals until they had narrowed the landing place down to five likely options. While Juan summoned his men, Inez telephoned the railway station and checked times of the late trains to Paris. None it seemed went after six pm so no chance of them going tonight, She then obtained the times of the morning trains, just in case.

Then, they settled down to wait for Juan's men to arrive, eating in a restaurant on the marina. By the time they had eaten, a dozen of Juan's men had arrived and were thoroughly briefed by him, photographs were shown of both Anna and her mother. During the wait, Inez had managed to get several photocopies of each which she distributed. They then split up and went to their allocated areas to watch for any boats landing passengers.

By eleven pm, Raul knew that they would not be coming directly into Barcelona, he called off the search for the evening, Juan ordered his men to be on duty the next morning at seven am. Some were to come to the marina, just in case, some were to watch the airport though Raul felt that this was a waste of time, however they would watch. A couple would go to the train station. Raul thought that they had well covered every eventuality that they possibly could. Now the wait to trap Patience.

At ten forty Tuesday morning, Juan received a telephone call from one of his men, Ignacio, who was at the station. The call was brief and to the point.

'We have them Raul,' Juan said after finishing the call. 'Carlos and Ignacio, two brothers have seen them at the railway station, they will get them and bring them to the side entrance to meet us.'

'Fantastic,' Raul enthused, a huge smile playing across his features. They ran for the car where Gonzalo sat waiting patiently. He took off for the station as soon as all had got in. The journey took them fifteen minutes, mainly because Gonzalo broke most of the rules of the road in his haste to get to the station. When they arrived, no-one waited at the side entrance. Raul, together with Inez and Juan, ran round to the main entrance and entered the station, Gonzalo had stayed with the car as usual.

Juan looked round for his men, they were nowhere in sight. Inez spotted some commotion across the station and with a feeling of foreboding, they made their way over.

It was Juan who spotted Carlos and Ignacio, they were being treated by a couple of paramedics, the two of them had blood on their faces. The Police were also in attendance. When Juan pointed this out to Raul, he swore savagely.

'Juan,' he ordered, 'No police. Quick.' Juan hurried over.

'Carlos, Ignacio, what happened to you, have you had an accident?' Juan emphasised these last few words. Ignacio, though dazed was alert enough to pick the vibes coming from Juan.

'Juan,' he began, 'My brother and I were standing here talking to two people when out of the blue, a crowd of thugs ran past. Without warning, they attacked Carlos and me and pushed us down the stairs. Is that not right my brother.'

'Si Juan. We were attacked for no reason.' Juan looked at the two policemen who were listening and watching the paramedics, doing little to hide the amusement on their faces. Both the brothers and Juan were well known to the Barcelona police in general and these officers in particular. The officers were quite pleased that someone had given Carlos and Ignacio a good kicking, the only thing that spoiled this was that Juan had not been there to get a kicking too. Once the paramedics had cleaned the brothers up, they recommended a visit to hospital which they declined. Once the paramedics had gone, the policemen left too, still chuckling about the beating the brothers had received.

Juan led the two over to where Raul and Inez waited.

'What happened.' Raul made his demand immediately, not bothered about the condition of the brothers.

'We had them Senor,' Ignacio answered. 'I had your daughter, Carlos had your ex-wife. As we said on the phone, we were bringing them to the side entrance to wait for you. Then, without warning, someone ran up. The next thing Carlos is on the floor and someone has a gun stuck in my face. He made me put my hands up, then he spoke to the lady, he spoke English so I do not know what he said but the woman and the child ran off.

He gestured for me to pick up my brother which I did, what choice did I have, he had a gun. We came to the top of those steps, then he hit me on the side of the head and I fell down the steps, then Carlos came down on top of me. I lost consciousness. We came round and the paramedics and police arrived, the rest you know.'

Raul thought about things for a moment or two. 'Who is this man who carries a gun? Where did he come from? Inez,' he directed, 'Go to the ticket office and see what you can find out.' As she left, Raul and Juan asked the people in the area if they had seen anything. Within minutes, Inez was back.

'An Englishman bought three tickets for Paris, two adults and a child. The next train leaves in fifteen minutes from platform eight.'

'Juan, let's go,' Raul ordered. The three of them ran to the platform leaving the injured brothers to fend for themselves. Quickly, they established that their quarry was not on the train.

Inez led the way back to the main concourse where the brothers awaited them. 'Ignacio, you were attacked just there,' she said pointing. He nodded. Looking round, she spotted a couple of stalls and rushed over. She was back moments later with some information.

'One of the stallholders saw these two grab Anna and the woman, then a man came up and dealt with these two. They then rushed out of the main entrance, where does that go?'

Juan answered. 'The Avinguda De Josep Tarrradellas which leads to the Placa De Francesco Macia and the Avinguda Diagonal.' Raul did not speak, he headed out to the car, the others trailing in his wake. Juan instructed the brothers to get their car, he would ring them with details of where to go.

In the car driving along the Avinguda De Josep Tarradellas, Juan put into words what they had all been thinking.

'Who is this mystery man who goes around armed?' he asked.

'Yes, I wonder,' Raul mused. 'Can we trust your men Juan?' he asked.

'Oh yes, if they say he was armed then he was.' As they cruised along, Raul phoned a friend in Paris and arranged to have the train met, just to be sure. As they drove, they saw no sign of Anna, her mother and the mystery man.

'They must be here somewhere,' Raul stormed. 'Where is that dammed bitch.' His temper was beginning to boil over. The others fell silent as he raved. Gonzalo continued to drive but they could see no sign of their prey.

Inez, risking Raul's rage said, 'They could have taken a cab from anywhere here, plenty of cabs are cruising the streets, but to where, that is the question.' Seeing the look on Raul's face, she continued quickly. 'If you were in a strange city and wanted to get away fast, and the train had been ruled out, what would you do?' She looked at him. 'You may hire a car.'

Raul brightened at once. 'Yes, if we can find a car hire place we can check there and see. If we can get details of the car they hired, then we can put guys on the road to find them.' Juan phoned his men and had them split up and check all the car hire firms in the city, Carlos and Ignacio began their search at the station.

They arranged to meet up in a couple of hours at a bar frequented by Juan and his gang. One by one they turned up at the bar, each with no reported sighting of Patience, Anna and the mystery man, or with news of hired cars.

To everyone's surprise, Raul did not explode, he merely asked them to give the matter plenty of thought, then sat back hoping someone would have some inspiration.

Chapter 22

Leaving the café with Patience, Anna and our bags, I led them round for a bit of a walk before heading into the car park where I had left the A6. To the best of my knowledge, no-one had shown the slightest interest in us as we made our way into the car park. As I loaded the boot, Patience settled Anna in the back before joining me in the front. I actually wanted Patience to crouch down in the passenger seat well but I thought that was probably a bit over the top so I kept quiet.

I had taken a look at the map and we headed for Albacete which as far as I could tell was about three hundred and sixty kilometres away. The first road we took was the A7 towards Valencia. I kept a close eye on the rear view mirror but saw nothing. It was a glorious day and the traffic was quite heavy, this didn't bother me like it might usually, I figured that we were safer in a crowd. We managed to get up to about 120 kph, the Audi hummed along giving the impression that it could do this all day, every day. Spain has two different fast roads, the Autopistas and the Autovias. The difference was quite simple really, on the Autopistas, you had to pay a toll, the others, you didn't. As far as I could tell, you picked up a ticket at a booth and paid when you came off and the cost was calculated on how far you travelled. I decided to keep to the Autovias, the toll free roads. Raul seemed to have quite a network of contacts throughout Spain and I was not taking any chances on him having contacts in their highway agency and finding us that way.

Patience and Anna seemed very happy, chatting away non-stop. Anna wanted to know about her grandparents among many other things. Then she spoke to me.

'I am glad that mum has met you Matthew, she has been lonely for too long but I can tell that she is very happy now. You are good for her.' This kid had her mum well sussed, she was eight going on thirty.

'Your mum is a special person Anna. She also makes me very happy too. I am glad that I have met her and I am glad that I have now met you.' I could see her in the mirror, grinning from ear to ear. Patience to looked happy, seems I said the right thing again which was becoming the norm around the Jameson women however old they might be.

As the traffic thinned, I pushed the Audi up to 140 kph and was passed the turn off for Valencia around three thirty, I could hear Anna talking about food.

'How about we look for a place to stop and have something to eat?' I ventured. As I had expected, that went down very well and it wasn't long before we saw a likely looking place. It was a small single story taverna set back from the road. Painted yellow with terracotta roof tiles, the place looked inviting. The owners had gone to great lengths to make their place look appealing from the road, plenty of flower beds dotted the car park which was not full but did have a few cars there. I parked our car at the side of a Chrysler Voyager which went some way to shielding the Audi from the road.

I think we were all pleased to get out and stretch our legs though the Audi was very comfortable. Patience led the way to the taverna and Anna walked just behind with me. As we walked, she took my hand, a small thing but for some reason this simple act pleased me.

We enjoyed a pleasant lunch and bought some bottled water to take with us on our journey south. It was four twenty when we started off again heading to Albacete. Before we went back to the car, we took a good look at a large map the owners had kindly put up. We would head to Albacete from here and in two or three hours, look for somewhere to spend the night, there was no hurry as we could not be picked up at Faro until Thursday morning. After a few minutes, Patience and Anna dropped off to sleep so I found some English music on the radio to keep me company as I drove. It was pleasant driving along in the sun, save of course for the constant watch in the rear view mirror for either Raul or his thugs. He would by now be aware that I was armed, I hoped that his men didn't carry guns, the last thing I wanted to have to actually fire the thing.

The girls woke up after an hour or so and carried on talking, they did have a bit to catch up on after all. We had to stop to fill with fuel in the late afternoon and topped up with water then carried on.

By seven, I was feeling a bit tired and after mentioning this to Patience, looked for somewhere to spend the night and soon saw a likely looking motel, the E57. They had plenty of room so I suggested that the two girls shared one and I had another but Patience was having none of it, her eyes betraying her feelings.

'No chance Matthew, I want you with us love. God, if you are not there I will never be able to rest. Please come in with us.' She looked at me, her eyes now pleading. How could I refuse, I did want to be with them but wanted to give Patience the choice. To be honest, I was pleased by what she had said. We took a twin room and discovered that the beds were a bit bigger than those we had slept in last night. The E57 had its own restaurant so we ate a good meal there, Patience and I had a couple of beers which was nice. When they went back to our room, I took the opportunity to ring Martin.

'Hi Matt, is everything okay? I am with Henry and Suzanne.'

'Everything is fine mate, don't worry. We are resting for the night and have just eaten. The girls are fine, as we speak, Anna is getting ready for bed.

As far as I can tell, we don't seem to have any undue interest in our movements which is good, I don't see how they could be on to us now, so with a bit of luck, it should be plain sailing from now on.

If you want to pass the phone to Henry, I will give this one to Patience so she can speak to her father.' I went in to the room and found Anna sat up in bed with the teddy. I passed the phone over to Patience. She spoke with her father and mother before passing the phone to Anna who spoke with her grandparents for the first time in a few months.

Anna settled down to sleep around nine thirty leaving Patience and I to talk softly. She was encouraged by the fact that we had not seen or heard of Raul since the incident at the station this morning.

By ten we were both yawning, time for bed. Being a gentleman I let her have the bathroom first. When I was settled in bed, she slipped in beside me.

'Hold me for five minutes please darling, I need to feel your arms round me.' I was happy to oblige and drew her close to me, stroking her hair with my free hand. After a few minutes she spoke again. 'I had better go love, I am so comfortable here with you that I could easily fall asleep. With Anna being here....' I put my finger to her lips.

'No need to explain, I understand.' With that, I kissed her then sent her back to the other bed.

The following morning, Wednesday, we were ready for the off by ten thirty. It was another hot sunny day, this of course meant more traffic on the roads, nothing I could do about it though. Today, we would head for Sevilla, over four hundred kilometres away. Pretty soon, thanks to Patience, we found the right road and headed towards Linares, from there, Cordoba then Sevilla.

The first hour or so passed uneventfully but around noon, we attracted interest from two guys in a white Seat. The car drew up alongside of us and the passenger took a good, long look. I saw him turn to the other guy and pull out a phone. Shit, shite and bewilderment, where had these guys come from? It looked like they had found us. Time for action. I looked for somewhere that I could pull off the road and see what I could do. Quietly, I told Patience what I had seen, to her credit she did not panic, just asked what she could do. I looked for the Seat in the rear view mirror, it was there, several cars back. No doubt they had phoned Raul.

'When we pull up off the road, take Anna and run, anywhere and hide, then wait till I ring. Then, just do what I say, okay?' It was, she trusted me totally.

We continued, then, in the distance, I saw a petrol station with a café, that would do. I turned off the road without signalling and drove quite a way from the buildings. A few cars were parked around but it was not busy, which was a bonus in view of what I had to do. As I stopped, Patience and Anna jumped out and went quickly towards the buildings. I left the car and hid behind a van about twenty feet from the Audi. The Seat arrived and parked next to the Audi, they got out and went towards the buildings. I crept over and stuck my Swiss Army knife unto each of the tyres in turn. Once that was done, and it didn't take long, I barged the Seat which set off its alarm, as I had hoped it would. From where I was hiding, I could see the two guys stop and turn round. Now I was keeping my fingers crossed. What I was hoping for was one of them to look in the services, the other to come back and see to the car. I held my breath then yes, it happened as I had hoped. One of them came back to the Seat. As he got to the car and saw the tyres, I stepped out from behind him and stuck the gun into the middle of his back. He froze but I pushed him towards the Seat.

'Open it,' I commanded, in English of course but he got the drift. As he did, I whacked him across the back of his head with the Glock and down he went. I was getting rather good at this. Then I bundled him into the back of the Seat, pocketing the keys. Then I went over to the buildings and rang Patience.

'Come straight out now love and head directly for the car. Don't stop or look round, just go for the car.'

'Understood.' That was all she said. What a girl. I hid again and waited. Within seconds I saw her and Anna come out of the building. The other guy followed, I hoped he was a bit uncertain as to what was going on. When they had all passed, I followed. Foolishly, I thought that it was like a scene from Benny Hill but soon put the thought out of my mind. At our car, Patience stopped, I was not there of course but she did not know that. Now for action. I rushed up behind the second thug and stuck the Glock in his back then motioned him forward.

'Patience,' I called softly, she heard and turned. 'Ask our friend here if he is working for Raul.' She did so and he confirmed that he was. She then asked him if he had reported to Raul that he had seen us. He seemed reluctant to answer this, I gave Patience the keys to the Audi and told her to settle Anna in the back, which she did. Then I told her to tell chummy to take a look in the Seat, she did and he did, seeing his friend in the back.

'Now tell him to answer your question or I will start on him, and his friend will be healthy by comparison.' She did but still he would not talk. Action boy. I moved quickly to the side and stamped down on the side of his knee which had the effect of getting him to his knees, then before he could cry out, I swiped him across the face with the Glock, breaking his nose and cutting open a cheek. Patience cried out but clamped a hand to her mouth.

'Ask again.' She did, this time he answered as I had expected him to. Yes, he had phoned and spoke to someone called Juan who was with Raul Martinez. He had told him where he had seen us and his instructions were to follow us and keep reporting our position. Shit. Still, it was no more than I had expected.

'Get in the car love,' I said to Patience, she did. As soon as her back was turned, I hit chummy and knocked him out before sitting him in the back of the Seat. I then sat his mate up. Anyone glancing might think they were sleeping, obviously a closer look would reveal the truth but I was hopeful that we would have the chance to get clean away. I quickly searched the two men and took their mobiles, I had the car keys.

When I got in, I handed Patience the keys to the Seat and the two phones.

'Strip the phones down and throw them and the keys away when we get going please love.' I could sense the questions forming so I decided to deal with things first. 'Before you say anything, please just listen for a second. As you know, he is Raul's man and had already reported where he has seen us and his orders were to shadow us, no doubt until Raul arrived.

Now, I'm sorry that I was a bit rough back there but I had a very good reason for that. Two reasons in fact, you and Anna. There is no way that I will let your ex-husband get his hands on you. You know what he is like, he sent people to get you at the station and I think they let you know what was in store for you and the little one, we have gone to a lot of effort to get her back, we are not giving up without a fight on that. And for good measure, I have only just met you so I'm not giving up on you yet. You mean too much to me already. That's why I did what I did, I just want to keep you safe.'

'I'm sorry darling, I should not question you, I know that what you are doing and did back there is for us for us and I am very grateful, I was just a bit shocked that's all. I'm glad you are not giving up on me, I feel that way too.' We both smiled, it seemed I was forgiven for breaking heads.

So Raul knew where we were, but he could not know where we were heading, unless he made an educated guess but that said, down the coast of southern Spain there was lots of places that we could be going too, for him to guess right would be an enormous stroke of luck, bad for us, good for him. The odds were with us so I did not worry too much. At least, we could not be followed yet. As I drove, Patience lowered the window and chucked the keys and the phones, which were now in pieces, away, they would never find them.

I hoped that we had seen the last of Raul's men, I did not expect any problems from the police, after all, Raul had killed someone and kidnapped his daughter so I hardly thought he would be in a position to go to the police. No, the problem was if they caught us, I had roughed up four of his men so they at least would not be happy, it would not be pleasant for me if they got us. Still, I had the Glock and knew how to use it. When I had used one at a shooting range in Florida, I had been fairly accurate but it would be different to shoot at people. Then I told myself that if it came to it, those people wanted to hurt Patience and take Anna away, not to mention hurting me. That made my resolve deepen, if I had to, I would use the Glock to protect them and worry about the consequences later.

An hour later and Anna was hungry, so was I for that matter. We stopped at the next services and whilst Patience and Anna purchased some food and drink for us to have on the road, I filled the car with fuel, we were on our way within ten minutes. The rest of the afternoon passed without event and for that I was grateful. Around five, I asked Patience to call Martin for me, I wanted an update on the plane which was going to be there for us in the morning. The Audi had Bluetooth.

'Hi Martin,' I said when he came on. 'We are in the general area of Sevilla, at the moment, things are quiet but we have had a bit of excitement which I will tell you about later. We are going to stop at a place called Huelva for the night, as far as I can tell, it's only about a hundred and twenty kilometres from Faro so we should be there round eleven in the morning. I assume that the plane will be there?'

'Yes, no problem, as far as I know, the pilot, Peter something, is going to be there early so he can get some rest in, flying hours, you know what I mean. I will ring you in the morning with all details you will need. How's Patience and Anna?' As they could both hear him, they answered for themselves.

'Bluetooth?' he asked, questioningly. Patience answered and confirmed that it was. It was just as well that he had made no comments about Patience and me.

We made Huelva around half six, I was hungry by then so Anna must have been starving, based on her appetite. Patience spotted a nice looking motel with restaurant so we pulled in there. Once we had checked in and taken our stuff to the room, I hid the Audi as best that I could. From the road, it was not obvious, not ideal but it would have to do.

After we had eaten, we retired to our room for the night, I had made sure that we got a room on the first floor. Again, it was a twin and again, the beds were a reasonable size. After Anna had fallen asleep, I took some basic precautions. With help from Patience, I dragged a chest of drawers across the door, then I balanced three bottles on the edge of the drawers then if anyone tried to get in, they would dislodge the bottles. Hopefully I would wake up at that point. That was the plan in any event.

Patience again came for a cuddle before joining Anna in bed. Despite being tired, I lay awake for a while listening. Eventually I dropped off but woke around three so I got up and had a prowl around the room and bathroom. Nothing to worry about so I went back to bed and dropped off, quickly this time.

I was rudely awakened around seven by a hungry little girl wanting breakfast. She was sat on the edge of my bed as she asked. This seemed a good idea so the kid went off happily to the bathroom to be replaced on the edge of my bed by her mother who greeted me with a nice kiss before telling me that I was very good with Anna. She seemed to be rather pleased by her observation but I didn't say any anything.

Chapter 23

Raul and his gang met up at nine on the Wednesday morning.

'Yesterday,' he began when they were all seated, 'We tried all the car hire people in Barcelona. Nothing. Last night, I phoned Marcel in Paris, he had the train watched, they did not get off it so clearly they were never on it. This means that they must still be in Spain. Now, has anyone had any thought on how they might have left Barcelona, if they have left at all?' He glared round the room at his men, and Inez.

Inez, feeling braver than the others said 'What about the bus? Please don't laugh. From the direction we are told they took when they left the railway station, they could quite easily have got possibly a taxi or indeed a bus to the bus depot, from there they could have gone almost anywhere.'

Raul looked at her scornfully then Juan spoke up. 'Inez has a point, who would expect anyone who was being hunted to take the bus? I like this idea Raul, I think it is one we should explore.'

'Okay, let's go to the bus station.' They left in three cars, it did not take long to get there. On the way, Raul devised his plan, they would talk to people at the bus station and tell them his English wife had run off with her boyfriend and taken his daughter with them and that he had to find her before they left Spain. At the bus station they split up, within minutes, Inez had an enormous stroke of luck, after describing Anna and Patience to a driver, he confirmed that he had taken a woman and a little girl who were travelling with an Englishman to Tarragona yesterday afternoon. Moments later, the three cars were racing south to Tarragona where they arrived just before eleven.

They immediately split up looking for car hire showrooms and again it was Inez who struck lucky. While Raul waited and fumed outside, Inez went in and spoke to the Penelope Cruz lookalike who confirmed that she had been on duty the previous day. Inez told the story about Raul's wife running off with her English boyfriend. When asked about a man, woman and child, she shook her head and told Inez that no-one fitting that description came in. She did however remember a handsome Englishman who said he was travelling alone and wanted to explore the Basque country.

'That may well be him,' Inez enthused. 'Could you give me the details of the car he hired please?' The young woman however could not, explaining it was not company policy. Inez urgently beckoned Raul inside and quietly told him the situation. Raul took over and laid it on thick about how much he needed to find his daughter. He could sense that the clerk was weakening and offered her a handful of Euros, which was a mistake. Realising his mistake, he offered her the money to donate to a charity of her choosing if she would give him the information, promising that he would not divulge where the info had come from. The charity clinched it. The clerk gave Raul the details of the Audi A6 that she had hired to the Englishman and happily took the cash which she placed in the ONCE collection box on the counter.

Outside, Raul called his team together for a powwow.

'We now know that this Englishman, who by the way is called Matthew Bentley, hired an Audi A6, a silver one yesterday afternoon. My daughter and her bitch mother were not with him so they must have been waiting somewhere nearby.' Ignacio tentatively raised his hand. Raul nodded at him.

'Senor, there is a café just down the road, maybe your daughter and the woman waited there while this Englishman Bentley hired the car. We could see if anyone there noticed anything.'

'Good thinking Ignacio. Take Inez with you and go and see.' The two of them left while Raul continued his briefing. They were back ten minutes later.

'Just so Raul,' said Inez when they returned. 'Anna and her mother waited in the café with their luggage while this Bentley left, he was gone about thirty minutes. Then he came back and they all left but no-one at the cafe saw a car outside. We saw an underground car park so we went there, it is unmanned but Ignacio saw an old tramp, for a few Euros for cheap wine, he remembered that around three, he saw a family, or what he thought was a family go into the car park and come out moments later in a silver car. They headed towards the road to the south.'

'Good work you two. So let's assume that Bentley saying to the car hire woman that he wanted to tour the Basque country was a rouse in case we found this place, they then have either gone south as the tramp suggests or north, back towards Barcelona and maybe on to France.'

'Or they could have headed towards the Basque country,' ventured Ignacio, feeling braver now he had been praised.

Raul regarded him thoughtfully. 'Yes, that's possible. Okay, this is what we will do, Ignacio, you and your brother go for the Basque country, see what you can find out. You others head back to Barcelona then on the France. You have the details of the car? Good. We now all know that this man Bentley is armed so be careful, I do not want any harm to come to my Anna. Let's go. Juan, you, Gonzalo Inez and myself will head south. I must say though that my former wife will almost certainly want to do the easiest thing. She is so lazy that I am sure she will order this person Bentley to get her out of the country as quick as possible. He is no doubt being paid by her father so will do as he is told therefore Juan, get men to the airports and train stations with orders to detain them if they see them. Now, who can we call and put on the road down there?'

'What about Xabi and his cousin Luis, they have always been reliable.'

'Yes of course, phone them please Juan and give them the information we need, have them cruise up and down the Autovias, I would think they would use those as there will be no record of them.'

For the rest of the day, Raul and his team headed south, fast. Juan kept in regular contact with Xabi and Luis who had the job of watching the roads heading south towards Andalucia. Every time they saw a silver Audi they relentlessly closed up on it to check the occupants. After a couple of hours of fast driving, Raul, scratching his head, checked the map.

'They must have turned off this road a way back. How far past Valencia are we?' he demanded of Gonzalo.

'About a hundred and thirty kilometres,' came the answer. Raul swore savagely.

'If they have turned off there is no way we could ever guess where. We have no real alternative other than to carry on and hope for the best.'

Chapter 24

Thursday morning and hopefully, the last leg of our journey. For the first time since I had been in Spain, it was raining, quite heavily as it happened. By nine thirty, we had had breakfast and were ready to go. It was still early back home but Martin was up and about. He phoned.

'Everything is arranged Matt. I expect that the plane will have been there two or three hours by now. The pilot is called Peter Hawkins, an old friend of Henry. He will re-fuel on arrival so when you get there you can set straight off.

Henry, Suzanne and I will be at Greenfield airport to meet you by the way, I will run you home.'

'By the way Martin,' I interrupted, 'What sort of plane is it, a Lear Jet or a Gulfstream?'

'It is not a jet at all, what it is, is a Piper-PA-42-720 Cheyanne 111 to give it its full name. Impressive isn't it?'

'Martin, what do you mean, it isn't a jet. Do you mean it has a little propeller on the front? I don't believe it.' I almost squealed in shock.

'Well actually it has two, it has two engines so it will have two propellers won't it. Don't worry, it is a real plane and can seat up to 9 people in comfort. It has a cruising speed of around four hundred and fifty mph so unless you fly into a strong headwind, it should take no more than five hours to get back. All being well. The plane is about forty feet long and has a wingspan of just short of fifty feet. It has got Peter to Faro and will get you three back to Greenfield. I know you don't like flying but just trust me, it will be fine.'

'All right Martin, seems like I have no option. I hope to see you later today.' It was the all being well which bothered me. I did not like flying at the best of times but at least in a proper plane you had four engines to keep you up. Still, no point in going on about it, I didn't want to scare Anna, it was enough that I was scared.

'I will text you Peter's number Matt then you can contact him when you get to the airport. Drive carefully.'

The girls were ready so off we went, heading for the Portuguese border. Apart from the business with the Seat yesterday, it had been an uneventful trip, in some ways I would be sorry when it was over. I had spent a week with Patience and had got to like it. That said, I was delighted that she had been reunited with her daughter, Anna was a lovely child and her presence had cheered up Patience, but the sooner we were back in England the better.

The rain stopped around ten past ten and I was able to pick up speed. We were in Portugal now, which looked the same as Spain to be honest. That is to say, nice, I had been to the Algarve before, to play golf with Martin and David Williams.

We arrived at the airport at ten forty, Patience soon spotted the Europcar bay so we parked the Audi up there. Inside the airport, I found the desk and handed in the keys. Then I phoned Peter, the pilot. It turned out that he was just fifteen feet away from me, he wandered over, still talking on the phone which reduced Anna into a laughing heap. By way of proof of his identity he showed me his passport and a letter from Claytons on their headed notepaper.

Peter had smoothed the way with the authorities but before we could make our way to the plane, Anna asked what we would have to eat on the way home. Typical of her, always thinking of her stomach. Patience and I went to buy some food and drink for all of us, Peter included.

Finally it was time, after our passports had been checked, Peter led the way to his plane. I regarded it with some suspicion but Patience playfully punched me on the arm. I tried a brave smile but failed miserably. It was however bigger than I had expected it to be. Peter loaded the bags into the hold then it was time to get aboard, Peter brought up the rear, closing the door behind him.

I was not looking forward to going up in the little plane but I would be glad to leave Spain and Portugal behind and get back to dear old England. Patience and Anna too were anxious to take off and leave this part of the world and head home to Little Thornley.

The three of us sat behind the pilot, I looked at Patience and could tell that she was thinking the same as me. Peter was very proud of his plane or kite as he insisted on calling it. Who did he think he was, Biggles? I half expected him to say 'Tally ho chaps' and was rather disappointed that he didn't to tell the truth. Anyway, he did his checks, contacted the tower requesting clearance for take-off. It must have been okay as he taxied the little plane to the runway where we looked to be third in a queue behind two proper planes. Once these real planes had taken off, it was our turn.

Peter gunned the engines and the little plane roared off down the runway. I found that I was holding my breath and gripping Patience by the hand, tight. All of a sudden, we were airborne. Peter climbed to whatever height he had been instructed to climb to, then settled on his pre-arranged flight path. He told us about the plane, not that any of us was in any way interested. Patience and I continued to hold hands, on the other side of her, Anna snuggled up to her mother not concerned in any way that we were holding hands.

We had been in the air no more than an hour when Anna decided that we should eat. I had to chuckle to myself. We had taken her from a market in Santa Ponsa, away from her father back to a mother she thought was dead. Then we took a boat trip to the mainland, got a lift and everything else and not once had the kid missed a meal. Incredible. Anyway, we ate our food after which I dropped off to sleep, waking just over an hour later. Both Patience and Anna had fallen asleep too.

'How are we doing?' I asked Peter, softly.

'Fine actually old man,' he replied. 'We are cruising at three seventy mph and you have been asleep for just over the hour.' He looked round at me. 'Was it rough in Majorca? Don't worry old man, I know what you were doing over there, Henry and I go back a long way so I am well aware what you have been doing for the Jameson's.'

I gave him the edited version of events which seemed to satisfy his curiosity. Even my editing must have made it sound a bit hairy as I caught him looking at me in a more respectful way. Then I remembered the Glock and mentioned it to Peter. I had completely forgotten it at Faro, good job they didn't search me. At his request, I passed it, together with the spare mags and rounds to him. He opened a widow and dropped the lot out over the English Channel. Nothing was in sight when he did so, it was a shame in a way but for the best. I was saved from having to say anything else about it as Anna woke up. As she stirred she disturbed her mother who also woke up.

Eventually, Peter told us that we had crossed the English coast line. That was the best news I had had in a long while. Yes, it was good of him to come and get us but the flight had been boring.

'Do me a favour old man, would you phone Henry and tell him that I expect to be landing at around four thirty GMT.' He passed me a phone and I did as he asked.

'Peter, how goes it?' I recognised Henry's voice.

'Henry it's Matt actually, Peter has asked me to ring to tell you he expects to land around four thirty GMT.'

'That's wonderful news Matthew, we shall be there to meet you. See you soon.'

As it happened, Peter was just out, we touched down at four twenty. Once down, he taxied to his place and switched off the engine. Silence is golden as they say, it certainly was, I had not realised until then just how noisy the little plane had been.

Peter got out first followed by me. As he unloaded our cases, I helped Patience down. Once on the ground, she hugged and kissed me.

'Thank you for everything darling, I don't know what I would have done without you. Please don't walk out of my life now we are home.'

I hugged her right back. 'No chance of that,' I said into her ear. I was glad that she looked so pleased. Just then a cough and a small voice interrupted us.

'Would someone help me down please.' She had tried to inject some severity into her voice but had not managed it. No wonder, she was grinning all over her little face as I lifted her down.

Peter led us inside where our passports were checked. It always seemed a damn sight harder to me, for British people to come back to their own country after a holiday, than for illegal immigrants to get in. Eventually we were through, the guy on passport control could find nothing wrong, despite what I thought were his best efforts, so had to let us through. There in the arrivals lounge of Greenfield airport, waiting for us was Henry, Suzanne and Martin. Henry and Suzanne saw Anna and Patience at the same time that Anna saw them. As she ran to them, the adults got down on their knees and the three of them hugged, all of them crying, Patience joined in as well, it was a touching scene and I was not far off crying myself but I managed to keep a stiff upper lip. Martin came over to me, his hand outstretched.

'Fantastic job mate, I'm proud of you.' As we shook hands, Suzanne detached herself from the huddle and came and hugged and kissed me. Henry pumped my hand until I thought my arm would fall off.

'Matthew, I can never thank you enough for bringing Anna back to us.' That was from Suzanne.

'Matthew has been wonderful,' Patience said to the others. 'Without him, none of us would be here now.'

Martin, Matthew, please come to dinner Saturday evening, Carole too of course,' Suzanne continued. 'We can celebrate this moment properly then and Matthew can fill us in with the details of what had gone on. What do you say?' Martin accepted straight away. I looked at Patience and smiled.

'Thank you Suzanne, I would be delighted to come.' Patience beamed with happiness. We walked outside to where Martin and Henry had parked. I loaded the girls bags into the boot of Henry's Mercedes, Suzanne kissed me again as she got into the front, Henry shook my hand again before taking his place behind the wheel. Then Anna hugged and kissed me before getting in. That left Patience, she kissed me properly, in front of her daughter, her parents and Martin.

'Thank you again Matthew. I can't wait for Saturday.' She looked me in the eye. 'I love you,' she said before kissing me again and getting in the car. I thought Jameson looked a bit shocked but Anna and Suzanne looked pleased.

Just before Martin closed the door, I heard Anna say, 'You know grandma, they call each other love and darling all the time. Oh and I think sweetheart too. I think it's nice.' I heard them laugh as the car pulled away.

'Wow,' said Martin. 'Love, now that's a turn up. I expected good friends but love. Do you feel the same way?'

'Yes I guess I do mate,' I replied. All of a sudden, I felt empty. Patience had been there, with me for ages, now she was not. It was a strange feeling.

As Martin ran me home, I told him that I would be in the office in the morning to work on my report.

'Meet me for lunch at the Lansdowne at one please Matt. I want to discuss with you the next step regarding friend Raul. Henry and I have spoken about it but I want your input too.'

'Fair enough mate, I will be there.' Martin dropped me at home, there was plenty to do. For a start, I had no food in the house so I had to pop to the shops to stock up. Then I phoned Daisy to tell her I was back and would see her in the morning. Then I thought about Patience.

Chapter 25

It was nice to sleep in my own bed again. Despite missing Patience, I dropped off quickly and slept quite well. I also enjoyed breakfast at home, then it was time to get ready for the office.

I left at eight forty but of course Daisy was already there when I walked in. She was delighted to see me and hugged and kissed me, it was nice to be made so welcome and be missed. She had not had breakfast so she went to get herself a bacon sandwich while I made the tea.

While I was waiting for the kettle I took a quick look in our work book, where we kept our record of each job that came into the office. While I had been away we had been very busy, I was aware of the problems of our main competitor and silently toasted Mike Weir, I was pleased that I had never liked the man and not in the least sorry for him, I would thank him if I ever saw him again.

Daisy returned, she had brought me a bacon sandwich as well, even though I had had toast I enjoyed it. She saw where I had been looking.

'Makes great reading doesn't it Matt. An awful lot of work that would normally have gone to EB has come to us. I made sure that things were dealt with straight away, most things got done, the odd job has stuck but that's normal. I'm pleased with the way things have gone, I just hope you are too.' Pleased, I was delighted with things. Over tea and sandwiches, we discussed the home based work.

Daisy said, 'Karen and Tony are pleased with the way things have gone too. They have enjoyed the extra work created by you not being here and the other stuff coming because of Weir's cock up has given them some good wages.'

'That's good because I expect to be going back to Majorca in a week or so.' That led us nicely into the Jameson job. Daisy of course had received the interim reports that I had sent back. What we had to do now was compile all the interim reports into one for Martin and eventually, Henry. To remind me of things, Daisy printed copies of the interim reports for me: it was all very clear though. All I had to do was start on the first of July and work through to the fourth, yesterday. No problem.

Daisy sat at her computer and typed while I dictated. This was not as slow as it may sound, we had been working this way for a number of years now and I knew how fast to speak. I was happy with this as it saved me money on expensive dictation and transcribing equipment. This took us up to twelve thirty. We would have finished sooner but for Karen and then Tony coming into the office. I ran through our escape from Barcelona for their benefit, and we talked about the extra work.

'Basically, we are a team Matt,' Karen answered. 'We have worked well together. Daisy has run the office with her usual efficiency and I have enjoyed being busier than usual. The extra money has been good too.' Tony agreed.

'Thanks for that guys. While you are here, I have a couple of things I want to say. First, I expect to be going back to Majorca in a week or so with Martin Keogh. We have to do something about Martinez. The second thing is that I want to thank you properly for what you have done while I have been away and for what you will do when I go again. As my thank you to you, I would like us all to go out for dinner one night next week, just the four of us. What do you think?'

They thought it a good idea, eventually we settled on Tuesday evening. I left it to them to decide where we would go. Daisy would book for us.

After Karen and Tony left, Daisy and I completed our report, she then slipped out to get her lunch and when she returned, I left to meet Martin at the Lansdowne.

We always met in the bar at the rear of the hotel, overlooking the last green of the golf course. As it was a lovely day, I found Martin sat outside with his jacket off looking very relaxed. As I sat down, Angela, one of the waitresses arrived with our drinks, a bottle of Coors for me, wine for himself. She took our lunch order then left. We then began to talk or rather, I did. I filled him in on the last part of our journey, from Huelva to Faro. As I finished, Angela returned with our lunch, as we ate, we watched the golfers coming up the final fairway and putting. It reminded me that it was quite a time since I had played.

Once we had eaten, Martin took over the conversation. 'I have spoken a few times to a Senor Almunia, he is the Mallorcan Minister of Justice by the way, the good Senor is rather interested to hear that we might have details of a serious crime committed on his island, one that included murder. When we have our case ready, Senor Almunia will afford us the opportunity to present it to him. He does however want everything notarised.' To notarise basically meant to certify. To have my evidence notarised, I would go to a notary public, who was a public official appointed to attest deeds. It was usually a solicitor and we had one or two in Greenfield we could use.

'No problem, the notarising I mean. As it happens, Daisy and I have spent the morning working on my report. She will, as we speak, be typing it as a first draft, I will read it over the weekend and do any amendments, we will not finish until next week though.' Martin accepted this.

'Once I have the report, I will prepare the documents for the notary, this will include the photographs you took over there. I will also prepare an affidavit for Patience to swear as well. I will exhibit the orders from her divorce and a copy of the police report into the accident.'

I was pleased that Martin was to prepare the documents for the notary as they could be quite fussy people.

'Now that we have finished the business part of lunch, tell me about you and Patience,' he said, a huge smile on his face.

'What do you want to know?' I asked. 'You heard what she said yesterday. What more can I say?'

'How about when, where and how it began. That will do for a start.' I had to smile.

'It started on the Thursday after I first met them with you, it was around six in the evening and I was still in the office tidying things up ready to go to Majorca. Patience came to the office and invited me for a drink. We went to the Hare and Hounds and had a nice time.

Then the day after, we went to their home for the second meeting. Patience stormed off as you will recall, she wanted to go out to Majorca with me. I went up to speak to her and talked her out of it. Next day, the Saturday, she rang me and we went out for a drink and a bite to eat to the Ship at Great Bidding. We got on well together and have interests in common, you know, books and the like.

Then she took me to the airport on the Monday and again we hit it off. When she came out to the island, we had the weekend together, with each other all the time, 24/7 and as you know, it can be easy to get on each other's nerves thrown together in a smallish apartment but it didn't happen to us. We were fine with each other all the time, it was just right. Then we grabbed Anna, the boat, the trip to Barcelona, the thugs, the whole thing was just right between us. I could not have wished for things to have been any different apart from Raul and his thugs chasing us of course.

On the trip down to Faro, we just seemed to grow closer together. The thing that concerns me, well I don't suppose it does concern me really, whatever happens, happens, but it is something Daisy said a few weeks ago. She said when Anna was back home, Patience would have no further use for me. A bit harsh but it is a point. I don't think that will happen but you never know but if that was to be the case, why say what she said yesterday? When she said that she loved me, it came as a surprise to me actually. There was no need to say that unless she meant it.

'I agree, I was aware of how she felt about you quite early on but said nothing, not wanting you to have her on your mind while you were working, well, not too much anyway. I am sure that everything will be okay. Oh, while I think on, dinner tomorrow night, Henry wants us to stay over so we can celebrate properly and have a drink so bring a change of clothes for Sunday morning. Wear a suit for dinner, don't bother with a tie. Carole and I will collect you from home at around seven if that's all right.' It was.

Back in the office, Daisy had typed up the first draft of the report and placed a copy in my briefcase for me to take home and read over the weekend.

'Martin has spoken to the Majorcan Minister of Justice who wants everything notarising so we need to get this report right as soon as possible The good thing is that Martin will prepare the affidavit for the notary.'

During the afternoon, I took a call from some solicitors from out of town regarding a new job. I agreed to do the work and asked them to fax over written instructions, that way, having instructions in writing would virtually ensure that we would be paid.

Then I just sat back in my chair to think. The subject was of course Patience. Was she interested or was it just the circumstances. In the past, I had helped many other mothers to get their kids back from fathers who were being awkward for one reason or another. Some had hugged me, some had offered more. The question was I guess, would I be disappointed if nothing came of this? The answer, yes I would.

Then Daisy came in to my room. 'What's up Matt?' she asked. 'I have asked five time if you want a cup of tea. What's on your mind, Patience?'

'Yes actually.' I told Daisy what she had said at the airport and what I had been thinking.

'I see where you are coming from Matt but don't let it get to you, I think she is interested.'

At five John, Daisy's husband came for her. He suggested a beer so we went and had a good hour in the local before I went home.

After I had eaten, I took out the report and settled down to read it. I was halfway through when the phone rang. It was Patience: I was immediately concerned, asking if everything was all right before even saying hello.

'Hello darling,' she began. 'Everything is fine, but I have missed you today and wanted to talk to you. I was going to ring earlier but I knew you would be busy so I waited until now and I can tell you, it took some doing.'

'It's great to hear from you, I just worried in case something was wrong. As for ringing when I am busy, don't think about it, ring me any time you want to.'

We spoke for over an hour before she rang off, time to sort Anna out and make sure that she got back into her old routine as soon as was possible.

Chapter 26

That night I slept like a log. The call from Patience had cheered me up no end. I finished reading the report and made a few minor alterations for Daisy then had an early night.

After breakfast I went to see my parents, I had spoken to them but wanted to see them of course. I had lunch with them before going to the Lansdowne. I kept fit but had not done any exercise whilst in Majorca unless paddling in the sea counted but I wanted to get back in the fitness routine.

I had a good hour in the gym and worked hard, at least it felt like I had worked hard. Time now to relax in the pool area. I was wondering where to sit first when the decision was made for me, Suzanne Jameson was in the Jacuzzi, I had to go over and see her. She was with some of her friends, all of whom I had seen from time to time in the leisure area but did not know.

Climbing down into the water, the woman on Suzanne's left made some room for me to sit next to Suzanne so I sat down between the two of them. She did not leave me much room but I was not complaining. Suzanne introduced me to her friends and told them that I was the man who had found Anna and brought her home safely. It seemed that Anna was a popular figure amongst these ladies as once they discovered who I was, were all over me, kissing and hugging me.

Suzanne said, 'We have all been friends for many years, all the girls have known Patience since she was small and have known Anna since she and her mother returned from Majorca five or six years ago.'

The woman on my left, I could not remember her name then spoke up. 'We have heard all about you from Suzanne, how you looked after her in here the other day when she became upset.' They were all grinning at me, I looked at Suzanne who was grinning along with them.

'Don't be embarrassed Matthew, I was a mess that day. You took the trouble to help me sort myself out. For that, I will always be grateful to you. In addition to that, you protected both Patience and Anna on the way back and again, I will never be able to thank you enough.' I heard one of the others say something about it not being every day one got to sit on a young man's knee. They all laughed again.

'I'm sure that what you have heard had been exaggerated, it was....' I got no further.

'Matthew, Patience has told me everything about the trip back,' Suzanne interrupted. 'The whole thing was fraught with danger, you were brave and resourceful, I don't think anyone else could have done what you did.' There was nothing I could really say so I kept quiet.

Then one of them wanted to know how Patience and I had got on together. I did not get a chance to answer as Suzanne answered for me.

'They seemed to get on very well indeed, thank you very much. I know this because of what I heard Patience say to Matthew at the airport, as we took our leave.' Needless to say, they all wanted to know what Patience had said. 'Before I tell you, let me say this, since she has been home, Patience has been walking round with a huge smile on her face, and not just because Anna is back. Anyway, to continue, I do believe that I heard the 'L' word.'

All these soppy women said aaaaaaaaaaaahhhhh at the same time. I was almost cringing with embarrassment but what could I do? Precisely nothing save for grin and bear it. They all seemed genuinely happy and I heard one of them say that Patience deserved to be happy.

It was then time for the ladies to leave. Suzanne was last out.

'I hope that we have not embarrassed you too much Matthew. I obviously told my friends about you and they all wanted to meet you. As you will know, they all love Anna and Patience very much and knew how the situation had been affecting all of us. You have solved the problem and they are happy for us. By the way, I hope that everything works out for you and Patience. You are good for her and I suspect that she is good for you. You know you are staying over tonight, good, see you later.' With that, she was gone.

I wandered into the steam room after that and found a couple of my pals there. We talked for a while before I left to shower and go home.

Chapter 27

By Thursday morning, Raul had become convinced that somehow, Patience had eluded him and had got clean away. Apart from himself, in Juan's car, Ignacio and Carlos in another, he had at least five other cars cruising round the roads of Spain looking for the silver Audi.

On Wednesday around lunchtime, Juan had received a call from Luis who, with his cousin Xabi, were checking the south. They had found them, heading towards Linares. Raul issued orders that the two men were to follow and observe, they would head down to join them, but Raul had insisted that they must keep in contact. Luis had readily agreed to this.

From then, there had been nothing. Gonzalo pushed his car as fast as he could due to the traffic conditions, Juan repeatedly called Luis and got no reply which caused Raul to slowly become more angry as each call went unanswered. Finally, at around two thirty in the afternoon, they reached the general area where Luis had originally called from.

'Try the fool Luis once more,' Raul instructed Juan. No answer.

A short while later, Juan received a call, he listened for a while before ending the call.

'Luis and Xabi followed your orders and followed the Audi to a petrol station and eatery where they were attacked, no doubt by this man Bentley.'

'Wait,' snapped Raul, before asking Gonzalo how far they were from the services.

'We are only four kilometres from the services, and can be there in minutes.'

Gonzalo made the services in five minutes and headed to the area Juan directed him. As they drove up, they spotted Luis standing there, Gonzalo pulled in behind the Seat.

'Juan,' Gonzalo hissed, urgently, 'The tyres, they are all flat.' The other three looked at the Seat and saw for themselves that Gonzalo was right. Raul swore again as the four of them climbed out of the car.

'Luis, what happened here?' Juan demanded.

'We were cruising down the road as directed, checking every silver Audi A6 we saw, I have to say that there are lots. Anyway, around noon we spotted the car, the registration tallied with that which we had been given, three people in the car, a man driving, a woman in the front passenger seat and a child in the back.

We fell back and followed, I rang you to report and received your further orders. Then the Audi pulled into this service area and stopped, we followed at a respectful distance and also parked. The people from the Audi had got out by the time we parked so we went to look for them. As we got to the service buildings, our car alarm went off. Xabi went to re-set the alarm, I continued inside to look for the people.

A few minutes later, the woman from the Audi came out of the toilet with the little girl, and they made their way out, I followed behind and they headed back to the Audi. When I got to our Seat, I noticed that all the tyres were flat. The child got in the Audi and then I felt a gun in my back.

I was questioned by the woman in Spanish but the man behind me with the gun was telling her what to ask but he was speaking English. They wanted to know if we were working for you Senor, at first I refused to answer, he hit me across the face with the gun, Senor, I had to answer. I told him yes we were working for you and we had reported the position. Then, he must have knocked me out because I woke up, sat in the car, only a few minutes ago. Xabi too had been knocked out presumably by this same man. We had both been sat in the car as if we were sleeping. He has taken our phones and the car keys so I had to ring from the payphone inside.'

'Shit, shit, shit,' fumed Raul. 'I am surrounded by incompetents. Who is this man with that bitch? Is he superman? I doubt it yet he takes out two men in Barcelona and another two here. Maybe I should get him to work for me eh?' The look on Raul's face was enough to ensure that nobody answered him. 'So, what are they doing in this area, where can they be going?' No-one answered for no-one had a clue.

Now, on Thursday, they were still in the Linares area having got no further forward. Raul had contacted all his men but none of them had had any success, it was as if they had vanished into thin air.

Finally, at mid-morning, Raul received a call from his man Carlos at Palma airport. As he listened, Raul grew red in the face as the rage inside him built up. When he put the phone down he launched in to a blistering tirade against Patience and the mystery man. Nobody spoke until he appeared to calm down, then Inez asked about the call.

'That was Carlos in Palma, he has been phoning the airports, just to check. For some reason, why I don't know, he phoned Faro in Portugal. A private plane is ready to take off any second now, flying to Greenfield in England, three passengers, a man, woman and child. No need to guess who the passengers are. As far as I can recall, Henry Jameson has friends who own their own planes, he will have had someone fly over for them. It seems I was wrong, I know my ex-wife and I say that she will have wanted an easy route, this man Bentley must have put his foot down and insisted they go to Faro. Well, they have beaten me. That will never do.' The others fell silent as Raul pondered the situation.

He had been proved wrong and had lost his daughter. Not only that, he had been outsmarted by Patience, something that was difficult for him to accept. She had made him look foolish in front of his men, he would have to do something spectacular to regain their respect, he would have to plan a big job in the next week or two.

As Gonzalo drove back up north, Raul and Juan worked their phones to call off the hunt for Patience and Anna. Eventually, they reached Barcelona and the helicopter that Carlos had sent back for them.

During the trip back to Palma, Inez tried to gauge Raul's mood. She was actually afraid, not just of Raul, though many times he had beaten her, no, she was afraid because of what they had done. Her conscience did not trouble her for she had none, what she did not want however, was the authorities looking into their recent activities. That could well become a major problem.

In the car, going back to the villa in Santa Ponsa, she finally plucked up the courage to voice her concerns to Raul. 'Do you thing that Patience will go to the police?' she asked.

'I have been thinking about this for the past couple of hours. Why should she? Anna is back with her, I am sure that this was all she would ever have wanted. Patience is not a vindictive woman and will probably want to revert to a normal life.

Her father, on the other hand, is vindictive but in all honesty, I cannot see him wanting to take this any further. After all, if they did go to the police, Patience would have to come back here to give evidence and there is no way that she will want to do that. Also, Anna will have to come too and that is something they will not risk. Further, she knows now what I am capable of, she would not dare to come back here as she will know for sure what would happen to her. Even if I was in prison, I have long arms, should anything happen to her then Anna would have to come to me and she will not risk that. Have no fear, we will hear no more of this matter that is until I decide what to do next.'

Inez, though reassured said, 'What about this fellow Bentley? He is resourceful, could he make trouble for us?'

'Why should he, what can he do? If he was paid to find Anna and get her back, then he has done his job. If he comes here making a nuisance of himself, I will have Caldano deal with him. We will hear nothing more of him. What we will do is this, we will do nothing for a couple of months. Let them think that they have got away with this. Then, maybe we go to England and take Anna back. This time we leave no-one to come here looking.'

Inez was actually afraid by the menace in Raul's voice and almost felt sorry for Patience at that moment. Almost. She recalled how Patience had looked down her nose at her and how the other Jameson's had treated her. It would be good to take Anna back then settle once and for all with that stuck up English bitch. Now, she felt better.

'One thing though,' Raul's voice broke into her thoughts, 'Salma Guttierez. I expect that by now she will be long gone from the villa. I want her found. When we get back, I will put some guys on it. Maybe Diego Calva has a hand in this, he is very friendly with Henry Jameson. If we cannot find Salma, I will have Calva followed, I am sure he will lead us to Salma sooner or later, that old bitch needs to be taught that it does not pay to cross me.'

Chapter 28

I was ready for Martin and Carole with half an hour to spare. To pass the time, I put some Santana on. As Martin had suggested, I was wearing a suit, a new charcoal Hugo Boss, and with it, I wore a light grey short sleeve shirt and thought I looked fine. My bag was packed with some casual clothes for the morning.

As usual, Martin was on time. I climbed into the back of the Q7 and Carole turned to give me a peck on the cheek. The two of us were old friends, she was slightly older than me by a couple of years. An attractive woman, Carole had brown shoulder length hair which she wore loose. Tonight, she wore a sleek, maroon dress and looked nice, which I told her. Then she turned round as Martin drove. She had on her face the kind of smile which suggested a lottery win, or something else. My money was on the something else.

'Okay, what has Martin been saying.' they both laughed.

'I don't know what you mean Matt, what is he supposed to have said?'

'Why are you smiling like that?'

'Because, as always, I am pleased to see you. I know what you have done over the past few weeks and I am, no we are, very proud of you. What you have accomplished is nothing short of miraculous, finding Anna and bringing her home safe and sound. It's down to your efforts that we are going for what will be a damn good dinner and evening out.' I was suitably mollified for all of a second. 'Oh and yes, I hear that you and Patience have become, shall we say, more than friends lately. Seriously Matt, I am very pleased for the both of you. I have known Patience for a few years now, she is a lovely girl. I hope everything goes well for you.'

'Do me a favour guys,' I pleaded, 'Don't say anything. We don't want to embarrass Patience in any way do we, or me for that matter. Plus, I don't want to annoy Henry, he might not approve and I have not been paid yet.'

That was enough to get us all laughing. Both of them knew me well enough to know that I was always conscious of my fees. They both promised to behave though.

Carole had, for a few years now, tried to fix me up with some of her friends, without success. At one time, she had been convinced that Daisy and

I would get together but this had never really been an option even when Daisy and I had been lovers, neither of us had wanted to settle down together. We were great friends now and that was all.

Once she had realised this, Carole had arranged for me to meet some of her friends. I had been out on numerous dates with her pals and, to be honest, had enjoyed myself. I had never met a woman though who made me feel the way Patience did.

By now, we had reached our destination. A strange guy opened the gates for us as Martin reached them, Martin didn't know who it was and was as mystified as I was. As he parked the Q7, the door to the house opened and a small whirlwind rushed out. Anna. As I got out, she jumped up into my arms to hug me. As my hands were rather full, Martin, grinning all over his face, got my bag out of the car and carried it in with theirs. I carried Anna indoors where the three adults were waiting, in the hallway. Patience wore a sleeveless black dress which fitted in all the right places, and looked fantastic. She came straight to me and kissed me even though I was still holding Anna. When I put the kid down, I gave Patience a hug. Then I turned to shake hands with Henry who, fortunately, was smiling. When he turned to greet the others Suzanne came to greet me. She also looked great in a navy silk dress that fitted her perfectly.

'You look lovely tonight Suzanne,' I said. 'That dress makes you look twenty years younger.' She burst out laughing and took my arm as we walked into the lounge. Before I could sit down though, Henry took Martin and I into the kitchen for drinks. The kitchen was enormous, my house would have fitted inside. In the centre was a huge island, around the walls, worktops with cupboards above and below, a huge Aga type thing dominated one wall and one of those massive American fridge freezers dominated another.

'I understand you like these Matthew,' Henry said, handing me a bottle of Coors, he passed another to Martin then got drinks for the women before leading the way back. Now I knew why they had those huge sofas in the lounge, Suzanne sat on one and Henry joined her. Carole and Martin had taken another leaving me to sit with Patience and Anna.

'I thought it would be nice if Anna joined us for dinner,' Henry said. 'After, we will speak of business if everyone agrees.' Everyone did. The talk was general until Aggi the maid came to tell us that dinner was ready. Very formal, we went through into the dining room, another room that I had not seen before. A large room with large picture windows overlooking the garden. The room itself was simply furnished, the table in the middle had room for eight though I suspect it could have opened out and seated more. It was, I think, beech and looked rather expensive. A matching sideboard stood against one wall. Henry and Suzanne sat at either end of the table, Martin and Carole at one side with Patience, Anna and I at the other.

The food was superb and would have done justice to many a restaurant, and we all enjoyed the meal. The conversation was general with everyone keeping off the main subject as Anna was sitting with us.

After dinner, Anna went up to bed, her mother taking her.

'How has she settled?' I asked Suzanne. 'On the way from Majorca, we had three overnight stops, as you know. She seemed all right to me but then, I don't know her.'

'She has been fine thank you Matthew. She is back in her normal routine, but we are all keeping a close eye on her. If need be, we will get some help but so far, so good. Patience then came back with a tray with more drinks, we moved back to the lounge and resumed our seats. When we were all sat, Henry asked if we might discuss the business at hand.

'We have some idea of what has gone on but perhaps you would take us through the events from the start Matthew. I know you will be sending a full report via Martin but I for one would like to hear all about things from the start.' How could I object, he was after all, paying.

'I will try not to bore you with all the details of my watching,' I began, 'So if you think I might have skipped over something, it will only be me sitting, watching. I never like to send my audience to sleep, too early.' That caused a laugh as I had hoped it would. 'The flight was just a flight so I don't intend to say anything about it. At Palma I met Diego and he took me to the apartment in Santa Ponsa that you had rented which gave me a good view of the garden at the Villa Borgosa though I could not see either the doors or garages.

When I arrived, Diego had put in a couple of tripods and a pair of binoculars for me to use.' I started to tell them of the first few days when Henry butted it.

'I understand that Diego provided you with a gun, is that really true Matthew?' Suzanne and Carole both had a look of horror on their faces, Patience, who knew that it was true, simply gripped my hand.

'Yes, that is true Henry. It was Glock 19, a 9mm semi-automatic as a matter of fact, it came complete with a very nice black holster actually.' I was trying to make light of the situation but they were concerned.

'Did you know how to use it and did you carry it around?' asked Carole.

'Yes and yes Carole. I have a pal who lives over in Florida called Scott. When I have been there visiting, he has taken me with him to the gun club and range he uses. As a matter of fact, he has a Glock too, the same model so I was not unfamiliar with it. I carried it with me all the time once Patience had joined me in Majorca.

'You never mentioned this,' Patience said, her face troubled. I smiled.

'It's not really the sort of thing you tell people Patience. I did have a permit to carry the gun. I said nothing because I didn't want to worry you. Unless your life was in danger, I would never have taken the thing out. I did use it on two occasions as you well know, but only because you and Anna were in danger.' That caused some commotion amongst those present and they all started to talk at once, that is until Henry called for quiet.

'Like you all, I would like to know more about this so may I suggest that we all remain quiet and allow Matthew to continue with his report.' That did the trick.

'With your permission, I will gloss over the time spent looking into the garden of the villa. For most of the time, I was sitting there looking at nothing at all.' I looked at Patience. 'You remember that I did say observations could be boring. Then one day, I saw Salma walking down the drive, early one evening actually so I decided to see if I could find her on the street and see what she was up to. I followed her into the local supermarket and watched her buy sweets and crisps which made me almost certain that there was a child living at the villa. Then a couple of cars arrived and some kids. I got pictures but none of the kids was Anna.

Then, on Monday the seventeenth of June as we all now know, I saw the two of them leave the villa. By the time they got down the street, I was waiting for them, camera at the ready. You have all seen the photos of them going to and coming out of the market, the fish stall to be accurate.

I wanted to watch for another week to see if they went the next Monday. I did so and they went on Monday the twenty fourth. That, plus the fact that I had seen Raul come and go at the same time on Tuesday made me sure that they were creatures of habit in the villa.

I was certain that Anna would go with Salma to the fish stall on Monday the first of July so I then wanted Patience with me so that between us, we could separate Anna from the nanny without fuss and beat a hasty retreat. In effect, I had three plans to work out. The first was to get Patience over to Majorca without anyone knowing. Diego had told me that Raul has many contacts throughout the island so I did not want her to fly in to Palma so she came by way of Valencia and a ferry from there to Palma. I wanted to keep her presence on the island a secret so to speak. I was fearful that if Raul got wind of Patience being on the island then she could well be in danger as, after all, he had either killed one person, or had her killed, I was not about to risk Patience becoming number two. In addition, if he was aware of us, he could have moved Anna off the island, that would have snookered us.

Secondly, we had to get Anna away from Salma, to be perfectly honest, I was going to wing that one, then Patience said that she felt that Salma would be on our side and that getting Anna away would present no problems, I am pleased to say that her assessment was spot on.

The last part of my planning was to get the three of us off the island. I thought if we could get a private boat to the mainland then we could probably take the train to Paris and fly from there. I discussed this with Diego, he liked the plans actually, he spoke to a pal of his, Sergio, who agreed to take us to a little place north of Barcelona, from there we would get a lift into Barcelona.

So Patience arrived on the Friday which was nice, I had not quite started to talk to myself but it was only a matter of time.' That brought a laugh, as I knew it would.

'Anyway, Monday came, we got Anna and left Santa Ponsa with Diego who drove us to Port de Soller to meet Sergio. As it happened, the guy who was to take us to Barcelona could not do it but we went anyway. I was sure we could sort out something when we got to Canyet de Mar. That was when we had some bad luck. On the way out of the harbour, Patience was seen and recognised by a friend of Raul who got straight on the phone to him.

Salma went back to the villa after we had been gone an hour or so and reported Anna missing. Unknown to her of course, Raul was already aware of the situation. With the use of force, he got out of the old lady what little information she had, fortunately, it was not much. He locked her in her room and it took her a few hours to get free. She phoned Diego who rang me and told me what Raul had put Salma through.

Then we landed at Canyet de Mar which for all intents and purposes was closed. Lucky for us, we came across a woman whose cousin took us, for a fee, to Barcelona where we spent the night in a hotel across from the station.

Next morning we went to the station, I went to get tickets, when I came out, Patience and Anna had decided to go for a stroll with a couple of the locals. I had to ask the locals to butt out.'

'It wasn't like that at all,' Patience interrupted. 'Two of Raul's thugs tried to drag Anna and I out of the station to where Raul was waiting, Matthew rushed straight over and saved us. He took the two of them on and sorted them out. I know that he is making light of the situation but if it were not for him then neither Anna or I would be here now. He was very brave.'

'Yes, well let's move on,' I said, a little embarrassed. 'We left the station rather quickly and walked for a few minutes then took a bus to the local bus station then took the bus out of Barcelona because who would expect anyone being chased to escape by bus.' Again they laughed. 'We went to Tarragona, hired a car then Martin spoke to Henry and arranged a plane to be waiting for us at Faro so we just drove down the road and here we are.'

'That is not all Matthew Bentley,' Patience again interrupted. 'I will tell them, I know you will not, because you will not make yourself sound good. On the way, we were spotted by two more of Raul's thugs who followed us so Matthew drove into a petrol station, then he sent Anna and I to the loo. He said only to come out when he rang and told me to. Anna and I were petrified as we waited though I should have known that Matthew would be on top of the situation.

He was of course. I got the call and Anna and I left and headed straight back to the car. The thugs car was parked close by, I noticed that all four tyres were flat, then Matthew appeared with one of the thugs, at the time I was not aware that he had the gun sticking into the thugs back. Anyway, between us we questioned him and he confirmed that he worked for Raul and that Raul knew where we were. Matthew sent me back to the car then joined me and we set off. On the way down the road, I threw the bad guys keys and phones out of the window.'

'What did you do to them?' asked Henry.

'I just knocked them out and sat them in their car as if they were asleep then we legged it so to speak. That really was that, we spent the night then drove into Faro where we met Peter and flew back here.' I sat back.

Everyone began to talk at once except for Patience who gazed at me admiringly.

'I think this call for champagne,' Henry decided and nodded at Aggi who was sat in the corner, I hadn't known she had been there. She nipped out and fetched a couple of bottles of Dom Perignon which Henry opened. After pouring Henry raised his glass. 'To Matthew.' We all drank, me too, despite wishing the sofa would swallow me up. I love champagne but was not too comfy being the centre of attention.

'I have arranged some security,' Henry continued. 'I will not take the risk of Raul trying something so until he is brought to justice, we are being looked after by an old friend of mine, Michael Fox and some of his friends. They are all ex SAS so we should be more than safe.' I was pleased by this news, it explained who the guy was who had let us in earlier. 'Martin and Matthew will work together to prepare the necessary documentation to take to Majorca to place before the authorities there. They will go in a week or so and remain there for however long it takes.' Then Martin took over.

'We will take with us an affidavit from Matt and one from Patience. Once there, I intend to take statements from Salma and Sergio and maybe Diego to, in any event, we will need him to translate for us.

We will see this Senor Almunia when we have the statements from the Spanish people, then it is down to him.'

Patience looked at me. 'It isn't over yet is it,' she said.

'Not quite,' I replied, taking her hand. 'Be strong for a week or two, then it will be. I don't think there will be any problems, your father has seen to that.'

It was now time to change the subject, Patience and Carole were old friends and they began to chat, Martin and Henry discussed our forthcoming trip, Suzanne asked me to come and help her with some more drinks, once in the kitchen, she spoke of the afternoon.

'I hope that we did not embarrass you too much this afternoon Matthew. The girls all mean well.' I smiled as well, nothing wrong with a bit of teasing. Then Patience came in and found us grinning like school kids.

'What's the joke?' she asked, smiling too. Her mother explained that I had met her and her friends that afternoon and that they had teased me over Patience.

'Oh you poor man,' Patience said, now laughing.

Suzanne and Henry retired for the night around half past eleven and were soon followed by Martin and Carole. Patience and I went through to the TV room. As soon as we sat down, I slipped my arm round her and pulled her to me for a kiss. When we came up for air, she snuggled into my side.

'What happens to us when this is over?' she asked.

'What would you like to happen?' I enquired.

'I would like us to have a normal, proper relationship and I would like to include Anna too, if you don't mind. What about you?'

'That's what I'd like,' I responded. 'I know that any relationship with you includes Anna and that is no problem to me whatsoever, to be honest with you, I would not want it any other way. The two of you come as a package, anyway, she is a great girl.' Seems that I said the right thing yet again. We kissed once more, just as nice as the last time. Then we heard a noise. Anna had woken up and had come to look for her mother. I made room for her on the sofa and she climbed on between us and sat with us for a little while.

We all went to bed. Anna and Patience showed me to my room before they both kissed me goodnight, then Patience took Anna back to her room. I got ready for bed wondering if maybe Patience would come back but discounted that thought virtually straight away. If Anna woke up in the night and wanted her mother, she would need her to be where she expected her to be, her own room.

I slept well and woke up around eight, and lay for a few minutes, just thinking. A knock came to my door, it was Anna and her mother bringing me some tea.

'I have a message from dad,' Patience said as Anna poured me a cup. 'Would you join him and Martin for breakfast in the kitchen at nine.'

'Of course,' I replied. 'By the way, thanks for the tea, I could get used to having tea brought to me in bed.'

'Best enjoy it then, it's your last,' she said, laughing.

I wandered into the kitchen at the appointed hour and found Henry and Martin sitting at the island, tucking into bacon and eggs, they looked great.

'Help yourself Matthew,' Henry said. I was not the sort to turn down an invitation like that.

'When can I expect your report Matt,' Martin said. 'Until Raul is locked up, Patience and Anna will not be safe from him. I know you are on hand to watch out for them but you cannot be here 24/7.' That was true enough.

'I took the draft copy home Friday evening actually and went through it, only a couple of small things to change. I will let Daisy have it first thing in the morning, when it has been amended I will go over it again. It should be ready to bring round to you straight after lunch, how's that?'

'That's fine Matt. I will forward you a copy Henry. Now Matt, can you come to the office Tuesday at half past two then the two of us can go through things and get the exhibits ready for notarising.'

'Yes of course, no problem at all.'

'Good, then by the end of Tuesday, we should have your affidavit and exhibits ready for engrossing for the notary. I will ring and make an appointment. Patience will come with us as she has one to swear too.

As far as I can tell Henry, Matt and I should be in a position to fly to Palma a week tomorrow. If you could speak with Diego, I would like, if possible, for him to arrange for us to have a word with Sergio on the Tuesday, I don't know if he can tell us much but I don't want to leave any stone unturned. Then, if he could arrange it, we could see Salma on Wednesday, then, if we can arrange this, I will try to get an appointment with Senor Almunia on Thursday.' It was a good plan, I could not see any way we could improve on his time frame. Once we had finished breakfast, Henry went off to phone Diego. Luckily for me, Anna came in for her breakfast then, I was sure that Martin was going to ask about last night. Saved by an eight year old. Patience and Carole then drifted in.

Henry returned after ten or so minutes. 'I have spoken to Diego,' he announced. 'He will make the arrangements as you suggest Martin, he sees no problems. In fact, he will meet you at the airport and drive you to your hotel, which ever you choose, we will need to let him have the flight details when we get them.' That was fair enough.

Carole wanted to be away by half ten as she had to pick up their kids. I went up to gather my things together, Patience came to.

'Would you like to go to the Lansdowne for a loaf around the pool tomorrow evening, just the two of us, then after, have a bite to eat?'

'I would love too,' she replied, smiling. 'There is just one thing though, dad does not want me to drive alone until all this is over, if I get a lift to your house, will you bring me home?'

'Of course I will. I would come for you but I have to get this report finished by tomorrow for Martin, but I will be glad to bring you home. What about Anna though, will she not mind?'

'No, not at all, in fact, she has already asked when you and I are planning to see each other.'

'Did she indeed, quite the little matchmaker eh. As a date it's not very glamorous but I just want to see you.'

'Me too, don't bother about glamour, that isn't important to me. Shall I be at your place for what, six?' That was fine. I took hold of her and kissed her, she sighed contentedly, which made me rather happy as Martin drove us away from Little Thornley.

Chapter 29

Once Daisy had completed all her normal Monday morning tasks, we settled down with the report. Before she would look at it though, I had to tell her all about Saturday evening; once that was out of the way, we were able to make a start.

As I had told Henry and Martin, I had gone over my copy and made a few amendments to the text. It did not take Daisy too long to transfer the amendments on to her computer, we then re-read the report together. I thought it was fine, she agreed and printed off the copy for Martin then did a covering letter, in the letter she mentioned that as I was going back to Majorca with Martin in a week's time, she would withhold our final bill until we had returned.

'That is Matt, if you are going to charge your girlfriends father,' she said mischievously. I ignored her which only made her laugh.

After lunch, I wandered over to Martin's office with the report as promised. He had left word with Gemma, the receptionist, that he wanted a quick word with me.

'Hi Matt,' he said when I entered his office. 'A couple of things, I have heard from Henry, he has booked us a room each at the Hotel Meliá Palas Atenea which is supposed to be the number one in Majorca. Diego has made the arrangements that I suggested, Sergio Tuesday, Salma Wednesday. I have also spoken to Almunia and we are to see him Thursday, so everything has gone right there. You will be here tomorrow at two thirty?'

'Course I will. One thing, you might ask Henry to ask Diego if he has a printer that we could take around with us, if so, we can type the statements from Sergio and Salma and have them sign there and then, save having to go back.'

'Good idea, I will get on to that. See, you can be clever now and again. Don't forget you are taking Patience out tonight.' Everyone was a comedian.

'No I will not forget Martin but thanks for the reminder old lad.'

Back in the office, I signed all the post that I needed to and generally helped Daisy, at least I tried but I was rather preoccupied; she noticed.

'Something on your mind boss?' she asked, eventually.

'Well yes actually. I am wondering how I can get out of the office without getting the third degree from you.'

'There's no chance of that boy. Why do you want to go now or should that be obvious to me.' I smiled weakly.

'I am meeting Patience at six, we are going to the Lansdowne to loaf around but she is coming to my place first. I need to tidy up.'

'It's about time you started to ask for my permission to leave, go on, clear off and get yourself ready. I'm happy for you.' She was too. I gave her a hug then I was off.

The house was not too bad but I vacuumed anyway, then I got out the polish, a good effort I thought.

All done by just after five. When I had got my loafing kit ready, I put Pink Floyd's 'Wish You Were Here' on the Hi Fi. That passed the time on nicely. Just after six, a Rover 75 pulled up outside the house. A guy I didn't know got out from behind the wheel and opened the passenger door for Patience, I went out to meet her and she greeted me with a kiss.

'Hi love, this is Michael Fox who is one of the men looking after us at the moment. Michael, this is Matthew, my boyfriend and the man who found and brought home Anna.' He smiled as we shook hands. He looked to be about forty, short hair and tough looking with a determined stare. Did they call it the thousand yard stare? I did not know but if they did, he had it. Everyone knew that our SAS guys were the best, I hoped that former SAS men were second best.

'Good to meet you Michael, thanks for bringing Patience over.'

'You too Matthew. Good job in Majorca by the way. I understand that you are to bring Miss Patience home?'

'Yes that's right Michael, sometime later, thanks for what you said.' He simply smiled and got Patience her bag from the rear seat of the Rover. Inside, we kissed, it had been a long time since Sunday morning.

We left for the Lansdowne in my Audi, I had contemplated using the van just for devilment but decided against it. She held my hand as we walked from the car, several people looked at us as they passed. Jealous guys in the main or so I thought. I was quite proud to be seen with her and by the same token she looked pleased to be with me.

The changing room was busy as it always was at this time, plenty of people stopped on their way home from work to use the facilities. I was first through into the pool area and waited for Patience to appear. It was worth the wait, she wore a one piece navy costume which fitted her like a glove, she looked gorgeous. More or less every guy in the place watched her walk over to me. A couple called out to her and got out of the pool to speak with her, I knew them by sight, they were not people that I would speak to, rich mummy's boys with flash cars. Patience it seemed was not in any mood to talk to them, she merely muttered something as she passed them without a glance. They looked round either to see who she was with or maybe at her bottom, or both. They were certainly shocked to see that she was with me, the shock plain on their faces. I resisted the temptation to stick my tongue out.

After the regulation shower, we went into the Jacuzzi. Three other people sat in the warm water, it left plenty of room for us to sit and talk without having to either whisper or shout. It was good to be out with her. Before I left for Majorca when we had been out, first she was my client. Then we had become friends. In Majorca, when we went out to eat, I had not been able to relax, carrying the Glock and looking out for Raul whilst giving the impression that everything was fine was quite stressful. Now, back in Greenfield I had none of those problems.

After a quarter of an hour, we went to the steam room which was busy. We sat, though we were thigh to thigh, which was nice. We could not really talk though as it was quite noisy in there. The steam was not so thick that we could not see or be seen, I nodded to a couple of people that I knew, as did Patience. I was sure that we would be the main topic of conversation all over the place once we had gone, or perhaps while we were still there. The Lansdowne was a good place to go but some of the people who used the place could be termed busybodies or maybe nosy bastards, one or the other.

From the steam room, we showered off before relaxing in the pool. I could not swim so we hung around at the side cooling down, then we tried the sauna. After ten minutes we cooled down again. It was seven forty.

'I will go and start to get ready now love, give me at least twenty minutes before you go out and I will meet you in the lobby.' A quick kiss and she was gone. The kiss was probably as much for the people who were openly staring at us as for me. As for me, well, I was really quite pleased.

When she had gone, I went back and sat in the Jacuzzi, intending to stay there until it was time to go. A few minutes later, one of Suzanne's friends came out of the changing room and headed over to the Jacuzzi, spotting me as she did so.

'Hello Matthew, good to see you again,' she said as she sat down beside me. 'Guess who I have just been speaking to in the changing room?' Then I think the penny dropped. 'Ah, I expect you already know. I'm such a fool, I should have realised when I saw you. Patience is a lovely girl, I hope you will both be happy.' That was nice of her. We chatted until it was time for me to go and get myself ready.

I was only kept waiting for ten minutes but the wait was worth it. Now, did we stop here for something to eat or go elsewhere?

'If we stay here,' Patience observed, 'we will have people staring at us and whispering over their drinks all night. Now, I'm not bothered about anyone else but what I do not want is for anyone to come over to us. By that, I mean anyone who knows either of us who might come over just for the sake of being nosy. Our relationship is our business and in any event, I just want to be with you. I vote that we go somewhere else.'

We settled on the Ship at Great Bidding. We had been there before on the Saturday before I left for Majorca. Not a bad choice as it was on the way to Little Thornley so easy for me to take her home after. In the car, she found a CD, Yessongs actually which she put on, softly so that we could talk.

At the Ship, we ordered food and drinks and settled down to talk. The food was good the company better. All too soon though, it was time to leave. We continued to chat on the way to her home.

The large gates were closed as I expected them to be but Patience had had the foresight to bring one of the remote controls with her. She expected me to come in and speak to her parents, which was no problem for me whatsoever. As we walked to the door from the car, I caught a movement in the corner of my eye, and tensed. Patience noticed too but it was Michael Fox who I had met earlier, doing I supposed, his rounds of the area.

Suzanne and Henry were in the TV room, Patience left me with them while she popped up to look at Anna.

'Have you had a nice evening Matthew? Good. Did you see my friend Rita, she was going tonight, I told her that you would be there?' I had seen her and said so. Anna it turned out was fine, fast asleep holding her new bear. The two of us went through to the kitchen where Patience made hot chocolate, very domesticated. We sat there drinking it, Henry and Suzanne came to say goodnight, Henry shook my hand, his wife kissed me. They both seemed perfectly at ease with me, seemingly accepting the fact that their daughter and I were becoming more than friends.

We went through to the TV room, it was on but we were not watching, we were soon kissing, passionately. All too soon though, it was midnight and time to go. She held me tight.

'When will I see you again?' she asked. It sounded like a song. I was getting really soppy now and would have to watch my step, still, Daisy would soon sort me out if I got soppy in the office.

'Tomorrow, I am taking the troops, Daisy, Karen and Tony out for dinner as a thank you for the extra work they did while I was away, and for what they will do next week. Why don't you join us.'

'I don't know any of them darling. If I came, it would spoil it for them and I don't want that to happen. What about Wednesday?'

'That would be great. Would you like to go for a drive in the country and have something to eat in a country pub. We can take Anna too if you think she would enjoy coming with us.'

'Enjoy it, she will love it. Thanks for including her. This Sunday, Anna wants to go to the Trafford Centre for the day, she has asked me to ask if you want to come too. What shall I tell her?'

'As for including Anna, that's no problem at all, she is a great kid and Sunday, please tell her yes, I will be pleased to come out for the day with the pair of you.'

'She will be so happy, she likes you a lot.'

'I like her too, she is a great kid. I've just said that haven't I.' Without thought, I had said the right thing once again. I was getting very good at that. It was true though and guaranteed me another kiss before I left. The last thing

I said was that I would be there to collect them between six and six thirty
Wednesday evening,

Michael let me out of the gate and on the way home, I put the CD on. It
had been a wonderful evening, the first of many I hoped.

Chapter 30

First thing Tuesday morning, Martin rang. 'Still okay for this afternoon? I could not get us before the notary until half past eleven Thursday morning, you will keep yourself free for that of course. It does give us that little bit longer to change things if we feel the need to otherwise I would be moaning about the delay. Before I go, how was last night?'

'Very nice thanks, we ended up at the Ship at Great Bidding having something to eat.'

'That's good. See you.' Then he was gone. I had quite a busy morning, the post brought several new jobs which was nice, then Karen arrived with some completed reports.

'Hello Matt,' she greeted me. 'I'm looking forward to this evening, what time are we meeting? I know we are going to 'Horizons' but that's all.'

'To be honest Karen, I don't know. This may sound a bit dozy of me but I didn't know that we were going to Horizons. Daisy only tells me what she thinks I need to know. If you ask her, tell her I would like to know too.'

'Okay boss, I'll go speak to her now.' Then Daisy came into my room followed by Karen.

'I'm sure that I told you Matt, you know, you have been rather preoccupied with the Jameson case in general and Patience in particular since you came back. I expect the poor thing forgot.' This last remark was addressed to Karen, not me. 'We are meeting at Horizons at seven thirty. Is that all right with you?'

'Yes, fine. I have not been there but I hear it's very good. For lunch, I had a sandwich in the office and got on with some paperwork before wandering up to meet Martin at his office.

His secretary, Lynn, was with him. Both of them had a copy of my affidavit in front of them, there was one for me, waiting on the desk.

'I thought Lynn might as well be here Matt, then, if we need to alter anything, Lynn can make a note of it on her copy. You have met Lynn before I think.' I had, we smiled and said hello, then I began to read.

My affidavit started with the instructions to look into a car crash that happened in Majorca which had allegedly caused the death of Anna Martinez. A copy of the death certificate and police report had been exhibited, together with a certified translation into English. I was then to look for Anna as it was thought that she was not the child who had been in the car at the time of the crash.

It continued with me saying that I had seen Anna on the seventeenth of June in Santa Ponsa and exhibited three of the photographs I had taken. The Nikon had a facility to date and time the digital image, an extra but one which was very handy in this case. Also exhibited was an earlier picture of Anna, there for the sake of comparison.

The affidavit further stated that I had seen Anna on the twenty fourth of June and the first of July, then it detailed the events of the first when Anna had been reunited with her mother. It described that the child returned to the jurisdiction of the English Courts on the fourth of July. That Anna should be under the care and control of her mother was evidenced by the parental responsibility order of the Greenfield County Court, and certified translations into Spanish, the affidavit concluded by saying that the child Anna Martinez had, at all material times, been alive rendering the death certificate and the police report, false.

That there was a body in the car was not in dispute as the statement of the fire fighter was referred to in the police report, which begged the question, 'Who was the child in the car?'

'That should do the trick Martin,' I said. 'Surely there is enough evidence there to convince this Almunia to act.'

'I agree, this, together with the affidavit of Patience and the statement of Salma Guttierez should be more than enough to do for friend Raul. Thanks Lynn, everything seems fine.

Now, enough of that, how did it go last night?' I had to smile at his persistence, but I knew that he was happy for me.

'We had a good time at the Lansdowne though I think it's fair to say that quite a few eyebrows were raised at our being together. Several jealous people in there last night you know, male and female.' He laughed out loud at that. 'We did intend to have something to eat there too but we decided to go to the Ship to avoid people staring at us. The Ship was good.'

'The Ship at Great Bidding, yes it's very good there, Carole and I have been a few times. When are you seeing her again?'

'Tomorrow as it happens. I am taking Patience and Anna out for a drive in the country for a pub meal. Tonight, I am taking Daisy, Karen and Tony out to Horizons for dinner as a thank you for their efforts while I was away. All this eating out, I will be getting fat before long.' He laughed.

'That's sounds good. Patience and Anna come as a pair as you well know. Right, Thursday, can you be here for say quarter past eleven then we can stroll up together?' I could and would.

'Daisy left early in the afternoon as she wanted to get ready for our evening out. I manned the office and for once, I was glad that no late work came in. Karen and Tony had both phoned when they were about to finish, just to see if anything else needed doing. They were good, loyal and trustworthy and I was pleased to have them on board.

I arrived home just after half five and headed straight for the shower. After, I put some Santana on to help me relax, which it did. For the meal, I wore a Hugo Boss suit in navy, white shirt and navy tie with small white spots, looking good, or at least I thought so.

I was first to arrive at the restaurant followed moments later by Karen. She looked nice in a pale blue sleeveless dress with dark tights. For work, she only ever wore trousers or sometimes jeans.

'You look very nice Karen,' I said. 'I never knew that you had such nice legs.' She smiled at the compliment.

'I am glad you like them Matt. I understand from Daisy that you are an authority on legs.' She had sat down opposite me and as she crossed her legs, I took a good look.

'Well, you know, everyone is good at something.' As she laughed, Daisy and Tony arrived. Daisy looked gorgeous in a short grey dress and black stockings. Her dress showed off her legs as she sat down, of course, I took my peek at them and was glad to see that they were as lovely as always. Tony looked smart but regimental in blazer and trousers.

Over dinner, the main topic of conversation was the Jameson case. I brought them up to date on my next visit to the island and the reasons for it. Daisy of course was already aware of everything so it could have been boring for her, if it was, she never let on.

When we had finished eating, I ordered a bottle of champagne for us as an extra thank you and to finish of what had been a really good evening out. I felt that the whole thing had been a success and a suitable thank you for the extra work they had put in, I would ask Daisy in the morning what she thought but the three of them seemed to me to have enjoyed themselves.

I arrived home just before eleven, just as I was going in, my mobile rang, Patience.

'Hello love,' she said. 'I hope you don't mind me calling, I wanted to know if you were having a nice time.'

'Hi there, I never mind you calling. Actually, I have just got in. It was a good evening and I think everyone enjoyed it.'

'You are home early.'

'Yes, I guess so. Having said that, we had done everything we had wanted to. John, Daisy's husband came to collect her and offered a lift to the others so it was a good time to finish. I grabbed a cab. I have had a good time, but I missed you.' There I was again, being soppy, get a grip lad.

'You say the nicest things. Anna is looking forward to going out tomorrow and thrilled that you are coming with us on Sunday.' We chatted for a few minutes longer before we hung up.

The following morning, we received an urgent job via the fax from a firm of solicitors in London. It seemed that one of their clients had come home from work one day only to find his wife had done one, taking their kid with her. Well, she would, wouldn't she. He was, seemingly, not to bothered about the wife but wanted to know where his son was, not unreasonable I guess. The client believed that his wife had gone to Greenfield though the letter of instruction did not say how he had arrived at that. They supplied an address which was not very far from the office, a photograph which was not too bad considering it came over the fax and could we ascertain whether the wife and child were in fact living at that address. Of course we could.

As both Karen and Tony were out, Daisy sent me out to do this one. To be honest, I was glad to do it, it was the first piece of work, other than the Jameson job, that I had done in a long while. It did not take me long, for once, the information provided was good, I had only been across the road for a few minutes, weighing up the neighbourhood before out of the house came Mrs Ronson and her son, Ronald. Ronald Ronson, I kid ye not. Some people eh.

Back in the office, Daisy rang the solicitors with a verbal report. They were mightily impressed at how quick we were able to do the job for them and report. Then she prepared the written report and our bill.

After lunch, Daisy and I sat and talked, she told me that she, and the others had really enjoyed the evening out and hoped that we would do it again one day.

'Matt, as you are going back to Majorca next week, would you like to come round for a meal with John and me tonight?'

'Sorry Daisy, tonight I have a previous engagement.' I could see the question in her eyes so I told her what I was doing. This was her opportunity to give me a bit of stick, which she quickly took.

'I expect it's easier for a man of your age to go for a ready-made family, saves you some effort and all those dirty nappies. You will have to move of course, you cannot expect a millionaire's daughter to live in your little house now, can you?'

By now, we were both laughing, no way could I take offence at what she had said. I stopped laughing suddenly. I had not thought of ready-made families or places to live. Was that what I wanted? It was early days so I decided to see how things played out over the next few weeks. Me being me, I pressed myself, yes, I suppose I did want it. There, I had told myself now. It felt good that I had and I felt happy.

I got myself ready to leave the office just after four. Karen appeared just as I was about to leave and looked quizzically at Daisy.

'He's going home to get ready,' she said by way of explanation. 'He is taking Patience Jameson out tonight so he needs all the time he can get to tart himself up.' Karen burst out laughing, Daisy soon joined her. I left with all the dignity I could muster, which wasn't much at all. Apart from the obvious pleasure of seeing Patience again I was looking forward to seeing Anna too.

I was on the road by quarter to six, the Yessongs disc was still in the car so I put it on again, a great album, possibly the finest live album ever, at least, I thought so.

Michael was hovering by the gate when I arrived so he let me in. Before I had chance to get out of the car, Anna was there to meet me.

'Hello Matt, mum's not ready yet. Come and say hello to grandma and granddad.' She took my hand and led me into the TV room where Suzanne and Henry were watching the early evening news. They seemed pleased to see me, apparently at ease with me taking out their only daughter and grandchild.

'Have you anywhere in mind to eat Matthew?' Henry asked me. I had not and told him so. 'Then may I suggest The White Swan,' he continued. 'It's in Rothmere which is about twenty miles from here.' I did not know where that was but before I could ask, Patience arrived, she looked good, white shirt with black trousers. She came straight to me and kissed me, which was nice but I wondered about Henry but the three of them all looked pleased which was a relief.

'Darling,' Henry addressed his daughter, 'I have suggested The White Swan at Rothmere to Matthew.' She looked pleased at the thought.

'Yes, it's nice there, have you been Matthew?' I confessed that I had not. 'Well, we could go there if you like.'

'It sounds good to me, if you know the way then we need not trouble the sat nav.' It took forty minutes to drive there through some very nice English countryside. Being July, the countryside was a mass of colour with flowers and the like blooming. Anna sat in the back and chattered away. It seemed that she was bored and wanted to go back to school, even though it was almost time for the summer holidays, but her mother was against the idea for obvious reasons, preferring to wait until the matter was settled once and for all.

'Do you know what they are going to do Matt?' she said, her voice so indignant that I struggled to stop myself laughing. 'They are getting me a tutor to come to the house. What do you think of that?'

'Well, as you are asking, I think it is a good idea.'

'Why?'

'Do you remember what happened twice while we were in Spain, first at the train station and then on the motorway?'

'Do you mean when those horrible people grabbed mum and me at the station and those other men on the motorway who were following us?'

'Yes, that's exactly what I mean. You do know who sent those men don't you?'

'Yes I do. They were dad's men. The one at the station hurt my arm as he pulled me along and the other one hurt mum. I heard mum tell grandma that it was a good job you were there to save us.'

'Yes well umm, at the moment, your mother and grandparents are rather concerned that your dad may send some more men to try to take you away from your mum again. Until we have sorted the problem out, your mum wants to keep you safe and the safest place is at home behind those big gates. The other reason is that you need to keep up with your school work, it really is important you know.'

'I understand, it's so dad can't take me away again. I see that now. I'm sorry mum for going on and making a fuss. I promise not to moan again and be good for the tutor.'

Patience looked at me gratefully, I interpreted the look to say thank you for explaining things so well, of course, I might have been wrong.

Rothmere, when we arrived, was a nice little village, in total about forty miles from Greenfield. Not much of it though, a few houses surrounding a well- kept village green. Large houses too, by the look of things. From the car to the pub, Anna walked between us holding each of our hands. The White Swan, by its appearance, had recently been renovated though it still had the beams in the ceiling and retained an olde world charm. We sat at a table overlooking a well-tended and colourful rose garden. Anna enjoyed the evening very much, after we had eaten, we took a stroll by the River Tron which flowed by the pub.

We were back at Little Thornley by nine thirty. The first thing that Anna did was to apologise to her grandparents about the fuss she had made over the tutor. They both looked surprised, but then she kissed everyone goodnight and thanked me for a lovely evening before going up to bed.

'Thanks Matt for tonight, I hope we can go out again soon.'

'Of course we can, don't forget we are going out Sunday. Then I have to go away on business for a few days, when I come back, we will go out then. How's that?' Her answer was to hug me again.

Henry said, after she had gone, 'I understand that you are to see the notary in the morning Matthew.'

'That's right, at half past eleven. Then we will be all set for Monday.' Patience came back and sat on the arm of the chair I was using.

'Do you anticipate any problems from Raul?'

'To be perfectly frank with you, no. I did wonder if he might come here and was going to suggest some security, but you were ahead of me there. Thinking about things, I would not be surprised if Raul thinks that he has got away with it, after all, it has been over a week since we got Anna back and the police have not been knocking on his door. I don't know him of course but Patience and Diego have told me an awful lot about him so I have a feel for the man. My impression is that he likes the easy way and expects that everyone will always look for the easy option. That said, he is like a snake, you never know what he will do'

Suzanne and Patience went to make a drink.

'What is your gut feeling Matthew, will Almunia help us?'

'I have not spoken to him Henry so it's a little hard to answer that. All I have to go on is what Martin has told me, the same as you I expect, but from what I have heard, yes, I think he will. Obviously he does not know what is going on but he must be aware that whatever it is, we must have sufficient evidence to back up our claim, and that it must be serious as we are coming to him and not the local police. And further, we are coming all the way from England.'

The two women that came back in with the hot drinks they had been making.

'How did you persuade Anna to accept the tutor?' Henry asked his daughter.

'I didn't, it was Matthew actually. He explained things to her rather differently than I had, she understood and accepted right away. All the trouble we have had over the past couple of days and along comes Matthew and sorts the problem out in seconds. I want to know how he does it.'

'I guess I was just lucky and said the right thing, but on the other hand, I might just have the knack with women of all ages.' Suzanne and Henry laughed though Patience looked a little unsure, until I laughed and then she joined in.

We all talked until ten, I was going to leave but Suzanne and Henry went up to watch TV in bed. We watched the TV too but did not see much as a bout of kissing broke out. I would have to get her alone somewhere then we could carry on with what had been developing back in Santa Ponsa. I think she read my mind.

'I can't wait to make love with you again Matthew, it was wonderful in Majorca. Hurry up and come back then we can go away for a holiday together.' Now that was what I call a good idea. 'Thanks for a lovely evening darling,' she continued. 'Anna enjoyed herself very much and told me that she asked if we could all go out again. She was thrilled by your answer, do you know, tonight was the first time that she has ever been out with me and a man. She likes you a lot, not that I can blame her for that.' It seemed a good time for a kiss. 'My parents approve too. I can tell that you are a little apprehensive around them but there is absolutely no reason to be. They want me to be happy, since I met you I have been happy. Mother thinks you are wonderful, if I didn't know better, I would say that she fancies you herself. What I am saying is that they are happy so you don't need to bother about that.'

'That's good to know. I was concerned because I came here as the hired help and am leaving with the daughter, what you said does make me feel better.'

When I arrived at the office in the morning, it was a full house and Daisy had made the tea, good timing. Over tea, we discussed a couple of jobs that had stuck, one each for Karen and Tony. We decide to swap them round, let a fresh face have a go, it usually worked.

Just after ten, the door buzzer sounded, Daisy answered it and I noticed a look of surprise on her face before she told whoever it was to come up.

'Someone for you Matt,' was all she said as she went to greet the visitor. Our office was on the first floor of a two story building, under us was an accountant's practice. Our floor comprised of a general office where Daisy sat, my office plus another two, one of which was empty, the other used for storage. We also had a good kitchen and a bathroom which had a shower cubicle in it. Daisy came back in to the general office with Patience, no wonder Daisy had looked surprised, I was too. She greeted me with a kiss before I introduced her to the others.

'I am going with you and Martin to the notary Matthew so I thought that I would come a little early and walk up to Martin's office with you.' She refused a cup of tea but sat down to chat with Daisy and Karen though after about ten minutes, Karen left as she had an appointment. Tony had already gone. Patience and Daisy seemed to hit it off from the start so I left them too it and went to my room to do some work. Just before eleven they came into my room.

'As you are going out Matt, I need to pop out and get some lunch so will you will listen for the phone.' As soon as she left, I took hold of Patience for a kiss.

'We have not arranged to see each other before Sunday, that's far too long to wait.'

'True, let's discuss it over lunch today shall we?' When Daisy returned, we left for the short walk to Martin's office. The two women hugged each other as women do. Outside, Michael sat patiently waiting in his Rover. Patience told him that she was going to be with me until after lunch so he could go and do whatever he wanted, she was to call him when she was ready to be picked up. He was happy with that, as long as she was with me, he knew that she was safe.

Martin was waiting for us in reception and we left straight away to go to the notary's office. We wondered about reading our affidavits but he said we could read them at the notary's office as he was bound to keep us waiting.

The notary was Christopher Wilkinson, a partner in a firm called Lyons and Metcalfe. I did work for this firm and knew Wilkinson. Martin was right, he did keep us waiting but it did give us the chance to read the affidavits which were fine.

Wilkinson shook hands with me and fussed over Patience when he found out who she was. Once we had signed the papers and Wilkinson had done his bit, Patience and I were ushered out while Martin paid. Solicitors did not like to receive payment for affidavits in front of the people that had sworn them. They were strange in that way, in my experience at least.

Once outside, Martin asked if Patience and I would like to join him for lunch at the Lansdowne, we did. As it was another nice day, we sat outside by the 18th green. The course was busy which reminded me that I still had not had a round, not much chance before Monday to play. Martin went off to order leaving Patience and I to chat. She wanted to come round to my place that night, we both knew why. Friday, we decided to go to the cinema.

'Matthew,' she asked, 'Saturday, would you like to come round and stay over so that we can set off to the Trafford Centre early, mum and dad are out so I will cook dinner for us.'

'Can you cook then?' I unwisely asked. The look on her face suggested that she could. 'I would love to,' I added hastily. I think it's a great idea. Where are your parents going?'

'They are at a dinner in Manchester and are staying over.' She looked me in the eye as she said this, oh good.

We spent an hour with Martin before he left to go back to his office. Patience phoned Michael and he agreed to come for her and drop me off at the office. On the way, she asked if he would drop her off at my place after tea, he couldn't as he was off but said that one of his team would, he also asked if I would be bringing her back. I would, I assured him. He certainly took his work very seriously, something I was pleased about.

Back in the office, Daisy was enthusiastic about Patience.

'She is lovely Matt. Beautiful but not flash and she has a great personality, she really listens when you speak to her. Not your usual type, I have to wonder what she sees in you.' Charming. Before I could reply, she continued. 'Just joking, she is great, just what you need. I think the two of you are ideal for each other.'

Patience arrived at eight in a Ford Mondeo, someone called Dan was doing the driving. I had some wine chilling in the fridge and poured her a glass, I thought she was a little nervous, I certainly was, anyway, the wine helped her to relax, I didn't have any as I was driving later.

The first of several kisses seemed to break the ice and I took her upstairs to bed. Our first time had been rather frantic, the second time, less urgent. This time it was just right. We were in no hurry and enjoyed loving each other. After, we lay in each other's arms talking.

'I'm glad that your parents will be out Saturday,' I said.

'Me too,' she agreed. We stayed in bed all evening and made love again before it was time for me to take her home. Before we left, she had a rummage through my CD collection and chose Tapestry by Carol King for the trip home. I took the Allman Brothers Live at the Fillmore for on the way back.

Dan, who had driven Patience over to my place was on duty in the grounds when we got back, Patience had again brought a remote control with her but he appeared to check us out when we got out of my car.

I didn't linger, she would choose a film to go and see and ring me with the details which was fine. On the way, I put the Allman Brothers Band on, it had been a while since I had listened to that one and I enjoyed it.

I was happy with the way things were going and expected that it would move up a gear once I returned from Majorca. I would be happy when this job was finished, no more dashing off to Majorca though the island was lovely. What was it she had said the other night, when this was over, we could go somewhere for a holiday. That would be nice, I could do with a holiday even though I had spent a few weeks in Majorca, it was certainly no holiday. Lazing on some quiet beach with Patience and probably Anna would be just the job. Anna would have to come too. Patience would not want to be separated from her daughter again, that I could understand. By the same token, Anna would not want to be parted from her mum again. No, Anna had to come, I would mention her coming though then Patience would not think that she was forcing the situation on me.

On Friday, Daisy sent me out to do a couple of jobs, it made a nice change, the sun was shining and I enjoyed the work. I was back in the office by lunchtime. While I had been out, Daisy had been to the bank and sorted the wages out for Karen and Tony. With going away again, I had left things as they were at the bank.

Out of the blue, Patience arrived at 4.15. Michael Fox had needed to pop into town so she had come over from Little Thornley with him. She wanted to surprise me and chat with Daisy again, they carried on where they had left off the other morning. When John came for Daisy, he was introduced to her, before they left, I reminded Daisy that I would not be in Monday, needless to say, she had remembered. Back at my place, I made us something to eat before getting ready to go and see Sex in the City 2, not what I would have chosen but Patience enjoyed it. We were back at her place by eleven, as usual I went in, Suzanne was alone, Henry had gone to bed with a headache. Patience went to check on Anna leaving us alone.

'Matthew, I just want you to know that Henry and I fully approve of your relationship with Patience. Please do not feel uncomfortable about coming here, you are always welcome.'

'Thanks for that,' I said, and meant it.

'By the way, I have a message for you from Martin concerning the flight Monday morning, he has booked the flight, from Manchester, it leaves at eleven thirty, and he will pick you up around eight.'

Patience came back to report that Anna was fine, Suzanne stood up and said that she was going to bed, she had only stayed up to give me the message.

'What message was that?' Patience asked after her mother had left the room. I told her what Martin had done. The reminder that this matter was still going on took the smile out of her eyes. I could do something about that.

'Do you remember on Wednesday, you suggested that after all this was over, we could go away for a holiday, well, I have been thinking about that and I think it is a great idea. The thing is though, I would like Anna to come with us too, if we do go anywhere. I think it would do her good after what she has been through and I don't think she would be too happy about being parted from you again, so soon after getting you back. I don't think you would want to leave her behind either love but obviously it's up to you, after all, you are her mother.'

'That's a wonderful thing to say love, thank you. Most people would not want a kid tagging along but then, you are not most people. It's no wonder that I love you. It's a deal. When this is over, the three of us will go away.'

We had a happy hour kissing before I got up to leave.

'I can't wait for tomorrow night my love,' she said to me at the door. 'Oh, by the way, is there anything you do not eat?'

'No, I eat pretty much anything. Except for cheese, I don't like cheese, it makes me ill. Oh, and oriental food, I don't like that, and curries and any Indian stuff, I don't like anything like that. Apart from those things, I eat anything.' She was laughing now.

'It sounds like it. Don't worry, I will not do any off that list, come any time, Anna and I will be here all afternoon.'

I intended to have a leisurely day Saturday, I had a late breakfast and was reading the paper when I realised that I was going to Majorca Monday and that I was out Sunday. Washing, ironing and packing needed to be done. Magic. I started by putting the washing machine on, while it was doing, I popped round to see my parents. The wash was done when I got back so out to dry. In the meantime I rang Martin to ask if I needed a suit, I did, and a tie too, for when we saw Senor Almunia.

One thing that was a disappointment, Daisy was not coming to do the packing for me so I had to do it myself, I took a suit and shirt and tie as I had been told, the rest was casual stuff. This took the best part of the afternoon, when I was done I got ready and went up to Little Thornley, listening to Led Zeppelin on the way.

Michael let me in to the grounds when I arrived and smiled at me, a first. Patience and Anna were delighted to see me which was just as well really. In the kitchen over a cup of tea, Anna told me about her tutor, Miss Chambers who, it turned out, she actually liked. After I had had my tea, Anna took me on a tour of the house.

'We need to leave the kitchen Matt, when mum's cooking she sometimes says things that she does not like me hearing, so I keep out of the way.' Patience looked horrified as I fell about laughing which in turn made Anna laugh.

Our tour was quite comprehensive and started in Henry's office on the ground floor. It was at the far end of the hall not that I had noticed the door before. It had a toilet next door which was rather handy. On the far side of his office was a guest suite, sitting room, bedroom and bathroom, decorated in plain white with blue carpeting. A rather nice set of rooms for a guest.

As I had seen the rest of the downstairs rooms, we went upstairs. First, a quick look at her grandparents room, large with a dressing room and en-suite. The family bathroom, three guest bedrooms, one of which I had used the weekend before. Then she took me to her mother's room. I did not tell her that I had been there before nor did we linger, Anna wanted me to see her room.

She had a lovely large room with its own bathroom. In one corner, she had a desk and chair for her school work. A large TV with a DVD player sat in another corner.

'This is probably the nicest room in the entire house,' I said which resulted in her beaming with pleasure. Then she took me to her mother's office which was on the far side of her room. I was quite interested in this room. Patience had a built in desk under the window and a very comfortable chair, I tried it for size. It was far more comfortable than the office chair I had, I made a mental note to ask where she got it from.

Over the garage block opposite the front of the house was where Aggi had her rooms, sitting room, bedroom, bathroom and her own kitchen.

Back at the kitchen, we peeped in tentatively, the air was not blue so we went in. Dinner was almost ready, Spanish chicken with rice, which gave off a delicious aroma. Hopefully, it would taste as good.

I was sent to open some wine that was chilling in the fridge. The meal was nice, Anna and I had ice cream after but Patience declined, watching her figure I was reliably informed by Anna.

Then we sat down and watched a DVD before it was time for Anna to go to bed. That night, I slept in Patience's room, not alone of course. We made love before falling asleep in each other's arms.

After breakfast, we went to the Trafford Centre in the Mercedes AMG which Patience wanted me to drive. It was nice but I didn't think I would bother with one, I would prefer one of the performance Audi's.

We had a lovely day just wandering around, though I have to say that I was keeping a close eye on the two of them, and the other shoppers but nothing out of the ordinary happened, thank goodness. Anna had some money to spend which she spent on books. I bought three paperbacks to take with me to Majorca, then it was time to go home.

Back in Little Thornley, Henry and Suzanne had returned from their evening out. Suzanne insisted that I stay for tea, something that I was happy to do. I ended up staying until ten, when I got up to leave, Suzanne and Henry wished me luck. Patience walked me to the door and clung on to me for an age before telling me to be careful which I promised to do. Led Zeppelin kept me company on the way back to Greenfield.

Chapter 31

Rather surprisingly, Martin was late in picking me up Monday morning. Only five minutes admittedly, but still late which was unusual for him. Not that it made any difference whatsoever, we were still at the airport in good time to check in. On the way, I had to provide details of our day out to the Trafford Centre. To my amazement, he made no sarcastic comment, my surprise must have shown on my face.

'Carole told me not to take the piss,' he said, sounding disappointed. I was saved having to reply by the ringing of my mobile. It was Patience who had rung to tell me to have a safe journey and to be careful. She also told me that she loved me and when I responded in the same way, Martin snorted with laughter.

'That noise in the background is your solicitor laughing at us.'

'He can laugh all he likes,' she retorted. 'We love each other and that is all that matters.' I had to agree with her. We spoke for a little longer before she had to go, the tutor, Miss Chambers was just arriving.

We arrived at the airport without any problems and checked in. We had a suitcase each, Martin had his briefcase of course with all the vital documentation inside. I had my trusty holdall with some books. Once checked in, we went through to the departure lounge and had some breakfast.

The flight itself was, as flights usually are, uneventful. After collecting our bags, I led Martin out into the arrivals hall to look for Diego and spotted him right away and went straight over, Martin behind me. His face seemed to light up when he saw me and we shook hands warmly, fortunately, we had none of that foreign kissing stuff. I then introduced him to Martin before Diego took us outside to where the Scenic waited. It was a glorious day, just as I had come to expect from Majorca.

Diego drove us into Palma, to the Hotel Meliá Palas Atenea where we had reserved two rooms. He told us on the way that this was the finest hotel on the island.

'Nothing too good for Henry's son in law to be,' joked Martin from the back of the Scenic. I managed a weak grin but Diego seized on the comment.

'Are you and Patience to be married?' he almost shouted in his excitement. 'That is wonderful news my friend, both my wife and I think that the two of you are made for each other.' In the back, Martin was laughing fit to burst.

'Diego, Patience and I are not getting married, at least not yet anyway. It's just Martin's way. He likes to tease me about Patience whenever he gets the chance.'

'Ah, the famous English sense of humour,' he said before starting to laugh. Great, now the two of them would be taking the piss at every opportunity.

He dropped us at the front of the hotel promising to pick us up at eleven the next morning for the trip to Port de Soller to speak to Sergio. In truth, Sergio could not say an awful lot about any abduction and so forth but he could confirm that he took us off the island on the first of July.

'I have a printer that I will bring with me,' Diego confirmed. Then, he handed me a parcel. 'Try not to lose this one,' he said dryly before driving off. I assumed that it was another hand gun but would look later.

The hotel had given us adjoining rooms on the fifth floor, I had unpacked and put my clothes away when a knock came to the door. Martin.

'Will you show me the gun Matt, and explain how it works,' he said as he came into the room. I had placed the gun, another Glock 19, bullets, spare mags and Fobus holster in the safe along with my passport. Now, I took them out, the first thing I showed him was the gun. It was unloaded, in fact, it had no magazine in. We loaded all three mags with the 9mm rounds. Then, after ensuring that the safety catch was on, I showed him how to insert a magazine and prepare to fire the gun. He handled it rather nervously and quickly passed it back to me, I removed the round from the breech and put everything away in the safe much to Martin's obvious relief. We arranged that we would go out to eat at eight that evening, Martin would give me a knock.

I read for a while then had a nap, waking at around six thirty. After phoning Patience to bring her up to date on things, apart from the gun, we chatted for a while then I went to get ready.

We left the hotel just after eight, Martin had spotted a couple of bars and restaurants as we had driven up to the hotel that afternoon so we went there to get a beer or two before eating. The first of the bars looked good, plenty of people having a drink and a good time so in we went. We sat at a table with three girls from Exeter and talked to them until they left to drink somewhere else. We found a traditional Spanish restaurant and had a good dinner. Then another drink. To my delight, Martin was chatted up by a drunken woman from, by the sound of her, Newcastle who wanted to take him back to her hotel room there and then. He tried to tell her that he was married but that made no difference to the girl whatsoever, all she wanted was sex. She realised after a couple of minutes that he was not going with her so she left and went looking for someone who would. I laughed at his discomfort, getting my own back for the teasing I had taken.

Breakfast the next morning was all right but I had to fill up with toast. Back in my room, I rang Daisy just to check in as it were. No problems back at the office which was good. I had decided to take the Glock with me, after all, I had a permit to carry the thing so I might as well use it. I had on a tee shirt so I didn't tuck it in. It was fairly long and covered the holster which was tucked down the back of my jeans in true American style. I did not tell Martin, no need to worry him.

Diego was on time but not in the Scenic as I had expected but in his wife's Seat Leon. I let Martin sit in the back of the car.

'Diego,' Martin asked when we were under way, 'Do you think we could stop for a moment at the scene of the crash if we go past it. I would like to see for myself where this affair began.'

'Of course we can stop Martin,' Diego replied. 'Matthew, you have been, I know it is on the road we have to take but you will need to tell me when to stop.' That was no problem. In due course, I directed Diego where to stop the car and the three of us got out and had a look over the edge of the cliff, each of us thinking our own thoughts. Mine was that if this had not happened, I would probably not have met Patience.

We did not linger there for too long before continuing into Port de Soller. Diego parked up and we strolled to the quayside to meet Sergio, Diego carried the printer in a holdall, Martin had his briefcase, all I had was the Glock. Sergio greeted me as an old friend.

'Matthew, good to see you again. I understand from Diego here that you gave a bit of a beating to some of that bastard Martinez's men the other day. Good for you, you are my friend for life.' Then he hugged me but stopped short of kissing my cheeks, thank goodness. These foreigners, I ask you.

Sergio led us away from the quay side to a little taverna where the owner had obviously been expecting us. Martin was able to plug in his laptop and take down the statement that Sergio was able to supply, as Sergio spoke only a little English, Diego translated for Martin. We ended up with a copy in both languages. Sergio said that he had been approached by Diego Calva and asked to take three English people, two adults and a child, out of Mallorca to the mainland because they were unable to fly as to do so would advertise their presence, which was something that they wanted to avoid at all costs.

He went on to say that he was happy to do this and we arrived at his boat on the first of July around one pm, we cast off immediately. He also recounted the story about being buzzed by a helicopter. His memory was very good and he was able to give the exact time that we landed at Canyet de Mar.

Once the statement was complete, Sergio read the Spanish version and pronounced himself happy. Martin then printed out both languages and had Sergio sign. Having completed the business, it was time to eat. A pretty waitress served us with tapas and ice cold beer, an excellent combination which we all enjoyed.

We left Sergio at three, he promised to do whatever he could if we needed any more from him, which was good of him. Diego then took us back to the hotel in Palma. On the way, we discussed the following day, Diego told us that Salma was living in an apartment that he owned, in a place called Banyalbufar, a small town on the island's west coast, not a great distance from Port de Soller actually; after the events of the first of July, Salma had stayed with him and his wife for a couple of days before she had wanted to return to the Villa Borgosa, it was the only home she knew and more or less, all her possessions were there. Neither Diego or his wife would hear of it. The enquiries he made revealed that there was nobody at the villa, they must have been chasing us around Spain so Diego and a couple of his pals took Salma back to the Villa and she was able to remove almost all her belongings. From there, they had taken her to the apartment in Banyalbufar and set her up there. Diego it seems had given her some cash to purchase the things that she needed, for example, the hair dryer she used at the Villa Borgosa belonged there. She did not want to take anything that was not hers. According to Diego, Salma was looking forward to seeing us and was keen to see Raul face the authorities to pay for what he had done.

Diego would pick us up from the hotel at the same time as he had today, eleven to go and see Salma. It was four thirty when we arrived back at our hotel, that night, Martin and I went out to eat and have a drink again. In between arriving back and going out, I again telephoned Patience, which was becoming the norm for me. Everything at home was fine, which was good news.

Chapter 32

Martin and I had breakfast together at nine in the morning and returned to our rooms to await Diego's arrival. I decided once again to take the Glock with me, I had not used the other one for anything other than to hit Raul's bad guys with and for that, I was quite grateful, carrying it though was like insurance. You rarely needed it but when you did, you were glad you had it. That had been the case on the mainland with the thugs.

When he arrived, on time, he was using the Scenic again. 'I spoke to Salma just before I left home,' he told us. 'She is looking forward to seeing us especially you Matthew and she has prepared lunch for us.' I had brought letters from Patience and Anna with some new photographs of the two of them for the old nanny.

It took us about a half hour to get to Banyalbufor. Salma's apartment was in a small block overlooking the sea. The town itself was a pleasant looking place, busy with holidaymakers as you would expect on such a lovely day however, the apartment block was just outside the town so it was much quieter. The block was three storey, Salma's flat was on the second floor.

She answered the knock to the door almost immediately, clearly, she had been waiting for us. She greeted me with a kiss to each cheek and Martin with a handshake. Before we got down to the business, I gave her the letters and photographs that I had brought. Salma, overcome with emotion, cried, we gave her time to compose herself and sat, silently. As she looked, I went to the window and took a look out, a force of habit really. A white Seat Toledo with two men inside was parked about forty yards from the entrance to the block. It had not been there when we pulled up. Interesting. I decided to keep this to myself for now and would keep an eye on the car as the afternoon wore on.

Once she was herself again, Salma poured us some home-made lemonade which was excellent. Then, Salma told her story.

'This business started several months ago,' she began, speaking in English, in a steady voice. 'Raul told me that Patience had agreed to let Anna come and stay for a week in April, I was delighted as I had not seen the child since her parents separated and they moved back to England. Without needing to be asked, I prepared a room for the child, a nice one overlooking the pool.

One afternoon however, I overheard Raul on the telephone although in truth, I could not hear everything that he said and I certainly could not hear what the other person was saying. I thought that I must be hearing things because I was sure that I heard him order a child of eight years which is Anna's age. I heard Inez coming so I left the area. Later, thinking over what I had heard, I thought that he must have been arranging a little playmate for Anna which I did think was a little strange because as far as I was aware, Anna did not speak our language. In any event, no child appeared so I thought that I was mistaken.

After Anna had been at the villa only two days, she was sent away to some friends of Raul. A Senor and Senora Hernandez who live somewhere in the north of the island but where, I have no idea. Anna did not want to go and became quite upset at the thought of going to strangers. I spoke to Raul about the matter and pointed out that Anna did not want to go and had become upset. He was not interested in her feelings and said that she would do as she was told.

He then told me that another child was coming to the villa the next day and that I was to tell no-one about this. If I mentioned it to a soul, I would be in serious trouble. Senor's, I have not lived at this villa for nearly forty years without knowing all about Raul and what he is capable of. If I had known what he was proposing to do though, I would have risked anything to alert the authorities and the hell with the consequences. At that time however, I had no suspicions about any wrongdoing and all I did wonder was why another child was coming to stay when Anna had been sent away.

Anna duly left, unhappy with the situation but I heard her father shout at her. Then this other girl arrived, a poor, underfed little thing she was too. She barely spoke and when she did, it was in a language that I had never heard before let alone understood. This child was afraid, afraid of everything, her surroundings, me but especially Raul and Inez.

Then, a day later, Inez took the child out in a car, an old BMW as far as I can remember. I don't know where the car came from but I had never seen it before. Inez did not return that day but came back the next day with Raul.

There was no sign of the child, I tried to ask Raul but instead of answering my question, they took me into, er what is the English? I am sorry, I do not know so I will have to use the Spanish, el salon, and told me to sit down. Raul then told me a story that chilled me to the bone and made me wish that I had not been born. What he said was this.

The car that Inez had been driving, the old BMW, had gone off the road on the way to Port de Soller the previous afternoon and had caught fire. I looked across at Inez but she just sat there, emotionless. As I said, the car caught fire and the little foreign girl had burned to death in the flames. He then said that the body had been burned beyond recognition. I was shocked and tried to speak but he would not let me. He went on to say that he had telephoned to Patience at her home in England and had told her about the crash and that he had said that it had been Anna who had died.

I was astounded and managed to ask him what he was playing at. He told me that it really was very simple, he wanted Anna to live with him and that he had arranged the crash so as to make everybody believe that it was Anna who had died.

He then said that Patience and her parents were coming to Mallorca for the cremation, a cremation that they thought was their Anna. I began to bluster, I said that Anna was not dead, that she was with the family in the north, that was when he became angry saying that I know that you old fool but if I were to speak out about what I knew, he would kill me. Then he said that if Patience found out from me about this, he would not only kill me but that he would kill her too. I believed him. Whilst I did not want to, I was afraid therefore I had no choice other than to go along with his scheme. I did so want to speak out but I dared not, he told me that Inez would be watching me all the time. Eventually I decided that I could not say anything as I was afraid for Patience.

When she and her parents arrived, I made myself scarce having decided that if I could not tell her what had happened, I would not speak to her at all. I hoped that if I did not speak to her, she would wonder why not and I hoped that she would suspect that something was amiss and try to find out what was going on.

I was right, she did as was proven when she and Matthew appeared at the market in Santa Ponsa to rescue Anna from her father.' She paused and poured more lemonade for all of us.

'After you left Santa Ponsa with Anna that Monday, I waited over an hour before going back to the villa to report Anna missing to Raul. His attitude was strange, he was far too calm as I told him my tale. Then he said something that scared me to my bones, he said Patience had been in Mallorca, he said that a friend of his, Rodrigo de la Pena had seen Anna and her mother on a boat leaving Port de Soller. He wanted to know where the boat was going but I said that I did not know, he then had Inez twist my arm up my back as he asked once again where the boat was going. Of course I could not tell him as I did not know, you did not tell me Matthew.' That was true, I never said anything. I felt awful that this old lady had been hurt because I had not given her some information.

'They began on the telephone, calling people before Raul had me locked up in my room. A little while later, I heard them leave, once they had gone, I tried to break out of my room. I looked out of the window, I was on the first floor and I admit that I was afraid to jump, it would have been no use to Patience if I was lying in the garden with a broken leg, my phone was in my bag in the villa. So I had really no choice, it had to be the door. It took ages but I got through and phoned Senor Calva with the news. And that Senor is all I can tell you.' It was more than enough for our purposes which was to have Raul Martinez locked up.

Martin completed the statement in both English and Spanish, printed the two off and had Salma sign the Spanish copy. Once this had been done, Salma went to the kitchen to get the lunch she had prepared for us. As we ate, she asked how Anna and Patience were coping, the letters had been good but she wanted to know properly. Martin was quick to suggest that she ask me for any news on Patience. Salma eyed me speculatively.

'Are you and Patience romantically involved?' she asked me. I was amused at her choice of words.

'Yes, I suppose we are,' I admitted. 'We only met through this unfortunate business and were introduced by Martin here. We began to see each other just before I came to the island, continued when Patience joined me and since we have been back in England, our relationship has grown considerably.'

'Is Anna comfortable with it?'

'Yes, I think she is. She does seem to like me and I like her too, very much.'

'That is good, I wish you much happiness. Tell me one thing please Matthew, do you think that one day, when this business has been resolved, Patience and Anna, and you too of course, will come back to Mallorca. I would very much like to see them in what would be normal circumstances.'

'I think I can speak for Patience and say that your help was invaluable to us and I am sure that coming here to see you would only be a pleasure for both of them. It would certainly be a pleasure for me.' She looked pleased by my words.

As we made our preparations to leave, I casually walked to the window and took a look out. The same Seat was parked in the same place with the same two men in it. Time to tell the others.

'Gentlemen, we may have a problem.' That got their attention. 'When we came into the apartment, you may remember that I took a look out of the window. A white Seat was parked about forty yards down the road from the entrance to the apartments, it had two men inside. The thing is, it was not there when we pulled up outside.

We have been here now for well over two hours and the car is still there, it is too much of a coincidence and I for one do not like coincidences.' Diego looked for himself.

'They could be Raul's people. What are we going to do?' They all looked at me.

'I guess they must have followed us, probably looking for Salma.'

'I have been watching for a tail since you left, I never saw them. They are either very good or they got lucky.'

'Well whatever, they are here now. It's my belief that they know you Diego but don't know who Martin and I am though they may have suspicions about me.

What I propose we do is this, we three leave as normal, we get into the Scenic and drive off. Diego, you stop just round that corner and one of two things will happen. They will either come round after us in a matter of seconds or if not, then it is Salma they want. For my money Salma, it is you. Now Salma, will you help us to catch these people, find out who they are working for and what they are up to?'

'Yes I will Matthew. What do you want me to do?'

'Thank you Salma. What we will do is this, we will go out and drive round the corner. We must give them time to get to your door but they will. It's not a big block, all they need to do is knock on a few doors and ask where the three men went, we saw one or two people as we came in so someone will have seen us come here and tell them in all innocence.

Anyway, when they knock at our door, shout to them that you will be there in a minute, count to a hundred then open the door. That will give us time to park round the corner and get back here. Is that all right?' She had a determined look on her face.

'It is fine, I am ready to help.' With that, we left the apartment. I reminded the others not to look at the Seat as we made our way to the Scenic. I got into the front, Martin the back and Diego behind the wheel. When he was ready, he started the car and drove off. He stopped round the corner and turned off the engine. We listened and faintly heard the sound of two car doors slamming. I had been right, it was Salma they were after. It could only mean Raul. Diego made to get out but I stopped him.

'Leave it a moment. They need to find the right apartment.' He stopped. I kept my eye on my watch, timing was critical. After five minutes I was ready.

'Let's go.' I was half out of the door when I spoke. I quickly sprinted round the corner back to the entrance to the block. Once through the door, I drew the Glock from the holster and quietly made my way up the stairs to Salma's apartment. The two men were at the door which I think she had just opened.

'You will come with us woman, Raul Martinez wants you.' That said, one tried to grab Salma by the arm but before he could I was across the gap and smacked him across the back of his head with the Glock, hard enough to knock him out. Before the other one could react, I stuck the Glock under his nose, hard and growled at him to be quiet. He may have not understood English but my meaning was clear enough. Then I motioned with the gun for him to get his hands up and again, he understood me. Seconds later, Martin and Diego arrived, I passed the Glock to Diego.

'Get this one inside,' I said to him, he did. 'Help me with this one,' I instructed Martin. Between us, we picked the unconscious thug up each taking an arm and dragged him inside. Salma closed the door behind us. Martin and I dropped our thug on the floor. Then, I took the gun back from Diego. Then I asked him to tell the conscious thug to lie face down on the floor, which he did. When the thug was lying down, I crouched at the side of him and as he looked at me, I lightly tapped his forehead with the Glock.

'We need to know who he is working for Diego and whoever it is, has he recently reported in.' Diego questioned the thug in rapid Spanish. I managed to pick out the words 'Raul Martinez' as the thug answered. Just as I thought.

'Right,' said Diego when our captive had finished speaking. 'As we suspected, these guys are working for Raul. They have been trying to find Salma for a couple of weeks. Yesterday, Raul told these two to follow me in the hope that I would lead them to Salma, and stupid person that I am, I have led them right to her.

They reported back to Raul as soon as we arrived that we had pulled up here. The order they received was to wait until we had left then check out the apartments in case Salma lived here and if they found her they were to take her to him. At least they have not reported that they have found her yet.' The lout that I had hit began to groan as he came round so I hit him again. Martin looked at me, I could tell that he was not too happy.

'Don't worry mate, we need to keep him docile until we can get this one tied up, I will not hurt him too much unless he tries to escape or he asks for it. He by the way, tried to grab Salma just as I got here, he would not hesitate to hurt her so don't waste any sympathy on him.'

'No, I guess I won't, it's just that I don't see this side of things normally.' Diego nipped back to his car where he had some rope, when he returned, he tied up our conscious guest before moving on to the second one. Once they were bound, I put the Glock away, much to Martin's relief.

'I hadn't armed it and the safety was on all the time, I was not going to shoot them.'

'What if they were armed?' he asked.

'That would have been different but as they are not, it makes no difference,' Then Diego produced his own Glock.

'If they had been armed, we could have dealt with the situation.'

The question we now had to answer was what to do with these two. Diego had a brainwave and phoned Sergio, the conversation, in Spanish of course, was brief.

'Sergio, his son and a couple of his friends are going to drive down. They will take these two back up the coast and keep them safe until this matter is over. Once their employer is in custody, he will release them. A good plan, no?' Yes it was. It solved the problem nicely though I suspected that our bound friends might not go free however, I kept that thought to myself.

It took Sergio and his merry men an hour to arrive at the apartments. His son I recognised as being with him on the Sunseeker when we left Majorca on the first of July.

'Ah, Rodrigo de la Pena,' he said when he saw the two thugs. It was a name I recognised, the guy who had seen Patience on Sergio's boat and told Raul.

'When are we going to move these guys out of here?' I asked Diego. He conferred with Sergio and his team then turned to me.

'It is quiet outside at the moment, we will take them to Sergio's van now. With you, Martin and I, we are seven. That will be enough to walk to the van without attracting attention.'

We left Salma packing a few things to take with her as she could not stay here now with Raul on the lookout for her. She was someone else who would be able to settle back to a life of normality when this business was finally over.

Before we moved out, Sergio searched the two men, he was looking for the keys to their Seat which he gave to his son when he found them. His lad would drive the Seat, Sergio his van with his men watching over the luckless thugs.

Fortunately for us, it was quiet outside when we moved out. We quickly had the thugs in the van which moved off straight away. In a short time, Sergio's son, Ramon, had the Seat heading after his father's van. Diego went for the Scenic and Martin and I went back in to get Salma and her things. Diego would once again take her back to his place until it was safe to return to the apartment.

As we drove, he spoke to his wife to tell her about the guest, we all ended up back at his place for dinner after which he said, he would run us back to our hotel in Palma.

Diego rang Henry when he got in, then Martin spoke with him before passing the phone to me.

'Hello Henry,' I said.

'Matthew, an exciting afternoon by all accounts.'

'Rather, however as you now know, it was all worthwhile as Salma provided us with a great amount of detail which is ideal for our purposes.' I could hear a noise in the background, down the phone line and did not need to guess who it was.

'Matthew, is everything all right? I heard my father mention a gun or two.'

'Yes love, everything is fine. Two of Raul's goons followed Diego, they wanted to find Salma. I saw them and we set a little trap for them which they kindly walked into. One of them was the guy who saw you on Sergio's boat and told Raul so it was his fault that we had the traumatic trip through Spain.'

'As long as everything is okay.' I assured her that it was then went on to tell her about the evidence Salma had provided us.

After a good meal and conversation where I again had to run through my relationship with Patience, this time for Diego's wife, Diego ran us back to Palma and the hotel. As we had eaten and had a drink, neither Martin nor I wanted to go out again and we retired to our respective rooms for the night.

I rang Patience again, this time we could talk without anyone listening at least to one side of our conversation.

Chapter 33

We had nothing to do Thursday morning as our appointment with Senor Almunia was not until three pm. Diego was going to meet us at the hotel at two and come with us.

After breakfast, Martin and I went out for a walk. I kept a careful eye open but saw nothing that caused me any alarm. We ended up after half an hour or so, in a nice shopping centre. Later on, I had the thought that Martin had somehow steered me here on purpose because when we arrived, he suggested a present for Patience and Anna. A good idea but what did one buy the daughter of a multi-millionaire?

'What it is makes no difference,' he said in answer to my question. 'What matters is that it is from you.' A fair point. After wandering around the place for an hour or so, I settled on a gold chain for Patience and a smaller, matching one for Anna.

We had some lunch before heading back to the hotel to change into suits for the meeting. Diego was on time as always and we sat in the lobby and Martin took a statement from Diego which detailed his involvement in the affair before Diego led us round to the Ministry of Justice. Martin had his briefcase with him with all the documents which was searched at the door, as we had expected. I had left the gun in the safe. Then we were taken to the third floor and shown to a waiting room where we had a five minute wait before we were shown into the office of Senor Almunia.

The good Senor rose from behind his desk and introduced himself to us. His English was good though we did have Diego with us to translate. He was a tall man aged about fifty. His hair, of which he had a full head, was grey and well cut, his suit was a tasteful blue pinstripe which he wore with a white shirt and blue tie. My first impression was that he was a smart, able looking man. He was not alone and introduced the three other people who were in the office with him. His deputy, Julio Romero and two others whose titles I did not get, a Senor Juan-Carlos Garcia and a Senora Consuela Banderas. Almunia incidentally was called Francisco and he explained that the others were his team and as we had said that this was a very delicate matter, he had wanted his team with him which, as far as I was concerned, was fine. The good thing was that the other three also spoke good English which would save time.

Martin performed the introductions on our part, we had decided prior to coming that we would leave the talking to Martin unless something was needed in Spanish when Diego would deal with any translations. If Martin needed me to clarify any points then he would ask, if not, I was to keep quiet.

He began by thanking Senor Almunia and his team for their time and promised not to take up any more of it than was absolutely necessary. Almunia nodded his head in acknowledgement.

'The story I am about to tell you is so fantastic that you may well have some difficulty in believing it however, everything that I am about to say is backed up with hard evidence. Firstly though, and for background, I am a lawyer practising in the English city of Greenfield, Mr Bentley is a private investigator working out of that city and who does a lot of work for me. Senor Calva is a resident of this beautiful island and has been of great and invaluable help to us in this matter, he is an old friend of my client.

Now to the facts. Let me show you a police report compiled, in good faith, by the police in Inca. I am sorry that I have only the one copy, had I known I would have prepared more. This report relates to a car accident which took place on the twenty seventh day of April of this year and refers to a BMW motor car which left the road in the hills above the town of Port de Soller. The car had been travelling from Santa Ponsa to Port de Soller and contained the driver, Inez Castillar and a passenger, an eight year old girl who was alleged to be Anna Martinez, the daughter and granddaughter of my clients. I say alleged for a reason which will be clear in moment so I ask you to bear with me.' Martin continued with his story, I sat quietly and watched the Spanish people. All were paying close attention to what they were being told.

'It was alleged that the child was Anna Martinez, the daughter of divorced parents, Patience Jameson of Greenfield, England and Raul Martinez of Santa Ponsa.' At the mention of Raul's name, the four people exchanged a glance. Martin either did not notice or more likely, chose to ignore it and carried on. 'My client was married to Senor Martinez but divorced him a few years ago, I represented her and presented the case in the Greenfield County Court in England where she was granted a decree absolute. In the course of those proceedings, my client was granted daily care and control of the child Anna with reasonable contact awarded to Senor

Martinez. Over the next few years, Senor Martinez visited his daughter in England two or three times a year.

In February of this year, Martinez asked his former wife if it would be possible for Anna to come to his home for a week during her school holidays.

After careful deliberation, my client decided to allow the visit to go ahead. The necessary permission was obtained from the Greenfield County Court and Anna duly came to this beautiful island.

When Anna had been here a day or two, Senorita Castillar allegedly took her for a drive intending to visit Port de Soller which is a lovely part of the island. That they never arrived is well documented as the car left the road and burst into flames. In the report compiled by the police from Inca, you will see a statement from a young couple, Senor and Senora Alves who stopped at the side of the road when they came upon a clearly distraught Senorita Castillar, indeed it was this Senor Alves who telephoned the emergency services. As I have said, the body of the child was eventually brought up.

As is normal, Senorita Castillar was given a breathalyser test at the scene, this proved to be negative. Also, there was no indication that she had been going too fast or driving recklessly. After fainting, she was taken to hospital in Inca and kept there overnight for observation. During the course of the evening, the police attended the hospital to take a statement from her. When they arrived, Senor Martinez was there too, he volunteered a statement, both are here for you to read. Both of them confirmed that the passenger in the car was Anna Martinez. With this positive identification and no suspicion of foul play, the police were satisfied and a death certificate was issued in the name of Anna Martinez and there is a copy of that certificate here for you.

Now, you may think this is satisfactory so why is the mad Englishman bothering us with this and what is delicate about it, a tragic accident, nothing more.' No-one spoke, Martin had their full attention. You could have heard a pin drop. 'I am here Senora and Senors because things are not quite what they seem. As I said, I am the lawyer for Patience Jameson formerly Martinez and her family. When they came here for the cremation, something happened which made Patience suspicious, something that made her think that perhaps, her daughter was not really dead.

In the weeks immediately following her return from the cremation, Patience had a strong feeling that all was not well. She discussed her feeling with her father who in turn discussed it with me. We could not approach you, the authorities, with the feelings of a mother. What was needed was some solid evidence which is where Mr Bentley comes in. He came to Santa Ponsa to look for Anna as we could not act upon the whim of a mother.

What Mr Bentley found in Santa Ponsa was Anna Martinez, alive and well.' Martin could not have dropped a bigger bombshell on the meeting even if he had stripped off. All four Spaniards began to talk at once, in their own language of course so I could not understand a word. Eventually, Almunia called for quiet.

'What proof do you have that Anna is alive and well,' was all he said. Martin delved once again into his open briefcase and removed some photographs which he passed to Almunia.

'These photographs were taken in Santa Ponsa by Mr Bentley. On the prints you will see the time and date, a facility available courtesy of Nikon. All the photographs are exhibited in the notarised affidavit of Mr Bentley. The first pictures are taken on the seventeenth of June of this year some seven or so weeks after Senor Martinez gave a statement to say that Anna was the passenger in the car which crashed on the road to Port de Soller, they were taken when the child accompanied Salma Guttierez to the local market.

The last of the pictures is one of Anna taken in March of this year and is there for you to compare to those of Mr Bentley. This I would say is conclusive proof that Anna Martinez is alive and well.

In some of the photographs, you will see Anna with an elderly lady. As I mentioned just now, she is Salma Guttierez who has been employed by the Martinez family for a great many years, She is totally innocent of any wrongdoing in this matter. She acted as nanny for Raul and his sisters Maria and Esther as they grew up, when my client married Raul, Salma was still resident at the Villa Borgosa and the two women became firm friends. When my client became pregnant, the nanny came into her own once again and when the child was born, the nanny was devoted to her.

On the twenty fourth of June, Anna again went to market with Salma, and they again went one week later, the first of July. In the market, my client approached her daughter who was overjoyed to see her mother again. Senora Guttierez was aware of my client and made no protest when my client said that she was taking her daughter back to England, in fact, she was highly delighted as it had been she who had put the seeds of doubt that Anna was dead into the mind of my client.

Being aware of the type of man that Raul Martinez is, Mr Bentley felt that it would be unsafe to try to travel back to England by conventional methods so they left Mallorca by sea from, coincidently, Port de Soller and landed on the mainland just north of Barcelona. From there, they intended to take the train to Paris and from there, fly on to England. As it happened, Raul Martinez became aware that they had left by sea therefore they had to revise their plans and hired a car and drove south, to Faro in Portugal and from there, flew back to England.

When Salma reported back to Raul, he was already aware that Anna had gone with her mother and both he and Inez Castillar assaulted the old lady, she was then locked in a room. She was able to eventually get free and alert Senor Calva who in turn alerted Mr Bentley.

At the railway station in Barcelona, men acting under the orders of Raul Martinez grabbed both my client and her daughter as Mr Bentley purchased tickets for the journey to Paris, luckily, Mr Bentley was able to effect a rescue and they left Barcelona by bus. Another attempt to grab the two women was made and again thwarted by Mr Bentley before they made it first to Faro and then back to England.

Here are notarised affidavits from both Mr Bentley and Patience Jameson, signed statements from Salma Guttierez, Sergio Bosko and Diego Calva. From the evidence before you, you will see that Raul Martinez and Inez Castillar kidnapped Anna Martinez, murdered an unknown child, falsified statements to the police, assaulted Senora Guttierez and tried again to kidnap Anna and her mother.

While Raul Martinez is at liberty, Patience Jameson and Anna Martinez will not be safe.' Martin had been pacing as he had spoken, now, he sat down. All four of the Spaniards were speaking at the same time once again and again Almunia had to call for silence. He picked up a telephone and spoke rapidly into it. Diego quietly translated for us. Almunia issued orders to the Palma police to immediately arrest Raul and Inez, that was great news, the good Senor had acted immediately. I expected that he would want time to review the documents and speak to his team.

'Senor Keogh, I am grateful to you for bringing this matter to my attention, I cannot say how badly I feel about what has happened but now, I am able to do something about it. Tell me, how long will you and Senor Bentley remain in Mallorca?'

'As long as we are needed, we will be happy to stay here,' Martin replied. When he looked at me, I nodded. Almunia took details of where we were staying and told us that he would visit us at the hotel around noon the next day.

I was surprised to see that it was almost seven thirty when we left the Ministry, how time flies when you are having fun. Diego left to go home, Martin and I went back and changed into casual clothes and went out to eat and get a couple of beers. While I changed, I phoned Patience to give her the news, she was of course delighted and now could see an end to the nightmare that she had been living since the end of April.

Chapter 34

Raul and Inez were enjoying a quiet drink at the Villa Borgosa. It was almost nine pm when the doorbell sounded. On the way from Palma, the police had worked out their tactics, normally, they would have smashed the door in and charged in looking for people. In this instance, they had decided to adopt a softly, softly approach. While several officers waited at the front, more made their way round the back. On a pre-arranged signal, one of the policemen rang the bell.

The couple inside the villa had been discussing the situation in general terms. In truth, following the failed attempt to prevent Patience and Anna escaping to England, they had both been rather afraid, expecting the police to turn up at the door at any time. However, as the days passed with nothing happening, Raul's confidence returned.

'I told you Inez, Patience would not go to the police. She will be happy to have Anna back and will not have the nerve to take things further, if she had, do you not think the police would have been here.'

'You are right my love, if they were coming, they would have been here by now. One thing does puzzle me though and that is since that call from Rodrigo in Banyalbufor where they had followed Calva, we have not heard from him. And, who were the two men with him.'

'Yes, that does puzzle me too. I have tried Rodrigo several times and he has not answered. I expect that it was a wild goose chase and he is still following Calva about trying to find Guttierez. I wondered if one of those other two men could have been this hired thug Bentley. I will ring Carlos at the airport in the morning and have him check back over the past few days on names arriving at the airport. Who can this be at this time?'

'I will get the door,' Inez said rising from her seat and leaving the room. She was back moments later with her hands in the air, followed by several heavily armed policemen, some had side arms, others Heckler and Koch machine pistols, whatever arms the police had, they were all pointed at Raul and Inez.

'On the floor, the pair of you,' the policeman in charge ordered. When the two of them were face down, they had their arms pulled behind them and handcuffs placed on, none to gently before they were expertly searched. 'Raul

Martinez and Inez Castillar, you are under arrest for the kidnap of Anna Martinez and the murder of an as yet unknown child. Take them out.'

As they were led out, Raul looked stunned but Inez was crying. They were taken to the police cars and pushed into the back of separate vehicles for the journey to the police station.

As the car drove off, Raul realised that Patience had surprised him once again, this was in fact the third time, the first was that she had the nerve to come to his island and take his daughter away. Then, with help from this Bentley, had fooled him and lost him at Barcelona and had managed to keep one step ahead all the time. Now this, how could this be? Someone must have put her up to it, he thought. It did not occur to him that Patience was perfectly able to think for herself and like almost any mother anywhere, would fight tooth and nail for her child. He had seriously underestimated his ex-wife.

As the car drove along he became more sure of himself. He had been arrested several times before and they had never made anything stick, why should now be any different, it was her word against his.

Then Raul received another surprise as the cars headed not for the local police station but for Palma. He had been sure that Caldano would have approved bail but now, he didn't know what was going on.

Once they arrived at police headquarters, he was told to remove his clothes and was given a paper suit to wear, then he was thrown into a cell. Down the corridor the same thing happened to Inez. It was now ten pm.

At midnight, Raul was taken to an interrogation room and formally charged with the kidnapping of Anna and the murder of an unknown person. The same happened to Inez in another room. They were told that they would be brought before a court in the morning and remanded in custody to await further charges. Then came two hours of intense questioning.

Both the prisoners were returned to their cells within ten minutes of each other. Inez managed to drop off to sleep but was awakened and taken back to the interrogation room at around four thirty. The questioning went on for an hour before she was taken back to her cell. They came again at nine.

The same thing was happening to Raul but neither of them talked.

Chapter 35

Martin and I hung around the hotel on the Friday morning after breakfast. Almunia was not due until noon but neither of us felt like doing anything. When he arrived, Almunia confirmed that both Raul and Inez had been arrested and taken before the court that morning and had been remanded in custody, Raul was sent to the island's prison, Inez kept at Palma police HQ.

'After the arrest, both were questioned at length by my officers, as yet, neither had said anything. A thorough search of the Villa Borgosa has been made and we have made some interesting finds. Some clothing which we are sure did not belong to Anna has been discovered, it had been put out to be burned but Raul had not yet got around to it, which is a break for us.

We also found a telephone number which one of my officers recognised as being a Naples number. At a civilised hour, I rang an Italian contact of mine who recognised the number as being that of a mafia man whose speciality is to provide young girls at a price. As we speak, he is being interviewed by the Naples police, I will keep you advised on developments from that front.

As a result of this, I got a warrant and we inspected the bank account of Senor Martinez. It seems that he drew out forty thousand euros on the fourteenth of April and he and Castillar took a road trip the following day, they went to Naples. What we think, and I am sure that the proof will be available soon is that the two of them drove to Naples and purchased a child from the mafia. They returned to Mallorca and kept the child hidden until it was time for her to take the place of Anna and die in the crash.' I was sickened, as was Martin. The poor kid. 'Raul denied the whole thing of course and actually tried to accuse your client of kidnapping Anna. Inez too denied everything but my chief interrogator believes she will crack under pressure and give the two of them away.' He paused as his telephone rang, which he answered. When he finished, he was smiling.

'Castillar has just come from yet another session in the interrogation room. This time, we were able to put to her the details of the case and the trip to Naples. This information turned her and she told the whole tale. They did buy a child, a Kosovan, from Naples though she is not able to furnish us with a name, they never bothered to ask.

You will not be surprised to know that it was all the idea of Raul, he came up with the plan, acquired the old BMW and found the location for the crash.

We need to bring them before the court again on Monday. By then, I am sure we will have more charges to bring. I would like you two to stay and attend court on Monday.'

Martin answered for the two of us telling him that we would both be happy to stay over the weekend and assist wherever we could. Almunia promised to send a car for us on Monday to take us to court.

Once he had left us, we sat and talked about it. It did seem that Almunia's team would have enough evidence to put Raul and Inez away for a long time. Good. I then rang Diego to bring him up to date with the news, he too was very pleased at the way things were going. Then I rang Patience to tell her what was happening. She listened in silence as I spoke. When I had finished, she began to cry but this time with relief as the nightmare was almost over.

'It is incredible love, how could I be married to a man like that? I suspected he was sometimes up to no good but something like this. It is beyond belief.

That poor child, please try to find out who she was Matthew then we can make sure her parents are notified, unless they know and sold her in the first place. What a world. When are you coming home, I need to be with you Matthew, more than ever.'

'We have to be here until Monday to speak with the prosecutors at court but after that, I can't see any reason that we would need to hang on here any longer so I hope Wednesday at the latest. I can't wait to see you and Anna again,' I said, meaning every word. We continued to talk for a little while then her father must have come in so we ended our call so that Patience could bring him up to date with all the developments there had been.

Chapter 36

The weekend dragged by for both Martin and I, it was something of an anti-climax after the rigours of the past few days. Fortunately, the weather was good and we were able to get out for walks one of which took us down to the marina. Martin it seemed quite fancied a boat so we had a potter round looking at them and at the ones for sale. Quite a lot were beyond his financial reach and a lot would have been beyond Henry, even with his money.

We spent some time by the hotel pool, reading in the sunshine which was good, I always enjoyed my reading especially in such plush surroundings. That too began to drag, Martin was of course missing his wife and kids and I was missing Patience and Anna. We went out to eat and drink each night, and to be honest, a few beers helped.

Each night I rang Patience and received calls from her during the day. The calls made me miss her even more, the sooner I was home, the better.

Eventually, Monday arrived. After breakfast, we got ready for our trip to court. The car we were promised arrived at ten thirty. Almunia had sent Senora Banderas with the car to prove it was from him. Though the good lady spoke English, she, after greeting us and enquiring after our health, said little else on the way to court, which only took ten minutes as it happened, We followed the good Senora into the building and to the court allocated for the hearing. Several people milled about but Almunia was there waiting for us, his face grave. After shaking hands, he took us to an empty room and made us sit down before he spoke.

'Gentlemen,' he began. 'I have news. You will recall that I said on Friday that Martinez had been sent to the island's prison.' We did, both of us nodded. 'On Saturday,' he continued, 'at about two thirty in the afternoon, Raul Martinez was stabbed in the stomach by another inmate. He received three stab wounds to the stomach and was taken to hospital where he died yesterday at three am.

He was unconscious most of the time but did regain consciousness briefly, it was clear to the doctors treating him that he would not survive so a priest was called to administer the last rites. He only said one thing before he died and that was that he loved his daughter.

We of course do have the man who killed him, he was already there obviously. His name is Miguel Romero. It seems that Romero was once part of the Martinez criminal gang and took the rap, if you will forgive my slang terms, for Martinez in respect of a drugs charge some three years ago. Martinez promised him that if he did take the blame then he, Martinez, would take care of the wife and children of this Romero. On that understanding, Romero took the five years for his boss.

Then, Martinez reneged on his promise to look after the family, as a result, Senora Romero and her two small children were thrown out of their home. Senora Romero even went to Raul to beg for the help he had promised but he had her removed from his villa so they were effectively on the street. As a direct result of this situation, Romero's little son Alvaro one day wandered away from his mother's grasp and was knocked down and killed. Romero naturally blamed Raul and swore to have his revenge. When he saw his former boss in prison, he realised that this might well be his only chance to avenge little Alvaro. Somehow, he managed to get hold of a knife and waited his moment. It came at exercise, he approached Martinez and plunged the blade three times into Martinez before anyone realised what was happening and could drag him away. He will be charged with the murder in due course.

This is not the end of our case however, we still have Castillar who, on receipt of the news of her lover's death, told us everything. She will plead culpable, which I think is guilty where you come from, that will be the end of the matter for you gentlemen. For us however, it is just the beginning. We will jail Castillar as a warning to anyone else that crime does not pay and with the help of our Italian friends will try to smash the slavery ring that has come to light.

I would appreciate it if you would come into court. If she does plead guilty she will be remanded in custody and that will be the end of it for you. If not, and one does not know until the plea is made, then the prosecutors will want to speak to you both.'

We sat in the back of the court. It was a bit of a stunner that it had ended this way. For the life of me, I had not seen this coming. I could not though feel any pity for Raul Martinez, he got what he deserved the evil bastard. The blood of two young children was on his hands and goodness knows what other blood was there too. Still, if he had not done what he did, I might not have met Patience so in one respect, he did me a good turn.

I did not relish the thought of telling Anna though, he was still her father whatever else he was. That would have to be a job for Patience though I would be with her when she told her daughter, if she wanted me to.

The case was called at eleven thirty. Inez, looking pale and not so attractive any more was brought in. The proceedings of course were conducted in Spanish, she spoke only to confirm her name and address and say 'Culpable' before she was removed. That was it, we could go home.

Outside, Almunia came over to us. 'As you know, she pleaded guilty to the charges. A date for sentencing will be set and I will let you know when this is Senor Keogh. I do not know if you or your client will wish to attend but if you do, you will be most welcome. All that remains for me is to thank you both for your very considerable help in bringing this matter to my attention. If I can ever be of service to you in the future, please do not hesitate to contact me.' He shook hands with us and left us alone.

We were just about to leave the building when two ladies approached us. I had seen them in court but had thought nothing of it.

'Are you gentlemen from England?' one of them asked, hesitantly, 'And if so have you had anything to do with the case against Inez Castillar that has just finished?'

'We have had some dealings with the case,' Martin replied cautiously. 'Would you mind telling me who you are?' he asked.

'My name is Maria Garcia and this is my sister, Esther Jiminez.' I butted in.

'Maria and Esther, are you the sisters of Raul Martinez?'

'We are Senor, may we speak to you for a moment?' I nodded and led them and Martin over to the refreshment room, invited them to sit down and left them with Martin while I went and bought four soft drinks. It appeared that nothing had been said while I was at the counter.

'Do you know Patience Jameson and if so, will you be speaking to her at all?' Maria asked.

'I am her lawyer and will speak to her sometime in the next few days. Matthew here is rather closer to her than I am and I am sure that he will be speaking to her very soon.'

'Ah, you are the partner of Patience, that is good Senor. Would you please tell her from the two of us that we are horrified at what our brother has done. To separate Anna from her mother was an act of unspeakable cruelty, despite him being our brother, we are both distressed by his actions and hope that Patience and Anna will be able to get over their ordeal very soon.

We cannot understand why this happened unless Raul was influenced by Inez but I do not think so. She wanted her own child, not another woman's.

Raul was stupid, Patience allowed him as much time with Anna as he required and of course, she had just allowed Anna to come here. If he had behaved properly, he could have had her to stay many more times so I am at a loss to understand why they did this terrible thing. Both Esther and I are just pleased that our parents are no longer alive to witness this.

After Patience had gone back to England, after the cremation, Raul told us that Anna was alive and well and that the whole cremation had been the idea of Patience who found Anna too much of a handful and wanted time to herself to see as many men as she wanted, and that she had begged Raul to help her out.' The shock must have shown on my face as Maria continued quickly. 'Senor, please believe me, neither Esther or I believed what he had said, not only do we both know Patience well, but we had seen how devastated she was when she thought that Anna had died. But what could we do? He forbade us to contact Patience and, I am ashamed to say, that the two of us are, or at least were, very frightened of him so our hands were tied.

We are also at a loss to understand what they did to that poor Kosovan child who was in the car. Was she dead when Inez let the car slip off the road? We shall never know the answer to that. As I said, I am glad our parents are not alive to see this.

It also seems that our brother had a life of crime, we did not know this for sure but both our husbands were suspicious of Raul but like us, they were afraid to get on the wrong side of him. Naturally, he never shared that information with us, nor I am sure did he share it with Patience when they were married. Well, he has paid for his life of crime now and that is another thing, that poor little boy, Alvaro, another innocent child the victim of our brother.

I cannot condone murder but I do understand why that man killed him.

Please pass on to Patience the sincere apologies of Esther and myself and tell her that if she ever wants to speak to either of us again, we will be more than happy to do so. We will pray for her and Anna and hope that we can still be friends.'

'Thank you for that. I do know that Patience in no way attaches any blame for this situation on either of you. When she has spoken to me of you, she speaks fondly, I think that her happiest memories of her time here were of the three of you.'

Maria smiled, sadly. 'One last thing Senor, Salma Guttierez, poor Salma. She still has some things in the Villa as for many years, that was her home. If she would get in touch with either of us, we will arrange for her to get the rest of her belongings from the villa. Here is my number for you to give her, I am sure you will be able to contact her. She was our nanny too.' There was nothing more to be said so they left.

'Well,' said Martin after they had gone. 'I did not think that they would have had any part in this business so I am pleased that they came over. It just clears things up.'

'True mate. I don't think Patience will want to come here for the sentence, if she does, I will talk her out of it. Best to let it lie now and get on with her life.'

'I agree. Let's go back to the hotel and while I try to sort out a flight home, you can ring Diego and bring him up to date and also give him Maria's number so that he can pass it on the Salma.'

Martin was able to secure seats for us on the two pm flight to Manchester the next day, I couldn't wait, nor I suspect, could Martin.

Then I phoned Patience to tell her that it was all over though I did not mention Raul's death over the telephone, news like that could wait until I was with her. She wanted me to come straight round and I was happy to agree. Diego invited us to have dinner with him and his wife that night and we were happy to accept. Again, Diego had proved very helpful whilst I had been in Majorca, and this time, I was able to return his Glock safely to him.

As we left, he wished Patience and I all the luck in the world, convinced that we were made for each other and wanted me to come for a holiday with the Jameson family as it had been too long since he had seen them. Not a bad idea now that the island was safe once more.

Chapter 37

At last it was time to go to the airport. Diego had wanted to drive us there but we had not wanted to put him out, after all, he had done loads for us already so we persuaded him to let us take a taxi.

The flight back to Manchester was boring with both Martin and I wanting it to arrive sooner rather than later. Eventually, it did. Then we had the drive back to Greenfield, the roads were always busy and today was no exception so it wasn't until just before six that Martin dropped me off. Pausing only to take the two gold chains from my case, I jumped in the Audi and headed out to Little Thornley arriving at six fifty.

I phoned Patience from the car when I was a few minutes away and when I arrived, the gate was open, Michael was waiting beside it. When I went through, he closed it and disappeared to wherever it was that he went.

Anna rushed out to greet me followed by her mother, it was clear that I had been missed. Inside, I received a third kiss from a Jameson woman, Suzanne of course, fortunately, Henry simply shook my hand.

'Is it really over Matthew?' Patience asked me as she hugged me in the hallway of her home.

'Yes, it really is over.' I was happy to say.

Once we were seated, I gave Anna her chain which she loved, putting it on straight away. Patience I knew did not have one so she too was delighted with hers. Then I looked directly at Patience then glanced at Anna who was busy showing her grandmother her new chain. Patience understood right away and asked Anna to pop up to her room while I talked business with her grandfather. On her way out, Anna hugged me once again and thanked me for the chain.

As soon as she had gone, Patience spoke up. 'Something is wrong Matthew, what is it, are you okay?' Suzanne and Henry looked at me, concern on their faces.

'I am fine, really. Come and sit down.' I took Patience by the hand and led her to one of the sofas, Henry and Suzanne sat on one of the others. I kept hold of her hand as I began to speak.

'On Saturday, Raul was stabbed three times in the stomach by one of the other prisoners in Majorca's jail. He died in hospital in the early hours of

Sunday morning. His killer was a man called Miguel Romero who used to work for Raul. Romero took a five year prison sentence which should have been Raul's, in return Raul was too look after this guy's family. To cut a long story short, he did not and as a direct result, this guy's little boy, Alvaro, was run over and killed. Romero took his revenge.' I felt Patience squeeze my hand.

'I am not sorry that he is dead, he was an evil man and I'm sure he has got just what he deserved. If that sounds harsh then so be it. He killed that Kosovan girl, was responsible for the death of that little boy and look what he put us through, no I'm not sorry at all. Thank you for not speaking in front of Anna.'

'When will you tell her?' asked Suzanne. Patience took a deep breath.

'No time like the present,' she said, standing up. I stood up too.

'If you want, I will come with you while you speak to her. Don't think I am trying to interfere, I'm not, I just want to be with you but only if you think it's a good idea.'

'Thanks love, I would like you with me, I was going to ask you. Is there anything else?'

'Just that Inez has pleaded guilty to all the charges oh, and as we left the court, Maria and Esther came over and asked me to tell you that they had no idea what had been going on. For what it is worth, I think they were genuine.'

Patience led the way upstairs to Anna's room, with me following on behind. Once there, we went in, Patience sat on the bed with her daughter, I stood. She did not beat about the bush and gave Anna the news quickly and concisely. She took it well considering though she did cry but after all, she is just eight years old.

'I am sorry that dad is dead but he did wrong mum. I did not want to see him ever again so I suppose that it is the same thing. Mum, I will need a new daddy now, do you think that one day I will get one?' The two of them looked up at me, expectantly.

The End

Acknowledgements

I would like to thank my children Deborah and Matthew for all the encouragement and support given during the writing of this book. Also thanks to my son in law Andrew for his work on the cover. I would also like to thank Claire Hughes for her technical help and my old friend Jeff Banks, without whose support, this book would not be available.

Disclaimer

All of the characters in this book and some of the places in this work of fiction are figments of my imagination. Any resemblance to any person either living or dead is purely coincidental.